CARTOUCHE CHRONICLES 1: THE CURSE OF THE MUMMY

ERIC CUTRIGHT

Copyright © 2018 by Eric Cutright

Visit the Official Cartouche Chronicles series website:

www.cartouchechronicles.com

ISBN 9781719961844

Disclaimer

This original book is a work of fiction. Names, characters, businesses, places, events, locales, and incidents are either the products of the author's imagination or used in a fictitious manner. Any resemblance to actual persons, living, dead, or undead, or actual events is purely coincidental. Historical, mythological, and archaeological references (except for Tutankhamun's new chamber contents – there is still ongoing archaeological work to determine if they actually even exist) are deemed by the author to be accurate but are not guaranteed.

Credits for all photographs and illustrations are provided in the References and Credits section at end of book.

All popular culture names and references are copyright of their respective owners and referenced under the fair use act of US copyright law with no intent for commercial gain or defamation. Please see the References and Credits section at end of book for full usage listing and copyright owners. All usage is intended as an appreciative homage to my favorite popular culture influences.

Finally, no living or undead creatures were harmed in the making of this book.

Dedication

This book is gratefully dedicated to my lovely wife (and high school sweetheart since she was 14) Marsha for indulging me in this crazy adventure, and to our four teenage boys Kyle, Marc, Luke, and Alec for providing so much daily insanity and seemingly infinite wild hijinks, many of which made their way into this crazy book. A special thanks is also due to the many friends and family members who were models, reviewers, editors (especially the amazing Ms. Grace T, my new lead editor for any of my future endeavors in this series), or simply the inspiration for one of the odd cast of characters in the book (and sorry for the horrible nickname for my beloved niece Becky!).

I would also like to recognize the amazing work of all the archaeologists, restoration experts, architects, engineers, and staff at the wonderful new Grand Egyptian Museum (GEM) in Cairo, Egypt. I have thoroughly enjoyed watching your exciting progress through TV specials and the GEM Facebook posts and awesome pictures. Needless to say, I look forward to visiting the GEM someday very soon!

What is a Cartouche?

A cartouche (pronounced car-toosh) is a way of signifying a formal name in ancient Egyptian hieroglyphics. It is traditionally drawn as an oval border enclosing the hieroglyphic characters of the name with three knots attached to a bottom bar, as shown below, and is typically drawn in either a vertical (with bar on bottom) or horizontal (with bar on right) arrangement. To the ancient Egyptians, names were extremely important and the cartouche symbolizes 'all that the sun encircles' as a way of giving them special prominence and power. A modern equivalent in the English language is our use of "Mr." or "Mrs." or "King" or "Queen" – when we see those characters we know the word following them is someone's name. In this way, the cartouche symbolism also made it very easy to find names in a long hieroglyphic passage. Cartouches were extremely important in ancient Egyptian religion and Pharaohs would carve their cartouche name into monuments that they constructed as a way of making their memory immortal so that they would not be forgotten by future generations. By doing so, they sought to live on in the memories of their people to ensure themselves a long and happy afterlife.

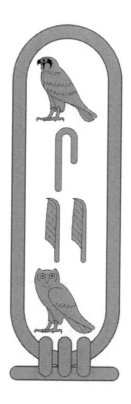

Writing with Ancient Egyptian Hieroglyphics

Hieroglyphics were the symbolic and phonetic written language of Ancient Egypt. The complete hieroglyphic language is very complex with thousands of different characters which roughly fall into three main categories: symbols representing individual phonetic letters (e.g. like an alphabet), symbols representing whole words or phrases (e.g. king, beast, all that is within), and symbols used to modify the other two categories to indicate an enhanced or specific meaning (e.g. his, hers, a specific type of bird, etc.). The precise meaning of all the hieroglyphic characters was forgotten long ago and it was not until the discovery and translation of the Rosetta Stone (check it out in the British Museum!) in the 1820s that they were again understood. The Rosetta Stone was a large black granite-like stone carved with the same decree written in 196 BC in three different languages: Egyptian hieroglyphics, Egyptian demotic script, and ancient Greek, which was a huge breakthrough for deciphering the meaning of the ancient Egyptian hieroglyphic language.

There are several variations of the hieroglyphic alphabet and numerous on-line translators where you can enter a name and the program will auto-magically generate the hieroglyphic version. This is my favorite version of the alphabet which I drew by hand on a computer while writing this book. My version uses cooler-looking variations of some of the letters (e.g. a falcon instead of a creepy-looking vulture for 'A') and also tracings of actual ancient hieroglyphics for several of the more complex symbols. Note that the letters represent sounds in the English language, and thus the symbol to choose depends on the sound that the letter makes in the word you are writing (e.g. a hard C sound would use C, but a soft C would use the symbol for S).

The cartouche of Tutankhamun was not directly spelled with individual alphabetic letters but also used other symbology to represent his name in nomen form as "living image of Amun, ruler of the Upper Egyptian Heliopolis." The most beautiful version of his cartouche (in my opinion) is on the front of his stunning second funerary casket in gold with exquisite blue, cyan and red inlaid symbols.

You can use this hieroglyphic alphabet for writing names, words, or whatever you like. Just for fun, see if you can translate the cartouche in the previous section.

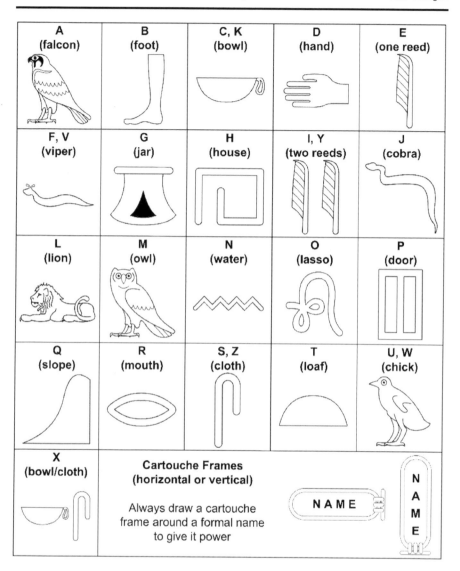

A (falcon)	B (foot)	C, K (bowl)	D (hand)	E (one reed)
F, V (viper)	G (jar)	H (house)	I, Y (two reeds)	J (cobra)
L (lion)	M (owl)	N (water)	O (lasso)	P (door)
Q (slope)	R (mouth)	S, Z (cloth)	T (loaf)	U, W (chick)

X (bowl/cloth)	**Cartouche Frames** (horizontal or vertical) Always draw a cartouche frame around a formal name to give it power	NAME — N A M E

Eric's Egyptian Hieroglyphic Alphabet ©

Prologue

Twins Marc and Sydney were completely surrounded and just *slightly* outnumbered by around ten thousand evil warriors facing the two of them. They had fought a long and valiant battle but the forces of darkness were slowly closing in upon them as they struggled to maintain their shimmer shields and keep up their offensive attacks. Then suddenly the army of the living and undead paused ominously and made way for their leader, the mummy Paatenemheb, who parted them like Moses parting the Red Sea. Slowly he staggered toward the twins as all his mighty warrior creatures moved out of his path in fear and respect of his horrible powers. One of the zombies who Marc had earlier slashed in half was too slow to crawl away and the mummy kicked him violently, scattering what was left of the zombie's rotten corpse across the ground.

"Well, this is it, Syd. He's finally found us. Let's light this nasty old snot rag up – on three," said Marc. "One ... two ... three!" The mummy waved one hand and both their best attacks fizzled out uselessly as he drew closer and closer. "Again!" yelled Marc but nothing happened.

"He's blocking our powers, I can't shimmer shield either," yelled Sydney in a panic. The mummy was now close enough that they could see him smiling grotesquely. "I guess we'll just have to do this the old-fashioned way," she screamed defiantly, raising both her fists as the mummy slowly lurched forward.

"OK, you take left and I'll take right," advised Marc who stood at the ready. The mummy waved his other hand and suddenly neither of them could move a muscle but stood completely frozen in place. This time they heard a dry chuckle from the mummy and were soon overwhelmed by the strong smell of natron, oils, and long-rotten flesh as he slowly reached for them.

"Well, it's been an honor fighting beside you. I love you and couldn't ask for a better sister," lamented Marc. "But crap, I wish I could see Akiiki again."

"Goonies never say die," said Sydney fiercely. "We are not giving up – as soon as he releases us - we smash him, so be ready. And I love you too, brother."

The mummy grasped their right arms firmly with his bony, rotten hands and they both blacked out instantly.

Table of Contents

Chapter 1. Discoveries

"Holy crap - HURRY UP, Lucas! We're going to be late," yelled Marc up the stairs to his annoying little eight year old brother's room.

"Yeah – just like always," moaned Sydney, Marc's fourteen year old twin sister.

"OK you guys have fun today – we'll see you tonight," called Mom from the front door as she and Dad were on their way out. "Say hello to the kids for us."

"Yeah we will – hey, dig up something cool today," Sydney replied with a laugh.

"Oh, that will definitely NOT be a problem - Mr. P has lots of cool bling," Dad replied. "Take care of Lucas you two – see you tonight!"

"OK - see you!" yelled Marc, now tapping his foot in frustration. "I'll take care of him, alright," he added, smacking his fist into the palm of his other hand. "COME ON Lucas, Asim and I have big plans today!"

"Yeah, whatever, hold your camels - I'll be there when I get there, you two stinky losers," yelled Lucas faintly from upstairs. Sydney rolled her eyes at Marc who was clearly getting quite agitated.

"I'm telling you – if we just lose the little twerp in the desert today I'm sure it would be AT LEAST a week before Mom and Dad even noticed," Marc pleaded excitedly, looking over at Sydney who had started to laugh.

"Maybe - we sure don't see much of them anymore so we could probably pull it off," Sydney giggled back at him. "But it would undoubtedly be BIG trouble for us if Mom and Dad ever figured it out."

"Yeah, I'm happy for them and all, but it will be nice to be back home in Charlottesville and back to a normal schedule," Marc replied with a frown. "Cairo is absolutely cool but I miss home and all our friends, plus even just hanging out more with Mom and Dad."

"Yeah, me too," said Sydney. "Another crazy summer off on some exotic dig around the world – same old, same old," she lamented. It had been this way for as long as they both could remember - each summer, their family was deployed on an archaeological field assignment to some exotic location across the world. Their parents were both archaeologists at the University of Virginia and had originally met on field assignment in Egypt so they were happy to return to Cairo this summer.

"And whenever we DO see them this summer, they are usually giving each other googly eyes," laughed Marc. "It's just downright disgusting."

Sydney chuckled. "Well you know what Dad always says - he and Mom had 'dug' each other at first sight," she added, unable to keep a straight face.

"Yeah, that's one of his classic archaeologist jokes," Marc replied, rolling his eyes. "Yet I suppose it's not quite as cringe-worthy as all his other bad jokes, or maybe I'm just getting used to it. They've definitely been reminding us all summer long with all the sickeningly romantic kissy-faces, hugs, and hand holding," he added with a low groan.

Despite all this chaos, Marc and Sydney had to admit that this summer was easily their most exciting so far. Their parents had been working with the UVA Electrical Engineering department for several years to develop a new type of high-resolution underground structure scanner based on ground-penetrating radar to scan potential archaeological dig sites. In the spring they had won their first major field project from the Egyptian Department of Antiquities to scan the mysterious new chambers discovered behind King Tutankhamun's tomb in the Valley of the Kings. These chambers were first suspected a few years ago after a high-resolution scan of Tutankhamun's tomb walls had revealed the outline of a door, and were then confirmed after a basic radar scan. The problem was that the Egyptian Department of Antiquities quite rightly refused to allow any destructive exploration of King Tutankhamun's tomb wall to reach the new chambers. Their parent's project had been to carefully scan the tomb area to develop a detailed map of the elusive chambers to allow an access shaft to be dug without damaging either the tomb or the new chambers. The chamber scanning project had already been an amazing success and brought worldwide attention back to King Tutankhamun and the Valley of the Kings. By the end of their first week in Cairo, his parents and their team had entered the new chambers and were absolutely astonished by their discoveries.

"I wonder what they will find today," Sydney asked thoughtfully. "It's pretty cool working right beside King Tut's tomb – it's still breathtaking every time we go in there; it must have been so cool to be Howard Carter to originally discover it when it was still full of bling like Mr. P's." This was the first excavation around King Tutankhamun's tomb since Howard Carter famously discovered it in 1922. Marc and Sydney visited Tutankhamun's tomb several times early in the summer, and looking into the face of his wonderful golden sarcophagus as well as that of his mummy was a breathtaking experience they would never forget. The solid gold and lapis lazuli funerary mask of King Tutankhamun that Carter found on his mummy in the innermost casket is now one of the most famous archaeological artifacts of all time and is instantly recognizable across the world.

Marc and Sydney had always wondered what had happened to King Tutankhamun and were amazed that he ruled all of Egypt when he was just a little boy about Lucas' age. He became Pharaoh around age nine and ruled for only about ten years when he abruptly died under mysterious circumstances at age eighteen or nineteen. Tutankhamun had spent most of his short reign undoing the legacy of his father Akhenaten who had radically shaken up Egypt by declaring that the old gods should be abandoned and that everyone must worship the one sun god, Aten. His father's action had resulted in great emotional and economic discontent across Egypt as the temples were a mainstay of Egyptian worship and a big business for temple priests whose jobs were then lost. Tutankhamun quickly restored the worship of the old gods and dismantled and erased the many statues and temples to Aten which were constructed under his father's reign. Even after

Tutankhamun's death, all of Egypt was still so upset by his father's legacy that the next several Pharaohs erased both Akhenaten AND Tutankhamun from all official records and monuments so that no one would remember them. In so doing, they attempted to ensure that these heretic Pharaohs would be doomed to be denied an afterlife.

In a strange twist of fate, this erasure of the Pharaonic records had likely been a primary reason that Tutankhamun's tomb had remained undiscovered for over 3,000 years – within a short while after his death, grave robbers did not even know he had ever existed. Tutankhamun's peaceful rest was also aided by the geographical location of the tomb in one of the lowest points in the Valley of the Kings. A great flood in antiquity had buried the entrance in deep debris which sealed over it almost like cement, and centuries of later grave robber digging of the tombs above it had further buried the long-forgotten tomb in stone chippings and dig waste. Now of course, the Boy King who likely had the humblest of Pharaonic tombs and most modest of treasures was now the most famous Pharaoh of all time and would live in human memory for all eternity.

"Well, Mr. P's sarcophagus sure was cool – it will be hard to top that!" said Marc seriously. "I think everyone is still shocked that it was Mr. P in there instead of Nefertiti," he laughed. Most Egyptologists had speculated that the chambers would be the burial place of Tutankhamun's famous "mother-in-law" Nefertiti, who had ruled as Pharaoh before him. Nefertiti was the wife of the heretic Pharaoh Akhenaten and the mother of Tutankhamun's wife Ankhesenamen, and she had ruled as Pharaoh after her husband's death until Tutankhamun ascended to Pharaoh as the boy king. However, what his parents found instead was quite remarkable and completely unexpected.

"I thought it was cool how the only entrance was so expertly hidden behind Tut's tomb wall," said Sydney. "It seems like they were trying very hard to keep the chambers a complete secret – like they were desperately trying to hide something extremely important. It's pretty wild that it took Dad's state-of-the-art imaging system to actually be able to detect it at all."

"Definitely," replied Marc. "The hidden chambers just get more and more mysterious the more that Dad learns about them – it's totally crazy. I just worry that maybe we weren't meant to actually find what was hidden there," he added nervously.

Much like Tutankhamun's tomb, the first hidden chamber was stocked with a wide assortment of traditional Egyptian grave goods. The sheer quantity and beauty of the goods was nowhere near that of King Tut, but nonetheless, there was an abundant store of food, drink, games, furniture, weapons, jewelry, papyrus scrolls, clothing, and even some mummified pets to sustain and entertain the deceased in the Egyptian afterlife. It would easily be enough to keep the team busy for several years classifying, documenting, and carefully preserving all of the discoveries.

The second chamber held the biggest surprise: a stunningly beautiful large sarcophagus completely covered in dense hieroglyphics and made entirely of a strange metal. In fact, the construction of the sarcophagus was absolutely unique in all of Egyptian archaeology and was utterly baffling to the entire team of expert Egyptologists on the project. The hieroglyphics seemed to be of a completely different and unknown language and no one on the team was able to make any sense of them. Most curiously of all, there was no sign of a lid seam or any way to open the sarcophagus. It was roughly the size of King Tutankhamun's outer golden casket, so Egyptologists were excited to see if it contained any similar magnificent golden inner caskets nested inside like Russian dolls.

"It was really cool being the first one to read Mr. P's cartouche," Sydney said wistfully. "I think Dad was mad that I beat him to it," she laughed. After they had removed the large and heavy sarcophagus, Sydney had been the first to discover the hieroglyphic cartouche with the name of the assumed occupant: Paatenemheb. This had led to great excitement within the team since Paatenemheb was known to be the commander-in-chief of the Pharaoh Akhenaten's army who had ruled before Nefertiti and Tutankhamun. Sydney and the boys thought his name was a bit of a mouthful so they nicknamed him "Mr. P" which was soon fondly adopted by the archaeological team. However, after weeks of further scrutiny, the only other hieroglyphics the team could decipher were a few random words and Egyptian names for colors including blue, yellow, orange, purple, and red. The purpose behind the extensive and strange sarcophagus hieroglyphics was proving to be elusive, puzzling, and quite frustrating.

"It's just awesome that now we get to take it back home with us to see if Mom and Dad can figure out how to open it," Marc replied. Not to be outdone by Sydney, Marc had been the first to notice the outline of the lid seam cleverly blended around the dense hieroglyphics but there was still no sign of how to actually open it. Several meticulously slow and careful attempts at prying it open along the seam were unsuccessful, as it seemed the lid was securely locked in place through some hidden mechanism and refused to budge in the slightest. To everyone's immense frustration, the strange metal and large size of the sarcophagus also made scanning the interior impossible. A portable X-ray machine was brought in but was not able to reveal anything of interest, and the sarcophagus was simply too large to fit in any of the CT scanners at any of the Egyptian hospitals. After exhausting all local options and based on the astounding success of the University of Virginia tomb scans, the Egyptian Department of Antiquities agreed to ship the sarcophagus to Charlottesville for detailed analysis using the advanced imaging equipment in the electrical engineering imaging and archaeology labs. This was a highly unusual move for the Department, and was approved only after the UVA team had developed a detailed security plan describing how the sarcophagus would be protected against damage and theft once it reached the university labs, and how the actual lab analysis would be coordinated with the Egyptian archaeological team. The Egyptian Department of Antiquities also requested that if the scans were successful, that the sarcophagus would not be opened until they could travel there to witness the event.

"Hey Lucas, are you coming or what?" yelled Sydney. "We're going to leave your butt here if you don't hurry up. We are all supposed to go to the GEM this morning!" To relieve their boredom after the summer's initial excitement calmed down, Marc, Sydney, and Lucas spent much of their time now hanging out with the family of one of the Egyptian archaeologists, Sallah Mohammed Faisel el-Kahir. Sallah had three children: twins Asim and Akiiki who were about 6 months older than Marc and Sydney, and son Mensah who was a year younger than Lucas. When they met at the very beginning of the summer, they all instantly became good friends and enjoyed each other's company immensely. It was actually a tremendously nice change of pace for Marc and Sydney that little Lucas now had someone else to hang out with instead of pestering and annoying them constantly as he usually did. In fact, he would never admit it, but Lucas, as the youngest of the family, thoroughly enjoyed having someone younger than himself in Mensah to be able to practice the role of being a big brother. The six close friends had many exciting adventures together around Cairo exploring museums, hitting all the tourist attractions, and eating exotic foods.

"Yeah, I can't wait until the GEM opens – it is going to be amazing with all of King Tut's bling together again, and now Sallah will have to make room for all of Mr. P's stuff too," said Marc. The entire world was eagerly awaiting the completion and grand opening of the giant new Grand Egyptian Museum (GEM) being constructed on the Giza plateau, practically in the shadow of the Great Pyramid. In its over 700,000 square foot footprint, the Grand Egyptian Museum will house more than 100,000 artifacts from all pharaonic periods and will finally, for the first time, allow the display of all of the almost 5,400 artifacts from King Tutankhamun's tomb. Most of these artifacts will be transferred from the Egyptian Antiquities Museum over 23 km away in Tahrir square near the center of Cairo. That small two-story museum was built around 1900 and with over 160,000 artifacts on display is absolutely bursting at the seams, with over 100,000 magnificent artifacts kept in storage with no space in the museum for public display.

As exciting as the first half of their summer was, the second half had quickly proven to be exactly the opposite. Their parents and the team were all extremely busy with removing, analyzing, documenting and preserving all the artifacts, holding meetings and TV/newspaper interviews, driving back and forth between Cairo, Giza, and the Valley of the Kings, and working through the huge stack of paperwork required to ship the sarcophagus to Charlottesville. It had all quickly become mind-numbingly boring so for the last half of the summer Marc, Sydney, and Lucas were mostly left alone in Cairo to entertain themselves. Marc and Sydney were looking forward to hanging out with Asim, Akiiki, and Mensah today to break up the monotony.

"FINALLY!" yelled Marc as Lucas appeared at the top of the stairs and made his way down to the front door, rudely pushing the twins aside. "What took you so long, twerp?" asked Marc, now extremely annoyed but relieved to actually almost be on their way.

"Sorry, I was trying to wipe all the ugly off your pictures in the hallway upstairs," Lucas explained as he walked past them. "But there was just WAY too much ugly so I had to give up," he snickered evilly.

Marc and Sydney both shot him murderous glares. "Well, it's a good thing you didn't look in the mirror then, because it would take you a year to wipe off all THAT ugly," Marc retorted angrily.

"Hmmm, wanna know a secret?" asked Lucas with a snort. "Mom said you two were both so ugly when you were born that she couldn't even tell what end to put the diapers on!" Lucas laughed uproariously at his own joke as the twins rolled their eyes and followed after him.

"Wow, that was SUCH a good one, dude," replied Marc sarcastically. "Such refined, sophisticated and highly intelligent humor," he added irritably.

"Yeah, since you two are probably too STUPID to understand - it means your faces are just as ugly as your butts, get it?" snickered Lucas, obviously pleased with his clever little joke. He continued laughing hysterically as they walked down the street.

"Just let it go, it's not worth it," Sydney said to Marc who was about to launch another verbal attack. "Isn't it just wonderful that he's always such a kind and pleasant person to hang out with?" Sydney grumbled sarcastically as the three of them continued the long walk to Sallah's house.

"Yeah, lucky us!" replied Marc with a groan. "Seriously Syd - think about my 'lose him in the desert' plan, I just know it would work!" Marc whispered conspiratorially to Sydney, as the twins both started giggling.

Chapter 2. GEM

Today as they had throughout the summer, the six friends were visiting Sallah to tour his team's work on caring for King Tutankhamun's treasures and to watch as the new exhibits at the Grand Egyptian Museum (GEM) were being assembled. Even apart from the new chamber discoveries, this was an exciting time for Sallah as he was involved hands-on in re-examining and preserving the priceless treasures and designing the new artifact exhibits and security enclosures. However, it was often difficult and time-consuming work, as some of the artifacts were badly deteriorating after being in storage at the Egyptian Antiquities Museum for almost a century. Sallah spent most of his time now in the state-of-the-art Conservation Center at the Grand Egyptian Museum, which was nearly complete and had everything his team needed for their critically important restoration and conservation work.

Marc and Sydney always thoroughly enjoyed visiting Sallah at the center since they were able to see something new and exciting at almost every visit. They had, of course, seen many pictures and read many books on King Tutankhamun, but seeing all his glorious treasures up close and personal was entirely different. Sallah was also very enthusiastic about his love of archaeology and was continuously amazed by the ongoing discoveries in Egypt which shed new light on the lives and legacies of his mighty ancestors. His enthusiasm was quite infectious and the six friends always learned many interesting new things at every visit.

The only somewhat annoying part of their visits was that Sallah and his staff were required to go over "the rules" every time the friends visited the lab or main museum floors, before they were even allowed to set foot inside the door. It was a bit unusual for children to tour the lab and museum during the ongoing construction phase, but since the friends all had professional archaeologist parents all working at the GEM, Sallah was able to vouch for their behavior. However, it was made abundantly clear to all of them that the first time any of them touched any artifacts or broke any of the numerous rules, the "special access" tours would be over forever. So everyone was always on their best behavior in the lab despite the constant temptation to reach out and touch the many glorious artifacts Sallah had shown them over the summer. At Lucas' suggestion (he definitely struggled with rules the most), they had all started the habit of keeping their hands in their back pockets whenever they looked closely at any artifacts in the lab as a further reminder to refrain from touching anything.

Today Sallah was working on an exhibit of Tutankhamun's favorite weapons which were found in his tomb. He was deciding how to best arrange his armor, daggers, swords, and several hunting bows plus over 200 arrows, which had long been in storage in the Egyptian Antiquities Museum. "All this weaponry found with Tutankhamun really makes me think that Egyptologists have gotten him all wrong," said Sallah. "Based on examination of his mummy, they assumed he was weak, frail, and disease-ridden but I really think he was truly a warrior Pharaoh who was right at the front when he led his mighty armies into battle. Just look at these bows, these are not ornamental," he said, pointing to the well-worn handles and arrow rests.

"Doesn't it seem like the arrows are a little too short for the bow?" asked Sydney, thinking of the many bows she had used at Scout summer camps. Tutankhamun's arrows all had sharp points and fine fletching, but most definitely seemed to be too short for a strong draw on the biggest of the bows. That bow was easily the most ornate and visually striking, with alternating stripes of gold and black over the entire bow. It was absolutely beautiful and Sydney day-dreamed about holding and firing it when it was new back in Tutankhamun's time.

"Maybe. He seems to have had several different types of arrows," explained Sallah, startling Sydney out of her day-dream. "There were probably different bows and arrows he preferred for hunting versus the larger ones used for battle. Since the bows were unstrung in the tomb, it is a little hard to determine the draw length to see which arrow lengths match. Of course the bows are too fragile now to risk trying to put the strings back on, so I'm just trying to sort the arrows by length to find their rough match to the bows."

"What's the story with this cool shirt of scale armor?" asked Marc. "It reminds me of plate armor used by medieval knights in Europe." The shirt looked like it was made out of hundreds of large fish scales about the size of Marc's fist, all pointing downward.

"Yes, that's exactly what it is," interjected Asim excitedly as his dad Sallah chuckled. "The scales are made out of pressed leather which they must have manufactured using molds to mass produce them to the exact same shape. The coolest part is these ridges on the back of each scale – they interlock with the scale underneath to make it stronger and prevent the scales from moving when struck. It's like a bullet-proof vest made out of Kevlar and would have been highly resistant to arrows."

"Wow," all the boys said in unison while Sydney and Akiiki caught each other's eyes and rolled them together, smiling and then laughing.

"Well, this awesome gold and iron dagger is totally my favorite by far," said Lucas as Mensah immediately nodded his agreement, looking at Lucas in admiration. The dagger was a stunning masterpiece of metalwork, with a beautiful golden handle inlaid with precious gems and a clear rock crystal pommel at the bottom of the handle, and sporting an elegant long double-edged iron blade. The sheath was equally magnificent and was decorated with an intricate fish-scale pattern that looked very similar to the shirt of armor.

"It's funny you should say that because we think it was Tutankhamun's very favorite weapon, too," explained Sallah. "It was found directly against the side of his body and had been wrapped up with embalming strips as the priests prepared his mummy. The most intriguing part is that the iron in the blade does not come from Earth – it was collected from many meteorites the Egyptians found in the desert and then forged into this iron blade. Iron was not very common back then in Egypt so this must have been particularly meaningful to Tutankhamun to have a blade made of metal from the heavens. A few years ago, we had a team do a spectral analysis of the blade to determine where the iron came from and this was their surprising conclusion. Pretty cool, huh?" Sallah asked.

"Yeah, really cool, Dad. Maybe it was even made by aliens!" said Mensah excitedly. "That would be so awesome!" he proclaimed as everyone chuckled.

"It just all goes to show that I think Tutankhamun had some pretty incredible weapons and must have really been a true warrior Pharaoh. Why don't you guys go check out the chariot and hunting exhibits and let me know what you think?" asked Sallah. "We're opening up the museum in a few months so I want to make sure we really tell the true story of King Tutankhamun. I think your mom and dad might even be out there today. They just dropped off another box of artifacts from Tutankhamun's new chambers for conservation," he said to Marc, Sydney, and Lucas.

They all said goodbye and ventured out to the two new Tutankhamun halls which, like the rest of the museum, were large and wonderful but a bit chaotic and jumbled as it was all still under construction. "Oh, hey guys!" said their mom who was there admiring the exhibit. "Are you all having fun today?" she asked, mussing up Lucas' hair to his great embarrassment as Mensah laughed. Lucas quickly poked her in the ribs to get his revenge, making her laugh as well.

"Definitely! Sallah just showed us the new weapons exhibit he is working on. It was really cool!" replied Sydney. "These new Tutankhamun halls are going to be just incredible," she said as everyone spread out to admire the recent progress on the exhibits. "Hey, where's Dad?" she asked.

"Oh, he's over in the atrium checking out the giant statue of Ramses II," Mom replied.

"Cool, I'll go grab him to let him know we are here," Sydney replied as she walked away. She found Dad admiring the 30 foot high red granite statue which served as a magnificent centerpiece in the museum's atrium.

"Oh hey, Syd, I didn't realize you guys were here," said Dad. "I just love this statue of Ramses II – I wish we could have been here to see them move it in, the whole process was just an amazing feat of engineering. This statue weighs over 83 tons and they had to transport it with special trucks and custom-built wrap-around bracing so it wouldn't get damaged."

"Where did they move it from?" Sydney asked curiously as she stood beside him to admire the beautiful details on the statue.

"Strangely enough, about fifty years ago it was placed in the middle of a traffic circle in Cairo near the main train station to make an imposing impression on tourists arriving by car and train," explained Dad. "But they were worried that the exhaust fumes were damaging it so they moved it to Giza in 2006 and just recently moved it into the Grand Egyptian Museum. Ramses II was one of the most powerful and influential Pharaohs of ancient Egypt about 3,200 years ago. His statue has had quite a journey and a fascinating history – it was quarried in Aswan and then installed in the Temple of Ptah in Memphis and then lost to the sands until 1820 when it was discovered by an Italian archaeologist who was excavating there."

"That is really cool. He will definitely make a great impression on visitors to the museum now," said Sydney excitedly. "Hey Dad, everyone else is over at the Tutankhamun halls – do you have time to come over and visit with us?"

"Sure, that would be great. Lead the way," replied Dad with a smile, giving the statue of Ramses II a last long admiring look.

Dad and Sydney found everyone else admiring Tutankhamun's world-famous funerary mask and fabulous innermost golden casket which were the centerpieces of the new halls. The mask was an absolute masterpiece of metalwork, crafted from solid gold and inlaid with beautiful lapis lazuli in shades of blue, red, and cyan. On the forehead of the wonderful striped headdress were the vulture and cobra, symbols of Upper and Lower Egypt, and an intricate beard under his chin identified the king with Osiris, God of the dead. Dad and Sydney joined everyone else in their awestruck admiration of the mask.

"Oh hey Dad, perfect timing – I have a question for you," said Lucas.

"Sure, what is it?" Dad responded.

"So why would they not bring Tutankhamun's mummy and his outer golden casket here to put with all his other treasures?" asked Lucas. "Isn't it weird that he's back in his tomb but all his afterlife bling is all here in the museum miles away from him? If I were him, I would be pretty pissed off without my bling," he added as everyone laughed.

"That's a great question," replied Dad, switching automatically to his professor voice. "Actually, his mummy is extremely fragile after unwrapping so it would be very risky to move it again. The Egyptian Department of Antiquities decided it was safer to keep the mummy and the outer golden casket in the special environmentally controlled glass enclosure they made for it in his original resting place. So Tutankhamun will likely stay there forever unless the tomb is damaged or at risk for any reason in the future."

"Sallah did a really great job with this poster here which shows all the layers of caskets and shrines around the mummy," Sydney said admiringly. "And they have everything on display and labeled – the four outer golden shrines, the quartzite sarcophagus which is back at his tomb, and then the three caskets and finally the mummy with the funerary mask, all stacked inside each other like Russian dolls."

"Yeah, this third casket is my favorite," said Mom, moving closer to admire it. "It is solid gold and intricately detailed with Nekhbet and Wadjet, the Gods of Upper and Lower Egypt, wrapping their wings around him protectively as he holds the rod and flail in his hands. It is just magnificent!"

"I like this display about Howard Carter when he first discovered the tomb in 1922," said Marc. Carter had been searching for the tomb for over six years and had almost lost his funding from Lord Carnarvon, a wealthy UK businessman and Carter's partner. Lord Carnarvon reluctantly agreed to fund just one more season and on the third day, Carter found the steps to King Tutankhamun's amazing tomb. For the next two years, Carter continued with the excavation and the long process of photographing, sketching, documenting, cataloging, removing and preserving all the wonderful artifacts within the tomb which would take him another eight years to complete. The tomb held a staggering wealth of exquisite objects to serve the pharaoh in his afterlife, including chariots, beds, chairs, weapons, games, statues, clothes, food, and drink as well as many other comforts of daily life.

"I love how you can see Tut's funerary mask from Howard's picture right here," Sydney said, starting at it in awe. Every time any of them saw the mask now, it seemed even more breathtakingly beautiful than they remembered, and they would always spend at least several minutes admiring it over and over again. The mask was simply impossible to walk past without being drawn in by its astonishing beauty.

The friends spent the next couple of hours touring the exhibit and were occasionally joined by Sallah or his team as they continued their work on the exhibits. The boys all loved Tutankhamun's chariots which had been reassembled in clear glass displays and were covered with intricate golden decorations of warfare and hunting scenes. He was buried with a total of six chariots, but two of the less exotically decorated ones were still being restored in the Conservation Center so were not yet out on display. The girls loved the three tall golden ritual couches of Tutankhamun, one decorated with heads of the hippopotamus God Ammut, one with heads of the cow-Goddess, and the third with heads of a gracefully elegant lion or leopard. Other favorites as they explored were the massive Anubis statue on a shrine with carrying poles, and the Pharaoh's huge golden canopic shrine which contained the elegant chest of alabaster jars holding Tutankhamun's mummified organs.

Everyone was quite saddened by the two small coffins from the tomb which had contained the mummies of Tutankhamun's two stillborn daughters. Sallah had told them sadly that the mummies had deteriorated very severely in storage and even with all their advanced equipment in the Conservation Center, they were not able to repair them. Instead, they had sealed them up with special chemical pouches to stop any further disintegration and put them in storage - in hopes that perhaps they could be repaired by future generations of archaeologists.

The sheer quantity of Tutankhamun's treasures was simply mind-boggling and they were all carefully and thoughtfully arranged in the two halls. Several exhibits were still under construction as some of the more delicate artifacts were in the process of being restored, including the two life-size guardian statues that had once protected the entrance to the burial chamber. Once everything was finished, Marc could easily see spending an entire week in just these two halls to explore and truly appreciate all the spectacular treasures.

"Well, kids, we need to get back to Tutankhamun's tomb in the Valley of the Kings," said Dad as they were wrapping up their tour. "Mr. P has lots more bling that we need to document and bring here for conservation."

"We'll see you later, and don't be late for dinner," Mom added. "Tarek has a big day planned for you tomorrow, so you need your rest tonight."

"Sure thing, no problem, Mom," Sydney replied. "We are going to head over to Sallah's house for the rest of the afternoon and then walk home afterward, so we'll catch you later."

"Say hello to Tutankhamun's mummy for us," added Lucas. "And tell him we all really love his cool afterlife bling!"

Chapter 3. Humps

"Are you ready for us, friend Tarek?" asked Akiiki.

"Oh yes, Mistress Akiiki, and good morning my dear friends," replied the old man. "But your usuals are out, so I have instead assembled all the mightiest Gods and Goddesses of Ancient Egypt to serve you today," he said with a deep bow and a grandiose flourish of his arms. Lucas and Mensah both started giggling. "Shall I introduce you?" Tarek continued, unfazed and smiling widely.

"Oh yes, please do, friend Tarek," responded Akiiki with a playful giggle.

They followed him past the many camel stalls and crowds of tourists into the back courtyard where six camels stood geared up and waiting for them. Tarek led them to the first camel, who was the largest of the group. "This is Osiris, one of the oldest and wisest of the Egyptian Gods. He shall serve the mighty Asim today," he said. Asim stood beside him and stroked Osiris' head fondly.

"Next, for the beautiful Mistress Akiiki, I have called upon Hathor, the Goddess of love and joy," said Tarek with another flourish. Asim snorted in amusement as Akiiki giggled and stood beside Hathor admiringly. She then squealed as Hathor suddenly planted a big kiss on the side of her face, as everyone laughed hysterically. "Yes, be careful – Hathor is very affectionate," Tarek chuckled, as Akiiki wiped the gooey camel slobber off her face as she laughed.

"Now, another beautiful lady to serve the lovely Mistress Sydney," he continued as he walked to the next camel. "This is the all-powerful Isis, Goddess of magic and weaver of fates," said Tarek as Sydney admired the gorgeous camel as she stood beside her.

Next was a camel who was much darker in color than the others. "Now for the brave Marc, I have Anubis, God of the underworld," Tarek continued. "He has a strong will so you must be firm and unwavering in your commands to make him cooperate."

"Oh, great, so you're saying I get the trouble-maker?" asked Marc, as he moved to stand beside Anubis and stroked his neck nervously.

"I sense great power in you, so I am sure that you can bend Anubis to your mighty will," replied Tarek confidently. He continued to the next camel, a magnificent tan male who held his head high as he observed the friends skeptically.

"Next for the young Master Lucas, I present the mighty Horus, the powerful and all-seeing Falcon, mighty God of the Pharaohs," Tarek said as Lucas jumped forward excitedly to greet his new friend.

"And last but not least, for the youngest Master Mensah, I have the mighty God Set, brother of Osiris and the dark God of chaos," Tarek said with a low bow.

"God of chaos – that is SO totally appropriate," snickered Akiiki. Mensah stuck out his tongue at her and clambered on board his camel excitedly with Tarek's assistance.

Tarek made sure they were all safely mounted on their camels and checked their water supplies and provisions. The camels were completely used to riders of all ages and sizes so accepted them easily, but were anxious to get started and pawed the ground impatiently.

"Now, I must warn you about these mighty Gods and Goddesses before you begin your adventure," Tarek announced loudly to get their full attention. "Do you know the story of these deities? Their names match their personalities so you must keep some of them apart if you wish to avoid trouble on your journeys."

"Yes friend Tarek, I will teach the story to our friends," replied Asim confidently. "Osiris is the brother of Set and husband to Isis. Set was insanely jealous of Osiris' power and murdered his brother, scattering the parts of his body all across Egypt so he would be denied an afterlife. But Isis gathered up the pieces to resurrect her husband and together they had their son Horus. But again Set murdered Osiris and banished him to the underworld where Set's son Anubis was the ruling God and could bend Osiris to his will. But Set's plan backfired as Osiris then wrestled dominion of the underworld from Anubis. Now Horus forever seeks his revenge and constantly battles Set for control of all of Egypt, and also to keep Set away from Horus' beautiful wife Hathor." Akiiki giggled as her camel jumped when she heard her name.

"Ah yes, very good, wise Master Asim," replied Tarek with relief. "So which of the camels must you keep apart?" he asked.

"So I imagine that Horus and Set like to fight each other all the time, and that both Anubis and Osiris will rush to their aid if threatened," replied Asim.

"But both of the goddesses will be fine together, and may calm down the always bad-tempered males if they argue," added Akiiki, as Sydney laughed.

"Yes, yes, very good. Remember that on your journey and you shall have a grand adventure today. Farewell and enjoy the glorious day, my dear friends!" Tarek replied as they made their way out into the hot desert sun.

The friends decided to take their usual route to visit all three of the pyramids in order and then finish at the Great Sphinx before riding back. The western and eastern sides of each pyramid were on a perfect true north-south alignment and the apex of each could almost be connected with an imaginary straight line from southwest to northeast, with the middle Pyramid of Khafre only slightly to the north of this shared centerline. Each pyramid had a funerary temple on its eastern side with a long causeway that connected to a corresponding valley temple further to the east. The largest Great Pyramid of Khufu was also particularly interesting because it had large ancient cemeteries on both the west and the east, with a row of mastabas along its southern side where key princes, princesses, and nobles had been buried in antiquity.

Tarek's camel stables were on the western edge of the Giza plateau, so the first pyramid they came to was the youngest and smallest at just over 200 feet tall –

the Pyramid of Menkaure. This was Mensah's favorite because he liked the three small Pyramids of the Queens which were built in a row just south of the pyramid. But actually, the main reason he liked it was because it was usually the least crowded of the pyramids, so he and Lucas loved to race their camels around it and normally would not get into trouble with the Giza guards. Today when they arrived it was still quite early in the morning so there were only a handful of tourists near the funerary temple taking pictures, so Mensah naturally challenged Lucas to a camel race.

"I'm not so sure about this, Mensah," said Akiiki worriedly. "Tarek warned us that Horus and Set are sworn enemies so this could get pretty ugly."

"Oh come on, it will be fine and they will enjoy the exercise instead of walking slowly like old men as they usually have to do with silly tourists," Mensah replied. "Are you up for it Lucas?"

"Duh, I just hope you can keep up – the mighty Horus flies like the falcon," Lucas bragged confidently. "Eat my dust!" he roared as he kicked Horus into action.

Not to be outdone by his enemy, Set leaped after Horus and the race was on. The two camels were neck and neck when they reached the first northwest corner of the pyramid and then ran close to the northern edge to take the shortest possible path. They rounded the second corner still close together and skirted around the eastern edge of the funerary temple, startling the tourists who had just started walking down the causeway. Both boys laughed and urged their camels onward as they approached the bottom corner of the Pyramids of the Queens and could see their friends on the western side. By this point, Horus had started to pull ahead which angered the struggling Set, who bit him in the butt as he passed by. Horus jumped and nearly dislodged Lucas who had to grab the saddle quickly to avoid being tossed. The camels quickly abandoned the race and started biting, spitting, and kicking each other in fury as the boys fought to control them. A few moments later Akiiki arrived on Hathor and wedged herself between them to break up the fight.

"See, I told you there would be trouble!" laughed Akiiki as Lucas and Mensah slowly regained control of Horus and Set, now both calming down but still giving each other the evil camel eye. Lucas and Mensah were both visibly shaken from the experience but were starting to giggle at each other. They had definitely both gotten a little more excitement than they had expected from the race.

"I clearly was beating you easily before Set cheated and bit poor Horus," bragged Lucas in between giggles.

"No way dude, I was just about to pass you slowpokes and Set was just trying to get your old grandpa camel to move out of our way," replied Mensah who was now laughing hysterically. Marc and Asim then arrived on Anubis and Osiris and they all laughed together about the crazy race.

"Whoops, we had better get moving," whispered Akiiki suddenly as she saw two of the Giza guards now looking in their direction. "Come on!"

The friends continued their journey northeast to the Pyramid of Khafre. This pyramid was much larger than the Pyramid of Menkaure at about 450 feet tall. The apex of this pyramid was the only one of the three which still had its smooth white limestone casing, hinting at the former grandeur of the pyramids which would have been fully encased in these stones with likely a mini-pyramid of gold or electrum at their peaks. It was thought that this pyramid was unique among the three since the bottommost layer of casing stones was made from an exquisite pink granite which would have contrasted nicely with the white limestone of the upper pyramid faces. There was also a mysterious very small subsidiary pyramid centered below its southern face, of which little remained other than the foundation. The Pyramid of Khafre also had the largest funerary temple which connected via a causeway to the Great Sphinx and the adjacent beautifully preserved valley temple to the east.

The friends took their time and circled casually around the entire Pyramid of Khafre, and tied up their camels at the halfway point to take a walk through the Funerary Temple of Khafre to stretch their legs and explore more closely. It was amazing to stand at the entrance of the temple and look eastward toward the back of the Great Sphinx along the perfectly straight causeway road. It was truly a mind-blowing feat of architecture, especially considering the tools available when it was constructed almost 4,600 years ago. Marc could not fathom attempting construction of the pyramid complex without the use of many computers in the skilled hands of modern architects to carefully lay it out with such unerring precision. The friends then rejoined their camels and rode along the southern side to check out the boat pits and the foundation of the subsidiary pyramid, before continuing northeast to the Great Pyramid.

As they approached the Great Pyramid of Khufu, they were simply astounded at its size. It was a bit taller than the Pyramid of Khafre at 481 feet, and had a base of 756 feet per side, a volume of over 90 million cubic feet, and an estimated mass of almost 6 million tons. This was the last surviving "wonder" of the seven wonders of the ancient world, and was by far the oldest. It was also the tallest building in the world for over 3,800 years until the Lincoln Cathedral was completed in 1300 AD. Even today with all but the bottommost layer of its smooth white limestone casing stones gone, exposing the much rougher interior construction stones, it was a truly beautiful and monumental achievement.

"I would have loved to see exactly how they built this," exclaimed Sydney. "Dad says it took 20,000 workers over twenty years to build it. What does your dad think – did they make a giant construction ramp to push up the stones on rollers, or use massive cranes to lift them from level to level?"

"Dad thinks it was probably a combination of both based on the archaeological evidence," replied Akiiki as she stared up at the apex in wonder. "It sure would have been interesting to see. I'll bet there was quite a celebration when they finally finished it, can you imagine?"

"I've always been curious about the casing stones," said Asim. "They were quarried across the Nile at Tora and had to be transported by boats to get here. And some of the interior granite came all the way from Aswan which at over 500 miles away must have been quite a difficult voyage on the river. I wonder how many they lost in boat wrecks?"

They stopped on the northern side to admire the view of the Grand Egyptian Museum which they could see less than two miles away to the northwest. It was truly a beautiful masterpiece of modern architecture and it was wonderful that it was so close to the pyramid complex and its masterpieces of ancient Egyptian architecture. The top of the museum was designed to be the same height as the pyramids, and they recalled that the view from the upper galleries looking towards the pyramid complex was truly spectacular. "I wish we could be here when the GEM opens," complained Sydney wistfully. "I can't wait to come back to visit once everything is finished."

"Yes, the whole world is looking forward to it," replied Akiiki. "I'm sure my dad can easily convince your parents to bring you guys back when it opens."

"But you would have to stay with us for a while to visit," added Mensah. Lucas nodded excitedly.

The friends then circled around to the eastern side where they saw the foundation of the funerary temple and to its south, the three small pyramids for Khufu's queens. There was also a long causeway leading to the northeast but the valley temple at its end was now buried under a modern village at the eastern edge of the Giza plateau. To the south of the causeway they could see the excavations of the eastern cemetery where Queen Hetepheres' tombs had been discovered. Here they lingered for a while to enjoy the lunch and snacks which kind Tarek had thoughtfully packed for them in their bags, and to give the camels a well-deserved rest after their labor.

Next they circled to the south to visit Marc's favorite stop – the museum housing Khufu's funerary boat. Archaeologists had found five long boat pits around the Pyramid of Khufu – three on the eastern side and two on the southern side. Four of them were very shallow and empty, but the fifth at the southeast corner had contained a perfectly preserved Lebanese cedar boat in a long chamber covered by heavy stone slabs. The boat was disassembled for burial into over 1,200 pieces and was originally held together by ropes, which was common for boats of this period so that they could be easily stored on land in the off-season. It was really quite ingenious - when the boats were reassembled, the water would expand the wood and tighten all the knots making the boat hull watertight again. A modern boat builder was able to restore, straighten, and reassemble the 143 foot long boat over a period of 14 years and it was now housed in a special air-conditioned museum directly over its original burial location. It is thought that the boat was a "solar barge" intended to carry the resurrected Pharaoh Khufu and the sun God Ra across the heavens in his afterlife, but it may have also been used by Khufu to travel on the Nile during his lifetime.

"This boat is just so cool! It is amazing that it survived intact for this long and was able to be put back together so perfectly like it was brand new," said Marc admiringly. "It is so long and sleek, although the blades on the ten oars seem far too narrow to work very well in water. And I love the high bow and stern, they look like rolls of papyrus."

"Yes, you can see many boats like this in ancient tomb paintings and papyrus scrolls," replied Akiiki. "Mom and Dad have taken us on several boat cruises up and down the Nile and it was really fun. I'm sure it must have been the same back then – only the sights to see on the land would have been very different," she chuckled.

"OK, come on guys, this boat is boring - I want to see the Sphinx," complained Lucas impatiently. The friends rejoined their camels and made their way the short ride south to the Great Sphinx. It was always such an impressive sight as they approached and none of them ever grew tired of visiting it again and again.

The sphinx was actually carved directly out of the limestone bedrock of the Giza plateau and the rock quarried away during its construction was used to build the adjacent excellently preserved valley temple and other nearby monuments. Lucas loved what he called the sphinx's "tiger stripes" which were a result of the many layers of soft and hard rock eroding differently over time, creating its unique weathered look. The 240 foot long Great Sphinx had the body of a mighty lion with the head of a man, which was theorized to most likely be the Pharaoh Khafre himself, although it was possibly much older. The face of the sphinx looks eastward toward the Nile river, and must have been an impressive sight to travelers arriving from the river in antiquity.

Lucas did his favorite trick of asking a riddle every time they visited the Great Sphinx. "OK, here is today's amazing riddle, you must answer it correctly or the Great Sphinx will eat you alive," he started excitedly. "What monument in the desert is wide and round and has a big crack in it?" he asked very seriously.

Everyone tried their best to humor him so they all shrugged their shoulders in defeat. "Oh mighty master of the Great Sphinx, we have no idea," relied Akiiki formally. "Please have mercy on our souls and do not let the Great Sphinx eat us."

"The answer is - your butt!" said Lucas, and he and Mensah started laughing hysterically.

"Yeah, good one. So clever and original, and of course the same answer as last time," whispered Marc as the older siblings chuckled at the silliness.

"Oh Lucas, that one was a real STINKER," Mensah finally got out between laughs.

"Yeah, I see it really CRACKED you up," Lucas giggled back as they both kept laughing uproariously.

"OK OK guys, we had better start heading back to Tarek's," advised Asim, checking his watch and shaking his head at the crazy pair. "Mom is making a big farewell dinner for you guys and she said she would feed ME to the Great Sphinx if we are late." They continued south from the Great Sphinx and then slowly headed back to Tarek's camel stables on the western side of the Giza plateau. When they arrived, Tarek was out leading a tour but their friend Evelyn helped them take care of the camels and feed them their dinner. Everyone asked her to thank Tarek for them for everything he had done to make such a wonderful last desert adventure for the six friends that day.

"Oh Marion, this is so wonderful – thanks for having us all over for dinner again," said Mom as they all sat around a huge table in her and Sallah's house enjoying their delicious food.

"It is our pleasure, we are always happy to have you here," replied Marion as Sallah nodded his agreement. "You are welcome at any time."

"Everything is just magnificent, I am SO going to miss your cooking," exclaimed Dad.

"Hey! What is that supposed to mean?" Mom asked with an evil look toward Dad as everyone snickered.

"Oh nothing, dear. Everybody knows your cooking is the bomb," replied Dad sheepishly with a wink. "Belly bomb, that is - boooom," he whispered conspiratorially to Lucas who cracked up laughing and snorted milk out of his nose. Mom then gave Dad the double evil eye and stuck her tongue out at both of them.

"We are going to miss you all very much – it's been such a wonderful summer together and such exciting times," lamented Sallah.

"Dad, so we were all talking on our camel ride today - can we all come back to visit the GEM when it finally opens?" asked Marc. "It would be so spectacular to see it when everything is finished and ready for the public."

"Oh yes, you simply must come back and stay with us," added Marion. "And I know Akiiki especially would love to see YOU again soon, Marc," said Marion with a wink.

"MOM!" whispered Akiiki as she turned a bright red and rolled her eyes. Sydney was watching her reaction quite curiously, and soon a wide smile spread on Sydney's face.

"Yeah, that would be great Mrs. e-K," Marc replied, completely oblivious to Akiiki's reaction, to her tremendous relief. "So what do you think, Dad?" he asked.

"Yes that sounds like a fantastic plan, and I'm sure we could swing it later this year or even next spring," replied Dad. "That would actually be a wonderful Spring

Break plan for next year so you guys wouldn't have to miss school," he added thoughtfully.

"Oh yeah, missing school would be just absolutely awful," moaned Lucas sarcastically as Mensah laughed.

"Yes, we would definitely love to – I can't wait," added Mom.

After dinner, the adults sat around the table still visiting while Lucas and Mensah ran up to his room like two thundering elephants. The four twins all walked to the backyard to sit and watch the beautiful sunset over the desert. "I will definitely miss Cairo and especially all of you guys," lamented Sydney. "This has been such an awesome summer!"

"Yeah, it will be soooo boring again when you guys are gone," complained Akiiki. "School is starting again soon and we are most definitely not looking forward to it."

"Same for us," replied Marc. "It's going to be hard to get back into our boring old routine again."

"So how is the packing going, guys?" asked Asim curiously.

"Don't even ask," complained Marc and Sydney simultaneously, as everyone laughed.

"Yeah, we haven't even started yet, so it is definitely going to be a long night!" Sydney added sadly.

"Oh hey Marc, I almost forgot - I want to give you something before you go," Asim said excitedly. "The GEM gift shop got in some cool Tutankhamun nesting sarcophagus models this week and I got one for you. I hope you have room for it in your suitcase."

"Awesome! That sounds cool!" Marc replied enthusiastically as the boys rushed inside to Asim's room to check it out, leaving the girls alone in the backyard.

"Soooooooo, apparently you have a giant crush on my twin brother," Sydney whispered to Akiiki, who immediately turned a bright red.

"Are you nuts? That's just ridiculous. I don't know what you are talking about Syd," Akiiki replied defensively. "What in the world makes you think that?" she added nervously, now obviously trying to avoid making eye contact with Sydney.

"Well, I have noticed the way you have been looking at him all summer AND your mom just confirmed my suspicions with her little comment at dinner, AND your reaction then AND just now is the icing on the cake," laughed Sydney as Akiiki started squirming uncomfortably.

"No, we're totally just friends and you have it all wrong," Akiiki replied weakly, still avoiding eye contact. Sydney raised her eyebrows skeptically.

"Yeah. Nice try. So do you want my help or not?" Sydney asked excitedly.

Akiiki looked up to stare at her for several long moments and then reluctantly replied "yes, please."

"That's more like it, girl!" Sydney laughed. "First of all, you DO realize that he's a total and complete doofus about romance and has no clue whatsoever that you have a crush on him at all, right?"

"Yes, I figured that out rather quickly on my own, thanks," laughed Akiiki. "That's why I need your help, obviously."

"Well, if it makes you feel any better, I'm in the same situation back home with a guy that I have a crush on," replied Sydney sadly. "He has no idea that I like him, and believe me, it can be really frustrating," she laughed.

"So what's your plan?" Akiiki asked excitedly. The girls huddled up for nearly an hour concocting several wild and crazy schemes together to hopefully ensnare the objects of their affection. Several times during the ride back to their Cairo house later that evening, Sydney found herself giggling uncontrollably as she reflected on the zany romantic plans ahead for both girls – IF they were brave enough to actually follow through on them, that is. Marc was starting to get very suspicious and a bit annoyed at her strange behavior, but luckily was quite pre-occupied with the awesome Tutankhamun sarcophagus model from Asim. He remained completely and blissfully oblivious to the giant heap of trouble he would soon be in for.

Chapter 4. Homecoming

After a long day of hard work and help from their Egyptian friends, the family finally had everything packed and ready to go. It was hard saying goodbye but they promised to keep in touch and visit each other whenever possible. Dad was actually hoping that Sallah and his kids might be able to come to visit whenever the UVA team figured out how to open the sarcophagus, which had started its long shipping journey about a week earlier. The entire family was sad to leave Egypt but definitely looking forward to being back home in Charlottesville. With some luck, hopefully the sarcophagus would arrive about the same time they did.

Unfortunately there were no super convenient flights for their trip back home, so they ended up booking flights from Cairo to Rome to Atlanta and then finally to Charlottesville. Everyone was dreading the first two flights which were going to be particularly long and uncomfortable at three hours and then ten hours, but it also seemed like each of their planned layovers along the way was overly long. Dad explained that he had booked their travel like this to give them some buffer in case any of their flights were delayed or cancelled, since he always seemed to have bad luck every time he traveled. Marc and Sydney just hoped that the trip would be over quickly so they could get home and get settled before school started in a few days.

The flight to Rome had not been so bad, but their second flight to Atlanta was starting to get miserable, mainly due to Lucas. "Dude, can you just try to relax and take a nap?" Sydney asked him as nicely as she could for about the twentieth time. He had been loudly chattering away about random stuff for the entire flight and was sorely getting on everyone's nerves, and was particularly aggravating Marc and Sydney - as usual.

"No way man, I don't want to miss any of the action," Lucas replied. "Plus I'm almost at the big boss level," he said, concentrating on his Switch and continuing his annoying video game play-by-play commentary which absolutely nobody wanted to hear.

Sydney looked over at Mom and Dad for backup but they were both holding hands and giving each other googly eyes, somehow completely tuning Lucas out. "Yuck," she said to Marc quietly after pointing out the romantic freak show to him.

"Definitely, they've been useless like that ever since we left Egypt. Disgusting," replied Marc. "I can't wait to get off this plane and actually walk around again. This is taking forever," he complained. "Hey are you going to eat those crackers?" he asked. "That airplane 'dinner' was terrible and I'm still starving."

"Sure, you can have them," Sydney replied, passing Marc the bag of crackers. "I don't feel like eating anything right now." She closed her eyes and tried again to take a little nap. Even with her earplugs in, Lucas was SO loud that it was very difficult to relax. Sydney finally nodded off to sleep and thankfully the next thing she knew she was awakened by their bumpy landing in Atlanta.

Everyone was extremely happy to finally be able to walk off the plane and breathe fresh air again. Unfortunately their plane was huge and the flight was very full, so it seemed to take forever to exit the plane as everyone was blocking the aisles as they retrieved their overhead luggage and gathered all their belongings in what seemed like extreme slow motion to Marc and Sydney. When the twins finally made it off the plane, it felt absolutely wonderful to walk down the jet way and actually stretch their legs for the first real time in over ten hours. After walking through a crazy seemingly never-ending maze of long corridors they finally arrived at Customs and were still so happy to be moving that they didn't even mind waiting in the long lines for nearly an hour. After dropping their luggage back off after the Customs inspection, they were all excited to make their way into the gigantic main airport terminal to locate their gate to Charlottesville. Lucas was complaining loudly and dramatically that he was surely going to collapse from total starvation at any moment, so they found a nice sit-down restaurant where they could grab a "real" dinner and hang out for a while as they waited for their next flight.

"I'm going to call Hailey to let her know we should be home on schedule," said Mom after dinner. Their cousin Hailey and her husband Jared were house- and cat-sitting for them again this summer, along with their dog Maisy.

"Ask how the cats are doing with Maisy," requested Marc and Sydney simultaneously, making each other giggle.

"Yeah, they were probably torturing poor Maisy again this summer," laughed Dad as Mom was talking to Hailey. Last summer was the first time the pets had all been together for so long, and their cats Yoda and Elle did not particularly like Maisy, a mini Australian Shepherd who was always trying to "herd" them throughout the house. When the cats did not cooperate the way she thought they should, Maisy would gently nip at them in an effort to make them follow her orders. Let's just say the cats did not take kindly to being herded and were quick to let Maisy know exactly how they felt about it. Hailey and Jared often had to intervene and on several occasions had to pull cat claws out of poor Maisy's nose. Earlier in the summer, Hailey had told them it was going much better this year, but that the pets were definitely all very wary of each other this time around.

"OK, Hailey is all set to pick us up at the airport," said Mom after a few minutes of gossiping over the phone with Hailey. "And all the pets are fine and there were actually no big injuries or fights this year, amazingly enough. They must be getting a little bit used to each other," she added, ruefully thinking it would sure be nice if her own kids could learn the same trick.

"I wish Maisy could stay with us forever," complained Lucas. "She lets me play with her and doesn't run away from me like the stupid kitty cats. We love playing fetch and tug-of-war together and I really like taking her on walks around the lake. She is so much fun to have around," he said sadly.

Marc and Sydney rolled their eyes at each other in amusement. The cats avoided Lucas for the same reason they did – he was usually extremely loud and annoying and hurt their kitty eardrums with all his constant racket and thundering around the house. He had also often been a little too rough with them when they were kittens – such as carrying them around the house like floppy beanbags with their poor little legs swinging back and forth wildly. So naturally they were now very wary of him and were always quick to scamper away whenever he got too close to them. Luckily, despite all the torture from Lucas, the cats were extremely attached to Marc and Sydney. Sydney was their older cat Yoda's favorite, and the younger Elle tended to gravitate toward Marc. The four of them always hung out constantly at home so Marc and Sydney had dearly missed their cat friends and couldn't wait to get back home to see them again.

"OK guys, we'd better head over to our gate. We should be boarding pretty soon," said Dad, looking at his watch. They gathered up all their belongings and started the long walk to their gate. They timed their arrival perfectly and only had to wait a few short minutes before boarding the plane.

This last leg of their trip was mercifully easy since the flight time home to Charlottesville was only about an hour. The airline attendants did not even attempt to offer a complicated beverage service, they just handed out cups of water along with some pretzels and almost immediately came back around again to collect the trash. Even the flight path was bizarre – by the time they climbed to cruising altitude, they almost immediately started their descent. A short time later, they landed at the small and cozy Charlottesville airport and started the short walk to baggage claim where they had planned to meet Hailey.

The kids all caught sight of Hailey and Jared as they entered baggage claim and rushed over to tackle them both to the floor in giant hugs. Dad helped everyone get slowly untangled and stand back up as they all laughed hysterically. All the other passengers arriving in baggage claim were staring at them quite curiously and chuckling at their joyous reunion. After catching up for a few minutes, Jared walked out to go get the family mini-van from the parking lot while they waited on their luggage. Soon the baggage claim announcement siren went off and the belt started moving. It took a long while for all their luggage to appear and Dad remarked that it had definitely multiplied over the summer. Jared pulled up just as the last bag appeared so soon it was all secured in the back of the mini-van and they all climbed in.

"Hello Betty, I've missed you," said Dad affectionately as he sat beside Jared in the front seat and patted the dash. For some weird reason, Dad always had to name their vehicles and this was about the fourth Betty they had owned so it must be one of his favorite vehicle names, mused Marc.

"Oh yeah, Betty's a real hot rod," joked Jared, rolling his eyes. "She's got so much horsepower, I don't know how you keep her under 150 mph."

"Dude, just you wait until you guys have kids," Dad replied sarcastically. "It will be bye-bye little sports car and hello mini-van to haul around all the baby, big kid, and pet gear. Plus when they get older you have to keep everybody separated by at least two feet so they don't poke each other's eyes out. You'll love it, trust me!" Hailey started laughing uproariously.

"Speaking of babies, where is Maisy?" Sydney asked.

"Oh we left her at your place to guard the cats," replied Jared. "Hopefully they don't have her tied up in yarn and half-buried in the litter box by now."

"Well, I wouldn't put it past them," snickered Marc. "Especially if she was trying to herd them again."

A short while later they pulled up to their house and could see that Yoda and Elle were watching from one of the front windows and Maisy was watching from another. As soon as Maisy saw the mini-van pull up and heard the garage door open she started barking her head off and both cats instantly scattered. "Welcome back home, guys," said Hailey cheerfully as they crawled out to unload everything.

"Home sweet home," declared Marc and Sydney as they carried in their first load.

"Lucas, get back here and help us carry all this luggage in!" yelled Mom as he immediately scampered off to give Maisy a big hug.

Maisy was supremely excited to see everyone – especially Lucas - but the cats were still hiding as they finally got the rest of the luggage stowed in the garage and headed inside to get settled. "Come on Maisy," yelled Lucas as he led the way up to his room with Maisy right on his heels. He shut his door and started a loud game of something crazy with Maisy as they could hear both of them thundering wildly around his room. It was impossible to tell which one of them was louder.

As everyone sat down to relax and visit in the living room, Elle and Yoda both peered around the corner of the doorway at them. Sydney and Marc both called them over but the cats hesitated comically in the doorway, obviously torn between being still mad at them for leaving and yet still being ecstatic to see them after the long summer. After a few seconds they couldn't take it anymore and meowed loudly and jumped in their laps.

Yoda was the older of the two cats by about six years, and was a beautiful fluffy Ragdoll they had gotten from a local breeder. He was all-white except for grey ears, back, tail and half of his face which made a cool looking white triangle over his left eye. Yoda had a very calm and easy-going attitude and didn't mind being picked up or carried around in the least - as long as it wasn't by Lucas.

Elle, on the other hand, was definitely the wild child of the two cats. She was almost two years old and had been adopted by Mom and Dad from a rescue shelter. Her back story was truly awful as she was found near-death abandoned in a ditch, and had already gone blind in her right eye from a raging infection. The rescue shelter had miraculously nursed her back to life and Mom and Dad had found her up for adoption at their local pet store. Sadly, she had been stuck there for almost two months because no one had wanted to take a chance on her. Mom had first played with Elle at the pet store and despite all her terrible hardships, found that she had an amazingly upbeat attitude and rewarded any kind human attention with loud purrs of joy. Elle was a beautiful Siamese mix with coloring very similar to Yoda's except for having brown features instead of grey, and some really interesting random coloring like tiger stripes on her left leg, black dots behind all her knees, a white triangle stripe on her nose, and all black foot pads on each paw. Her left eye was a gorgeous blue but her right eye was totally clouded and a strange opaque pink color. It was obvious that she had little or no vision out of that eye as she would constantly move her head back and forth to "scan" with her good eye whenever something interested her. Mom filled out the adoption papers immediately and brought Dad to the store to see her the very next day. Of course emotional sucker Dad was instantly smitten, so home with them she came, and that evening was a complete and fantastic surprise to Marc, Sydney, and Lucas. And after a careful introduction process and a lot of initial hissing, she and Yoda quickly became good friends.

As the cats curled up for naps in their laps, Marc and Sydney were excitedly telling Hailey and Jared about all their adventures in Egypt over the summer. They of course had heard all about the Tutankhamun chambers and the new sarcophagus on the news so were keen to hear all the latest details. In return, they shared all their crazy pet adventures from over the summer. Elle had of course been up to her usual mischief and Jared reported that she had hunted down and destroyed every single one of Lucas' Nerf gun darts, which made everyone laugh since they had all seen Lucas sneakily shooting her with them on many occasions. It was also particularly funny to hear that Hailey and Jared had both tripped over

Elle about a hundred times, as she had a dangerous habit of darting between their feet as they walked.

"Yeah, she does the same thing to us all the time," explained Marc. "I think it's because she is blind in one eye and just doesn't see where she is going very well sometimes. Or maybe she just doesn't care, who knows? It's a real miracle nobody has crushed her yet." At that moment Elle opened one eye and hissed quietly up at Marc, making everyone laugh hysterically.

"And she's obviously quite the character," giggled Sydney.

"That is totally true, she reminds me of Hailey with her crazy attitude," replied Jared snickering, as Hailey punched his arm.

At that moment they heard Lucas' door open as he and Maisy came thundering down the stairs. Both cats awoke instantly and ran for cover. Lucas and Maisy both jumped over the back of the couch and landed heavily on the other side, getting a stern look from Mom.

"Lucas, you know I hate when you do that – you are destroying our furniture!" Mom scolded.

"And the rest of the house, for that matter," Dad snickered as Lucas stuck his tongue out at them both in reply.

"Hey Hailey, can Maisy stay in my room tonight?" he asked excitedly.

"Sure, no problem, but she snores like crazy, kicks all night, and hogs the bed," Hailey replied laughing.

"Hmmmm, just like her momma," joked Jared as Hailey smacked him again, smiling. "Yes, two for two, I'm on a roll," he whispered, as he smiled back at her with googly eyes.

Marc and Sydney both looked away awkwardly. "What's with all the goopy love-struck adults around here?" they both wondered. Yuck.

"Oh no problem Hailey, I don't mind. She's my best buddy. Thanks!" Lucas replied as he ran off again with Maisy close behind.

"Those two are a perfect match for each other," said Marc as he rolled his eyes. He and Sydney visited with the family for a while longer and then quickly made their way up to their rooms. They were happy to see that everything was just as they remembered leaving it (except for a thin layer of dust everywhere), and they wandered around their rooms fondly remembering all their treasures and adding a few souvenirs from Egypt in key locations. Marc excitedly placed the amazing Tutankhamun sarcophagus model from Asim as the new centerpiece of his archaeology display. That night, it felt absolutely wonderful to finally sleep in their own cozy beds for the first time in months.

The next morning, everyone was very sad to see Hailey and Jared leave, but knew they had to get back home to Charleston, SC, after the long summer away. Lucas was particularly sad to say goodbye to Maisy, but both the cats were obviously completely ecstatic. Marc and Sydney were sure they saw them both hissing and sticking their tongues out at Maisy as she drove away, to everyone's great amusement.

"OK kids, let's get ready to go - we have a big day today. There are only a couple of days before school starts so we need to go shopping for school supplies – hooray!" said Mom sarcastically as everyone groaned. "And Marc and Syd I swear you both have grown six inches over the summer so we'll need to find some new clothes for you too. Come on, follow me."

"Oh joy, what a glorious day this will be," they both exclaimed sadly as they headed up to their rooms with Mom to try on their old clothes and make their school shopping lists.

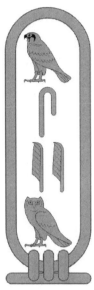

Chapter 5. Trouble

Marc and Sydney were hanging out with Dad in his lab in the UVA Department of Archaeology. They were both excited to see Mr. P's sarcophagus which had arrived from Egypt that morning. Dad and his team had spent the entire day unpacking, weighing and measuring it, and giving the sarcophagus a thorough and careful top-to-bottom inspection and cleaning to check for any damage during shipping. Everything appeared to be in perfect condition so afterwards they maneuvered it onto a custom-built adjustable elevated stand in the Archaeology lab which would allow for easy, safe, and unhindered study of the entire sarcophagus.

"Wow, it is even more beautiful than I remember," said Sydney, examining the sarcophagus. "The hieroglyphics are so amazing – I wish we could figure out what they mean."

"Yeah, me too," said Dad. "Today was the first time I've gotten a good look at the underside of the sarcophagus – the hieroglyphics are just as complex underneath which is pretty strange considering it was resting flat on the floor of the tomb chamber where no one could readily see them. Hmmm, except in the Egyptian afterlife, I suppose. Anyway, I've never seen sarcophagus decorations this densely packed and complex, it really is breathtaking. Tutankhamun's outer golden sarcophagus had exquisite and intricate patterns all over it but really just a few hieroglyphics, and mainly just on the top."

Marc and Sydney both stretched out on the floor underneath the sarcophagus to get a better look. "Ohh, these are really neat. Hey, I think I see Mr. P's cartouche again down here too," said Marc.

"Yes, that's definitely it," confirmed Sydney. "I don't recognize anything else though. So what's next in the investigation, Dad?" she asked eagerly.

"Well, tomorrow the EE department is bringing over their 3D scanner so we can get a comprehensive scan of the exterior," said Dad. "That will probably take a couple of days to process and render as a full 3D computer model in our tools. They also want to take some further measurements to see if their big imaging scanner will be able to fit in this lab or if we need to move Mr. P again. That scan will hopefully finally let us have a look at the inside so we can discover how to open it without damage."

"Wow, I can't wait to see what is inside," Marc and Sydney both declared simultaneously.

Dad glanced down at his watch. "Definitely! Hey I guess I need to get going to teach my Archaeology 304 class. Tonight I'm introducing one of my favorite archaeological sites - the Minoan Palace of Knossos on Crete, so it should be pretty exciting I hope. Will you guys be OK hanging out here until I get back?"

"Sure Dad, no worries. I think we'd both love to keep looking over Mr. P's sarcophagus if that's OK," said Marc.

"Oh, absolutely," said Dad. "But everyone has left for the day so just be careful and remember not to touch or disturb anything. You are under the exact same no-touch rules as back at the GEM – so I'm trusting you guys. I'll lock the lab door on my way to class, but text me if you need anything. Call the UVA Police if you see anything suspicious; they are making special patrols around the archaeology buildings for us while Mr. P is here. I should be back in a couple of hours, depending on how many questions I get after class. The first test is next week so I might be stuck there for a while."

"OK, see you later. Have fun at class!" they both chimed as they quickly returned to their examination.

"Man, I wish I could read hieroglyphics better – you'd think I would have caught on a little faster after spending the summer in Egypt. Akiiki tried to give me some lessons but she wasn't very good at it either," Sydney complained. "The only thing I really easily recognize is Paatenemheb's cartouche here. See how it is surrounded by an oval border with three knots attached to a bottom bar? The cartouche is supposed to symbolize 'all that the sun encircles' and means it is someone's formal name."

"Well, you are much better at it than I am," said Marc, looking carefully at Mr. P's cartouche. "I've tried to read a bunch of Dad's 'Hieroglyphics for Dummies' books but I still can't really recognize the characters to have it make sense as English words in my head. I guess it just takes a lot of practice, even Dad is pretty slow at it and has to keep looking up the symbols."

"Hey, why don't you grab those translation papers off of Dad's desk over there?" Sydney asked excitedly. "The GEM staff had been working on a translation of the top and sides, so maybe we can use that to figure out some new hieroglyphic texts on the bottom."

"Oh yeah, great idea!" replied Marc enthusiastically. "Hang on a second, I'll grab it and some pencils and more paper too," added Marc as he jumped up and headed over to Dad's desk, returning quickly with the requested items.

"OK, see this?" asked Sydney. "The GEM translation is arranged according to the different sections of the top and sides of the sarcophagus which have these faint separating borders between them, as if they were different topics or some sort of unique subject matter."

"Well, they sure don't have very much translated so far – mostly just some color names it looks like," remarked Marc, studying the translation papers and trying to coordinate them with the different subject zones of the sarcophagus.

"Yeah, here I found blue, other there is yellow, then orange underneath that and purple and red over here," said Sydney as they walked around the sarcophagus inspecting it closely and pointing out the symbols. "It seems like the color is one of the first words in each section, but I'm really not sure if that means anything important or not," she added.

"Oh, here they found some non-color words," Marc said excitedly. "This looks like 'tap' and maybe 'twice' but I can't find it on the sarcophagus."

"Oh, I just saw that one – it is over here near the right shoulder," Sydney said. "And this one beside it seems to have a bunch of animal names at the end – here they wrote ibis, monkey, cat, snake, tiger, crocodile, bull, and hippopotamus."

"OK I think we have the general idea, let's see if we can find anything new on the bottom," Marc instructed enthusiastically. They both carefully crawled back underneath the sarcophagus stand and started a close examination of the dense hieroglyphics. Marc made a detailed drawing of the different zones on the bottom of the sarcophagus while Sydney started looking for matches to any of the previously translated hieroglyphics from the GEM papers.

"Oh nice job, Marc," Sydney declared a few minutes later as she admired his detailed drawing. "I think I found a new color – see this? I'm pretty sure this says green," she said excitedly as she pointed to a set of symbols near the top of one of the zones.

"Oh cool, let me write that on my drawing," Marc said excitedly. "Hey what is this one over here with all the scarab beetles and the weird looking thingy?" asked Marc, pointing to the area right beside the green zone.

"Hmm, beats me," replied Sydney in frustration, after studying it for several seconds. "I can't read any of that at all, except maybe for these two parts which MIGHT say 'beetle' and possibly 'hide'."

"OK, nice! I'll put that on my drawing," Marc replied. "Hey this is good, we're actually making a little progress!"

"Yeah, this is pretty fun – I think Dad will be excited with our discoveries!" replied Sydney proudly. The twins spent the next hour carefully looking over the different areas of the sarcophagus and excitedly pointing out their finds to each other. They kept working at it diligently and were able to match several more of the color names and found lots of 'taps' and what they thought might be numbers, but overall it was very slow going and extremely frustrating and tiring work.

Marc moved around to the feet of the sarcophagus to continue his investigation. "Hey Syd, check this out – I think I found another cartouche!" he said excitedly. The new cartouche was in the exact center of the foot panel and consisted of four characters: a falcon, a draped cloth, a double reed, and an owl from top to bottom all surrounded by an oval border and bottom bar just like Mr. P's. Neither of them had noticed this before, and it was definitely not on the GEM translation diagrams. To their great astonishment, the cartouche itself was glowing a faint blue. Without thinking, they both reached out and touched it. The cartouche immediately began glowing a brighter blue and suddenly they could see a blue rectangular border appear around it and several of the adjacent symbols. Without warning, this section of the sarcophagus popped forward revealing a small secret drawer. Spellbound, they both leaned over to curiously peek inside.

The secret drawer contained two magnificent golden bracelets, each crafted from dozens of tiny, intricately woven wires of solid gold topped with a stunning blue lapis lazuli gemstone exquisitely carved into the shape of the cartouche from the outside of the drawer. The bracelets were absolutely breathtaking to behold and they both automatically reached for them. Despite the warnings from Dad and all they knew about the cardinal rule of archaeology of not disturbing artifacts until they could be fully analyzed and documented, they were both filled with the undeniable urge to immediately place the bracelets on their wrists. The bracelets fit perfectly on their right-hand wrists and they turned their hands over and back to admire the bracelets' beauty from different angles. "These are just superbly crafted and magnificent – I don't think I've ever seen anything so beautiful in my entire life!" Sydney exclaimed in total awe.

"Umm, I totally agree but suddenly I'm getting a very bad feeling about this. We should take them off NOW," said Marc reaching for his wrist. At that exact moment the cartouche gemstone on both bracelets starting glowing a brilliant bright blue and they found that they were unable to move a single muscle. The tiny golden wires on the bracelets then began to quickly unwind and then dissolved into the underside of their wrists. The process did not hurt at all but gave them both a strange, warm, tingling sensation. When the wires had all been absorbed into their arm, the cartouche gemstone also dissolved into their skin and spread out as a glowing blue liquid on the underside of their forearms to form the sparkling cartouche symbol just under the surface of their skin. The cartouche was slightly taller than the width of their hand and slowly moved to center itself lengthwise perfectly between their wrist and elbow before locking in place there and pulsating like a living thing. It was a totally bizarre and terrifying experience and they both started to panic and hyperventilate as their muscle control began to return. Then several things happened at once. They first heard a loud scratching from inside the sarcophagus followed by a loud crack, and then the new cartouche symbol on their arms began to glow a blindingly bright blue and they both immediately blacked out, falling hard to the floor.

They both awoke to find that the sarcophagus cartouche and the secret drawer had both completely vanished and worse yet, the hinged sarcophagus lid was wide open. Marc and Sydney jumped up to look inside but it contained only a large amount of dust and some scraps of embalming wrappings. They also noticed the clever latch mechanism on the underside of the lid which had so far eluded discovery by the imaging scans. Then they both simultaneously looked down at their forearms and saw that the blue cartouche in their skin had faded almost to nothing and then disappeared completely before their eyes. That was when they noticed a trail of dust covering the lab floor. "Oh crap, crap, crap. Dad is going to kill us," wailed Marc.

"Yikes, I think I hear Dad at the lab door. We must have been out cold for a long time! Hurry up and help me close the lid!" whispered Sydney. They both grabbed the side of the sarcophagus lid and it slowly closed on its own and sealed with a hiss of air and a loud click. They took a few steps back and tried their best to look completely innocent as Dad entered the lab.

"Hey, where did you guys go?" Dad asked.

"Nowhere, why?" they both responded cautiously.

"Well, the lab door was unlocked when I got back here just now," said Dad curiously.

"Oh yeah, I forgot. Umm, we just went over to the vending machine in the break room for a quick snack," Sydney said, thinking quickly. Marc gave her a relieved glance.

"Oh right, we should get back home for dinner," said Dad. "These night classes make it hard to keep a normal family schedule sometimes, sorry about that. By the way, where did all this dust on the floor come from?" he asked. They both looked down and saw that there was quite a bit of dust all around one side of the sarcophagus.

"Sorry Dad, I knocked over the trash can by accident when I was throwing our trash away. I'll clean it up. We both got so excited checking out Mr. P's sarcophagus and I wasn't paying close enough attention to what I was doing," said Marc trying to refocus the conversation elsewhere.

"No worries," said Dad. "I completely understand - it is definitely the most fascinating and mysterious artifact I have ever seen, and by far the biggest discovery of my career. This was actually the first time ever that I did not want to teach a class – I just wanted to stay here to keep studying the sarcophagus. So did you guys make any more exciting new discoveries while I was gone?" he asked.

"No not really," they both said a little too quickly.

Dad gave them both a funny look. "Well, if you want, we can all keep investigating tomorrow after school. You guys have a big day tomorrow – woo hoo, first day of school! Clean this up while I grab my work papers and then let's get home for dinner," he said.

After cleaning up the dusty floor, Marc and Sydney followed him out of the lab looking around carefully. "Look," whispered Marc, pointing at the floor in the main hallway. There was definitely a light trail of dust all the way down the hall and right up to the lab door, where they both noticed a tiny scrap of embalming wrapping on the floor. Marc quickly covered it with his foot and carefully slid it outside as Dad locked the lab door behind them. Then when Dad was not looking, he picked it up and gently placed it into his pocket on top of the handful of dust he had already secretly collected. Marc and Sydney shared a long and very worried look with each other as they followed Dad to their car.

Chapter 6. Champion

Neither Marc nor Sydney were particularly thrilled about being back in school the next day. They had both enjoyed a fantastic summer and were not quite ready for it to be over, plus in the back of their minds they were extremely worried about what had happened in the lab yesterday. But there was no sign of their forearm cartouches, so this morning it had all almost seemed like waking up from a bad dream. They both had a glorious reunion with their friends during and between their first few classes and then over the long lunch break it was great to REALLY get caught up with everyone's adventures over the summer. But the rest of the day so far had been downright boring and they could already tell that eighth grade was going to translate into a lot more homework than last year. At least they were both in all the same classes this year which was a bit unusual for them. It seemed like in the past the schools had given extra thought to keeping the twins mostly apart, so it was nice to know they would finally be together in everything this year.

"OK, bad news," said Nick, Marc's best friend. "I hear McGregor is making everyone play dodgeball in PE today. I swear that is his favorite sport!"

"Crap," said Marc. "I hate dodgeball. We must be the only school in America that still plays that barbaric sport, if you can even call it that. I think I still have bruises where Knuckles pummeled me with the ball last year," rubbing his arms and neck from the sudden bad memories.

"Thank goodness for Becky, that's all I have to say," said Sydney's best friend Kelly, referring to what had become known as the "Becky Incident." That was the day last year when they were playing co-ed dodgeball and Alec "Knuckles" Nichols had badly broken Becky Johnson's nose with a particularly vicious shot to her face. Ever since then, Mr. McGregor had mercifully kept the boy's and girl's games completely separate, and all the girls were immensely grateful towards Becky for rescuing them from the usually quite painful games.

"Well, it's great for you ladies but it just means that now all the guys get to be the full target of all his fury," said Nick. "I think it really pissed him off - the first few games after that were particularly ugly," he remembered painfully.

The lunch bell rang and they all got up and gathered their backpacks to head to PE. "Well, this should be loads of fun," complained Marc sarcastically.

After a few mandatory laps around the gym to get them warmed up, Mr. McGregor separated the boys and the girls and had them divide up into teams of about 12 players each for dodgeball. As luck would have it, of course Marc, Nick and their friend Tyler were on the team playing against Knuckles and his entire band of cronies. As the whistle blew, they all quickly ran to either pick up a ball or to find a good slow person to hide behind. As he stooped to pick up a ball, Tyler made the terrible mistake of making direct eye contact with Knuckles who was casually seeking his first victim.

"Welcome back to target practice, ladies," heckled Knuckles as he launched a ferocious fast ball directly at Tyler's face. Tyler valiantly tried to duck but was too slow and took a hard hit to his shoulder. Nick saw his opening and jumped in front of the ricochet to get himself out as well. "YES, two losers with one shot!" screamed Knuckles as all his cronies laughed.

"Sorry Marc!" whispered Nick as he quickly ran off the court beside Tyler who was busy nursing and stretching out his sore shoulder.

"Yeah, thanks a lot buddy!" whispered back Marc sarcastically, keeping a close eye on Knuckles. He found himself getting more and more infuriated as the taunts from Knuckles and his cronies escalated as they systematically took out all of

Marc's team. All of his teammates had been carefully concentrating on hitting everyone else on Knuckle's team to avoid massive retaliation hits from the cronies, and they were all quickly picked off one by one. Soon it was just Marc left against Knuckles and three of his worst cronies – Kyle, Will, and Harlow. With Mr. McGregor now watching the game intently with an overly excited smile on his face, Sydney and all the girls quietly agreed to quit their game and quickly came over to watch the showdown. Something inside Marc finally snapped and he dabbed and laughed at Knuckles tauntingly. "Bring it, Mr. Big Guy!" he yelled at Knuckles which drew gasps of horror and disbelief from everyone watching the game.

This was a first. Knuckles was not used to being taunted and definitely did not take it very well. "You're going down, loser!" he yelled at Marc. "McGregor is going to have to scrape you off the wall with a spatula when I'm done with you. Get him, boys!" he yelled at his cronies. Kyle, Will, and Harlow viciously launched their dodgeballs at Marc simultaneously as Knuckles snickered evilly. Sydney screamed loudly which echoed badly inside Marc's brain, nearly distracting him as the three dodgeballs bore down on him at high speed.

Marc's body took over automatically and he could see the path of each dodgeball clearly in his mind as if everything were in slow motion. He twisted to easily avoid the first dodgeball heading for his face and reached instinctively for the other two dodgeballs, catching them both effortlessly. He then instantly spun around to maintain their momentum and wind-milled the two dodgeballs back at the three surprised cronies. The first dodgeball hit Kyle in the side and spun him around like a top. The other hit Will in the stomach and ricocheted hard into Harlow, knocking them both to the floor and sliding out of the game. "How do you like that – three cronies down, one big ugly bully to go!!" yelled Marc. The crowd started cheering emphatically. "Nice shot," Marc heard in Sydney's voice inside his head which startled him. He risked a quick glance at her and thought back "Thanks!" Now it was her turn to be startled. They both grinned widely.

Knuckles gasped in complete shock at how quickly the game had turned against him. He had never lost a game of dodgeball and was not about to start now, especially against this nerd who he had always crushed so easily in the past. He quickly turned a bright red and totally blew his top. Knuckles wound up a massive shot and yelled "Oh yeah, well dodge THIS, nerd!" viciously launching his dodgeball straight for Marc's head as hard as he possibly could.

Marc easily stepped out of the way just in time and the dodgeball smacked the wall behind him with a huge crash and bounced back towards him. Marc caught it easily from behind without even looking and re-launched it directly at Knuckles like a bowling ball, yelling "Right back at you, buddy!" The ball hit Knuckles directly in the chest and knocked him backward several feet as he stumbled to the floor. The crowd went crazy and they all instantly rushed Marc to congratulate him. This was the first time in his life that Marc had actually enjoyed playing a game of dodgeball and it was definitely the only time he had ever won in ANY sport against Knuckles. "What a crazy wonderful feeling," he thought to himself as he returned high fives to the admiring crowd.

Mr. McGregor rushed over excitedly and raised Marc's arm high into the air and yelled "Our new champion! Dang, that was well done, kid. What the heck happened to you over the summer? We might actually make an athlete out of you yet!" The crowd cheered wildly. Tyler and Nick both broke through the crowd and clapped him on the shoulders in congratulations.

Marc started to feel a bit guilty and walked over to a still-sitting Knuckles to see how he was doing. "Are you OK, Alec?" he asked timidly. Marc realized this may have been the first time he had ever used Knuckles' real name, much less talk to Alec willingly.

"Umm yeah, nice game Marc. I see you must have been practicing over the summer. I'm looking forward to a rematch," he said grumpily as Marc reached out his hand to help Alec to his feet. "Hey, what's on your arm, dude?" he asked, noticing the cartouche symbol now glowing a bright blue on Marc's right forearm.

Marc looked down in shock but recovered quickly saying, "Oh, it's just one of those temporary tattoos I got in Egypt over the summer. I'm having trouble washing it off so I'm kind of stuck with it." Alec held tightly onto his arm and looked closely at the cartouche.

"Well, dang that's pretty cool. I've never seen a tattoo glow that brightly in the day time," Alec said as his cronies Kyle, Will, and Harlow all crowded around to look at Marc's arm.

Sydney rushed over to Marc's side as the bell rang and said urgently, "Come on, let's go!" grabbing his other arm. Marc twisted his arm out of Alec's grasp and casually clamped it against his side to hide it from all the curious eyes.

"Ahh, how sweet. Look, his special twinnie Sydney has a matching tattoo on her arm too," teased Alec.

Marc and Sydney both glanced down at her right forearm and realized her cartouche was also glowing brightly, although both were now slowly starting to fade. Sydney quickly covered hers with her left hand and snickered "Ha ha, very funny" sarcastically back at Alec, rolling her eyes in contempt.

"Anyway, nice game Marc, see you!" said Alec, as he and his cronies huddled together as the twins walked off. Marc and Sydney could hear them whispering loudly to each other, complaining about their aches and wondering how Marc had managed to cheat his way to a victory and especially if the weird matching glowing tattoos had something to do with it.

"What was that all about?" asked Tyler as he pushed between them and put his arms around their shoulders. "Are you guys OK? That looked a little dangerous," he said. At his touch, Sydney's mind immediately turned to mush and she could only smile back at him awkwardly. She had always had a giant crush on Tyler and of course he was completely clueless to her affections. Although she thought bitterly, her not being able to actually talk to him coherently was probably the biggest reason her affection was not being returned. She took a deep breath to steady herself.

"Oh yeah, no worries," said Marc. "I was just helping him up. That was a pretty nasty hit - how's your shoulder?" he asked as Nick and Kelly joined them.

Tyler released them both and flexed his shoulder painfully. "Well, not too bad I suppose – he's definitely given me a lot worse last year," he laughed. "That was an amazing game, Marc. You're going to have to give me some lessons," he chuckled as Nick and Kelly voiced their agreement.

As they reached the hallway and separated from their friends, Sydney turned and urgently whispered to Marc, "Holy crap, seriously though - how did you do that? Those were totally savage moves. You always totally STINK at dodgeball! Not to even mention - how in the world did you talk inside my head like that? I heard you clear as a bell and your lips were definitely not moving."

Marc responded excitedly, "I have no idea. I just started to get mad at always losing to him and my mind just took over. Somehow the game was suddenly incredibly easy and I could see EVERYTHING in slow motion. I knew they would not be able to hit me and I knew exactly where every dodgeball in the room was located at every second. And I heard your voice in my head too, what WAS that? I think these new cartouches are much more than they seem, I'm getting really worried about last night. I'm afraid something freaky bad is happening to us."

"Yeah, me too. When we get home tonight we need to try to figure out what this all means," agreed Sydney. As they walked to class, they both stared worriedly at their blue cartouches which had now nearly completely faded away again.

Chapter 7. Dreams

Mom, Marc, and Lucas were all at Marc's soccer practice so Sydney was hanging out with Dad at home. For the past hour, he had been focused intently on his laptop screen and had a large stack of hieroglyphic books open on his desk. Every now and then, she would hear him muttering something to himself and then frantically turn a few pages in one of the books. Finally Sydney's curiosity was triggered and she walked over to his desk to see what he was doing. "What are you working on, Dad?" she asked, moving around to see his screen.

"Oh, sorry. Have I been totally ignoring you?" he asked. "Sallah emailed me some cool pictures of one of the papyrus scrolls from Tutankhamun's tomb which he has been restoring," Dad said. "Somebody back in Howard Carter's time had glued it to a piece of cardboard in a horribly shoddy attempt at conservation and then it sat untouched in the bottom of a drawer for almost 100 years. It was deteriorating badly and it was a real miracle that Sallah was able to repair it. Come check it out." Dad dragged the picture up to his larger monitor screen so that Sydney could see it more clearly.

"I've been translating it just for fun to brush up on my hieroglyphics. I've got the first line translated and it only took me about an hour," Dad proclaimed proudly. Here, let me read it to you. 'I am the mighty warrior Pharaoh Tutankhamun. Today in the seventh year of my reign,' well, that's all I have so far," he read from the screen proudly.

"Today in the seventh year of my reign," Sydney continued to read quickly, "'I was victorious in a great and mighty battle against my enemies and I brought great honor to the mighty Horus, falcon god of the Pharaohs. All shall praise the mighty warrior Pharaoh Tutankhamun and give thanks to his father the Pharaoh Akhenaten who was treated so unjustly by his people. Today vengeance and great glory in both our names is mine, for I faced many thousands of evil and well-armed Nubians who were aided by the God Anubis and his army of jackal headed shadow warriors. Together my Grand Egyptian Army and the mystical magic warriors of Asim smote them all back to dust and sent their souls to the underworld with no guide to be forever there lost. My almighty...' Oh, hey Dad, can you scroll down for me?" she asked excitedly, motioning her finger downward.

She realized that Dad was sitting there frozen in complete amazement. "Holy crap, since when are you fluent in ancient Egyptian hieroglyphics? That was like speed-reading, were you just making it up to troll me or is that really what it says?" he asked very suspiciously.

"Oh yeah, I forgot to tell you that Akiiki gave me lessons over the summer. She's really good at it and was a great teacher," Sydney backtracked quickly, now feeling in shock herself at what she had just done so automatically. Reading the scroll felt completely natural and easy just like she was reading one of her favorite books. She glanced quickly at her forearm and saw that her cartouche was glowing purple so she hid it quickly from Dad. "Crap, so that's how I did it," she thought to herself as a growing panic started to well up inside her.

"Really? Well read it to me again so I can write this down," demanded Dad who was still staring intently at the screen. "I'm going to double-check you to see if you are right," he said, obviously more than a little annoyed that Sydney was so much better at reading than he was.

"Sure, Dad," Sydney said sheepishly and started reading the entire passage to him again. However, when she got halfway through she stopped on the cartouche for 'Asim,' realizing in shock that it was the very same symbol that was now glowing brightly on her forearm which she still held carefully behind her back. Dad looked up at her questioningly as she suddenly paused so she quickly pulled herself together and finished the passage for him. "Did you get all that, or would you like for me, the lowly untrained barely teenager to read it again, Dr. Professional Egyptologist Expert, sir?" she asked sarcastically.

"Ha ha, very funny. No, I got it thanks. Very impressive, you must get those amazing language skills from your mother because you're obviously lightyears ahead of me," Dad said, feeling a bit depressed. "Come back later when I'm done checking and you can read the rest of it for me - IF you got this first part right - that is. We shall see."

"OK, cool. Thanks Dad - that was really fun!" she said as she quickly bolted for the door and ran upstairs to her room. Her mind was racing frantically. What did "mystical magic warriors of Asim" mean and why was it the same name as Akiiki's twin brother? She desperately needed to talk to Marc. Stupid soccer practice! Her cartouche was still glowing a bright purple. "My cartouche – of course!" as she quickly formulated a plan. "I'll try mind-linking to Marc again! How did I do it the first time? I have absolutely no idea," she thought frantically to herself.

Her pulse was racing wildly so she fought for several minutes to calm her body and to concentrate with her mind to focus only on one thought – talking to Marc. She closed her eyes and thought meekly, "Marc, can you hear me? I need to talk to you." Nothing. "Crap! How do I do this?" she yelled in frustration. Still nothing. "Marc, are you there? Marc. Marc. Roger, roger. Come in Marc. Come in Marc. Over!"

"Dude, what's with the walkie-talkie talk? You sound like a blithering idiot in my head," she heard Marc say while laughing hysterically in her mind. She could instantly feel they had a strong mind-link connection and she nearly fell over with relief.

"Stop laughing doofus, I need to talk to you! I just figured out what our arm cartouches say!" she mind-yelled back at him. "They are hieroglyphics for the name 'Asim' and I just read a really creepy scroll from Tutankhamun's tomb that talked about his 'mystical magic warriors of Asim,' whatever that means!"

"What? Slow down!" Marc mind-yelled back in return. "How did you figure that out?"

"It's hard to explain. Dad showed me a scroll that Sallah had emailed him and I was able to read it without even thinking. Oh, I'll just have to show it to you – when are you getting home?" she asked.

"Maybe twenty minutes," Marc said after a brief hesitation. "Practice is over but Mom is talking to Coach Carlos about something. And Lucas is running around the field like a total and complete idiot - surprise, surprise!"

"Well, tell them to hurry up! Over and out," said Sydney angrily as she broke the mind-link connection and sat down on her bed to gather her thoughts. Elle jumped onto her lap and loudly meowed demandingly at her several times. "Oh, hey girl," said Sydney distractedly as she gave Elle a nice chin rub, which was always her favorite. Elle gave her an affectionate nibble and lick on the finger. She could feel herself slowly calming down as Elle purred loudly and curled up in her lap. Before very long, Yoda came bounding in her room to see what he was missing and jumped up beside her. Then he also wormed his way into her lap and made himself at home, halfway lying right on top of Elle who didn't seem to mind in the least. Before Sydney knew it, both cats were snoring loudly and still somehow managing to purr at the same time. "Crazy cats!" she chuckled to herself.

It was well over an hour before Marc returned home. "What the heck, dude?" she mind-yelled at him when she heard the garage door finally open.

"Sorry, I know." Marc replied. "Mom had to stop to get groceries and it took forever. Lucas also threw a giant hissy fit in the candy aisle so look out – they are both in a REALLY bad mood," he warned.

Sydney could hear the noisy commotion downstairs as the rest of the family came in from the garage. "Well, fine. Just get up here as soon as you can," she told Marc. Both cats woke up in her lap and stretched lazily before racing off together down the hall to investigate all the sudden noise.

A few minutes later Marc came bursting into her room. "OK, I finally made it here. What's up?" he asked eagerly.

Sydney recounted the entire Dad/scroll experience for Marc and recited the translated hieroglyphic message several times as they both tried to process what it might mean for them.

"Did you ever ask Asim what his name means in ancient Egyptian?" asked Marc suddenly.

"Oh yeah, that's a great idea. Maybe I could text Akiiki since it would be a little weird asking him directly," replied Sydney.

"Well, maybe, but there's a seven hour time difference between Cairo and Charlottesville – they are ahead of us so it's the middle of the night there now. Why don't you just google it on your phone?"

"Crap, great idea – duh!" said Sydney as she typed quickly into her phone. "OK, got it!" she said as they both looked at the screen together.

Asim (also spelled Aasim or Asem) is a male given name of Arabic origin, which means "protector, guardian, and defender." This same word also means "a word, a message" in Akan, spoken by Akans and by inhabitants of Suriname.

"Protector, guardian, and defender," repeated Marc excitedly. "Do you think that means us with these new cartouche powers?" he asked.

"Yeah, I think it does but who or what are we supposed to be protecting, guarding, and defending? That's the million dollar question," she wondered. "And how are we supposed to figure it all out?"

"Beats me!" exclaimed Marc. "Why don't you look up Akiiki and Mensah to see if they mean something that might help?" he asked. Sydney typed them into her phone but both had much more normal and totally unrelated definitions:

Akiiki – friend, female name of Arabic origin

Mensah – third born, male name of Arabic origin

"Well, that is pretty cool I guess but doesn't really help us," said Sydney bleakly.

"Mensah's name is pretty funny though – that would be like naming Lucas 'Number Three,'" chuckled Marc.

"Yeah, Lucas would love that," Sydney laughed along with him. "He definitely thinks he's number one around here!"

"Kids, dinner!" Mom yelled up the stairs impatiently.

"We're on our way!" Sydney replied immediately. She and Marc looked at each other quickly and then hurried downstairs, not wanting to worsen Mom's already bad mood.

That night neither of them slept very well. When she finally fell asleep, Sydney found herself in an intense and vividly real dream. She immediately knew she was back in ancient Egypt since she could clearly see the Great Pyramid nearby which was completely covered in smooth beautiful white limestone casing stones rather than the ugly filler stones that remain in modern times. The pyramid was blindingly bright in the hot desert sun of Egypt and was topped with a glorious golden mini-pyramid. It was truly an impressive sight to behold and looked absolutely spectacular.

Sydney quickly realized she was surrounded by many other people in her dream. She seemed to be part of two large and distinct armies. The first army was obviously ancient Egyptian which she could immediately tell from their armor, weapons, and headgear. She seemed to be standing amongst the second army which was a bizarre mix of people from many different races and time periods, including medieval knights, crusaders, Inca warriors, Roman soldiers, Vikings, Japanese samurai, American Indians, Mongols, British Redcoats, towering Amazon warriors, and many she could not even recognize at all. Several of the more contemporary-looking people nearby would have even looked right at home back on the streets of Charlottesville. She then excitedly noticed that her Egyptian friends Akiiki and Asim were standing not far away and she called to them. Akiiki caught her eye and smiled back in return. She nudged Asim who waved enthusiastically. Sydney immediately noticed that he also had a forearm cartouche which was glowing a fiery orange. Looking around quickly, she realized that everyone in the second army had glowing forearm cartouches. She glanced down quickly at her right forearm and saw that her own cartouche was glowing the same fiery orange, blazing brighter and warmer than it ever had before.

Sydney then noticed a handsome young Egyptian in the distance at the front of the two armies, holding a familiar bow which she immediately recognized. "Holy crap, that's King Tutankhamun," she thought to herself excitedly. From this distance, she could also make out the plate armor shirt from the museum which was now shimmering brightly in the hot sun, so she knew it must surely be him. Tutankhamun was surrounded by many large and fierce looking generals who were deep in conversation. Looking past Tutankhamun, she could immediately guess what they were talking about. Looming in the distance, two much larger armies seemed to be approaching them slowly. She could make out an army of dark-haired men but the other army seemed to all have the heads of jackals, unless her eyes were deceiving her. She was quickly filled with a sense of foreboding and pending doom.

Then suddenly, she felt a soft, gentle hand on her shoulder. Turning slowly, she realized it was Tyler. "I've always loved you too, Sydney," he said fiercely. "But I've been too afraid to tell you since I didn't know how my best friend Marc would react. But I don't care anymore – I've waited far too long to do this," he said reaching gingerly for her face, then kissing her intensely as she melted into his arms in complete and total bliss.

Sydney instantly woke up from her dream and was extremely angry it was over so abruptly. "Arrgghh, you have GOT to be kidding me," she yelled. "It was just getting to the good part!" She clamped her eyes shut and tried to force herself back to sleep to continue the wonderful dream, but her body was now just too worked up and anxious to cooperate.

"What are you yelling about over there?" asked Marc sleepily in her mind. "Are you OK?" he asked.

"Oh, I'm fine. I just had a really weird dream," Sydney replied, rubbing her forehead in extreme annoyance and frustration.

"It didn't happen to be about Tutankhamun leading an army of cartouche warriors against a bunch of ugly bad guys, did it?" Marc asked tentatively.

"Yes, that was it exactly! Did you just have the same dream?" she asked excitedly.

"Yep, I guess so. It was pretty creepy, here take a look," Marc said, playing back through the entire vivid dream in his mind for her. "I woke up when I heard you yelling."

Sydney realized it was exactly the same as her dream - up to a point. "Yep, exactly the same as mine. Umm, did the end of your dream happen to have Tyler in it?" she asked timidly.

"No, why do you ask?" Marc replied in confusion.

"Oh, no reason I guess," Sydney replied quickly. But she couldn't stop herself from thinking of Tyler's amazing words and his magical kiss. Her heart started fluttering again and beating wildly.

"OH MY GOSH THAT IS DISGUSTING!" mind-yelled Marc. "He's my best friend, what were you two thinking? Turn the horrible romantic dream replay off, please! Holy crap, it is still burning my eyes! Aaarrrggghhh!"

Sydney was instantly mortified and defensive. "Well, so sorry to disappoint you but I have always had a giant crush on Tyler and I can't help it. Didn't you dream about Akiiki in YOUR dream? I saw the way you were looking at her fondly," she mind-yelled back at him.

"Ewww, gross, what are you talking about? We're just friends – she's not my type. I was just happy to see her and Asim in the middle of all the bizarre people. You're completely insane. Good night, crazy sis! Over and out!" he said, breaking their connection angrily.

Marc tried his best to relax and go back to sleep but now he kept thinking about Akiiki and the way she had smiled at him in the dream. She was even more beautiful than he remembered, with her long black hair, lovely face, gorgeously striking green eyes, and full pretty lips. Her wonderful green eyes were always his favorite of her features, and he remembered fondly how they always lit up whenever she laughed at one of his jokes. He thought back to Sydney's strong reaction when dream Tyler was kissing her, and he wondered (admittedly not for the first time) what it would be like to kiss Akiiki.

"HA I KNEW IT!" Sydney mind-yelled at him, laughing hysterically.

"Oh, just shut up and go to sleep. You know, this mind-link with you is a real pain in the butt," he replied, rolling over and trying desperately to think of something else.

"Well, I'm your sister so you have to love me anyway," Sydney chuckled at him.

"Hummph," he grunted back at her and tried to fall asleep again so he could rejoin Akiiki and maybe try out that kiss.

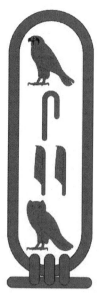

Chapter 8. Crush

Marc and Sydney met in the kitchen hallway on their way to breakfast the next morning, and smiled at each other sheepishly. "Well, last night sure was interesting," Sydney laughed as Marc chuckled in agreement. They walked into the kitchen where the rest of the family was gathered.

"Shhh," said Mom, pointing to Dad who was in a heated conversation on the kitchen phone. Sydney was planning to ask him to show Marc the papyrus scroll pictures from Sallah, but quickly changed her mind when she saw his expression.

"Yes, I realize you had yours calibrated three months ago, but they calibrated mine less than two weeks ago," Dad said, raising his voice. "Can you just check your reading again and get back to me? They can't be that far off from each other – something is really wrong with one of them. Are you sure yours is rated for something that heavy? Yes, well OK please just do me a favor and check it again. OK, thanks," he said, hanging up the phone and rubbing his forehead in annoyance.

"Is something wrong, Dad?" Marc asked immediately. He and Sydney could sense that something was really bothering him since Dad never easily lost his cool like that.

"Oh, it's Mr. P's sarcophagus. We had to move it to the Electrical Engineering lab this morning since their imaging equipment would not fit in my archaeology lab," he replied.

"Oh CRAP, did it get damaged on the way?" asked Sydney worriedly.

"No, no it was totally fine but the problem is when they re-weighed it on their lab scale it came in at over 200 pounds lighter which can't be right," Dad replied. "I just had our scales recalibrated by Lab Services two weeks before Mr. P arrived, so I think the engineering scales must just be way out of calibration but of course they are claiming mine are off. There is absolutely no reason for the sarcophagus to be that much lighter all of the sudden."

Marc and Sydney looked at each other in horror with their eyes wide open. "Are you thinking what I'm thinking?" he mind-linked to Sydney.

"Well, that's probably the only reasonable explanation. The sarcophagus was empty when we saw it, so there must be a 200 pound mummy on the loose," she replied over the mind-link. "Remember the trail of dust and that embalming wrapping you found?"

"Yep, this is not good," Marc replied.

"Well duh, that's the understatement of the century, Sherlock," she snickered back at him worriedly. He stuck out his tongue at her.

"OK, are you guys ready for school?" Mom asked a short while later as they were all finishing breakfast. "Sydney – I have to leave early to get back to work so you're with me this morning. Marc and Lucas - Dad is going to drop you two off at your schools a little later. Let's roll, time to get this show on the road."

A few minutes later Sydney was riding to school with Mom in her car, still deep in thought about last night's dream. "Mom, can I ask you something a little weird?" she asked tentatively.

"Well sure, honey, what's up?" Mom asked, keeping her eyes on the road and especially on the idiot car that was now trying awkwardly to pass them.

"Well I have a little crush on someone and I need some advice I guess," she said timidly.

"OHHH, I need all the juicy details, Syd!" Mom exclaimed excitedly. "I was beginning to wonder when you guys were going to start dating," she laughed. "Oh my gosh, I've been waiting forever for this wonderful day! This is SOOO exciting! What's his name? When do I get to meet him? Somebody please pinch me, I must be dreaming. Oh my gosh, I can't wait!"

Sydney was suddenly extremely embarrassed and very much regretted bringing up this topic with Mom who was a die-hard romantic through and through. "Hey slow down your horses there, Mom!" she said with great annoyance. "Well see, I have always liked this guy but I don't think he has the slightest clue as to how I feel," she continued quietly. "I see him almost every day but I just get too nervous around him to even speak. My mind just turns to mush and I can never seem to say more than hello to him without sounding like a crazy grunting Neanderthal woman. And last night I started dreaming about him."

"Hmm, I see," said Mom thoughtfully, putting on her romantic advice columnist thinking cap. "Well, I think you just have to relax and be yourself. If you stop putting so much pressure on yourself, always trying to say the perfect words, your mind will relax and he will soon be able to see the real you shining through. When you get to that point, tell him how you feel and you may learn that he feels the same way about you. My mom always told me that in matters of love, there is no reward without a little risk. Sometimes it just takes a few moments of sheer bravery in the face of all your terror and doubt, and afterwards true love will always find a way."

"Easier said than done," Sydney thought bitterly to herself. "What was it like with you and Dad?" she asked, hoping to shift the conversation topic away from herself and Tyler.

"Well, you know it is one of Dad's worst archaeologist jokes, but we really did 'dig' each other at first sight," Mom replied. "It was almost as if we both had known each other forever and were already the best of friends. It was so amazing – we both just instantly KNEW it was our destiny to be together. I don't know how to explain it but I've talked with many of our friends and it was definitely NOT like that for any of them. Something just magically clicked for us and we have been happily together ever since, and now we are blessed with you three wonderful children. It really was such a delightful miracle."

"Wow, I hope I have that someday," Sydney replied wistfully as Mom pulled in to the school parking lot. Sydney looked around the parking lot and school grounds and was suddenly hyper-aware of all the couples holding hands and greeting each other happily.

"Honey, you will. You just have to be patient and you will find your soul-mate, I have no doubts whatsoever," said Mom.

"Thanks Mom, you made me feel better. See you after school – love you!" Sydney said as she wrestled her heavy backpack out of the car.

"Love you too, Syd! Have a great day!" Mom replied as she drove off.

Of course, as luck would have it, Tyler was almost the very first person she saw as she left her locker and walked to class. He ambled up quickly beside her and asked, "Hey Syd, how's it going? Where's Marc?"

Sydney's heart instantly started fluttering but she tried to relax and quickly worked up her courage to get her lips moving coherently enough to speak. "Oh, hey Ty. Dad is dropping him off today, but they have to drop off Lucas first. He should be here soon," she said casually, smiling up at Tyler. "Wow, I actually did it," she thought proudly to herself. "That was probably the longest conversation I have ever managed with Tyler without sounding like a stupid Neanderthal. Way to go, me! I rock! I can do this!" she thought to herself happily.

"Oh, OK, cool. Hey do you mind if I walk with you to class?" Tyler asked. "I can't find any of my buddies this morning but everybody knows you're my favorite girl in the world anyway," he continued, winking at her mischievously with his gorgeous blue eyes.

Sydney's mind instantly melted into complete mush again. "Duuuhh, sewer, dat beee oootay" was all she could awkwardly get out as Tyler walked happily beside her down the hallways, chatting away about his favorite TV show he had watched the night before. Her mind was racing almost as fast as her heartbeat and last night's kissing dream kept replaying over and over again in her head which made everything that much worse. Her ears were now buzzing loudly and she could not make out a single word that Tyler was saying to her. Luckily he didn't seem to notice as he was gesturing wildly to reenact some of his favorite scenes for her. She tried her best to look like she was paying close attention to him and randomly nodded excitedly every now and then. She was intensely relieved when they finally reached Mrs. Baker's class and then split off to their desks, exchanging a quick smile. Sydney was glad she sat a few rows in front of Tyler as she was absolutely sure her face HAD to be a brilliant lobster red. She slumped over in her desk in embarrassment for several minutes to recover her senses. "Come on, this is ridiculous - you can SO do this, girl!" she finally said to herself as she sat back up.

They had arrived a bit early and there were only a few other people in the classroom, so thinking back to Mom's advice, Sydney had a crazy impulsive scary wonderful idea. She slowly turned around to look at Tyler and concentrated deeply, touching her right forearm where she knew her magical cartouche was hidden. "Kiss me," she mind-linked at him as forcefully as she could muster with a fierce look in her eyes.

Tyler turned to look at her a bit confusedly and smiled timidly. Then a piercing heat wave burned her arm as she yelped in pain and reactively grasped it tightly, sure that it was scarred beyond all recognition from what must have been molten lava. She looked down carefully at her arm but it was completely normal and her cartouche flashed a bright red and then blinked out.

Tyler came running up to check on her. "Are you OK?" he asked worriedly as he knelt down beside her. At that exact moment Marc came walking into the classroom with a deep frown and gave her a stern look of warning. Surveying the scene carefully, he immediately pointed at his eyes and then back at her with two fingers. That thoroughly pissed her off to no end and sparked her courage as never before.

"Sorry, yes, I'm fine. I just twisted my wrist," she replied, looking Tyler straight in his gorgeous eyes. "Hey, would you want to go to the movies with me tonight?" she asked bravely.

"Well, sure, that would be great," Tyler replied with a wry smile, taken a bit aback but not missing a beat. "Just text me the details," he winked. They both looked at the doorway as Mrs. Baker walked in just as the bell for class rang.

"OK folks, I know this is Language Arts, but let's have a little less spoken language and more written language instead," joked Mrs. Baker as she moved to the front of the class. "Everybody get out your notebooks and our fantastic textbook. And remember what Jedi Master Obi-wan always says: metaphors be with you!"

"Crap, gotta go. See you after class," whispered Tyler with another charming smile, chuckling just a little at Mrs. Baker's terrible joke.

As their eyes met again, Sydney smiled widely back and then gave a huge sigh of relief as Tyler returned to his desk. Wow, she had done it. Now she would have to spend two hours alone with Tyler on a Friday night in a possibly not-so-crowded movie theater. "Oh CRAP, what did I just do?" she thought to herself nervously as her heart raced wildly in total panic.

Marc projected loud ambulance sirens into her mind. "Oh shut up, very funny," she mind-yelled at him. "I don't care if you like it or not but you are going to help me," she said furiously.

"As if. Keep dreaming! No way, sis! I told you to stay away from him," replied Marc.

"Alright, class – everybody calm down and get to your seats," said Mrs. Baker loudly to get everyone's attention. "Before we get started I have a great joke for you: The past, present, and future walked into a bar. It was tense!" Mrs. Baker cracked up laughing but the entire class just moaned miserably. They all could already tell it was going to be a LONG school year...

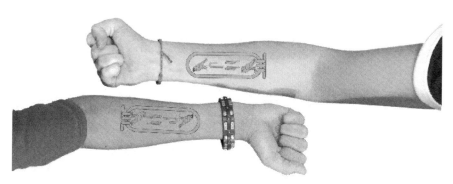

Chapter 9. Powers

Marc refused to talk to Sydney for the rest of the morning, and he was even acting a little weird around Tyler which had her worried that all her spontaneous hard work and bravery would be utterly ruined. Marc had even somehow managed to block all her attempts at mind-linking which added to her growing frustration. Hmm, she would definitely have to ask him about that later after she calmed down a bit. Sydney finally cornered Marc at lunch. "Dude, come on. What's your problem? Mom said I should talk to Tyler, just be honest and brave, and then see how it goes. Why are you so mad at me - what's the worst that could happen?" she asked defensively.

"Oh, great so now Mom's conspiring with you to creep out my best friend, is that it? You are going to totally gross him out and scare him away from both of us, that's what's going to happen," he replied bitterly, stubbornly refusing to look at her.

"Oh give me a break, if he were creeped out then he would have just told me 'no,' right? It's just the movies but I'm really nervous about being alone with him for that long and really could use your help, please?" she pleaded intensely, nearly crying.

Marc finally turned to look at her and saw the deep worry and tears starting in her eyes. "Oh fine then, just promise me no kissing OK? I do NOT want to see that gross vision ever again. And definitely don't creep him out with all your weirdness either – I don't want to lose my best friend," he said angrily. "So you have to promise to keep your freakitude under control, OK?"

"Awesome, thanks bro! I promise both – I'll be way too nervous anyway," she said in relief. "Although maybe a little kiss would be a delightful way to end our first date," she thought to herself pleasantly.

"I heard that, gross!" mind-linked Marc. Whoops. She was definitely going to need to learn that mind-link blocking trick.

They reached their desks in Spanish class just as the bell rang. Senor Poolay walked to the front of the class holding a stack of papers. "OK, put everything away except for your pencils – it's pop quiz time!" he announced gleefully. "I want to see how much Spanish you guys remember after rotting your brains away all summer - doing absolutely nothing educational I'm sure."

There was a simultaneous loud groan from the entire class. Knuckles, who was sitting in the back with all his cronies who were groaning the loudest of all, yelled out "Oh come on, Senor P, it's only the second day of school, isn't this just a little evil?" Marc and Sydney (and the rest of the class for that matter) were quite inclined to agree with Alec for once.

"Yep, it sure is a LOT evil but that's how I roll, baby!" Senor Poolay declared with a mischievous grin. "Quizzes build character, and you guys could all use some more character," he snickered. "Come on, it will be fun, I promise."

"I seriously doubt that," Marc mind-linked to Sydney, making her snort in suppressed laughter. As Senor Poolay handed out the quizzes, Marc had a great idea. "Sydney, you are incredible at Spanish, why don't you help me on my quiz?" he pleaded. "Senor Poolay is right, I don't remember any of it. This summer was way too exciting and I didn't even think about Spanish for one second. Please?"

"I don't know, Marc," she replied nervously, thinking about her earlier red cartouche experience with Tyler which she did not dare tell him about. That would definitely push him over the edge and he would surely not help her at all tonight on her date. She quickly pushed that memory out of her mind so he wouldn't see it by accident. Luckily he was too distracted to notice.

"Oh come on, why on earth would we be gifted with amazing magical powers if we're not supposed to use them?" he asked over their mind-link.

"Well I think we are supposed to use them for the right reasons to protect, guard, and defend and all that stuff. I don't think we are supposed to use them for personal gain or to cheat on quizzes," she chided. "And aren't you a Scout, anyway? What about our 'do your best' motto and I could have sworn 'trustworthy' was the first of the twelve points of the Scout Law. How many others are you planning to break today?" she retaliated.

"Fine, be that way, if you won't help ME, then I won't help YOU later," Marc said quite viciously.

"That's so unfair," she complained. "Fine then, I'll help you ONLY if you get stuck but this is ALL on you if we get in trouble," she replied angrily. "AND you have to promise to help me later no matter what happens."

"Deal," said Marc eagerly. "Thanks sis, you rock!" Sydney snorted back in disgust. Some Scout he was!

Senor Poolay finally reached their desks and gave them their quizzes with an evil wink. "Buena suerte, folks! You may start," he said with an annoying little chuckle.

Marc scanned over all the quiz questions and groaned at how many there were. Holy crap, this was going to take them the whole class time to finish. He scanned the quiz and actually found with relief that he thought he could probably answer about two thirds of them fairly easily. "I guess something did stick from last year, after all," he thought to himself proudly. After about twenty minutes he had finished all the questions that he could easily answer without racking his brain. "OK sis, what does 'castigo ardiente' mean? I don't have the slightest clue," he mind-linked to Sydney.

"What number is that one?" Sydney asked distractedly. She was nearly done with her quiz and was going back through to check her answers.

"Number 011," Marc replied, holding his pencil at the ready.

"011, 011, let me see. Oh yeah, 'castigo ardiente' means…," she started to say as a piercing heat wave burned both their forearm cartouches. Marc yelped in pain but this time she was halfway expecting it and was able to stifle her yell. She looked down at her arm and then over at his, but both were completely unburnt and their cartouches flashed a bright red and then blinked out.

From his desk, Senor Poolay looked up at Marc inquisitively. "Sorry teach, paper cut!" whispered Marc, shaking his arm. Senor Poolay nodded and returned to excitedly reading a Spanish soap opera gossip magazine.

"What the heck was that?" Marc mind-linked in pain and surprise, now rubbing his forearm gingerly and feeling amazed it was not burnt to a complete crisp.

"See, told you so, smart guy. We're not supposed to cheat," she replied as she walked forward to turn in her quiz to Senor Poolay.

"Hmmm, I guess you're right, sis. Looks like I'm on my own," he said sadly as he returned to continue his work on the quiz. At the end of the class, he turned his in with everyone else with a strong feeling that he did not do very well on several of the tougher questions, but that he had done his very best which is all that really mattered.

"OK, I turned mine in so tell me now, what does 'castigo ardiente' mean?" he mind-linked Sydney. "I had to just randomly make something up for that one."

She laughed. "Well, ironically enough it means 'fiery punishment' which is just what we both received for trying to cheat!" They walked out of class giggling with Tyler and Kelly close behind them.

When they got home that afternoon, they both went up to Sydney's room to formulate a plan for her date with Tyler later that evening. "OK, give me Tyler's number so I can text him the plan," demanded Sydney excitedly, as Elle and Yoda both circled their laps eagerly looking for a good spot to settle in for a nice nap. "And Kelly is walking over later to help me get ready, so please be nice to her."

"Well, I don't know, if you have Tyler's number anytime you want it this could all get very dangerous..." Marc said evasively. She shot him a fierce look and he knew she wasn't in the mood for teasing. "Oh fine, here it is," he said quickly, showing her his cell phone. She typed in Tyler's contact info and started looking up the movies playing that night.

"OK, it looks like two romantic comedies, a sad movie, a war movie, a superhero movie, and an action flick," she announced, looking over the entertainment options.

"Well, I assume the romantic comedies would be too much for you to handle without fainting when he looks at you, so I guess those are automatically out," he laughed.

"Ha ha, very funny. But yes, you are totally right. So I think it's either the superhero movie or the action flick, do you know if he has seen either of those?" she asked.

"Yeah, I think he saw the superhero movie last weekend with Nick, so I would say go for the action flick," Marc replied. "Although I did hear there is a little romance in that one, so you'll need to prepare yourself," he snickered.

"OK, action flick it is, let me text him the time," she said, ignoring his little jab and ordering their tickets. "I guess I'll need to ask Mom to take us there and pick us up," she continued with dread.

"Ha ha, Mom is going to go freaking CRAZY on you, you know that, right? First date for anyone in the family, that's a MAJOR mom milestone," he chuckled.

"Oh shut up, she's going to be awful of course. I wonder if Dad could take us instead?" she asked hopefully.

"Too bad, so sad. You're out of luck – Dad is teaching class again tonight, remember?" Marc laughed.

"Crap, you're right, I know. Well, wish me luck," she said dejectedly as she went downstairs to make arrangements with Mom.

After about one hundred loud squeals of joy from Mom and probably just as many teasing songs and jokes from Lucas, Sydney returned to her room with her face completely red. "Don't -- you -- dare," she said sternly to Marc as he watched her enter.

"Not a word," he promised, chuckling. "So what's next in this crazy plan of yours?" he asked.

"So first of all, teach me how you shut me out of mind-link today," she demanded, slowly calming back down. "I need to keep you from snooping around in my head any time you please."

"Oh yeah, that was actually pretty easy. I figured out the mind-link is much like a door – you can close it, open it just a little, open it half way, or keep it all the way open. Just think of it like making a phone call, you can choose to answer a call or just ignore it, but then you also get to decide how much to let the other person see.

That's what I did to you most of the morning – I just hung up on you every time you called," he laughed.

"Fine then, let's practice," said Sydney grumpily. They practiced for about twenty minutes by visualizing objects and then controlling if the other person could see them or not. By the end of the exercise they both had it working pretty well. "OK, so no more snooping around each other's minds without permission, deal?" she asked sternly.

"Heck yes – it's a deal," said Marc, shaking her hand formally. This was good - he didn't want her snooping around about his growing feelings for Akiiki and he definitely did not want to see Sydney kissing Tyler again. Gross.

By this point, Elle was getting furiously annoyed at being ignored for so long so she meowed loudly at both of them and started nibbling at their fingers. Marc and Sydney both laughed at her. "Hmmmm - I wonder what else we can do?" Marc asked with a mischievous look on his face. Suddenly Elle was floating through the air across Sydney's room flailing her legs and meowing in alarm. Yoda quickly scampered far under the bed to hide.

"Hey, be careful with her," said Sydney in astonishment. "How exactly are you doing that?" she then asked curiously.

"I don't know exactly, I just visualized what I wanted to do and it happened," said Marc. He looked down at his forearm cartouche which was now glowing a pleasant green color. Elle was getting used to flying and started purring and trying to grab all of Sydney's stuffed animals as she flew past them. Yoda peeked out from under the bed curiously but very cautiously.

"Let me try," said Sydney impulsively as she spotted Yoda. He noticed her looking at him, panicked, and then tried to run back under the bed, but soon he was floating around the room chasing Elle. "Oh, this is so much fun," Sydney exclaimed. Both cats were soon having a great time and purring loudly. Marc and Sydney had levitated a bunch of cat toys into the flying mix so the cats were eagerly trying to capture as many as they could, and were twisting and flipping around comically.

They heard a thundering noise outside her door and Lucas came crashing in loudly, as all the toys fell and both cats dropped to the floor gracefully. "What are you losers doing in here all evening?" he asked rudely. "Are you getting ready for your super-hot date, Syd? Mooochas smooooochas, baby. Ohhh Tyyyyler, I luuuv you!" he teased, making loud kissing noises and pretending to hug and kiss someone.

"Oh grow up," Sydney yelled back, resisting the strong urge to send him flying into the ceiling. Instead she threw a stuffed animal at him and he ran out of her room laughing. "Holy crap, how can something so little be so annoying sometimes?" Sydney complained.

"Yeah, tell me about it," Marc agreed. "But he's probably right – don't you need to get ready for a hot date with a certain someone? I'm just saying - it sure you looks like you have a LONG way to go in the beautification process!" She shot him a venomous look as he hastily jumped up to exit the room. She slammed the door shut behind him with her mind, feeling very satisfied with her handy new power.

Marc got downstairs just in time to see Mom letting Kelly in the front door. She had a large bag of make-up and hair products and looked quite frazzled. "Out of my way please, I've got a LOT of work to do on Syd to make her beautiful," she said to Mom who started laughing. She grinned at Marc and bounded up the stairs to Sydney's room.

"Well, good luck. You're going to need it," whispered Marc up the stairs after her.

"Tell me about it," said Kelly, chuckling as she reached Sydney's room.

Marc quickly assessed that Mom was a total wreck and had obviously just been crying bucketfuls of tears of joy. "Mom, you've got to pull yourself together. Syd is already nervous and you are going to push her over the edge," he told her worriedly. "It's just the movies – it's not like they are going to prom or running off to get married or anything."

"I know, I know," said Mom. "I'm just such a romantic and I want her to be happy. We had a really nice talk this morning on the way to school and then suddenly everything worked like I said it would and now she's going on her first ever date. It's just happening sooooo fast," Mom sobbed.

"Well, you've got about an hour before you have to drive them to the movies so please try to relax for Syd's sake," Marc instructed sternly. "Hey, where did Lucas run off to?" he asked as he looked around carefully. Marc knew he was going to have to keep his kid brother far away from Sydney or else she would either completely crack into an emotional meltdown or smash Lucas through a wall with her powers, either of which would likely cancel her date.

"Oh, he's off playing the Switch somewhere in the house. I can't seem to pry him away from some sort of screen or another. If it's not the Switch then it's the computer or the TV. I feel like he is rotting his brain. At least he doesn't have a cell phone like you and Syd – it could be worse I suppose. But I really wish you and Syd would play with him more," she said sadly.

"Well, you know sometimes it works OK but sometimes he just stirs up trouble and starts a fight. But we'll keep trying, I promise," Marc replied, as Mom shot him a worried look. "Maybe with some luck he'll grow out of his super annoying stage soon." Secretly, Marc seriously doubted it.

"OK, my work here is done," Kelly announced about an hour later as everyone else gathered at the bottom of the stairs. "I now present the new and improved Sydney," she announced proudly as Sydney smacked her hard in the arm as she walked by.

Sydney's hair looked amazing as she came walking down the stairs, and she had just enough makeup on to look nice but not overdone. Even Lucas was in total shock and could not think of anything to tease her about, which had to be a first. Mom started sniffling badly so Marc stepped on her foot as a reminder for her to behave herself. "Wow, you look fantastic, Syd," said Marc in amazement as she reached the bottom.

"Thanks," she said tentatively, wondering if he was being serious or if she should smack him.

"Yeah, your hair actually looks like you didn't wash it in a diarrhea potty like you usually do," teased Lucas, recovering from his momentary shock. Sydney rolled her eyes and shot him her meanest look, again sorely tempted to send him crashing into the ceiling.

"Lucas!" Mom chided. "Syd, you really do look just lovely. Are you ready to go?" she asked in a shaky voice, trying her best to hold herself together as Marc had pleaded.

"Yep, let's do this thing," Sydney said bravely as she and Mom walked to the car.

"Keep an open connection, dude. I'm a total wreck," she mind-linked to Marc. "And thanks for talking to Mom – so far so good. Oh, and give Lucas a good smack for me, that was even ruder than his usual. Dang little twerp."

"I'm on it, sis," replied Marc over their mind-link.

"1 ... 2 ...3 ... Good luck, guuurrrrl!" yelled Marc and Kelly together, laughing. Marc helped Kelly gather up all her beauty products and then held the front door open for her. "Thanks – see you later, Marc!" she said, as she started the short walk back home.

They stopped to pick up Tyler from his house and he hopped in the backseat with Sydney. "Wow, you look absolutely stunning!" he said, without taking his eyes off her. She felt her mind quickly turning to mush again but clamped down on her emotions instantly. Somehow it was a little easier with Mom in the front seat to keep her grounded.

"Thanks - you too!" she replied quite calmly for once. Tyler flashed his dazzling smile. Yikes, this was going to be tough.

"Hiiiiii Tyler, I'm SO excited for you two," Mom gushed from the driver's seat. "This is Sydney's FIRST EVER date, so thank you SO much for being the first guy to actually like her. But she's REALLY nervous, so please be nice to her," she added shakily, as Sydney immediately turned a bright red, with her eyes wide in shock and embarrassment.

"Well, Sydney is totally awesome and thanks a lot for taking us, Mrs. C," replied Tyler. "And this is MY first ever date too, so I know exactly how she feels," he added, rolling his eyes and smiling at Sydney, making her completely lose control of her racing emotions once again.

"Aw, that is so sweet," Mom replied excitedly. "You two make a wonderful couple; I am SO happy for you both," she added enthusiastically.

"HEY - COOL IT AND CALM DOWN," she heard in her mind from Marc. "Just ignore Mom – she obviously can't control herself."

"I'll try – thanks for having my back, bro," she mind-linked back gratefully, as she fought to get herself back under control.

"No worries, and PLEASE just remember your promises tonight," Marc mind-laughed back at her as she snickered in response.

"So much for the calming factor from Mom," she thought to herself bitterly as they drove off.

The ride to the movie theater was really nice, and she found that Tyler was surprisingly easy to talk to if she just kept herself relaxed. For most of the ride they talked about Tyler's favorite TV show "Stranger Things" which Sydney also loved, so the conversation was easy and fun. Marc was a super-fan of the show so he helped her out whenever Tyler asked her something she couldn't remember.

"Yeah, we named our cat Elle after Eleven on the show," Sydney said casually. "She is such a cool and unique character with all her super powers and 'don't mess with me' attitude, so it was a pretty easy name choice." Sydney looked down at her arm nervously, wondering what Tyler would think if he knew about HER crazy new powers.

"Yeah, Eleven is really cool. I wish I had powers like that, it would be so freaking incredible!" Tyler said wistfully. "I can SO see myself throwing vans and knocking bad guys out of my way like she does!"

Sydney breathed a little sigh of relief. "I know, right? It was funny with the cat name too - we tried to call the cat straight-up Eleven for a while but all of Mom and Dad's friends got really confused and thought she was our 11th cat or something, so we switched it to Elle for short. Mom was worried everyone would think she was the crazy cat lady with eleven cats," Sydney explained as Tyler laughed hysterically. "Oh, and Lucas wanted to name her One-Eyed Willy, or even One-Eyed Wilma, from 'The Goonies' but Mom vetoed that name since she thought it was too mean. Marc wanted to call her Luna from Luna Lovegood in 'Harry Potter and the Order of the Phoenix,' and then tell everybody it was just short for Lunatic which actually fits her attitude nicely. Dad wanted to name her Leeloo from 'The Fifth Element,' and Mom wanted a Star Wars name like Rey or Padme. But when the dust all settled, we all finally agreed on Elle as the very best option so that's her name now."

Soon they arrived at the theater. "OK, Syd I'll pick you up at 9:30 at the coffee shop beside the theater, and Tyler dear, your mom is meeting us there to get you," Mom said.

"OK, thanks again Mrs. C!" said Tyler graciously.

"Yeah, great, thanks Mom! See you later," said Sydney as they both scrambled out of the car as quickly as they could manage.

"Oh Tyler, I am SO sorry about my Mom's behavior," Sydney said awkwardly to Tyler as Mom drove away. "She's a hopeless romantic and this is all just a little too much for her," she added sheepishly.

"Ha ha, no worries," Tyler replied laughing. "Believe it or not, my mom was even worse before you picked me up tonight – a total wreck!" Sydney smiled back gratefully.

They had just enough time to get some popcorn and drinks at the snack bar before heading into the movie. As they sat down and got settled, Sydney could feel herself getting nervous again. "Dude, chill out and relax," said Marc inside her head. She snickered, so Tyler looked at her curiously and smiled. The lights dimmed and the previews started playing so they both turned to watch the screen.

The action movie was actually pretty good and they both enjoyed it. As Marc had warned her though, there was a big romantic backstory mixed in with all the action so there were definitely more than a few awkward moments. At one point Sydney confidently decided to reach out to hold Tyler's hand but then chickened out at the last moment and grabbed a handful of popcorn instead. He saw her movement and smiled at her again before turning back to the screen.

"Wow, that was pretty awesome," Tyler said excitedly a little later as they exited the theater. "It got some pretty bad reviews so I wasn't sure what to expect. The love story was pretty nice too," he chuckled, winking at Sydney and reaching for her hand.

"Yes it was nice," Sydney smiled, as their hands joined and her knees went weak. "Help me! Red alert! I'm totally losing it," she mind-screamed to Marc.

"Just count to ten and concentrate on walking. You won't impress Tyler very much if you fall flat on your face," Marc warned. He played the ambulance noises for her again which snapped her back to reality.

Sydney concentrated on walking carefully step by step as they approached the coffee shop. Tyler held the door for her and they walked in together without releasing their hands. Tyler ordered them both a soda and they sat down. Sydney refused to release her Kung-Fu death grip of his hand so Tyler laughed as he was forced to sit down awkwardly while almost spilling his drink.

"Thanks for coming with me, I had a lot of fun tonight," she said breathlessly, taking a sip of her soda.

"Oh yeah, me too. This was great. We need to do it again very soon," he winked mischievously.

Sydney smiled and stared at their intertwined hands, quickly starting to lose it again. There was one thing she was sure of though – she absolutely never wanted to let go.

"Hey focus, stay with me!" Marc mind-whispered to her. She pulled it together and looked up at Tyler who was watching her face with keen interest. Big mistake. She looked away again shyly.

The silence stretched on for a few minutes which made Sydney grow more and more nervous with every passing second. Tyler seemed perfectly content to sit there and stare at her and squeeze her hand occasionally which made it worse. "You have to say something quick, Syd," Marc mind-yelled. "This silence is getting too weird and he's going to freak out. Ask him if he saw the Patriots game last Sunday!"

"So how about that Patriots game on Sunday?" Sydney asked nervously.

"Oh yeah, that was incredible. Did you see that amazing one-handed touchdown catch by Gronk in the third quarter?" he asked excitedly.

"Yeah, that was awesome – I couldn't believe he caught that one," bluffed Sydney, now in full panic mode.

"I didn't know you liked football," Tyler said, looking at her curiously.

"Oh yeah, well mainly just the Patriots – they are my favorite team. Marc's and Dad's too," she replied. "We all like to watch together," she added for good measure, even though truthfully she had never been able to watch a football game for more than a quarter before getting bored.

"Marc, give me something else about the game to say, I'm blowing it! Quick!" she demanded. Marc hurriedly sent her a mind image of the key play from the end of the game.

"My favorite part was when Tom Brady kicked the game-winning field goal at the end," she said proudly as she heard Marc groan. Whoops.

Tyler cracked up laughing hysterically and Sydney was just really confused. "Brady's the quarterback! Oh my gosh, you totally crack me up Syd," he quipped and squeezed her hand gently.

Luckily Sydney was saved by the arrival of their moms which instantly caught their full and complete attention. Their moms were gossiping happily as they walked through the door but both fell ominously silent as soon as they saw the kids. "Hmmm, not a good sign," Sydney whispered to Tyler as they both casually but reluctantly released each other's hand. Of course both moms immediately noticed the movement thanks to their built-in mom advance warning romance detection systems. Crap. Their moms exchanged a sly glance and smiled broadly as they came over to talk to them excitedly for a few minutes. Sydney and Tyler looked at each other nervously during the awkward conversation. Apparently his mom was as crazy happy about this date as hers.

"OK, let's hit the road, Tyler. I'll meet you outside," she winked at Sydney as both moms walked out together, giggling loudly.

"Sorry about that, like I said, my mom is acting more than a little weird about this whole first ever date thing," Tyler apologized with a grin.

"Yeah, mine too, obviously. Well, good night," replied Sydney looking deeply into his eyes, and now wishing the wonderful evening would continue.

Tyler hesitated and then leaned over timidly to kiss Sydney on her cheek but her mind took over and instantly twisted her head so that their lips met in an awkward full kiss. "Whoops, that wasn't where I was aiming but that was nice," Tyler said a few seconds later, his head now spinning dangerously. Sydney was very pleased that it was apparently now HIS turn to appear breathless.

"Crap, that's it, I'm out," Marc said disgustedly.

"Goodnight," Sydney said to Tyler with a huge smile on her face as they departed.

Chapter 10.   Visitors

Marc was infinitely glad that he had now mastered the mind-link connection with Sydney. He was now very careful to "call her" formally and to wait a few seconds after she answered before opening up his mind to give her a chance to clear out all her thoughts about Tyler. He had quickly learned that lesson the hard way a few weeks ago after they first started dating. Gross. Sydney had also confirmed what she and Marc had both suspected – the mind-link only worked between the two of them and not with other people. Sydney had been subtly trying for days to get it to work on Tyler but he was starting to get creeped out whenever he caught her staring at him in deep concentration, so she was finally forced to admit defeat and stop.

Although Marc was really nervous about the whole Sydney/Tyler dating deal at the beginning, he had to grudgingly admit that he had never seen either one of them any happier in their entire lives. Sydney had quickly overcome her fears and seldom needed any help or encouragement from Marc anymore when she was around Tyler, except occasionally when he would say or do something uber-romantic and she would have to instantly call Marc for emotional backup. And he had to admit that they were also both very good about keeping their public displays of affection to a tolerable minimum when Marc was around, which he very much appreciated.

Sydney's dating bravery and constant bliss had spurred Kelly into action and she quickly snared his other best friend Nick. The four of them had started going on double dates together and even though they always invited Marc, whenever he went along he inevitably ended up feeling like a fifth wheel, particularly when everyone else was holding hands and giving each other googly eyes. He was genuinely happy for all of them but was definitely starting to feel a little lonely and left-out.

In his growing free time, Marc had been helping Dad translate some more of the hieroglyphic scrolls from Sallah and it turned out that he could read them just as easily as Sydney thanks to the power of his purple cartouche. Dad was quite annoyed at the beginning when Marc breezed through the first scroll just as quickly as Sydney had, and lately had started the habit of pestering both of them constantly to give him lessons. None of the other scrolls were as directly interesting as the first one, but Marc liked to stay involved in the work just in case anything else came up about their powers, and of course it was fun just hanging out with Dad.

Dad also kept Marc up-to-date on the latest news about Mr. P's sarcophagus. Luckily the weight discrepancy problem had seemingly worked itself out since after scanning, Dad re-weighed it back in his lab and got the same weight as the engineering lab, even though it was still 200 pounds lighter than Dad's first measurement. Luckily nobody had thought to ask the Egyptian team what the sarcophagus weighed when it left Egypt. Sydney was convinced that Dad suspected something fishy had happened but was too scared to bring it up to the team in case he was right and 200 pounds of precious ancient Egyptian artifacts had been stolen out of the sarcophagus under his watch.

Marc followed that situation carefully and he and Sydney had even started searching widely for the mummy whenever they could find time to sneak off. So far, they had not seen any sign of where it might have gone after it left the archaeology lab. For the first few weeks after its release, they were sure the mummy would turn up in the evening news on a horrible rampage of mass destruction, but so far it had been keeping a low profile. However, the embalming wrapping and mummy dust hidden in a box under Marc's bed was a constant reminder that something mysterious was out there, and they had no clue of its whereabouts or intentions.

The imaging scans had worked out really well, and the team had been able to discover the latch mechanism for the lid but were unfortunately also quite certain that the sarcophagus was empty (which of course he and Sydney knew quite well was indeed the case). That had been an exciting but also disappointing day for the whole team when Dad first reported the news. However, he and Sydney had both been totally creeped out when Dad was mystified that the latch appeared to be made only for someone from INSIDE the sarcophagus to open it up. A few days later though, after poring over the scan images the team had found what Dad called an "emergency release button" on the outside which they were fairly confident would open the lid. The Egyptian Department of Antiquities was very excited and Sallah was on his way to perform the actual opening while the local TV station was going to film it in case something exciting might just be revealed against the odds.

Marc and Sydney were particularly thrilled because Sallah was bringing his daughter Akiiki with him. They would both be arriving tomorrow and staying for at least a week to get the sarcophagus ready for shipment back to Egypt after the grand opening. Sallah did not want to intrude on their hospitality but they had both begged and pleaded for Akiiki to stay at their house and share Sydney's room. Mom got a little suspicious that Marc seemed to be begging much harder than Sydney but she was looking forward to seeing Akiiki too (and also to raise the female balance in the house as well), so had helped Dad secure the deal with Sallah and Marion. By a lucky coincidence, tomorrow was their last day of school before Fall Break so they would have almost the entire visit time off from school to hang out with Akiiki.

Marc and Sydney had also made excellent progress with their new powers over the last few weeks. However, it was extremely and continually exasperating that there was no "instruction manual" for their powers which would have made the learning process infinitely easier. They had accidentally discovered that swiping their wrist while concentrating made the cartouche appear, and that they could touch the individual hieroglyphics which would make them change colors. Unfortunately, they were not able to determine the next steps afterwards to activate a power or to make something interesting happen. So they found themselves limited to powers that they could activate by concentrating and visualizing what they wanted to happen. The problem was that they had to first think of what they wanted to do but they had no real ideas of the rules, possibilities, or limitations of their powers. However, despite the frustration, they were both having a glorious time exploring the depth of their mysterious new abilities.

"So, any bright ideas for powers to try today, dude?" asked Sydney at their next practice session. "I'm getting pretty aggravated and feel like we just keep hitting dead-ends. I think I've turned my cartouche every color of the rainbow now but we've got no new powers to show for it. Why didn't these stupid things come with an instruction manual?" she added in annoyance.

"Well, we're getting pretty good at levitation, and I was wondering if it would also work for bigger objects," Marc replied excitedly.

"OK, that sounds somewhat interesting – what did you have in mind?" Sydney replied enthusiastically.

"Well, it's just us here today, so follow me outside," Marc said. "I've got a little plan for an experiment," he chuckled. He led Sydney out the front door to the driveway. "OK, I think all the neighbors are at work, but help me make sure the coast is clear," he instructed.

Sydney looked carefully up and down their street and did not see any cars coming or any signs of activity from their neighbor's houses. "OK, it looks clear at the moment, what is the plan?" she asked.

"Let's try to lift Betty, the family mini-van," he whispered. "Just a little bit at first to make sure we can do it."

"Are you nuts?" Sydney replied. "Betty weighs over two tons, we could never lift that!"

"Well, we will never know until we try," Marc scolded. "Where's your sense of adventure? You said you were frustrated with the cartouches so let's try something fun for once."

"OK fine then. Just be careful not to hurt her or we will be in big trouble with Dad," Sydney replied nervously. "How do you want to do this?"

"I've been thinking about it, levitating the cats is really easy and automatic, so size should not make a difference," Marc explained excitedly. "So on the count of three, just visualize Betty rising up about 6 inches off the ground, and we will hold her there for a few seconds. Are you ready?"

"Sure, let's do this," Sydney responded, getting a little more enthusiastic about Marc's crazy plan. "One, two, three..."

To their immense satisfaction, Betty rose up off the ground and hovered in place just as they commanded. "See, that was just as easy as floating a cat, right?" Marc said in proud amazement.

"Hang on, you keep hovering her but I want to try something," Sydney said with a huge smile. She rotated her finger in a spinning motion, and Betty obediently started spinning in a circle.

"Hey, that is pretty cool," Marc said happily. "But let's put her down before someone sees us. Mini-vans don't usually spin in place like this," he laughed. Betty slowly sank back to the ground in the same spot where she had started. "OK, come on – that was too easy," Marc added proudly. "Let's see if we can lift the house!" he said as he turned his concentration to their house.

"Dude, no way! STOP!" yelled Sydney, breaking his concentration.

"What?" Marc replied angrily. "I know we could do it!"

"Well yeah, I'm sure we could too, but did you stop to think about all the electrical, water, and sewer connections which would likely break in the process?" Sydney asked. "Not to even mention all the nasty sewer stuff which would likely spray all over us if it worked. I don't think Mom and Dad would appreciate that level of destruction to our poor house."

"Oh yeah, sorry," Marc replied sheepishly. "I didn't think that through very well, I guess," he added, now quite embarrassed.

"Well, that was a close call so let's agree to plan carefully together before trying anything too crazy with our powers, OK?" Sydney laughed.

"OK, it's a deal!" Marc replied, but then quickly fell silent and looked around nervously. "Hey, I have an eerie feeling we are being watched, do you see anybody?" he whispered. "It's like my Spidey Sense is tingling or something."

"No, but I suddenly get the same weird feeling," Sydney replied, scanning their surroundings carefully but failing to notice a large dusty spy hiding in their bushes. "Let's get inside and keep practicing, I don't feel safe here at the moment."

Marc followed Sydney back inside and up the stairs to Sydney's room. "OK, that was a little creepy, do you see anybody out of your window?" Marc asked as he shut the door behind them.

"No, the coast is still clear," Sydney replied, closing her window curtains after checking the yard. "That reminds me – I've been getting worried about how we would defend ourselves if the mummy ever reappears and ends up attacking us."

"Yeah, we should probably keep working on those shields from last week," Marc agreed reluctantly. "They are not very exciting, but we need some defensive strategies first and then we need to start on some weapons development for offensive retaliation."

"OK, that's a good idea, shields it is," Sydney agreed. They both could now reliably and consistently produce a shimmering power shield on either arm, which moved automatically with their arm and could be angled slightly up or down with their minds. They both raised their shields easily with a little concentration, and walked around the room blocking imaginary blows, and then smashing into each other's shields like human battering rams. "I think we have got these down fairly well, show me again how you did that shimmer shield bubble thing," Sydney asked breathlessly, turning off her shield with a swipe of her cartouche.

"Ah, OK. I'm still not very good at it though," Marc replied, swiping off his arm shield and taking a few deep breaths. "So I swipe the cartouche and then think 'shimmer shield' and try to visualize a bubble around myself, but you have to really concentrate and block everything else out of your mind. Hang on for a second, let me try." Marc swiped his cartouche and concentrated deeply for several seconds. A beautiful shimmering honeycomb shield suddenly flickered into place around him, pushing a surprised Sydney back several feet, knocking her onto the bed.

"Whoa, that's new!" Sydney exclaimed. The shield was much larger than the last time Marc had conjured it, and seemed to be made of interlocking hexagonal honeycombs that shimmered and flashed in a slow rotation around Marc.

"Whoops, sorry about that," Marc said. As soon as he took a step forward the shield flickered out and disappeared. "Crap! See? That happens every time I move at all," Marc exclaimed in frustration. "Are you OK?"

"Yeah, I'm fine," Sydney laughed, getting up from the bed. "It didn't hurt at all, but it just felt like a solid wall of force that simply pushed me right out of its way.

Pretty cool! I wish it would work for me!" she lamented. "I can't even get it to appear at all."

"Well, I've been tinkering around with it a bit for over a week, so it just takes more practice," Marc replied reassuringly. "I think it is supposed to move with me, though, so I definitely do NOT have that part of it down yet. How about some offense now - any more luck with that fireball of yours?"

"No not really," Sydney replied. "I've been too scared to try it inside, but last night in the backyard I managed to conjure a stream of a few sputtering sparks. Definitely not the big green fireball from D&D which I was going for," she chuckled.

"Well – keep trying, I want you to teach it to me once you figure it out. Force punch is always pretty fun, though," Marc said thoughtfully. "Let's practice that on some of your stuffed animals."

"Hmmm, maybe we should try it on some of your precious Star Wars action figures instead, why do you always want to beat up my stuff?" Sydney countered angrily.

"Oh just deal with it, your stuff is already here," Marc replied, levitating several of her stuffed animals into a lineup on the edge of her desk.

"Fine then, but next time we practice in your room," she replied, as they took turns knocking the animals off her desk one by one. "This IS pretty cool, I must say," she said excitedly.

"Yeah, we're getting pretty good with this, I think my best range is around ten feet so far, but I think we can go much further with more practice," Marc replied, concentrating on his next victim. Suddenly they heard a loud scratching at the door, and two mournful meows.

"Rut row, they found us again," Sydney laughed, opening the door for Yoda and Elle to come bounding in, both meowing angrily. Their recent practice sessions had an unexpected and sometimes entertaining side-effect - Elle and Yoda now always demanded to participate and had started the bad habit of always jumping up and down around Marc and Sydney, constantly demanding more flying time. Both cats were now hopping up and down madly trying to get their attention.

"You two are just pitiful," Marc said as he launched them both into the air in a slow circle around Sydney's room, as they both started purring loudly.

"Yeah, remind me to talk to Dad – he has been noticing them hopping around us lately and is beginning to think that something is wrong with them," Sydney chuckled. "Yesterday I heard him muttering about taking them to the vet to get checked out." Both cats instantly hissed when she said the "v" word, making the twins start laughing hysterically. Sydney made a mental note to herself to definitely talk to Dad at some point soon to keep the cats from being needlessly poked and prodded by the vet, which both cats obviously absolutely hated. Sydney floated a few cat toys into the orbiting chaos around her room, and the twins both hooted in laughter at the cats trying their best to catch everything.

The next day after school Marc was helping Sydney clean up her room to make space for Akiiki tomorrow night. "Honestly, you are such a slob," he said. "Look at all this trash under your bed – empty water bottles, candy wrappers, chip bags – I mean, this is just ridiculous."

"Oh shut up, your room is worse than mine and you know it. Your room has more layers of trash debris than one of Mom and Dad's archaeological digs," Sydney quickly retorted.

"Ha ha, you're such a comedian," Marc chuckled. "But maybe you're right. Hey, so why didn't you invite your friend Jean over to help? She loves organizing big chaotic junk piles like this at school."

"Clean Jean, are you kidding?" Sydney asked incredulously. "She would have a heart attack if she saw all this mess. I'm sure she would unfriend me instantly as a bad influence on her!"

"Ha ha, you're probably right. Hey, here's another cat toy!" he said as he tossed a catnip mouse into the cat toy bucket. Elle instantly dove after it and scattered all the cat toys again making Sydney groan. They had been finding cat toys in all sorts of weird places in her room - wherever the cats had knocked them out of the air during their frequent flight times.

"Elle, come on, girl! We're trying to clean up, and you're making more of a mess for us," Sydney complained bitterly to the cat.

Elle just meowed back at her innocently and flicked her tail, as if to say "Who? Me?" Elle then viciously pounced on her favorite yellow stuffed princess pony toy which she had stolen from Sydney months ago, and started kangarooing it with her back paws. She had the hilarious habit of dragging the pony - as well as a large stuffed brontosaurus she had "acquired" from Lucas – all over the house. Dad always laughed at her and said he had never seen a cat drag big toys around like a dog. Mom always thought it was funny too, because whenever she did it, Elle would always try meowing with her mouth full which sounded absolutely bizarre. Elle also had the curious and inexplicable habit of stashing her two favorite toys into closets and laundry bins all over the house, and none of the family had been able to figure out a good reason for this strange behavior.

After the twins had the floor relatively clear, they ran the vacuum to clean up the smaller debris and had to empty the vacuum canister several times since it filled quickly with cat hair, dust, chips, candy, and random nastiness. "Syd, this is really gross, how can you be such a slob?" Marc asked her in disgust.

"Let's just run it in your room if you want to see who the bigger slob is," Sydney retorted angrily. Marc raised his hands in surrender with a big smile. "You know, actually you SHOULD clean YOUR room as well so you don't gross out poor Akiiki if she happens to wander in there by mistake," she added seriously.

"Maybe you are right," Marc replied thoughtfully. "It's in nearly pristine and immaculate condition so it wouldn't take long to clean at all," he added, as they both started laughing hysterically.

After their monumental cleaning job was finished, they carried over the spare bed mattress from Lucas' top bunk bed and arranged it across from Sydney's bed. "Perfect, this looks great," Sydney declared. "I hope she likes it."

Admiring their work, Marc noticed they had amassed an impressive collection of dirty cups, plates, bowls, containers, and spoons which had been lost in the debris for who knows how long. "You had better stick these in the dishwasher quickly before Mom finds them – remember she is charging five dollars an item now for any dishes she finds in our rooms, and that would break your piggy bank for sure with this many!" Marc chuckled. "And I suggest you just throw away these sandwich containers with the rotten moldy whatever-it-is inside – they are probably deadly to open at this stage," he added.

"Yeah, that's probably a good idea," Sydney reflected with a frown. "I've been hiding them so she doesn't see them, but then I forget where I put them," she admitted grudgingly. "It's like they get sucked into a black hole."

"True that! Hey, I'll go check to see if the path to the kitchen is clear, and then come back to help you carry them," Marc said, chuckling at her messiness. "Then you can help me clean up MY room," he added cheerfully, as Sydney moaned in despair.

The next day at school was a real drag. None of their teachers felt motivated to start on any new material since they knew everyone would just forget it over the week-long Fall Break anyway. For two of their classes, they ended up watching a semi-educational movie which was just mind-numbingly boring with at least half of the class actually falling asleep in the dimmed classroom. The only somewhat entertaining part of the day was health class where they were wrapping up the state-mandated study of human reproduction systems. The entire class was immensely relieved that it was the last day they would cover the topic this year and were actually looking forward to switching back to gym class, even if it meant more dodgeball. The boys and the girls had been in separate health classes the entire week but were now back together for the wrap up. Sydney and Tyler had made the HUGE mistake of looking at each other during one of the extremely awkward class discussion sessions and had instantly given each other a very bad case of the giggles. Naturally, this highly agitated old Mrs. Varley who was teaching the class for probably the millionth time and was tired of such teenage nonsense. She gave both of them "a talkin' to" as she liked to put it, which absolutely mortified both of them with undoubtedly the worst embarrassment of their lives. Marc found the whole situation completely hilarious and actually downright entertaining but was trying his best not to laugh, or worse yet, to mind-tease Sydney. He could tell by her miserable expression that any teasing whatsoever would surely bring him a swift and painful payback later.

Around mid-afternoon they both got a text from Dad that he had picked up Sallah and Akiiki from the airport and was taking them back to their house. Having their reunion with Akiiki to look forward to made the rest of the day go a little faster, so almost before they knew it, school was out. Unfortunately Marc had to go to soccer practice right after school so they parted ways as they walked outside. Normally he didn't mind going to practice in the least, but today let's just say he was not terribly pleased with Coach Carlos' practice scheduling skills. "Practice on the last day of school before a big break – come on, Coach!" he thought to himself in frustration, even though he knew they did actually have a game tomorrow. But still – he didn't think they needed any more practice. Sydney waved goodbye as she hopped on the bus and mind-wished him good luck at practice.

Once the team got into the right mood after a few minutes of drills, their practice was fun as usual. Marc was thoroughly and absolutely enjoying soccer games after his cartouche power gift, and even regular practices were no exception. He had always been a good player, but now he was hands-down the best player on the team. It was much like the dodgeball game with Knuckles – he was easily able to watch everything on the entire field at the same time and was adept at making amazingly precise passes to his teammates. He definitely preferred passing and was reluctant to score many goals on his own since it honestly felt a little bit like cheating now that his powers made the game so easy. However, he still usually ended up scoring a handful of goals each game whenever he found himself too near the goal with no teammates nearby and no good excuse not to shoot.

His team was gloriously undefeated in all their games so far this season, and Coach Carlos said he had never been more proud of their awesome team play, particularly with their phenomenal selfless passing and excellent ball movement. Marc thought a big part of their success was that before last season, Coach Carlos had assigned them homework of watching as many professional soccer games as they could. The style of play was very different than Marc's team so it was a great learning experience. Marc's team had tended to just charge to the goal whenever they got the ball and hope that somebody was behind them to back them up. Unfortunately, what usually happened is that they almost immediately lost the ball to the other team when they overconfidently tried to juke through several of the other players instead of passing to an open teammate. The flow of the professional soccer games was much more strategic, with extensive passing in and out to test the defenses and set up scoring plays, with only occasional mad charges on the goal when there was a rare breakaway. Marc's team had all picked up much better patience and now looked to pass quickly before the defense converged on them, and to take their time to properly set up their plays which had resulted in many more scores.

Marc's favorite player was Mohamed Salah from Liverpool FC in the Premier League. Salah was an Egyptian forward who Marc had discovered through Akiiki's twin brother Asim. Salah was Asim's all-time favorite player and he and Marc had watched several Liverpool games together over the summer and they both admired Salah's amazing footwork and crazy accuracy with both passing and goal shots. Marc had bought himself an awesome Salah Liverpool jersey for practice and now tried his best to emulate Salah using his newly acquired cartouche skills.

Marc's core team had been together for many seasons, and Marc actually could not remember a time when the teamwork and outstanding game play from everyone all came together into such a well-oiled soccer machine. The whole team was really looking forward to their upcoming games, and chatted excitedly as practice ended and they parted ways.

Mom and Lucas picked up Marc and drove him straight home since they knew he was anxious to see Akiiki. As the garage door opened, Sydney mind-linked him to warn him that a bunch of her friends were there for an impromptu slumber party that night. "Arrgghh, you have GOT to be kidding me," he complained. "I was looking forward to us spending some quality time with Akiiki – we haven't seen her for ages."

"Well she's here for a whole week so just suck it up for tonight," Sydney replied. "Kelly and Becky are both here, and Eleanor, Ellie, Jean, and Caroline too, so there is nobody that you don't like hanging out with. We'll play some cool games and it will be really fun, you'll see."

Marc snorted in disgust as they walked inside. Eight girls playing games at a slumber party – he was going to avoid that like the plague. When he got inside to the kitchen he could already hear the loud squeals and giggles from whatever girly craziness they were up to in Sydney's room. Lucas stared up at him with pure terror in his eyes, so Marc looked at him very seriously and said "Yes, be afraid, be very afraid." Lucas nodded in complete agreement.

"Some very fine big brother advice if I do say so myself," Marc thought to himself proudly.

Lucas went running off to his room to find his Switch. "Mom, have you seen my headphones?" he yelled loudly even though Mom was standing nearby. "It sounds like I'm going to need them tonight! Oh never mind, here they are," he yelled happily just a few seconds later, as Marc and Mom both rolled their eyes at each other.

Marc took a deep breath and walked upstairs to say hello to Akiiki, with the noise from Sydney's room getting ever louder and louder with each approaching step. He hesitated for several long moments at her bedroom door but decided there was just no easy way out, so he knocked loudly. The noise stopped immediately and Sydney giggled "Come on in, Marc!" Marc steeled himself and opened the door slowly.

"Well, hello ladies," Marc said as he walked through the door. "And hello, beautiful," he thought as he saw the gorgeous Akiiki across the room. Whoops, he had said that out loud.

"Well, hello AND hello," said all the girls at once, giggling loudly as Akiiki jumped up excitedly to greet Marc.

"Hello, crazy fool. How have you been?" Akiiki asked as she gave Marc a giant hug, releasing him and then catching both his hands in hers. She stepped back a little and looked him in the eyes with a little giggle.

"Good I guess, but I've missed you and your brothers," said Marc as he focused completely on her amazing face. She was even more breathtakingly stunning than he remembered and he could not stop looking at her gorgeous green eyes. Now he understood what Sydney went through with Tyler as his knees suddenly started shaking. "Pull it together, dude," he thought desperately to himself.

"Well, I've missed you guys too. And Sydney has been telling me some VERY interesting stories about you," Akiiki said mischievously with a cute little grin.

Marc looked around her at Sydney in a panic and asked worriedly "Oh, really? Has she now?"

Sydney smiled widely and mind-linked back to him "Nothing about our little cartouche secret and nothing about your muuuchhaaass smmooocchhaass thoughts for her," she giggled.

"Whew, well thanks SO much for that," he replied out loud, now returning his attention to Akiiki and feeling instantly mesmerized by her sparkling eyes again. All the girls were starting to giggle again as they watched him staring so intently at Akiiki. Yikes - he knew he was going to have to make a hasty exit before things got out of hand, but he did not want to leave Akiiki. Stupid slumber party! He finally released one of Akiiki's hands gently and raised the other to his lips for a quick kiss before releasing it as well, never looking away from Akiiki's beautiful face. "Well, I'll leave you ladies to the big crazy girl party then. Come see me later," he said to Akiiki as the giggles got louder and a few "woo-hoos" were thrown in.

"Sure, it's a deal," Akiiki replied enthusiastically, and then carefully mouthed "save me" so that none of the other girls could see her. Marc smiled and nodded slightly to let her know he understood, making his way carefully to the door.

"Oh yeah, Akiiki, I almost forgot. Dad said he wanted to talk to you about something important later, so he wants you to come down when you can – but soon," Marc winked slyly as he reached the door.

"OK, thanks!" she said with a little sigh of relief as Marc quickly shut the door to make his retreat. Instantly the noise level in Sydney's room went through the roof and he quickly scampered for the stairs. The last thing he heard was several of the girls saying "Ooooohhh, somebody's got a crush!" and laughing loudly.

Crap, he was only in there for two minutes and they were totally on to him. "I knew that kiss on the hand was over the top, dang it! That was so stupid, why did I do that?" he thought to himself in frustration.

Then he heard Akiiki respond very faintly to the girls "Sorry, I can't help it! Was I that obvious?" as the room erupted into total chaos again and Marc stumbled badly down the stairs, his knees giving out from under him in complete shock.

The girls stayed in Sydney's room for most of the evening, and only occasionally ventured out in pairs to fetch snacks or new games to play. At dinner time, Dad bravely delivered a large stack of pizzas up to her room and afterwards was happy to make it back downstairs still in one piece, getting congratulatory high-fives of relief from Mom and Marc. Lucas was still deeply scarred emotionally from the "let's dress up my little brother" game from one of Sydney's last slumber parties a few months back, so wisely kept his distance and ended up playing video games in his room until he finally drifted off to sleep. The noise level upstairs had been WAY too much for Marc to handle so he was hanging out downstairs on the couch watching TV. Dad and Sallah visited with Marc for a while before Dad drove his friend to his hotel which was conveniently quite close to their house. Marc was able to catch up on the latest news on the Grand Egyptian Museum and also Mr. P's sarcophagus, both of which were set to open soon he reflected, laughing at his own joke. Dad and Sallah had just taken off when he heard footsteps on the stairs behind him.

"Hi Marc, mind if I join you?" asked Akiiki. "It's getting a bit too wild and crazy upstairs and I'm so tired. My body is still on Egyptian time and I would normally be sleeping right now," she yawned. Marc noticed that she was starting to shiver badly. "Plus the flights today were so long and boring, I'm just feeling totally wiped out," she complained.

"Of course - no problem," he said. "You take the couch and I'll find you some blankets to warm you up," running off for the closet to see what he could find.

"Okay, thanks. That would be great. It's just so much colder here and I'm not used to it yet," Akiiki explained as she sat down on the couch still shivering. Marc returned with several fleece blankets and helped her get settled in a nice warm cozy nest, and then made a similar nest for himself on their big chair beside the couch.

"I remember having the opposite problem when we first got to Egypt at the beginning of the summer," Marc replied. "It was so overwhelmingly hot when we got off the plane that I thought we were all going to melt right on the spot," he chuckled.

"Yes, it can definitely get hot but I suppose you just get used to it after a while. I really don't even notice much anymore," she laughed. "But here in the cold – wow, that's much different!"

A few seconds later both Elle and Yoda came in and jumped up on Akiiki's lap making themselves right at home. Akiiki giggled and scratched both of them under the chin affectionately. "I just love your cats, they are so cool and friendly," she said happily as both cats started purring loudly. "They came into Syd's room to check out Ellie's pet rat Chadley for a while, but I think the girls were too loud for them so they left pretty quickly. I really haven't seen much of them until now."

"Yeah, they definitely do not like loud noises. That's probably the main reason they avoid Lucas – he gets annoyed and tries to carry them around or lock them in his room with him, but they always escape at the first chance they get," Marc observed. "Lucas has been wanting a cat of his own for ages but Mom and Dad think it would just end up avoiding him too, so they haven't let him get one yet," he laughed.

"Oh, that's really awfully sad. But hey, I've really missed you guys, how has everyone been?" Akiiki asked, her green eyes sparkling mesmerizingly. "Mensah was so upset for weeks after Lucas left, I was beginning to think he would never get back to normal. Well, normal for him, that is."

"Yeah, Lucas was the same way – I think he really enjoyed being a big brother for the summer," Marc replied. "But we're all doing OK I guess. School is going fairly well and I'm enjoying soccer and Syd has her first boyfriend. That was probably the biggest news – I thought Mom was going to keel over, she was so excited and worked up."

"Ha, that's hilarious. Yeah, Syd told me a little bit about Tyler before the girls got here – he sounds really nice and I can't wait to meet him. I'm definitely dreading what my mom is going to do if I ever get MY first boyfriend," she said worriedly.

Marc suddenly started to get overheated and had to move out from under some of his blankets. Akiiki was so remarkably beautiful that he was really surprised to hear she had never had a boyfriend yet. Maybe things were different in Egypt than they were here. Maybe dates were even arranged by the parents - that sure would be strange. He found himself getting mesmerized yet again by her gorgeously striking green eyes which were now staring at him intently. He glanced down at her lips and wondered what it would be like to kiss her. He quickly shook his head to break her spell. "So do you have anyone in mind?" he finally asked her curiously.

She laughed cutely which made her eyes sparkle even more intensely, to Marc's great delight. "Oh, maybe someone I have a little crush on," she teased with a wink. "That is, if Mom doesn't scare him off with her craziness."

"Oh, your mom is a total sweetie-pie, I think he would be just fine," Marc chuckled. "My mom quickly got used to the idea of Syd and Tyler dating and she is pretty chill about it now."

"Well, maybe," she said thoughtfully, staring intently at Marc. "I guess I'll have to ask him if he feels the same way about me."

"Yeah, you probably should. Honesty is definitely the best policy for stuff like that," Marc replied in a serious voice.

"I'll keep that in mind the next time I see him," she said mischievously as Marc's dad came in the front door.

"Oh hey kids, I'm back. How's the slumber party going, Akiiki? Uh oh, did they scare you off?" he asked with a big grin.

"Ha ha, no. It was just getting a little loud and I'm so tired from traveling today. I think I may just crash here on the couch tonight to get some decent sleep," she replied. "I was just getting caught up with Marc."

"Sounds good, well, let us know if you need anything," Dad replied. "Oh, and hey sometime this week I want you to give me some hieroglyphic lessons. Marc and Sydney say you taught them over the summer and they both speed-read circles around me now. They have been refusing to give me any serious tutoring so I'm getting pretty frustrated - so I'll just bypass them and go straight to their awesome teacher," Dad explained with a smile.

"Hmmm, I actually stink pretty badly at hieroglyphics," she said confusedly, and then saw Marc winking at her frantically. "But I'll sure give it a shot, Mr. C," she ended enthusiastically.

"OK, thanks, that will be great," replied Dad, looking over at Marc a little suspiciously. "Well, good night, I'll leave you guys to it. Just turn off the TV and lights before you conk out."

"Sure thing, Dad," Marc replied quickly. "Good night!"

Akiiki shot him a curious look. "What was that all about?" she asked suspiciously.

"Oh, it's a long story. Syd and I have gotten pretty good at hieroglyphics and it bugs him to no end that we are better at it than he is," Marc explained. Akiiki was not convinced and made a mental note to herself to ask Sydney about it later.

"Hmmm, OK," Akiiki replied, trying to stifle a big yawn. "Sorry, I'm fading out fast here," she apologized.

"No problem, it's been a long day for you, so get some rest. It's still crazy up in Syd's room so you might as well just stay here with me. We can keep talking in the morning," he said.

"Yes, that sounds very nice," she replied, settling into the warm covers sleepily.

Marc decided to try a little experiment while she was still partially awake. He concentrated with all his might to try to open a mind-link with her. After several attempts with no response, he was reluctantly forced to admit defeat. "It sure would have been nice to have a mind-link connection with her," he thought sadly. "I wonder if there is a distance limit, I might have been able to even mind-link with her back home in Egypt. That would be so freaking cool." He contented himself with watching Akiiki finally fall asleep, which was quickly making him very sleepy as well.

Marc was awakened by a beam of morning sunlight sneaking through the curtains of the front window. Akiiki was still asleep on the couch with both cats deep under the covers with her, their noses barely sticking out and both snore-purring loudly. Akiiki looked even more beautiful in the bright morning sun as it sparkled off her long glistening black hair. Marc sat watching her for long time, deep in thought about her apparent feelings for him which he learned just yesterday. This was getting VERY complicated.

"Hey, where's Akiiki?" asked Sydney sleepily over mind-link.

"Oh, she's down here on the couch asleep. I think the slumber party was too loud for her last night," he chuckled.

"So what are YOU doing, then?" asked Sydney suspiciously.

"Oh, just keeping an eye on her to protect her from the wild beasts," Marc replied slyly. At that moment they both heard a door open and thundering elephant footsteps racing down the stairs – boom – boom – boom. "Great, right on cue," Marc said with annoyance as he turned to watch the stairs.

Lucas came flying into the room and launched himself high in the air to tiger pounce on Akiiki. Marc reacted quickly and slowed him down enough with his powers that Lucas wouldn't break her when he landed. Lucas landed right on top of her and both cats growled loudly and scattered in a panic, looking for somewhere to hide. Akiiki awoke instantly and wrapped him in a big hug as they both laughed hysterically. Marc felt an intense wave of jealousy as he jumped up from his chair and stood there awkwardly.

"No fair, everyone has been hogging you!" Lucas squealed loudly as he released her just enough to look her over carefully. "I missed you so much! How's Mensah?"

"I know, right? I've missed you too, and so has Mensah," Akiiki said as she struggled to sit up under his weight. "It's so good to see you again, little brother," she smiled.

"And you too! What are we going to do today?" he asked her excitedly. "I need some Akiiki time."

"Well, I think Marc does too, so you might have to share me a little," she said, winking at Marc playfully with her gorgeous green sparkling eyes, making Marc's mind quickly race out of control. "Oh, I almost forgot, Mensah sent you a letter," she said very seriously.

Lucas's jaw dropped and he jumped up quickly. "Really? Where is it? Where is it?" he asked excitedly.

"It's in my backpack in Syd's room, shall we go get it?" she asked. "But we'll have to be quiet so we don't wake up the girls." He hurriedly grabbed her hand and they headed for the stairs, with Akiiki doing her best to slow him down and keep him semi-quiet.

"Yeah, fat chance of that," Marc thought. "Hey Syd, did you get all that? You should move that backpack unless you ALL want to be awakened rudely by the beast," he mind-linked.

"Yes, I'm on it," she said as Akiiki's backpack floated out her door and landed in the hallway just before Lucas and Akiiki arrived. Akiiki pulled out the letter and handed it to Lucas who ran back downstairs loudly to open it. The thundering footsteps awakened the slumber party crew who started to stir reluctantly as Sydney and Akiiki both laughed.

Marc saw that "letter" was an understatement. Mensah had sent Lucas a huge stack of papers including drawings, pictures, newspaper clippings, some cool mummy bookmarks and papyrus postcards from the GEM gift shop, and pages upon pages of handwritten letters for Lucas. Lucas was absolutely thrilled and looked everything over with great excitement.

"Dude, you should take that to your room to spread everything out," Marc suggested quietly as Akiiki came back in the room giggling.

"Great idea!" Lucas shouted, gathering everything up and thundering back up the stairs loudly.

"Well, that should keep him busy for a while," Akiiki laughed as she darted out of his way.

"Yeah, but I hope you have a bunch more of those for later in the week – we're going to need them," Marc replied chuckling.

Soon all the girls had all emerged from Sydney's room looking tired and disheveled. Mom and Dad made a giant breakfast and soon everyone was eating and gossiping merrily. All the girls were teasing Akiiki and asked her where she went last night, giggling as they looked over at Marc. "Oh, sorry about that," Akiiki explained. "I was just tired so I ended up accidently falling asleep on the couch when I was visiting with Marc." All the girls giggled loudly.

"Yeah, 'accidently,' I'm so sure," teased Kelly which made all the others start woo-hoo-ing. Marc chuckled and watched with growing amusement as Akiiki started turning red from embarrassment and refused to look in his direction. This was getting very interesting indeed.

"No, it's true. I can vouch that she was really tired and we actually had a VERY nice visit - before she started snoring like a camel and shaking the whole couch," replied Marc seriously, making all the girls start laughing uproariously again.

"Hey!" exclaimed Akiiki, now giving him a stern look and trying unsuccessfully to suppress a smile.

Chapter 11.   Rematch

As the morning wore on, one by one Sydney's friends were picked up by their parents, and soon only Kelly was left. She lived within easy walking distance so was helping Sydney to clean up all the party remnants and straighten up all the mess they had made. Luckily most of the real mess was limited to Sydney's room so Mom and Dad were pretty chill about the whole process since they didn't have to see it. Marc had been chuckling to himself all morning because Sydney's friend "Clean Jean" had been the first to leave, since she was totally triggered and overwhelmed by all the mess the girls had made. When everything was mostly restored to normal, Sydney, Marc, and Akiiki walked Kelly to the door and said goodbye and thanks. Kelly gave Marc a weird look when he was standing in the doorway beside Akiiki, and he wasn't quite sure what that was all about. He decided to try to figure it out later as he had to get ready for his soccer game which was fast approaching.

For the first time this season, Marc was a little bit worried and anxious about his upcoming soccer game. Today they were playing against Knuckles' team which was stacked with several of his biggest and meanest cronies. Luckily Marc had not had to play dodgeball against Knuckles in gym class since the first day of school, although he strongly suspected that Mr. McGregor was trying to keep them from playing against each other again by always placing them on the same team or in totally different matches. Knuckles had been taunting him all week about their upcoming "rematch" at the soccer game in an effort to intimidate Marc, or to make himself feel better because Marc now intimidated him – Marc wasn't quite sure. He had not seen Knuckles' team play yet this year, but could easily imagine that it was a "brute force" versus "skill" approach which was reinforced by the rumor that their team always received at least a couple of yellow and often red card penalties at every match. Marc wondered briefly if his cartouche shield would be too obvious to use during the match, assuming he could actually maintain it while running, which had so far eluded him. Or maybe some well-placed mini-fireballs would do the trick to keep him from getting walloped. He definitely had lots of options to think about.

"What's wrong, Marc?" asked Akiiki. "You look a little worried about something."

"Oh sorry, I was just thinking about my soccer game this afternoon," replied Marc. "We're playing the school bully Alec's team which has a lot of his brutish buddies on it and they always play too rough and bend the rules. I think it will probably get pretty ugly and I'm hoping nobody gets hurt," he lamented.

"Isn't there a referee to keep it fair?" Akiiki asked with concern. "That does not sound right."

"Well yes, but in our league there is usually just one referee to keep an eye on the entire field, so it is not very hard to get away with unsportsmanlike play if you are not too close to the ball where the referee is watching," Marc explained. "And all of the referees are just volunteer dads who do it for fun, so some are much more observant and stricter than others, but unfortunately you never know who you are going to get."

"Hmm, that does not sound good at all. Please be careful, I would prefer that you not be damaged or broken," said Akiiki with a mischievous wink.

"Yes definitely, I would prefer that as well!" he laughed. "I'll do my best to stay out of trouble. So what are you and Sydney going to do today?" he asked.

"I'm not sure. Your mom said we need to go the grocery store, so that should be interesting since I've never been to one here," Akiiki replied.

"Well, just don't take Lucas or else he will throw a fit about wanting candy or a toy or something stupid," Marc advised. "He can be quite embarrassing when Mom lets him get into full meltdown mode," he chuckled, as Akiiki nodded with a smile.

"Yes, Mensah has his moments like that too, usually at the worst possible time," she laughed.

At that moment, Sydney walked into the room. "Holy crap, what in the world is that?" she asked, pointing to a large green beetle nearly the size of her fist which was crawling on the ceiling above them. If it were not so freakishly large she would have thought it quite lovely as it was a bright, shimmering, green metallic color.

"Crikey, he is so beautiful," said Akiiki, not scared in the least and moving closer to get a good look. "I have never seen a beetle as large and pretty as this one. We do not have such beetles in Egypt – are they common here?" she asked curiously.

"I've never seen one like this," replied Marc. "He looks like a jeweled green scarab beetle but I didn't think they got that large. Are you sure you didn't bring him from Egypt?" he asked Akiiki. "He reminds me of the temple and tomb carvings we saw there this summer."

"No, this is unlike any beetle that I have ever seen at home," she replied. "This is very interesting, I love insects so you must show me other curious types you have here."

"Do you think the beetle has something to do with the mummy?" Sydney mind-linked to Marc, who looked back at her nervously.

"Well, I certainly have never seen one this big. I still think it looks EXACTLY like the tomb paintings and hieroglyphics we saw in Egypt over the summer," Marc mind-linked back in reply. "It's a little strange to just be a creepy coincidence - we should definitely keep an eye on it."

Elle and Yoda had both just entered the room and noticed the giant beetle immediately. They instantly crouched into their hunting position and watched every tiny movement of the beetle with keen interest.

"Well, it looks like the cats may take care of the beetle for us," Sydney laughed. "This should be a good hunting challenge for them. I just hope the beetle doesn't eat THEM."

"Oh hey Marc, Dad was asking if you were ready to head to the game," Sydney said. "And I heard you are playing Knuckles so I'll keep in touch if you know what I mean," she added as Akiiki stared at her curiously.

"Thanks - that will be great. I'm afraid I'll need all the help I can get," Marc replied, heading off to gather up his gear. "And I might need to use some powers to keep from getting walloped," he added to Sydney via mind-link with a quick wink.

"Good luck, and don't get damaged!" Akiiki added seriously.

"I'll try – thanks. See you lovely ladies later!" yelled Marc from the other room.

A few minutes after Marc arrived at the game, Coach Carlos had everyone huddle up for a strategy session. "Now listen up, these guys are known for playing rough and bending the rules, but we are not going to stoop to their level, is that understood?" he asked sternly. All the players nodded their heads. "So no smack talking the other team, no arguing with the ref, no flopping, and just play a good clean game. At least I DO have some good news - Mr. Thompson is the referee today which is awesome because he is a first-class ref and REALLY strict so that should keep the other team from playing too dangerously. Remember to keep moving the ball and pass quickly before you get surrounded. So everybody, here are the game positions – three forwards: Jorge, Nick, and Lodi; three middies: Vincente, Marc, and Hadrian; and three defense: Joe, Davin, and Adam; Tommy you are sweeper; plus Nathan is goalie. The only change from normal is Marc - I'm switching you with Nick so you play center mid as a rover and Nick you're center striker. Marc - you'll need to follow the ball and play both defense and offense, and try not to get worn out. I think this way the other team will focus on you and it should free up everyone else to pass and get into scoring position. Everybody got it?" Everyone nodded nervously. "OK, on three, one, two, three, break!" All the players ran out on the field to take their positions.

Marc mind-linked Sydney to let her know the game was about to start. "Be careful!" she warned him and promised to stay on-line.

As soon as they took the field, Knuckles and his cronies Kyle, Will, Matt, Drew and Harlow all started taunting and smack talking everyone but Marc's team all put on their game faces with a smile and did not respond. Nick took the opening ball downfield with Marc and the two forwards close behind. Knuckles quickly bore down on Nick and blatantly knocked him over, stealing the ball and drawing an instant angry whistle from the ref, who came running over immediately. "Are you OK?" he asked Nick as he held up a yellow card to Knuckles who was protesting mightily. "That's one," said the ref sternly to Knuckles. "You pull that again and you are out of the game!" Knuckles stomped away in a huff as the ref placed the ball on the field.

Marc helped Nick get gingerly back up to his feet as he signaled to Coach that he was OK to play. "Wow, a yellow card in the first ten seconds, that has to be a record for Knuckles," whispered Marc as he and Nick both started laughing. "I'm glad the ref is going to be strict. You sure you're OK?" he asked, looking down at Nick's grass-covered knees.

"Yep, I'm good," Nick replied with a fierce look at Knuckles. "It will take more than that to knock me out!" he yelled as he kicked the ball back into play. He immediately charged toward the goal with Jorge and Lodi spread out left and right and Marc right behind him as the defense sprang forward to intercept them. Knuckles was about to smash him again when Nick cleverly back-kicked the ball to Marc, who couldn't resist taking a beautiful shot to hit the upper right corner of the net, just beyond the keeper's outstretched fingers. Knuckles roared in anger, Coach Carlos jumped and fist-pumped for joy, and Marc's team all rushed to congratulate him as they returned back to midfield. "Nice shot, Marc!" said Nick. "Maybe that will make them think twice about playing dirty!"

"Well, they ARE pretty thick – so probably not!" replied Marc as his team all started laughing quietly as they awaited the kick off from an angry and obviously agitated Knuckles.

"One to zero," Marc mind-linked happily to Sydney. "And that was my first shot!"

"Yeah, I know," Sydney mind-linked back. "I can see the whole field around you somehow, this is a really crazy start to the game! Be careful – Knuckles looks really mad."

When the ref blew his whistle, Knuckles tried to force the ball through their defense by pushing defenders away from him, but he was easily picked off by Vincente. All the cronies immediately converged to cover Marc which left Jorge and Lodi wide open, so Vincente was able to easily pass to Lodi, but their keeper just barely blocked his fantastic shot from the left and fell onto the ball to recover it. Knuckles' coach was screaming at their team from the sidelines, but all the cronies completely ignored him and continued to focus on Marc.

The keeper punted the ball downfield to crony Kyle, who immediately looked around for Knuckles to pass him the ball. Hadrian was able to steal the ball easily when Kyle was distracted, and passed back to Adam who gave it a beautiful high kick all the way down the field to land practically on Jorge's toe as he ran in full stride and then juked around the sweeper in front of him. The move was too fast for the defense who were still swarming around Marc at midfield, so Jorge was able to score easily on a quick kick he squeaked just inside the left post.

"Two to zero," Marc mind-linked again to Sydney. "Jorge got that one."

"YES!" Sydney yelled with a fist-pump back in the middle of the grocery store, startling Mom and Akiiki who were both now looking at her curiously.

"Did you find the cereal you wanted, or what?" Akiiki laughed. "I usually don't get that excited during grocery shopping," she chuckled. Sydney smiled back at her, now a bit embarrassed. This was going to be a little tricky.

Knuckles kicked off again from midfield, and was able to find his crony Will down the left sideline. Tommy quickly moved to intercept him but Will passed to crony Drew who then blatantly smashed into Davin, the smallest player on Marc's team, knocking him to the ground roughly. The ref instantly blew his whistle and gave a yellow card to Drew who was arguing loudly against the call and getting a serious scolding from the ref. Marc ran quickly over to help little Davin back on his feet.

"Davin, are you OK dude?" asked Marc as his teammates all crowded around to check on their player.

"Yeah, I'm fine, just knocked the wind out of me," Davin replied cautiously. "What a rotten sport! He totally saw me planted right in front of him and he just aimed right for me."

"THOSE STUPID JERKS!" yelled Sydney angrily before she could stop herself, then quickly put her hands over her mouth. Akiiki and Mom both turned to look at her again in confusion as they all stood in the middle of the health and beauty aisle.

"What's the matter dear, did they raise the price on your best lip gloss – Tyler's favorite flavor?" Mom giggled as Akiiki started laughing uproariously. Sydney's face quickly turned a bright red.

The game continued and it was easily the ugliest game any of Marc's teammates had ever played in. Their superbly talented keeper Nathan had several amazing saves against the ugly onslaught as the cronies tried to man-handle their way through the defense. Nick was knocked over two more times and now had a bad limp, and the cronies were all just blatantly trying to trip or push Marc whenever he happened to be in their vicinity, whether or not he even had the ball at the time. Luckily Marc was able to easily dodge all the attacks and had retaliated by now nutmegging everyone on the other team every time he had the ball, deftly passing the ball between their feet even while they were running at full tilt. Knuckles was getting angrier and angrier as the game wore on, and after two more yellow cards the ref stopped the game to go talk to Knuckles' coach on the sidelines.

"LOOK OUT BEHIND YOU!" yelled Sydney, causing Akiiki to turn around quickly thinking she was about to be hit by a rogue grocery cart or maybe a charging hippo (waving his credit card wildly).

Marc quickly jumped out of the way as Knuckles and four of his cronies crashed together violently on the spot where he had been standing a second before. "Thanks sis!" Marc mind-linked back to Sydney. "I was watching the ref and didn't see them coming!" The five players were now all lying on the ground moaning as the ref came running back over to see what had happened. He immediately ejected Knuckles from the game with a red card, and gave his cronies Kyle, Matt, Will, and Harlow all yellow cards and a long talk with all of them about good sportsmanship. The ref then called an early halftime and ordered both coaches to meet him at midfield. Marc could not hear their conversation but judging by all the gesturing from the ref, it was a really heated exchange and seemed to be all directed at Knuckles' coach. Coach Carlos was obviously quite angry as well at the mistreatment and abuse of his players and was almost as animated as the furious ref. Marc's teammates all watched intently as they broke out the oranges and drinks for their halftime snack. None of them had EVER seen Coach Carlos this angry.

"Are you OK, Syd?" Mom asked tentatively, as Akiiki now stared at her worriedly. "You seem a little distracted."

"Whoops, sorry Mom," Sydney replied sheepishly, pulling her cell phone out of her pocket in a sudden inspiration. "Marc has been texting me updates from the soccer game during breaks and it is pretty ugly."

"Is he OK?" asked Akiiki urgently. "He said he was worried that Alec's team of big brutes was going to play too rough."

"He's fine so far, but Nick got whacked a few times and has a bad limp," Sydney replied. "It is halftime now and Coach Carlos is probably going to have to pull Nick out of the game – it's pretty bad."

"Oh, that makes me so mad," Mom said angrily. "Alec and his little gang of cronies are such horrible bullies – I hear it from all the other moms. Somebody needs to teach them a good hard lesson. I hope Marc knocks his big ugly head right off!"

"MOM!" yelled Sydney in surprise, shocked to hear her mom talk trash about anyone. Akiiki let out a nervous giggle as she watched Sydney's reaction.

"Sorry, it just burns me up!" Mom replied furiously. "Are you girls almost ready to check out? I'm going to call Dad to have him help Coach Carlos keep it under control so nobody else gets hurt."

"Sure Mom - that sounds like a really good idea," replied Sydney with a quick glance at Akiiki who was looking very worried. "It's OK Akiiki – Marc can take care of himself – he'll be just fine – trust me." Akiiki smiled back at her, obviously unconvinced.

The cronies' coach was utterly furious with his team over halftime, and Marc was quite heartened to see that Knuckles was still getting a severe chewing-out on the sideline as the ref blew his whistle to start the second half. Since he was officially kicked out of the game, the cronies coach sent Knuckles off the sideline to sit with his agitated parents. Now thanks to Knuckles' red card, Marc's team was up by a player. Since they had no substitute players today, Coach Carlos had switched Nathan and Nick's positions so Nick was now playing keeper and Nathan had moved to center striker. Within the first five minutes of the second half, cronies Kyle and Drew had both been ejected from the game with red cards so Marc's team was suddenly three players up. The other team was simply no match for the concerted effort from Marc's team and they scored three more goals within the next five minutes.

"Five to zero, Joe got the third and then Adam got the last two goals in a row!" Marc mind-linked excitedly to Sydney, who was careful to mask her reactions as she was sitting beside Akiiki on the ride home from the grocery store, pretending to be watching her phone for more texts from Marc.

The game had turned into a runaway, to the immense satisfaction of Coach Carlos and the entire team. Marc scored twice more, as did Jorge and Lodi so by the end of the game the score was eleven to zero.

"Awesome game guys! I'm so proud of your level-headed play against all that nastiness today," praised Coach Carlos as they gathered together on the sideline at the end of the game after shaking hands with the other team and the ref. "It was a great showing of good sportsmanship in the face of adversity," he added.

Marc's team all gave each other high-fives and dug into the after-game snacks and drinks. He noticed that Nick was now limping pretty badly and asked Coach to check on him.

"Game's over – final was eleven to zero," Marc mind-linked to Sydney. "We should be home in about 30 minutes, and Coach Carlos is checking on Nick's knee right now," he added.

"Yes! The game just finished - eleven to zero!" Sydney proclaimed as she sat with Mom and Akiiki in the living room. They all sighed with relief after being so worried about Marc and his friends.

"Nick, I think your knee got worse from not moving around when you switched to keeper," Coach said as he looked closely at Nick's injured knee and had him try some different motions. "Here, put some ice on it and rest it when you get home. You probably should skip the next practice and the next game if it still hurts."

"OK, thanks Coach!" replied Nick enthusiastically, still beaming from their amazing win as he gave Marc a last high-five.

"How's Nick?" asked Akiiki, trying to see Sydney's cell phone screen.

"Coach says his knee is sprained so he will need to sit out the next practice and probably the next game," Sydney replied, carefully moving her phone so that Akiiki would not see the blank screen.

When Marc and Dad arrived home a little later, they all gave him high fives and then Akiiki gave him a giant hug in relief. "Oh Marc, I was so worried about you!" she said as she released him but held gingerly onto his hand for a few lingering moments as they drew slowly apart.

"Yeah, it was definitely the ugliest game we have ever played," Marc replied breathlessly, his head spinning from the sudden unexpected contact with Akiiki.

"Knuckles and two of his cronies all got ejected – Coach Carlos said he has never seen that many players ejected in ANY soccer game of any level. If they would have ended up with fewer than seven players they would have had to quit and forfeit the game."

"Oh man," Akiiki gasped. "At least the ref was strict, I suppose it could have been much worse," she added worriedly.

"I just hope Nick is OK, his knee was pretty gnarly looking at the end of the game," Marc replied. "Syd, you should probably tell Kelly to go check on him this afternoon to make him rest it completely per Coach's orders."

"Yeah, good idea," Sydney replied, sending Kelly a quick text on her phone. "He's a bit stubborn about following directions - just like the rest of you guys!" she giggled as everyone except Marc started laughing hysterically.

Chapter 12.   Butterflies

Today was the official opening ceremony for Mr. P's sarcophagus, so Dad and Sallah were simply beside themselves with excitement. They had taken off early this morning to get the UVA Archaeology lab ready for the big event and coordinate with the TV news crews who would soon be arriving to set up their gear. Mom, Akiiki, and Lucas were also quite excited to attend the event, but Marc and Sydney had both declared last week that they had no interest in seeing the grand opening and had made other plans. In reality, the sarcophagus simply gave them the creeps after their cartouche incident, and they both would be perfectly happy if they never saw it again for the rest of their lives after all the chaos it had brought to them.

"Are you sure you guys don't want to go with us?" asked Mom for about the tenth time that morning. "I know Dad and Sallah would love to have you there with the rest of the family."

"Yeah, he's making me live stream the whole thing back to Asim and Mensah and Mom so they can 'be there' too," complained Akiiki. "It might be fun and if it's empty we're going to roast them with a fake mummy doll in front of the camera. Lucas made me an awesome paper cut-out mummy - it will be hilarious," she added, as Lucas giggled excitedly.

"No, we're good, thanks," replied Marc. "That sounds like a funny prank, but Dad said the imaging showed that the sarcophagus was empty, so I think it will just be a tremendous letdown for everyone all around."

"Plus we've got some homework to catch up on for after break anyway," added Sydney sadly. "This way we don't have to waste our Akiiki time working on it later this week. You guys go on ahead and you can tell us all about it later." The others waved goodbye and headed out to the car.

"Homework? Good one, Syd," laughed Marc once they were alone. "So what are we really going to do instead, oh mighty mastermind?" he asked.

"Practice our powers, of course, duh!" she replied. "We haven't done anything since Akiiki has been here, and I have a bad feeling we're going to need those shields we've been working on. That mummy is bound to show up sooner or later and we need to be ready."

"OK, cool," replied Marc. "We have the house to ourselves for once so where do you want to practice? I'm getting tired of your tiny room."

"Let's go to the game room, we can close the blinds so that nobody can see inside," replied Sydney after thinking over their options for a second.

"Good, I have something new I want to show you," replied Marc as they walked upstairs to the game room. "I'm pretty good with my arm hex shield, but I've been getting really frustrated with the shimmer shield – it just keeps blinking in and out, especially when I try moving around."

"You just need more practice, my shields are both slowly getting better," replied Sydney.

"Well, I was getting too aggravated so I wanted to try something totally different," Marc explained. "I was actually trying to craft a lightsaber, but watch this." He swiped his cartouche and then concentrated for a few seconds with his eyes closed. Suddenly a glowing blue Egyptian sword appeared in his right hand

and he opened his eyes. "See, pretty cool, huh?" he asked. "And I get an awesome orange cartouche," pointing to his right arm.

"Wow, how did you do that?" Sydney exclaimed, admiring the glowing sword. "It looks just like Tutankhamun's from the GEM with the weird hook shape on the end – I think Sallah said it was called a 'khepesh' sword. But it seems too transparent, does it cut anything?" she asked.

"Well, yes it definitely does. The first time I crafted it, I tried it out on my bed without thinking, and it chopped straight through my bed post clean as a whistle just like a lightsaber," Marc laughed. "Luckily, I found some of Dad's wood glue and was able to fix it, so hopefully Mom doesn't notice."

"So how do you craft one?" Sydney asked seriously. "I want to try."

"Well, I just swiped my cartouche and then visualized the word 'sword,'" he explained. "I've tried thinking about other types of swords, but I always seem to get this one."

"OK, cool, let me try," replied Sydney excitedly. She swiped her cartouche and then concentrated as Marc had instructed. Suddenly an identical glowing blue sword appeared in her right hand. "Freaking ... awesome," she said in amazement, admiring the wonderful sword. She carefully touched the blade which felt completely solid, even though the sword seemed almost ghost-like.

"Nice job, Syd!" said Marc enthusiastically. "It took me a few tries to get it, you are amazing!" They both swung their cartouche swords around, attacking imaginary enemies.

"You know, I have a strange feeling that we are supposed to throw these like boomerangs, do you sense that too?" Sydney asked.

"Yes, I think so, but I was too scared to try it in the house," Marc replied. "We need to find somewhere secluded outside to practice that."

"Yeah, you're right. Let's remember to try that next time. I want to try the force punch again where we have more space, too," said Sydney. "Hmmm, I wonder? I love Dad's Samurai swords, let me try something," she said as she closed her eyes. She visualized her favorite sword from Dad's collection – a beautiful curved long katana with a blue handle ito wrap and golden tsuba and kashira. She carefully thought about every minute detail from the sword and tried to create a clear picture in her mind. She then felt something change in her right hand, and opened her eyes excitedly. A perfect blue ghost version of Dad's sword had replaced the Egyptian one in her right hand. "Wow," was all she could say.

"Syd, that is incredible. How did you do that?" asked Marc quietly. "Crap, I tried to make that exact same sword but it didn't work for me," he said bitterly, admiring her wonderful creation.

"I'm not sure. I just very carefully tried to picture exactly what I wanted it to look like in 3D from top to bottom, and then I felt it change in my hand," she answered in awe.

"OK, you're making me SO jealous right now," Marc said bitterly. "Why don't you just go ahead and make my misery complete and craft a lightsaber? How about Dad's blue one?"

"OK, I know the one. Let me try," she said, concentrating carefully as she visualized the lightsaber. She opened her eyes but the glowing katana was still in her hand. "Nope, sorry - it didn't work. Maybe it has to be a REAL weapon," she added.

"What do you mean? Lightsabers ARE real weapons," Marc replied seriously, and then immediately started laughing. "Oh, hey, looks like we have company," Marc added. Both Elle and Yoda had just stormed into the room meowing angrily.

"I think they are annoyed that we are practicing without them," laughed Sydney. They both swiped their cartouches to make the swords disappear. "Sorry about that, guys," she said as she knelt down to pet both of the cats, who were now meowing inquisitively and jumping up and down.

"Looks like they want to fly again," chuckled Marc. Both cats started purring in response. "OK, I guess practice time is officially over," he said as they launched both cats into the air.

Later that evening the rest of the family returned from the opening ceremony all feeling a bit dejected. Naturally, the sarcophagus was indeed empty except for some dust and a few scraps of embalming wrapping, just as Sydney and Marc of course knew it would be. One bright side was that Akiiki and Lucas were still giggling conspiratorially about their trick with the fake mummy cut-out because it had fooled Mensah completely until Asim and Marion had started laughing hysterically. Mensah was sure the mummy had been walking around the room trying to eat everyone, and was at first embarrassed at being tricked but then laughed along with everyone else at how horribly fake it had looked when they played it back for him again.   He and Lucas had then visited over the video connection for a couple of hours while Dad and Sallah were inspecting and filming the hieroglyphic-covered interior of the sarcophagus and helping the news crews take down their gear.   The news reporters were still excited despite the lack of a mummy and had given the whole story a positive spin, so overall it was a great day for the project.   Starting in the morning, Dad and Sallah would begin the long process of carefully re-packing the sarcophagus for shipment back to the Grand Egyptian Museum in Cairo.

The next morning Mom had everyone up early and out the door for a long day of sightseeing.   The twins soon realized that Mom apparently thought it was her civic duty to take Akiiki to every sightseeing location within a 500 mile radius, but Akiiki was actually really excited so they played along.   This morning they were on their way to Washington DC for a museum and zoo run, after first swinging by Tyler's house to pick him up.   It was still dark outside, so within minutes Marc and Mom were the only ones awake on the two hour drive to DC.   Tyler and Sydney were sitting beside each other and had fallen asleep holding hands, as had Akiiki and Lucas to Marc's supreme annoyance with his cheeky little brother.   This was going to be a long day, he thought ruefully.

Mom did not at all enjoy driving in the crazy Washington DC traffic and Lucas loved to ride the Metro train anyway, so they parked at an outlying Metro station and hopped on the train to the city.   It was still quite early in the morning so the train was packed with commuters heading to work, therefore Mom nervously kept an eye on everyone to make sure they all stayed together.   They reached the National Mall stop without any trouble and exited the station, walking the short distance to stand in the center of the National Mall.

"Ohhh, there is so much green," said Akiiki admiringly, looking around as they walked.

"Yes, this is a lovely park," explained Mom.   "It is over two miles long from west to east and over a mile wide, with the Lincoln Memorial on the west end, the Washington Monument in the middle, and the US Capital building on the east end. There are many fantastic museums all around the mall which we absolutely love."

"It is still a little cold in the fall, but in the spring and summer this place is crazy with people and all sorts of cool outdoor activities and festivals, especially when all the cherry blossoms are in bloom," said Sydney.

"And they have an awesome carousel which is my favorite in the whole wide world," proclaimed Lucas proudly.

"Akiiki, this is your first time here so where would you like to start?" Marc asked.

"Let's walk to the Washington Monument – it reminds me of all the ancient obelisks back home in Egypt!" Akiiki said excitedly, as she saw the top of the monument from where they were standing.

"OK, great, it is not far at all," said Lucas, grabbing her hand and pulling her along while the others followed chuckling.

"He never holds my hand like that," Sydney said sadly.

"Why would you want him to?" asked Marc in disbelief. "He'd probably drag you down the stairs or over a cliff if he did," he added as Sydney and Tyler laughed while Mom frowned sadly.

"Don't let it bother you Syd - I would love to hold your hand," exclaimed Tyler as he reached for Sydney's hand, getting a big smile in return. "I love you," he whispered to her quietly.

"Right back at you," Sydney winked back.

"I wish Akiiki would hold my hand," thought Marc to himself, feeling a bit dejected and left out, but trying his best to hide it from the girls. "But I feel stupid asking her, and Lucas would tease me to no end," he thought ruefully.

Mom looked over at him thoughtfully for a few minutes as they walked and then quietly said "Marc, I would love to hold your hand if you are feeling lonely."

"No, that's OK," Marc replied a little too quickly, which made him instantly feel guilty. "So don't take this the wrong way, Mom, because I do love you, but when guys are my age it is just too weird to hold your mom's hand anymore. It kinda makes me feel like a toddler again, if you know what I mean."

"Yeah, I figured you would say that," Mom replied with a smile. "It's OK – no worries. I know you're not my little baby anymore," she sighed sadly.

Before long, they all stood at the base of the tall Washington Monument admiring the dizzying top 555 feet above them. "Ohh, it's beautiful. But I'm used to seeing obelisks like this all covered with hieroglyphics, so it looks strangely plain to me," Akiiki observed, laughing.

"To the north you can see the White House, and to the west past the World War II Memorial is the Lincoln Reflecting Pool and then the Lincoln Memorial, and to the east is the US Capital Building," said Tyler, pointing out the major landmarks for her. They all spent some time walking around admiring the sights, but Akiiki was getting chilly so they decided to hit some of the museums so she could warm up inside.

Their first museum stop was the Smithsonian National Museum of American History, which was one of Lucas' favorites. He had been there many times, so he dragged Akiiki by the hand along his favorite route, acting just like an official (but high-speed) museum guide pointing out what he thought were all the best highlights for her. He started with Edison's light bulb from 1879 on the first floor, and then took everyone upstairs to see the tattered Star-Spangled Banner from 1814. Sydney then insisted they see Dorothy's ruby slippers from the 1939 Wizard of Oz movie, so Lucas reluctantly agreed to the detour - but only because Akiiki wanted to see them as well. After that, Lucas took them up to the third floor to see George Washington's army uniform from 1789. Finally, they went to see the adjustable-top desk that Thomas Jefferson had used to draft the Declaration of Independence in 1776, which was definitely a cool artifact from American history. Mom reminded everyone that they would be going to visit Thomas Jefferson's home called Monticello back in Charlottesville later that week, so they all felt a special hometown connection with the desk. Lucas then declared that the tour was over and they should immediately proceed to the next museum. Everyone laughed and then slowly made their way back down to the entrance, stopping along the way to admire some exhibits which Lucas had skipped over in his personal high-speed highlights tour.

Their next stop was Smithsonian National Museum of Natural History, which was Lucas' absolute favorite museum on the National Mall. He first took them directly to see the Tyrannosaurus Rex skull on the ground floor and then rushed them through the Ocean Hall on the first floor. The Ocean Hall had an amazing full-size blue whale model hanging from the ceiling which Akiiki absolutely loved, so she managed to get Lucas to reluctantly stop for a few minutes so she could check it out.

"You're quite good at managing him," Mom whispered in her ear. "I always have a hard time diverting his attention off his next target," she chuckled.

"Oh, it's not a problem," Akiiki replied quietly. "I'm used to Mensah dragging me around everywhere so I don't mind in the least. It's very nice to have another little brother, and he's just so irresistibly cute," she said happily, as Marc observed the exchange irritably.

"OK, so it's a big blue whale, can we go now?" Lucas asked impatiently, still holding tightly onto Akiiki's hand. "We're SO close to the Dinosaur Hall and it's killing me," he added quietly.

"Sure no problem," said Akiiki kindly. "Thanks for slowing down for me little brother, I think the whale is really cool," she added, kneeling down to kiss Lucas on the cheek. Sydney and Mom laughed at his reaction, torn between smiling and wanting to wipe his cheek, as he did a little of each. Marc wondered if Mom would notice if Lucas were to suddenly float away and smack into the whale. Probably so, he thought to himself bitterly.

At last they reached the Dinosaur Hall, so Lucas was quickly and completely enthralled. After a while, everyone else sat down for a rest as he dragged Akiiki from one dinosaur exhibit to the next and back again over and over. Tyler and Sydney were giggling and giving each other googly eyes, so Marc was feeling even lonelier and getting quite irritated.

"Hmmm, I think I need to rescue Akiiki," said Mom wisely. "Hey Lucas, do you want to check out the dinosaur gift shop?" she asked as they passed nearby.

"Sure!" yelled Lucas, dropping Akiiki's hand like a rock and running over to meet Mom, who walked with him into the gift shop. "We'll meet you guys a little later," she said with a wink.

Akiiki joined them and could sense that something was bothering Marc. She looked over at Sydney quizzically and caught her eye. Sydney very subtly motioned to her hand, and Akiiki nodded wisely. "Marc, can you please check out the mummies with me? They are just around the corner but I couldn't escape from little Lucas," Akiiki asked, grabbing Marc's hand gently in hers.

"Sure, I'd love to," Marc said with a giant smile, following her obediently.

"By the way, you do know that I have two hands, right?" Akiiki asked with a giggle. "This one gets lonely sometimes," she said mischievously as she squeezed his hand tightly. Tyler and Sydney both started snickering as they followed them to the mummy hall, but Marc was completely oblivious and felt truly happy for the first time that day. Akiiki's hand felt warm and delightful inside his own.

The mummy hall was quite small and unimpressive after seeing the Grand Egyptian Museum, but there were several very interesting human and animal Egyptian mummies on display along with some shabti figurines and other cool funerary offerings. There was also a really exquisite Horus falcon statue and a beautiful winged scarab pendant which caught everyone's eye. However, they were all immediately drawn to a cat mummy in one of the glass-enclosed exhibits. The mummy was tightly wrapped in a cool crisscross pattern and would have been unrecognizable as a cat except for the lovely painted cat head which had been added on top. As they all stared at it admiringly, Marc and Sydney both noticed a blue Asim cartouche symbol which appeared and started pulsating brightly over the cat's chest area. They looked at each other in a panic but it did not seem that Akiiki or Tyler were able to see it.

"Ummm, can you guys see any cartouche markings on the mummy?" Sydney asked nervously. "I wonder if the cat had a name that maybe they wrote on the wrappings," she added quickly.

"Hmmm, no I don't see anything," said Akiiki as she bent over to examine the mummy more closely.

"Nope, I don't see anything either. The wrapping is really cool, though," added Tyler as he looked from a different angle. "I wonder how they did that pattern so neatly. It must have taken forever."

Marc and Sydney looked at each other nervously and breathed a sigh of relief. "What do you think it means?" mind-linked Marc.

"I think there is probably another Asim cartouche bracelet hidden inside," Sydney mind-linked back to him, surveying the hall carefully to make sure no one else was nearby.

"What should we do?" asked Marc over the mind-link.

"I think we just have to leave it, I don't know how to retrieve it without breaking the mummy and setting off the alarms, not to mention that it will probably knock us out cold again if we touch it," she replied. "And we are not exactly alone at the moment," she added.

"Crap, I guess you're right. Let's get out of here so we don't draw any more attention to it," he said quickly. Akiiki had started to look at both of them suspiciously, as had one of the burly museum guards who had just entered the exhibit area.

"Hey Akiiki, you like insects, right? Want to check out the insect hall with me?" asked Marc.

"Sure, that would be cool," she responded with a smile as they started moving again, still holding hands as Marc's mind continued to race over both the cartouche and his close proximity to Akiiki.

The museum had a live insect zoo and also a live butterfly exhibit which everyone enjoyed immensely. There were several large beetles in the zoo, but nothing that looked like the huge green scarab beetles that had invaded their house back in Charlottesville. The closest insect they saw was a large black Rhinoceros Beetle that had a really cool massive horn on the back of its head and another protruding from its nose, together looking almost like a giant pincher. Marc thought it looked very heavy and awkward, and wondered how the beetle was able to fly with such a heavy weight on its head.

The sealed-off butterfly exhibit was wonderful but also quite nerve racking as they had to be very careful where they stepped and moved (which was the main reason Mom never let Lucas come in, Marc thought to himself). For some reason the butterflies seemed attracted to Akiiki, and at one point when she stopped moving there were almost a hundred of them all over her head, shoulders, and outstretched arms. She giggled excitedly and twirled slowly, sending all the butterflies flying off casually in different directions in a mesmerizing kaleidoscope of shimmering colors. She had never looked more radiantly beautiful, Marc thought to himself as he watched the amazing spectacle in total and complete awe.

"Oh, that was so fun," Akiiki giggled as she spun over to give Marc a giant hug and gently collect his hand again. She smiled at him widely as her gorgeous green eyes twinkled brightly in joy, reflecting the colors of the nearby butterflies. Marc's mind had already turned to total mush several seconds ago and he could not find the words he wanted to say, to tell her that she was the most beautiful girl he had ever seen and that he was madly in love with her from the very first time he saw her in Cairo. Instead he only smiled back timidly and desperately tried to concentrate on walking carefully to not disturb any of the butterflies as they moved through the rest of the exhibit. It felt like a whole swarm of them had flown into his belly as he wobbled awkwardly ahead, completely under Akiiki's wondrous spell with his heart beating wildly. Behind him he could hear Sydney snickering, and then suddenly he heard loud ambulance noises in his mind.

"Very funny, sis!" he mind-linked back to her grumpily.

"I'm just happy that now you know how it feels, brother," she mind-linked back. "Love is a wonderful thing."

"Geez, you sound totally like mushy Mom!" he replied with a chuckle. "And don't you dare tell her, she will be freaking out enough today with Akiiki holding my hand. I'm sure Mom's built-in advance warning romance detection system is beeping like crazy right now," he added sternly as Sydney giggled. They reached the exit area of the butterfly exhibit and had to wait in line to be de-butterflied before exiting through the sealed door.

"You should just be brave, tell the truth, and let Akiiki know exactly how you feel," Sydney advised. "It worked for me and I know she has a crush on you too."

"I'm too chicken," Marc mind-linked sadly. "And besides, in a few days she'll be halfway across the world again and we'll be lucky to see each other once a year. That will just make me even more miserable."

"Isn't that still better than nothing?" Sydney asked. "Just be happy in the time you have together. You can still email and text her all the time, you would just have to work at it."

"It just seems impossible, I don't think we could ever be happy not actually being with each other like this," Marc mind-linked sadly.

"What are you two up to?" asked Akiiki suspiciously. "I can swear that you are talking but I can't hear anything." Marc and Sydney were startled and both looked over at Akiiki and Tyler who were both watching them curiously.

"Oh, sorry, it's a twin thing," Sydney replied apologetically. "We have a special mind connection," she added awkwardly.

"Really? Because I have a twin too and we don't usually talk without speaking," Akiiki said suspiciously. "What's really going on?"

Acting on a sudden crazy impulse, Marc held out his arm to show Akiiki his cartouche which was still glowing a light blue from his mind-link with Sydney. "OK fine, the truth is, we got these magic cartouches from Egypt so we now we can mind-link and have other magic powers," he said, grabbing Sydney's arm to show Akiiki and Tyler her matching glowing cartouche as well. Sydney gasped in shock. "They change colors like a mood ring and disappear when we're not using them."

"That's not what I meant when I said tell her the truth, you idiot!" Sydney mind-yelled at Marc. "You're probably putting whoever knows about our powers in grave danger, fool!" Marc frowned back at her in response.

Akiiki and Tyler both stared at them unbelieving. "Yeah, Knuckles was asking me about those but I told him I had never seen them before. May I?" Tyler asked as he reached for Sydney's arm. She nodded nervously and he held her arm gently to look more closely at the cartouche.

"Oh, it is really cool. I love the detail and it even looks like it is glowing," said Tyler admiringly. "Amazing, Syd. And it matches my eyes," he added, giggling.

Akiiki then grabbed Marc's arm a little roughly and looked at it closely. Suddenly she started laughing hysterically, startling everyone else. "Oh you guys are too much! You realize this says 'ASIM,' right? My big brother Asim is totally trolling you guys with one of his crazy practical jokes," she chortled. "I can't believe you fell for it – these are probably just temporary color-change tattoos, right? Mensah and Asim are going to love this!" she laughed.

Sydney and Marc both looked at each other cautiously and giggled nervously. Their butterfly check was over and the exhibit guard told them they could leave through the exit door, so everyone started walking out together holding hands again.

"That was a close call, Marc," Sydney mind-linked. "You shouldn't have done that. I guess we're going to have to wear long-sleeved shirts all the time now. That's going to be a real fashion challenge for me," she added sadly, as Marc chuckled.

As they exited the butterfly exhibit, Mom and Lucas were waiting excitedly for them. Lucas was proudly wearing an enormous foam T-rex hat and looked absolutely ridiculous, plus he was holding a huge bulging bag of assorted dinosaur souvenirs from the gift shop. Marc, Sydney and Tyler all started laughing uproariously as soon as they saw him, but Akiiki was of course much nicer.

"Oh, Lucas, that is an amazing hat," she said. "You look very scary in it though," she added thoughtfully.

"Thanks, I'm going to wear it EVERYWHERE from now on," Lucas proclaimed proudly while he ignored the giggles from everyone else. He then noticed Marc holding Akiiki's hand and gave him the evil eye. "I'll take care of Akiiki again now," he said sharply, trying to knock Marc's hand away.

"No, that's OK," said Akiiki, moving their joined hands out the way before Marc could react. "I have two hands and I would love to share them both with my two favorite boys, errrr men, in the world," she said, catching Lucas' hand with her other one as Mom chuckled. "So where are we going next, guys?" Marc and Lucas stuck their tongues out at each other and then looked away, not offering any suggestions. Akiiki rolled her eyes at their silly stubbornness.

"Well, we should probably grab some lunch next but then we could hit the National Gallery of Art which is my favorite, but actually I'm not sure if they will let a rampaging T-rex into the galleries," Mom said, still giggling.

"And we need to visit the Smithsonian National Air and Space Museum which is my favorite," added Tyler.

"Plus you said we could go the zoo to see the tigers," added Lucas, now feeling better since Akiiki was squeezing his hand.

"OK then, we had better get moving – it's going to be a busy day!" exclaimed Mom. They took a quick vote and headed for the Air and Space Museum where they had a quick lunch and a dessert of the somewhat strange but still interesting Astronaut Ice Cream. After that, they cleaned up and then started exploring the museum, with Tyler leading their tour.

"Are you sure all these planes are safe?" Akiiki asked nervously, worried about all the planes and spacecraft suspended from the museum ceiling.

"Oh yeah, don't worry, everything is suspended by steel cables or steel beams, and over-engineered for safety," Tyler said reassuringly. "I've been here dozens of times and have never heard of any problems."

"Well, OK," Akiiki replied, obviously still not totally convinced.

"It's OK - I'll protect you," said Lucas, grabbing her hand and pulling her along to catch up with Tyler and Sydney, leaving Marc and Mom in his dust.   They looked at each other and rolled their eyes.

"You had better catch her – I think you have some stiff competition," Mom said, now giggling again.

"Very funny, Mom," Marc replied quietly, as he rushed ahead to take Akiiki's other hand.

Their first stop was to check out the models of the Space Shuttle Columbia and the International Space Station, and then the Hubble Space Telescope in the next exhibit area.   Next they came to Tyler's favorite – a model of the USS Enterprise that was used in the filming of the old Star Trek TV show.

"I love this model," exclaimed Tyler admiringly.   "The special effects in the old Star Trek were pretty cheesy by today's standards, but my Dad got me into the show and the stories were really cool," he added.

"Yeah, my Dad made my brothers and I watch them too," laughed Akiiki. "Asim always pretended to be Captain Kirk and Mensah always liked Spock the best.   It was pretty funny to watch them trying to re-enact all their favorite scenes from the show."

Next they visited the Apollo Lunar Module, Viking Lander, and a cool touchable moon rock before heading upstairs to see the 1903 Wright Flyer, the world's first successful airplane.   It seemed so small and flimsy compared to all the other aircraft and spacecraft in the museum, but it was fascinating to think that they all evolved from this revolutionary airplane created by the Wright brothers so long ago. Their last stop on Tyler's tour of favorites was the "Apollo to the Moon" exhibit, where he showed them the Apollo Command Module and the Lunar Rover.   After that, they wandered around the rest of the museum checking out all the other fabulous exhibits.

"OK guys - that was fun, thanks for the tour, Tyler.   We should probably hop back on the Metro to go to the zoo before we run out of daytime," Mom said.   "I don't think we will have time for the National Gallery of Art this time.   And I'm pretty sure they don't want a crazy T-rex Lucas eating all the artwork and visitors."

"Wait, wait!   We have to ride the carousel before we leave!" yelled Lucas in dismay.

"Oh, sorry! I almost forgot," replied Mom. "It's on the way, so no problem," she added.

They had seen the carousel in the distance several times that day, but as they approached to take a ride they were struck by its beauty and wonderful charm. Akiiki was particularly fascinated since she had never seen one before in real life, and was laughing at all the young children enjoying their ride as the friends approached. There was a wide assortment of horses, each of which was colorfully painted with an old-fashioned fantastical theme. Akiiki was immediately drawn to the wonderful shimmering blue twin-tailed seahorse which she followed around in a circle as the ride was coming to a stop. She hopped on as soon as the ride finished, and Lucas climbed on a tan horse right beside her, still wearing his crazy T-rex hat. Marc was too slow in reaching them and reluctantly hopped on a zebra a couple of rows behind them so he could keep an eye on them. Sydney found a cool American flag horse and Tyler was not far away on a Medieval knight horse. As the ride started up again, Mom followed them around taking pictures with her phone.

"Wow, Lucas, that WAS really fun – thanks!" said Akiiki excitedly as they exited a few minutes later. "I just love that beautiful sea horse - crikey, he is just gorgeous! That is my very favorite color of blue, too," she added, turning to admire the seahorse as the next group of riders were clamoring to select their rides. "Why is this carousel here?" she asked. "It seems a little out of place among all these museums and huge monuments."

"Come here and check out this sign," said Marc. "It was moved here from an amusement park in Baltimore to celebrate Rev. Dr. Martin Luther King Jr.'s 'I Have a Dream' Civil Rights speech that he gave at the far end of the mall at the Lincoln Memorial back in 1963. The first African American child got to ride it after segregation ended at the park that same day, so it is a great symbol and reminder of his dreams."

"Yes, it is a wonderful history," Mom added. "His speech was before I was born but he was an amazing man and I always loved visiting this carousel as a child, too."

"I learned a little about him in school back in Cairo, so it's cool to actually be here to see this place," replied Akiiki solemnly.

"OK guys, not to rush you off, but we need to hurry up if you want to hit the zoo today before it gets dark," Mom said.

Chapter 13.   Tigers

Lucas and Marc both grabbed one of Akiiki's hands and they walked back to the Metro station to catch the train to the National Zoo. They got lucky and made it to the platform just as their train was arriving, so a short while later they hopped off at the zoo exit and rode a long, steep escalator up to street level. After walking for a few blocks along Connecticut Avenue, they arrived at the zoo entrance and of course Lucas made a bee-line straight for the tigers.

"Lucas, you are missing everything," laughed Akiiki as she was being dragged along rapidly. "Slow down, please!"

"We're going to see the tigers first, and then you guys can visit these other boring animals on the way back, duh!" replied Lucas, totally focused on his objective.

"Sorry Akiiki, this is the way we always have to go, so it's easiest to just humor him," said Mom apologetically. "But we can definitely take our time on the way back."

Marc had gotten tired of Lucas' crazy pace so dropped Akiiki's hand. She looked back at him curiously as Lucas dragged her onward. He smiled and said, "No worries - I'll catch you again later when the beast slows down."

As they were passing the Elephant Outpost, they heard a loud commotion to their right and suddenly saw a beautiful, large Peregrine Falcon flying directly towards them, with several zoo staffers clamoring behind in distant pursuit. Marc instinctively held out his right arm and the huge falcon landed gently on his arm, obviously being extremely careful not to hurt him with its massive yellow talons. It turned its head to stare directly at him with its sharp yellow and black eyes and let out a short piercing shriek. Everyone slowly gathered around him to admire the gorgeous bird as it started casually preening its wing feathers, still keeping an eye on Marc.

"Oh, crikey he is gorgeous," said Akiiki admiringly. The falcon's head and wing feathers were dark brown and he had a beautiful white feathered chest speckled with dark feathers and an all-white neck up to his sharp, curved, yellow beak. "I didn't know you were a falconer, Marc."

"I didn't either, but he is totally amazing and so gentle," replied Marc in awe as Mom was taking a video with her phone. The falcon let both Akiiki and Marc gently stroke his head and back, and seemed to really enjoy their attention as he made soft cooing noises. "He sounds like one of our cats purring," Marc laughed, as the others joined in the falcon petting action.

"Hmmm, what's on your arm, dear?" asked Mom curiously. "Did Mensah send you some temporary tattoos?" Marc and Sydney both looked quickly at his arm to see that his cartouche was glowing a warm brown. Crap.

"No, I bought a bunch of them in Egypt, so I put one on every now and then just for fun," Marc replied in a panic. "Sydney got some too," he added. Sydney looked quickly at her own arm and was relieved to see that her cartouche was not activated. Tyler and Akiiki both looked at the twins very curiously and were obviously about to say something.

Luckily at that awkward moment he was rescued by the zoo staffers who had finally caught up with the falcon. "Are you OK?" one of them asked in obvious amazement. "We don't know how he escaped but thank you for catching him," she said. "Are you a trained falconer? He seems so calm and happy on your arm." There was now a large crowd of people gathering around him to admire the wonderful falcon.

"Nope, this is my first time. I think he just wanted to make some new friends today," Marc said as he stroked the falcon. "What is his name?"

"Oh, his name is Horus," she replied. "We named him after the Egyptian Falcon God of the Pharaohs." The twins and Lucas and Akiiki all started laughing as the staffer looked slightly confused at their reaction.

"Oh yes, we know that name quite well," Marc explained. "We were in Egypt this summer and my little brother Lucas here took a crazy ride on a camel named Horus," he chuckled. "Do I really have to give him back?" he asked reluctantly.

The zoo staffers all laughed. "Yes, I'm afraid so. We need to get Horus back to his enclosure so he doesn't get hurt. Come on, Horus." She reached gently for the falcon and he hopped to her arm gauntlet with a last look at Marc and another piercing shriek. Marc could swear that he saw the falcon wink at him happily. They all said goodbye to Horus as the zoo staffers took him back home, with most of the gathered crowd now following the amazing falcon.

"OK, that was probably one of the coolest things that has ever happened to me," said Marc happily as Akiiki grabbed his hand again excitedly.

"And I got it all on video!" Mom declared proudly. "Dad is going to freak out, he loves falcons."

"Just don't post it anywhere, Mom," ordered Marc worriedly, staring down at his cartouche which was slowly fading. That would probably not be good to have everyone checking out his freaky arm in the video. Mom looked at him curiously.

Now that Horus had departed, Lucas was getting anxious to see the tigers. "OK, OK, cool bird but COME ON, let's keep moving people. I want to see the tigers!" he complained grumpily.

"Lead the way, little brother," chuckled Akiiki as he grabbed her other hand, much to Marc's annoyance. They soon passed the bats, great apes, and reptile buildings in their mad rush to reach the great cats enclosures.

"Hey Lucas, I definitely want to see the snakes on the way back, OK?" Akiiki asked, looking back longingly at the reptile building.

"Yeah, yeah, no problem. Just hurry up, we're almost there," Lucas replied quickly as Akiiki rolled her eyes in amusement at Marc with a cute wink.

"I want to see the snakes too, so we'll double-team him – no worries," whispered Marc.

"Make that a triple-team," added Tyler, now swinging Sydney's hand as they followed close behind. "I love snakes, too."

"Yuck, no thanks," added Sydney. "Snakes creep me out, I'll just wait for you guys outside when we get there," she said disgustedly as Tyler laughed.

"Oh Syd, you are hiiiiisssssss-terical, snakes are awesome," chuckled Tyler, as everyone except Lucas cracked up at his silly pun.

As they reached the tiger enclosure, Lucas excitedly dragged Akiiki out of Marc's grasp to the viewing fence to introduce her. "These are my friends Damai and Sparky - they are both Sumatran Tigers," he said hurriedly as he pointed to each. "And over there is Pavel, he's a Siberian Tiger which is the largest cat species in the world. But he's only a couple years older than me so he is not full grown yet. Some people call them Amur Tigers too, but I like saying Siberian Tiger better," he explained excitedly. The three tigers were strikingly magnificent with beautiful orange fur all over with black vertical stripes and white highlights on their face, ears, tail, and belly.

"Oh Lucas, your friends are so breathtakingly lovely," said Akiiki admiringly as Sparky yawned widely and let out a small roar. Damai and Pavel both roared back quietly in response.

"See, they missed me!" said Lucas proudly. Mom rolled her eyes and chuckled. Lucas started into a long conversation with his tiger friends so Akiiki was able to escape and return to Marc after a few minutes.

"He is so excited about the tigers, it is so cute," Akiiki said to Mom, as she reached for Marc's hand which he happily offered.

"Yeah, I'm just always worried that he is going to jump IN the enclosure to be with his buddies," Mom laughed in reply. "Are you guys having fun? Akiiki, you and Marc definitely seem to be holding hands a LOT today," Mom observed excitedly.

"MOM!" yelled Marc and Sydney simultaneously, but Akiiki just giggled.

"Yes, I'm having a wonderful time, thank you so much, Mrs. C," she said as she smiled widely at Marc, temporarily stunning him again, which unfortunately for Marc this time did not escape Mom's notice.

"I'm so happy you are able to stay with us Akiiki, it is lovely having another daughter around," Mom replied happily as she hugged Akiiki tightly.

"Are you guys up for another carousel ride today?" Sydney asked awkwardly to change the subject. "It's probably the only way we will get him away from the tigers anytime soon," she added nervously.

"That's a great idea," said Mom. "Lucas honey, try to wrap it up with your tiger friends soon and we can ride the zoo carousel," she called out.

"OK, OK, Mom," Lucas responded in agitation. "I'll be there in a few minutes, I was just talking to Damai to get some advice on dealing with our cats Elle and Yoda. And I asked Sparky if he knew of any cats that could come live with me, but he said he didn't know of any," he added sadly. "But I'm going to ask Pavel next, so fingers crossed!" he added excitedly.

Quite a bit more than a few minutes later, Lucas was finally finished with the tigers and they walked over to the nearby zoo carousel. "Wow, this is so cool!" exclaimed Akiiki as they stood outside the carousel gate. Instead of being mostly horses like the National Mall carousel, this one quite appropriately had an amazing menagerie of colorful zoo animals including a tiger, giraffe, cheetah, antelope, birds, dolphin, alligator, armadillo, fox, lion, ostrich, and even a pink flamingo among many others.

When it was their turn, Lucas of course jumped on the tiger, while the others spread out to pick their favorite animal to ride. Akiiki picked the cool green alligator which reminded her of the Nile crocodiles back home, and Sydney went for the pink flamingo. Marc picked the armadillo which was right beside Akiiki, and Tyler selected the crazy ostrich which was just in front of them. Naturally, Mom walked around as they rode, taking pictures with her phone and embarrassing them all mightily.

After the carousel, they toured the nearby Amazonian Rainforest exhibit and then worked their way back to the reptile center. As promised, Sydney refused to go in, so Mom waited outside with her while everyone else went in to find the snakes. "Are there any venomous snakes here?" asked Akiiki excitedly as they entered. "I'd love to see the ones you have here – we have MANY back home in Egypt," she added.

"Yes, I think they have all three venomous snakes in Virginia – the timber rattlesnake, copperhead, and water moccasin," replied Marc. Sure enough, they were soon able to find all three and Akiiki found them very interesting, especially the very large timber rattlesnake who was a bit grumpy as they watched him.

"It is strange you have only three, Dad made us learn all the venomous snakes in Egypt and we have three dangerous cobras plus six smaller vipers which are even worse because they are so hard to see," Akiiki said. "He made us learn them all because we often go on archaeological digs with him in Egypt, and we've actually seen almost all of them in the wild."

"Which one is on Tutankhamun's golden mask?" asked Lucas interestedly.

"Oh, that is the Egyptian Cobra which is the symbol of Lower Egypt and the winged cobra God Wadjet," answered Akiiki. "That is also supposedly the snake that bit Cleopatra. He's probably our most famous snake but Asim likes the Red Spitting Cobra because he had a close call with one a few years ago."

"What happened?" asked Tyler curiously.

"Well, Asim and Dad were on a dig and they accidently disturbed one who was nesting in the ruins," explained Akiiki. "Let's just say the snake wasn't very happy and spat venom at Asim, but luckily it missed his eyes but did hit his shirt. I think it almost scared Dad, and especially Asim, to death but now Asim has a weird fascination with them. They are actually quite pretty – usually a fairly bright scarlet with a really cool and wide cobra hood."

"Wow," said the three boys simultaneously. The friends wrapped up their tour of the reptile center after checking out some cool turtles and lizards and met Mom and Sydney back at the entrance.

"Is anyone hungry for dinner yet?" Mom asked. "The zoo is closing in a couple of hours so we should probably find something to eat soon," she added.

"Yes, I'm DYING of starvation," Lucas said grumpily as everyone laughed. "The tigers already ate most of their dinner and they wouldn't give me any."

"Well, we're pretty close to the Panda Plaza if you want to eat there and then check out the gift shop," Mom replied. "But if you get anything else Lucas, you are going to have to carry it. I've been lugging around your dinosaur souvenirs all day and my arms are getting tired," she chuckled.

After dinner, the friends took their time exploring the exhibits and stayed until the zoo closed that evening. Lucas was getting very tired from the long day of exploring so was too tired to complain or rush them like he did earlier. Afterwards, they took the Metro back to the station where they had parked their car early that morning, and started the drive back home to Charlottesville. Lucas had insisted on sitting between Akiiki and Marc, but Akiiki somehow convinced him that she should sit in between Lucas and Marc instead as a compromise.

"How sweet," Mom thought to herself, as everyone had quickly fallen asleep. Lucas and Marc were both holding one of Akiiki's hands and she had fallen asleep leaning on Marc's shoulder. In the back, Sydney and Tyler had also passed out holding hands.

"What an amazing family and great friends they have," Mom reflected happily. "But I am going to miss Akiiki terribly when she goes back home – I just wish she lived closer to us," she thought sadly. And Mom also knew that she would most certainly not be the only one in the family who would soon be missing dear Akiiki.

Chapter 14.   Godzilla

"Guys, come on! It's almost 10:00. Are you all just going to sleep all day?" yelled Dad up the stairs. "The kayaks are loaded and we're ready to go – you're wasting a beautiful day! Get your butts down here and let's roll."

"I think the DC trip wore them all out yesterday," laughed Sallah.

"Probably so," agreed Dad. "Mom's all-day tours can be pretty brutal, that's for sure," he added.

Slowly Lucas and the teenagers emerged groggily from their rooms and made their way downstairs, sleepily rubbing their eyes. "Where's Mom?" Lucas asked in confusion.

"She's at the lab covering for us so Sallah and I can take you guys kayaking today," Dad explained patiently. "Remember how we've been talking about this for days now?"

"Oh, yeah I guess," replied Lucas. "Hey Sallah!" he added, noticing him for the first time.

"Hey back, Lucas," Sallah replied. "And how's my sleepy little princess?" he asked Akiiki, mussing up her hair.

"Good morning Dad!" Akiiki replied cheerfully. "Sorry – I think we all overslept. I just can't seem to get on the right schedule with the time difference from back home," she explained.

"No worries," Sallah replied. "Hey we made you guys a quick breakfast and we already have a lunch packed, so grab something to eat and we will hit the road."

The kids all ate a little breakfast and then went back upstairs to get dressed and gather what they wanted to take with them for the trip. Almost an hour later - much to Dad's frustration at their slow pace - they were finally on the road.

Today they were heading to nearby Walnut Creek Park which was one of their favorite places to kayak, bike, and hike. There was a large beautiful lake, lots of great biking and hiking trails, and a nice swim beach there - although the water would be far too cold today to actually go swimming. Dad and Sallah had loaded their three two-person tandem kayaks on the trailer which they hooked to Betty, the family mini-van. Of course, Dad had given all the kayaks names which was one of his weird traditions. The kayaks were all uniquely colored and their names were Godzilla (blue), Mothra (yellow), and Rodan (red) after Dad's favorite Japanese movie monsters. They also had a white, blue, and silver stand-up paddleboard named R2-D2 but they left him at home since the water was sure to be frigid and someone usually fell off at least once (except for Marc who had mastered it long ago).

Once they arrived, Dad and Sallah unloaded the kayaks while everyone else spread out the life jackets, paddles, and all their other gear. Marc and Sydney helped Lucas and Akiiki get their life jackets adjusted properly while Dad and Sallah carried the three kayaks to the water's edge.

"OK Marc, I don't think Akiiki and Sallah have kayaked very much, so you had better give them the safety speech before we start," advised Dad with a smile. Marc and Sydney had both earned the Kayaking Merit Badge with their Scout Troop and had been on dozens of crazy kayak adventures, but Marc was the Troop Instructor who always trained new kayakers so usually gave all the safety speeches for friends and family. Lucas had heard "the speech" a million times so he promptly drifted off along the shore to look for frogs and turtles to chase.

"Well, living in the middle of a desert does somewhat limit one's options for recreational boating," chuckled Sallah as everyone laughed.

"And Mom won't let us take small boats on the Nile because of the crocodiles and grumpy hippos," lamented Akiiki.

"Well, we have none of those here, so we should be OK today," chuckled Marc. "Your biggest danger today is probably getting rammed and capsized by Lucas since he doesn't steer very well."

"Hey, I heard that!" yelled Lucas angrily from off in the distance, holding a frog he had just caught.

"OK Lesson 1 is getting into the boat," began Marc in his instructor's voice as he approached Godzilla. "The rule is to always maintain three points of contact with the boat – so two hands and a foot, two feet and a hand, two knees and a hand, you get the idea," he continued as he climbed into the blue kayak gracefully.

"Lesson 2 is closely related and comes from Assistant Scoutmaster Mr. Warring – you NEVER stand up in a boat unless you are George Washington crossing the Delaware," he said with a chuckle. "It's a perfect way to lose your balance and end up soaking wet," he added as Akiiki started giggling.

"Lesson 3 is the paddle," he continued as he held up his paddle. "Kayak paddles have two blades, so you hold it with both hands like this with the logos on the blades right-side up and the blades curving toward you. Then you simply dip into the water on one side and then dip into the water on the other side in a nice smooth motion," he said as he demonstrated the proper technique. "If you want to turn right, you paddle on the left side, and vice versa. If you are going fast and need to turn quickly, you can jab your paddle down into the water on the side you want to turn to and hold it there to create drag," he explained. "These are two person kayaks, so you have to work together as a synchronized team to steer correctly. OK, any questions?"

Akiiki and Sallah looked a little nervous but did not ask any questions, so Marc came back to shore and climbed out to help them get settled.

"OK honey, blue is my favorite color, so we'll take Godzilla. You take the front and I'll take the back," said Sallah as he motioned Akiiki towards Godzilla. Akiiki looked back apologetically at Marc as she held the kayak steady while her dad climbed in. "OK, your turn," Sallah said excitedly as he reached for Akiiki's hand. She followed Marc's instructions and soon was seated comfortably in the front seat.

Lucas and Sydney climbed into Mothra and Marc and Dad were last in the water in Rodan. "OK, everybody ready? Let's move out to deeper water," said Dad.

Lucas and Sydney were used to kayaking together so they forged ahead quickly and easily, with Marc and Dad close behind. But Sallah and Akiiki were having major trouble moving and were soon both laughing uproariously. Sydney turned back to watch them, and it looked like they were doing everything correctly but their kayak mysteriously just kept going in a big circle. She happened to look over at Marc to see if he could offer some advice, but she noticed that he appeared to be concentrating intensely on Godzilla.

"OK, what are you doing? I can see your cartouche from here," Sydney mind-linked to him suspiciously.

"Oh, I'm just helping them steer," replied Marc calmly over the mind-link.

"Well, it looks like you are not doing a very good job," mind-laughed Sydney. "What exactly are you planning, oh incredibly helpful one?"

"I have a wonderful and amazing plan, watch and learn, sis, watch and learn," Marc replied, chuckling.

"Hey Sallah, maybe it is not such a good idea to put two beginners in the same kayak," yelled Marc. "Would you mind if you and I switched places?" he asked as Akiiki tried to stifle her giggles.

"Well, we sure are NOT getting anywhere like this, so that sounds like a great plan," replied Sallah, still laughing. They took the boats back to shore and Marc helped Sallah climb out to join Dad, while he settled into Godzilla behind Akiiki.

"OK, I'm not sure how you did that, but thanks," she whispered to him with a dazzling wink of her gorgeous green eyes. "I suppose I have my brother's magic cartouche to thank for it?" she asked, giggling.

"As a matter of fact, you do! And rescuing you was my pleasure," he chuckled back to her. "And thank YOU very much," he thought to his arm cartouche which was now quickly fading.

Dad and Sallah now paddled away easily from shore. "Wow, this IS much easier," Sallah said. "I'm not sure what I was doing wrong before," he added, a bit puzzled. Marc and Sydney both tried to stifle their laughter. Soon the dads caught up with Lucas and Sydney, leaving Marc and Akiiki behind.

"OK, the key is to keep a good rhythm and work together as a team," instructed Marc. "Since you are in the front, just start paddling on one side and then the other, and I will match your rhythm." Akiiki started paddling and she and Marc were able to develop an easy rhythm and quickly caught up with the others. "There see - we are perfectly matched," Marc added proudly.

"I have always thought so too," replied Akiiki with a quick wink back at Marc, making his head suddenly start spinning wildly.

"OK, where do you want to go, Lucas?" asked Dad as the three boats gathered in the middle of the lake.

"Let's go the first inflow branch across the lake to look for turtles," Lucas responded immediately, pulling out his net which he had stowed in the kayak. Catching water turtles was one of his favorite activities at the lake, but the turtles had quickly caught on to him and now fled into the water instantly whenever they saw him coming. "Follow us!" Lucas yelled as he and Sydney started paddling away. They soon reached the other side and drifted slowly along the shoreline, looking for the turtles who liked to sun themselves on floating logs and fallen trees near the shore.

"What does he do with the turtles?" Akiiki asked Marc curiously. "He doesn't hurt them, does he?"

"Oh no, he just tries to catch him with his net, plays with them for a bit, and then lets them go," replied Marc. "But they are scared of him now and always jump in the water as soon as they see him coming in the kayak, so he doesn't catch very many anymore."

"Which gives me an interesting idea," Marc thought to himself mischievously.

Marc steered Godzilla close behind Lucas and Sydney in Mothra as they all scanned for nearby turtles. Dad and Sallah had fallen behind in Rodan watching a large four foot long carp swimming near the shore. As they rounded a fallen branch, they all saw a large group of ten Red-Eared Slider turtles of assorted sizes happily sunning themselves on a floating log. Lucas immediately grabbed his net at the same instant the turtles caught sight of him. All the turtles jumped off the log, but instead of hitting the water they all leaped toward Lucas and landed directly in his lap, to the complete surprise of everyone except Marc.

"Marc, quit it!" yelled Sydney, totally startled by the flying turtles as Lucas started hooting for joy, Marc started laughing hysterically, and Akiiki watched it all with confused amusement. Akiiki then turned around to look at Marc and noticed his arm cartouche glowing a bright green, as she stared at it thoughtfully.

"I've done it! I've done it!" yelled Lucas happily. "Did you see that? I've discovered a new species of turtles – I'm going to call them Kangaroo Turtles! I'm going to be famous – the cover of National Geographic here I come!" he yelled proudly. "This is the best day EVER!"

"Yeah, you'll probably get rich and make loads of money!" Marc laughed.

"And I'm sure you'll get lots of babes, too!" Akiiki added seriously, trying hard to stifle her laughter.

"Oh yuck, thanks for ruining the moment, Akiiki!" Lucas replied as he gave her a disgusted look of total revulsion. Marc and Akiiki both started laughing hysterically.

Dad and Sallah had now joined the group to see what all the yelling and commotion was about. The turtles were now scampering all over the inside of Mothra trying to make their escape, so Lucas and Sydney had to catch them all individually and release them back into the water. She gave Marc a murderous glare for startling her like that, which then turned to a mischievous smile.

"DID YOU SEE THAT, DAD? It was incredible – all the turtles jumped about ten feet and landed right in my lap!" Lucas yelled with excitement. Dad looked over at Marc and Sydney in confusion and they both shrugged their shoulders. "I've discovered a new species – Kangaroo Turtles - I'm going to be famous!" Lucas added proudly.

"Yes, it was quite amazing - I saw them jump," declared Akiiki with a strange look back at Marc, who returned the look with his best smile of total innocence. "You are truly a master turtle catcher, Lucas!" she praised.

"Thank you! You know, sometimes I even amaze myself!" replied Lucas, absolutely bubbling with pride and excitement.

At that moment they all heard a loud splash and a giant bullfrog smacked hard into Marc's face, making him scream shrilly in shock and drop his paddle. The slimy frog slid down his life jacket and landed partially stunned in his lap. Everyone immediately burst into laughter, and Marc's face turned bright red with embarrassment.

"Wow, the wildlife around here is almost as dangerous as the grumpy hippos and Nile crocodiles back home!" Akiiki declared with a giggle as she looked directly at Sydney with a sly smile. Sydney smiled back innocently and added a little wink. Akiiki reached backward to rescue the slowly recovering frog and laid him gently back in the water. "Crikey, he's a beautiful frog – I love his colors!" she added, still laughing, as he swam away quickly.

They all kayaked at a casual, relaxed pace for a couple of hours and saw lots of wildlife, but there were no more flying creatures, much to Lucas' disappointment. Akiiki was now suspiciously watching the twins quite closely so they decided via mind-link to call a truce and be more careful around her. They all landed on the deserted swim beach for a mid-afternoon lunch on the cool white sand. Mom had packed a couple of small coolers of food and drinks plus a blanket and other picnic supplies which they had stowed in the kayaks, so it was a wonderful spread once they had it all laid out. Lucas quickly devoured his lunch and ran off to check along the beach shoreline for critters to catch. The others all ate their lunch leisurely and chatted for a while about the gorgeous day and the latest work news from Dad and Sallah. Soon the dads were engaged in a detailed conversation about packing up Mr. P's sarcophagus so Akiiki and the twins were starting to get restless and bored.

Akiiki looked around to see where Lucas had gone and then stood up quickly, reaching her hand down to Marc. "Would you like to go for a walk?" she asked him with a dazzling smile as he stood up slowly. Sydney had started to get up as well, but Akiiki gave her a covert shake of her head, so Sydney quickly sat back down - smiling widely.

"Good luck," Sydney mouthed to Akiiki. Akiiki made an "L" with her finger and thumb, and Sydney mouthed back "Got him." Akiiki smiled and nodded back.

"Sure, that would be great!" replied Marc, totally missing the exchange between the girls, and now happily holding Akiiki's hand. Akiiki led them off in the opposite direction from where she had last seen Lucas, and both dads instantly snapped out of their conversation as the pair walked away.

"Hmmm, this could be trouble," said Dad with a big smile towards Sallah.

"Yes, Marion warned me Akiiki had a giant crush on Marc, and that she and Sydney would be scheming something," laughed Sallah in reply. "Akiiki begged us mercilessly for weeks to come on this trip with me, and now I think I know why," he added thoughtfully. "Should we follow them?" he whispered to Dad, starting to stand up.

"NO ... WAY. You two just cut it out and leave them alone," Sydney ordered fiercely. "Lucas was glued to Akiiki all day yesterday, and she just wants to talk to Marc. It will be fine, trust me," she added seriously.

"Well, OK – I guess," Dad replied reluctantly. Soon he and Sallah were deep in work conversation again so Sydney kept an eye on the pair as they walked on the far end of the beach.

"This is a beautiful lake and it's been so nice kayaking with you," Akiiki said, her gorgeous green eyes flashing brightly and making Marc's insides squirm. "I just love being on the water, I wish we could do this so easily back home," she added.

"Yeah, this is a perfect day for kayaking, and Lucas always keeps himself busy catching critters so it is usually fairly peaceful – as long as you're not in the same boat with him," Marc responded with a chuckle. Lucas had re-appeared on the other end of the beach and was slowly walking in their direction, scanning the shoreline for critters.

Akiiki caught a glimpse of Lucas and suddenly stopped walking and turned to face Marc, grasping his other hand gingerly as he stared at her quizzically. "Marc, so there's something I've been wanting to tell you but I have not been able to find a good moment," she explained shyly, now obviously quite nervous.

"What is it?" asked Marc, who was now quite confused by the sudden change in Akiiki's behavior. Unfortunately, Lucas had just seen the two of them and was now moving quickly towards them, with Sydney hot on his trail to intercept him.

"Well, it's just that ... well ... you see ... I really like ... I have a ... Oh never mind, it's not important – I'll tell you later," she said as Lucas had now caught up with them and was actively wedging himself between them and trying to grab one of Akiiki's hands away from Marc.

"OK, cool," replied Marc, completely oblivious and now starting to get annoyed at Lucas. "We can never get a minute's peace with him around," he added.

"Come on, Akiiki, let's take a hike around the lake – Dad said we all could," Lucas begged, trying to pull her away from Marc.

Sydney now joined them as well, breathless from running. "Crap, you move fast Lucas," she complained with an apologetic glance at Akiiki. "Lucas, here – hold my hand and we can hike together," she said, offering her hand to Lucas.

"Ewww, gross – no way Syd," Lucas replied, giving her a look of sheer disgust as if she had totally lost her mind. "I'm walking with Akiiki, obviously. You can hold hands with Marc if you want," he added with a snicker.

"Holy crap - he is SO annoying sometimes," she mind-linked angrily to Marc.

"Tell me about it," Marc mind-linked back. "I think Akiiki was trying to tell me something important, but we got rudely interrupted of course. I wonder what it was? I hope she's not mad at me..." he trailed off.

"Yeah, sorry – I tried to intercept him but the little twerp can move fast when he wants to," Sydney mind-linked back. "And no, she's NOT mad at you, you big doofus," she added, annoyed at his cluelessness.

Marc finally gave up the struggle with Lucas and let him take one of Akiiki's hands as he kept a firm grip on the other. "OK - we'll share Akiiki again," Marc said to him grumpily.

"Fine then," replied Lucas as he tried to drag Akiiki away. Akiiki smiled awkwardly at Marc and rolled her gorgeous green eyes, obviously frustrated but seemingly resigned to her fate.

"Just go a little slower, Lucas," she instructed, pulling back on his hand. They met up with Dad and Sallah who had packed up lunch and re-stowed everything into the kayaks but left out a water bottle for everyone. Marc grabbed his daypack from Godzilla and they headed off together to the trailhead for the lake loop hike.

"Looks like you have a fan club," Sallah whispered to Akiiki as she walked by with the boys locked on to her hands.

"They're two of my favorite men – so it's OK," she chuckled back at him with a smile. Both dads started cracking up as Marc and Lucas both covertly tried to pull her away from the other. "Besides, what's a girl to do?" she asked, rolling her eyes at the dads as Sydney joined in their laughter.

The hike around the lake was very nice and enjoyable, but it took them almost 90 minutes to complete the loop since they walked at a leisurely pace and Lucas stopped often to look for critters to harass. They also had trouble at a few of the tight turns in the trail since Marc and Lucas both refused to let go of Akiiki's hands, making navigating the bends quite challenging. When they returned to the beach they hopped back in their kayaks and then boated to the mini-van and trailer. The kids stowed the gear while Dad and Sallah dumped the water out of the kayaks and loaded them back onto the trailer. Everyone hopped in the mini-van once everything was put away and tied down for the trip home.

"Wow, thanks guys – that was really awesome," Akiiki said appreciatively.

"Yes, that was definitely lots of fun," added Sallah. "I haven't boated in ages."

"It was our pleasure – this is always one of our favorite family outings," replied Dad. "I'm glad you guys could join us!"

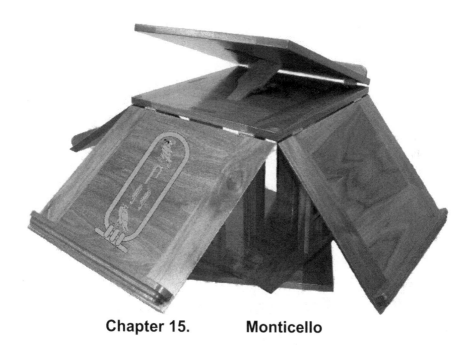

Chapter 15.   Monticello

Mom gave them the next day off to rest and relax at home, but the day after they were headed to their final sightseeing adventure – a tour of Monticello, the home of Thomas Jefferson. Sydney had cleverly made covert arrangements to have Lucas invited over to his friend Hobie's house for the day, and had then invited Tyler to join Mom, Akiiki, Marc, and herself. In her mind it was almost like a double date, and with some luck she hoped to get Marc and Akiiki to actually admit their feelings for one another and stop all this ridiculous avoiding-the-obvious nonsense so they could both just be happy.

When they stopped to pick up Tyler, he hopped in the mini-van beside Sydney and they greeted each other awkwardly. They had gotten into a heated argument on the phone yesterday over the whole Marc and Akiiki situation. After inviting him to Monticello for today, Sydney had asked Tyler to talk to Marc to help her convince him to admit his feelings to Akiiki, but Tyler had politely refused.

"Syd, it is Marc's decision to make and I'm not going to pressure him," Tyler had replied. "I can see his point too – in a few more days she'll be back in Egypt and chances are good that they will see each other what, maybe a couple of times a year?" he added. "Think how hard that would be for us to deal with – we would both be miserable not being together."

"But Tyler, they are both together NOW and I know if they work hard, they can make it work and be happy," Sydney had countered. "They have to think long-term, who knows what the future will bring?"

"You sound just like my mom, Syd," Tyler chuckled. "She's a helpless romantic too."

"So you're saying you won't help me?" she asked furiously. "You know - I think he would listen to you, since he's not listening to me."

"Sorry, no – I won't help. It's his decision," Tyler had replied firmly. Then for the first time ever, Sydney had hung up on him.

They now smiled at each other awkwardly as Tyler reached for Sydney's hand and gave it a nice squeeze. "Are we good?" he whispered, flashing a dazzling smile.

Sydney tried to remain angry with him, but found it impossible now that he was sitting beside her. "I suppose, but I still want your help," she whispered back.

"Good, but my answer's still no," he replied with a smile. Marc was now looking over at them curiously, so Sydney stuck out her tongue at Tyler and dropped the subject.

Akiiki had really enjoyed their hike at Walnut Creek (despite the crazy hand-holding), so Mom parked at Kemper Park so they could hike the Saunders-Monticello Trail up the mountain to Monticello. It was about a three mile hike but the trail had an easy uphill grade and was nicely paved with elevated boardwalks over some of the trickier terrain. The leaves on many of the trees were just starting to show hints of their bright colors as the fall season was just around the corner, and the weather was just perfect for an outdoor adventure.

"Wow, what a gorgeous day for a hike," exclaimed Akiiki as they got out of the mini-van. It was a little cooler today, so she had borrowed a light jacket from Sydney, although everyone else did not need one. Marc took her hand with a smile as they walked to the trailhead across the parking lot. Sydney accepted Tyler's hand a bit reluctantly and followed them, with Mom bringing up the rear, feeling very happy about the blossoming romances ahead of her on the trail.

"And it sure is nice to not have to share you with Lucas for once," Marc chuckled.

"Yes, it most certainly is," Akiiki replied with a lovely wink, squeezing his hand. "My hands are still sore from the last hike where you guys both held on too tightly and tried to tear me in half," she laughed.

"Sorry, I'll try to be extra gentle with your hand today," he replied apologetically. "Or does it need a break today?" he asked worriedly, loosening his grip.

Akiiki hesitated dramatically before responding. "Hmm, I think it should be just fine if you can behave yourself," she giggled, with a quick wink at Marc.

"Well, I'll try - but no promises," Marc whispered back mischievously. "You are quite irresistible, you know," staring at her thoughtfully.

"Well, perhaps you should stop trying to resist me then, and see what happens," Akiiki whispered with a dazzling smile. Marc's head started spinning dangerously so he quickly changed the subject.

"Hey Syd - I thought Lucas WAS coming, what happened?" asked Marc, looking back at Sydney awkwardly.

"Let's just say I made other arrangements for him," she whispered back with a smile. "You're both welcome, and I hope you use the alone time wisely," she added. They all started giggling as Marc and Akiiki both turned a bright red.

Everyone thoroughly enjoyed their hike up the mountain. It took about an hour but they stopped often to admire the beautiful scenery and of course for Mom to take a bunch of obligatory pictures of the two happy couples with her phone. Sydney also caught Mom several times unabashedly texting both Tyler's mom and Akiiki's mom to give them constant romance updates, so she warned everyone to be wary of the triple mom spying. When they arrived at the Visitor's Center they all looked around the gift shop while they waited for Mom to get their tour tickets. Akiiki asked Marc to remind her to look for a little souvenir for Mensah at the end of the day when they would be leaving.

The shuttle bus arrived quickly and it was just a short ride up to the front of the house at Monticello. Their house tour was starting soon so they walked directly up the sidewalk to the East Portico to wait for their guide. Akiiki was thrilled to finally see Monticello in person.

"It is not quite as large as I was expecting, but the architecture is so beautiful and interesting. I love the columns and all the wonderful old trees," Akiiki said admiringly. "It reminds me of the Rotunda and the Lawn at the University of Virginia – I can't wait to see the rest."

"Yes, it is pretty spectacular," Marc agreed. "The other side of the house is the more famous view from the back of the US nickel, and Lucas always loves the fish pond back there. Remind me to show you later," he added, smiling at Akiiki.

Their tour guide, a young college-aged woman, exited the house and started walking over towards them. "Hi guys, my name is Grace and I'll be your guide today," she said pleasantly. "I'm an undergraduate archaeology student at UVA and have been working here for a couple of years leading tours. You guys are in luck – your timing was perfect so I think it's just the six of us today. What are your names and where are you from?" she asked, looking at Mom curiously as if she recognized her from somewhere.

They each introduced themselves and Mom said she was a professor of archaeology at UVA.

"I thought I recognized you from somewhere, Dr. C!" Grace responded excitedly.

"Nice to meet you, I teach mostly graduate level courses so you haven't been in any of my classes yet," Mom replied. "This is an absolutely perfect job for an archaeology student – you are so lucky! Oh, and obviously we are all locals except for my beloved beautiful future daughter-in-law Akiiki here who is visiting us from Cairo, Egypt," she added, giving Akiiki a giant hug and kissing her on the cheek.

"MOM!" yelled both Marc and Sydney simultaneously, as Akiiki turned a brilliant red and Tyler laughed hysterically.

"Wow, Egypt is number one on my archaeology visit wish list – have you ever been to the Grand Egyptian Museum?" Grace asked Akiiki enthusiastically, completely ignoring the romantic chaos bomb Mom had just dropped.

"Well, yes, my dad and mom both work there as archaeologists," Akiiki replied, recovering her composure quickly, as Marc squeezed her hand cautiously. "My dad is in charge of the new Tutankhamun exhibits, so I've seen all his artifacts up close – it will be SO amazing when the GEM opens," Akiiki added breathlessly.

"WOW, that is so cool," replied Grace in total awe. "Can you PLEASE tell me more about it after the tour? After you guys, I've got a break for 30 minutes and in return, I can show you around my favorite places here at Monticello if you like."

"Sure, I would love that," replied Akiiki.

"Fantastic. Oh and Akiiki, when we go in the house, be sure to look on the mantel above the fireplace in the entrance hall – you will see something familiar," Grace added with a smile.

Another of the tour guides was now waving to Grace from the entrance. "OK, they are almost ready for us, so I have to give you the safety speech," she added apologetically. "Please remember not to touch anything inside the house, and do not sit or lean on any of the furniture. Much of the furniture is original or an old reproduction, so can be quite fragile. Do you guys have any questions before we go in?" Nobody did so they walked up the steps to the East entrance, and Grace held the door open for them to all enter. "Please feel free to ask me anything - anytime you want," said Grace. "Tours are much more fun with a small group, so don't be shy."

As they entered, the East Hall was a bit overwhelming to take in, and was full of artifacts highlighting Thomas Jefferson's many varied interests and hobbies. To the right there was a display of elk and moose antlers, several giant wall maps, three display cases of mastodon and other fossils, and a large old portrait of Jefferson. On the left there was a huge wall display of Native American weapons and artifacts and decorated hides arranged over the second floor bannister, a beautiful fireplace with a lounging statue in front, and a huge map of Africa. Then Akiiki saw what she was searching for on the fireplace mantel, just below a large portrait of the signing of the Declaration of Independence.

"The Great Pyramid of Khufu!" she said excitedly, moving closer to a large detailed model of the pyramid which was deeper than the mantel and hung out over the edge a bit awkwardly. "What is that doing here, I wonder?" she asked, as Grace came over to stand beside her. The model was well-done and quite accurate, and even had sand around the base which made it very realistic.

"Jefferson used the Westernized name of Cheops instead of Khufu, so he called it the Great Pyramid of Cheops," explained Grace. "The original was given to him by his French explorer friend Constantin-François de Chasseboeuf in 1802," she added.

"The original?" asked Akiiki.

"Yes, the original disappeared mysteriously after Jefferson's death, so this is a modern recreation per his own descriptions," Grace replied. "It's made from cork and real sand from Cairo, of course. Jefferson called this his 'Egyptian Corner' with the map of Africa to your right, and he mistakenly thought this was a statue of Cleopatra for a while until he realized it was Ariadne."

"We noticed the pyramid the very first time we came here when we were little," Marc added. "I've always wondered if Jefferson had a deeper connection with Egypt – his tombstone is shaped like an Egyptian obelisk, and he designed a cool double obelisk clock in his bedroom. It seems a little curious but Dad didn't really have any insights or more information."

"Yes, actually I have wondered the same thing too," Grace replied. "I'm sure he must have visited Egypt several times, and I hear that once you see the pyramids and temples in person you will never forget them. They HAD to make a great impression on him, especially since he had such a passion for architecture and engineering."

"Well, that is certainly true," laughed Akiiki. "They are also a little hard to miss – the scale and magnitude is amazing. We were all there over the summer – well, except for Tyler – and rode camels around them. Seeing them up close really makes you wonder how on earth they were built so long ago with no modern tools or equipment."

"I REALLY hope to see them someday," Grace replied wistfully. "Well, do you guys have any questions before we move on?" she asked.

"Please tell Akiiki about the Great Clock – that's one of my favorite Jefferson inventions," Marc replied. Everyone turned around to look out the way they had entered and gazed up at the large clock above the door, with two cables leading to a series of hanging weights on the North and South walls.

"Oh yes, he worked with a clock designer from Philadelphia to design this beautiful custom clock," Grace explained. "There is the inside face you see here which shows hours, minutes, and seconds, plus the outside face on the East Portico – which you may have missed above the door – showing just hours which Jefferson felt was accurate enough to manage the work on his plantation. It's really quite ingenious – if you notice the weights on the South wall, they even mark the days of the week – starting with Sunday - and extend through that hole to the floor below to show Saturday. Be sure to look for it when you walk around the basement."

"Yeah, the Great Clock is one of my favorites, too," added Tyler. "Jefferson's rotating bookstand is my very favorite of his inventions, though. We'll see that later in his Cabinet," he added, squeezing Sydney's hand as she smiled at him.

Grace led them on the house tour in a clockwise direction, starting from the South Square Room. This was one of Mom's favorite rooms since it had a collection of small family portraits on the walls and two lovely large portraits of his eldest daughter Martha Jefferson Randolph, as well as her eldest daughter. Martha had used this room for sewing and reading books to her many children. The library was next and was a comfortable room with several chairs, desks and tables where it was easy to visualize Jefferson reading intently from his vast collection of books. Grace said that most of the books on display now were not his originals, since he sold almost his entire collection to the Library of Congress in 1815 to rebuild it after it was burned by the British in the War of 1812. The Monticello researchers had matched most of the titles based on Jefferson's records but he had never actually touched most of these books, but it was an impressive collection nonetheless.

"Whoops. Hold on a minute, guys, looks like we're stuck behind a slow tour," said Grace. "Feel free to look around in here a bit, some of the book titles are pretty interesting to peruse," she added. "The tour ahead has several kids and believe me, sometimes it is like herding cats," she whispered as Mom laughed in complete understanding.

One of the boys in the next room was about Lucas' age and kept staring back at Akiiki, so she waved back at him and winked. "Don't encourage him," complained Marc, giving the boy the evil eye and covertly shaking a fist at him. The boy just stuck out his tongue at Marc. "Oh great, he definitely reminds me of bratty Lucas!"

"Hmm, is someone jealous?" Akiiki whispered in his ear, startling Marc and making him jump.

"Maybe," Marc responded gruffly, his ear now tingling wildly. "I just don't like sharing my girlfriend," he added quickly, without thinking.

Akiiki's eyebrows raised in a look of intense interest. "Hmmm, what did you say I was?" she asked coyly. Marc's face instantly turned a bright red.

"Well, you're my friend, and you're also a girl – so girl … friend," he replied awkwardly.

"Wow, two for two. You are indeed amazingly observant, Sherlock. But is that all I am to you – a friend?" she asked with a sly giggle. Marc was starting to panic, but was saved answering by Grace who was now leading them to the next room – Jefferson's Cabinet. At a loss for the right words, he just shot Akiiki a quick smile and shook his head "no" sheepishly.

"OK, here we go," said Grace, as they walked past the South Piazza which Jefferson had used primarily as a greenhouse. "Past the South Piazza, this is Jefferson's Cabinet room which is adjacent to his bedroom through those doors on his bed. Here he loved to relax, read, write correspondence, and tinker with his many scientific instruments away from all the hustle and bustle of the main house."

"Oh yeah – there's my favorite Jefferson invention – his revolving bookstand," exclaimed Tyler excitedly, pointing across the room to the curious cube-shaped bookstand beside the green sofa. "Check out the top of the stand – all four sides tilt upward plus there's a tilt on the top so he can read five books at once. The whole thing even rotates so he can move around easily between his readings."

"I don't think I've ever actually read five books at the same time, that would be pretty crazy confusing," laughed Sydney, as she admired the bookstand. Suddenly she froze in shock.

"Marc, do you see that on the bookstand?" she mind-linked. A glowing blue Asim cartouche had just appeared on the side of the bookstand facing them. "It's just like the one on the cat mummy at the museum in DC," she mind-linked excitedly.

"Yeah, I see it, but I guess we're the only ones who can," Marc mind-linked back to her. Tyler was still going on and on about the cool features of the stand, so obviously he didn't see it and Akiiki did not react as if anything unusual were happening. "What should we do?"

"Well, I don't think we can do anything – we can't get over there very easily and there's another tour right behind us," Sydney mind-linked back worriedly. "I don't really see any guards though, I hope it is safe here," she added, looking around the room carefully. "Plus it would be a little awkward blacking out as soon as we touched the cartouche bracelet inside. I'm honestly not sure how to pull that off without bringing down some serious trouble on us."

Akiiki was now staring at the twins curiously, so they broke off their mind connection and smiled back at her innocently. Grace had now started leading them back down the hall and into the main doorway of Jefferson's bedroom. "OK, here you see we are on the other side of Jefferson's bed through the main doorway. Note the lovely large window and the cozy fireplace." The bed was built into an alcove, opening to the rest of the room, and they could see the Cabinet room behind the bed. "Above the bed was a large closet space which Jefferson had designed for efficient storage, with stairs behind the door back there for access," Grace explained. "Beside the bed are his original riding boots, and on that shelf over his bed is the obelisk clock that Marc mentioned earlier. As you can see, it was the first thing he would see every morning when he woke up."

The clock was very interesting. It was about two feet tall and had a beautiful circular brass clock work in the middle supported by two dark Egyptian obelisks on either side, which looked to be made from granite with some brass trim. "The clock was obviously one of Jefferson's favorite possessions since he wrote about it often and used it for all his time references when he was working either in here or in his Cabinet room," Grace explained.

Next they passed the large roughly octagonal Parlor with its comfortable looking chairs, game tables, numerous portraits adorning the walls, several bust sculptures, the beautiful piano-like harpsichord under a lovely mirror, and the odd-looking camera obscura which Jefferson used for making sketches on a center table. "This room is the Parlor where Jefferson liked to entertain and visit with his most special guests in a large relaxed space," Grace explained. "The glass door at the back leads to the West Portico and a grand view of Monticello's West Lawn."

"Next we have the formal Dining Room," Grace continued as they followed. "It was painted this chrome yellow color in Jefferson's time and the table is set and chairs are arranged for a formal dinner. Note the dumbwaiters which are small sets of shelves on rolling casters which Jefferson liked to use for holding the various dinner courses and all the service items needed for dinner, which minimized interruptions from the dinner staff. There is also a clever wine dumbwaiter built into the fireplace frame, which acted like an elevator for bringing wine up from the cellar below."

"Ohh, I have always loved that invention. Maybe Dad could rig up a dumbwaiter system in our house for me," Mom said wistfully.

"Mom, we don't need a dumbwaiter – we already have Lucas," Marc quipped. "He's about as dumb as it gets. The only problem is convincing him to bring us stuff like a waiter when we want it," he laughed.

"Ha ha, very funny, Marc. You're always SO nice to your brother," Mom replied dryly as she and Akiiki both gave Marc a disapproving look. He shrugged his shoulders but Tyler and Sydney at least enjoyed his joke and were still chuckling.

They wrapped up the house tour after checking out the cozy Tea Room and the North Octagonal and North Square rooms which were set up as bedrooms for guests with alcove beds and period furniture. Grace led them all back outside. "OK, I've got thirty minutes until my next tour, can I show you guys around some of my favorite places?" she asked.

"Sure that would be great, and in turn, I'll tell you about the Tutankhamun artifacts," replied Akiiki enthusiastically.

First Grace took them on a tour of the West and East Ranges and also the basement of the main house where they saw the main kitchen and other household work areas, plus the ice house where ice was stored for food preservation in the days before refrigerators. She also took them to the middle of the West Lawn and held up a nickel to show them the view of Monticello. As they walked between the different areas, Akiiki told her about her father's work with the Tutankhamun artifacts and gave a run-down of the latest and greatest plans for the opening of the Grand Egyptian Museum.

They spent the rest of their time with Grace exploring Mulberry Row to the south of the main house which was dominated by a huge and beautiful garden, work areas for ironworking, joinery, and other skilled crafts, as well as housing for Jefferson's household slaves. They toured the tiny wooden Hemmings Cabin which had been reconstructed to illustrate a typical single-family slave cabin.

"I can't imagine a whole family living in here – it is such a contrast to Jefferson's gigantic mansion," Akiiki said sadly. "I just don't understand how slavery could ever be deemed acceptable," she added angrily.

"Yes, Jefferson was an interesting contradiction on slavery," explained Grace. "On the one hand he was a very vocal opponent of slavery, but on the other, he held over 600 slaves in his lifetime and vitally depended on them to work on his plantation and in his household. He did fight for change but I suppose the timing in society during that period was just not right, particularly with the slave-fueled cotton boom in the South coming near the end of his lifetime and entrenching slavery even further until the Civil War. At least he tried to improve his own plantation practices – he moved from growing labor-intensive tobacco to more seasonal wheat which allowed his slaves to learn skilled crafts and sometimes earn money for their work in the off-season. He seems to have made efforts to treat them well, but he was often away from Monticello traveling, and many were treated poorly in his absence. When Jefferson died, he wanted all of his slaves to be free, but in accordance with Virginia law at the time, over 130 were sold off and separated from their families to pay off his massive debts. Jefferson had fought hard to repeal that law but was defeated by a single vote. It was definitely a terrible time," Grace added sadly.

"Yes, I cannot even imagine," Mom agreed as everyone reflected on their own sad thoughts.

"Well, thanks so much for hanging out with me, but I need to get back to the house for my next tour," Grace said. "It was so nice meeting all of you, and thanks for all the exciting news Akiiki! Please email me some pictures and keep in touch," she added, handing Akiiki a card with her email address and cell phone number scribbled on it.

"Definitely," replied Akiiki. "Thanks again for the tour – I really enjoyed it."

They all thanked Grace graciously and then spent another couple of hours exploring the Monticello grounds, and walked down to see Jefferson's grave with its large Egyptian Obelisk tombstone. From there, they took the trail back down to the Visitor's Center and finally ended up in the gift shop where Akiiki wanted to get something for Mensah. Grace had given her a 50% off coupon as thanks, which Akiiki thought was very nice of her.

"Hey Akiiki, how about this?" Marc asked, holding up a wooden wheel cypher secret decoder. "It's a Monticello exclusive and Lucas has one so they could write each other secret messages. Lucas' has just been stuck on a shelf in his room since he doesn't have anyone else with one to communicate."

"Oh that's a great idea," replied Akiiki excitedly. "I also found some candy sticks and this model of Jefferson's camera obscura which I think he might like. That should be enough with what I already got for him in DC."

"Cool, sounds good," Marc replied. "Are you ready to start the hike back down to the van?"

"Yes, let's check out and then we can find everyone else," Akiiki replied. "This was been a wonderful day – I really love this place. Thanks for bringing me, and being with me today."

"Oh it was my pleasure, my lady," Marc replied with a giggle and a low formal bow.

The next morning Marc and Sydney helped Akiiki start packing up all her belongings for her flight home that afternoon. They found it quite challenging as she had accumulated some significant souvenirs and extra random "stuff" during her visit. In the end, Marc and Sydney had to both sit on her suitcase as she barely managed to zip it shut.

By sheer coincidence, Mr. P's sarcophagus was also set to ship back to Egypt that evening, and Dad asked the twins if they wanted to see it in person one last time. They both decided not to see it, but preferred instead to spend all their remaining time with Akiiki before she left. The sarcophagus was also an awkward reminder of the mummy that was wandering around Charlottesville somewhere, so not going to see it was an easy call. "Hopefully we'll see Mr. P's sarcophagus next time at the Grand Egyptian Museum with Akiiki," Marc had declared enthusiastically to Dad.

It seemed to Marc that the precious moments with Akiiki were just falling through his fingers like grains of sand, even as he desperately tried to hold on to them in vain. He could not bring himself to tell Akiiki how he really felt about her, which was making him miserable. It seemed as if Akiiki was having similar feelings and shared his misery. "If she did not live so far away, things could be SO different," he lamented to himself sadly. "It's just not fair."

Finally it was time for Sallah and Akiiki to depart with Dad for the airport, so everyone exchanged hugs and promised to keep in touch. They had all laughed at Lucas who had come running in with a stack of letters for Akiiki, Asim, and Mensah.

"Now you have to promise not to open yours until you get home, OK?" he asked Akiiki sternly. Akiiki took the three letters and stowed them carefully in her backpack. The letter for Mensah was huge and thick compared to the other two, but she was pleased to see that hers was still much bigger than Asim's.

"Yes, my Pharaoh, it shall be as you command," Akiiki said with a flourish of her arms and a deep formal bow. Lucas giggled and gave her a last giant hug.

"I love you big sister, come back soon," said Lucas.

"I love you too, little brother," Akiiki replies. "Come see ME soon for the museum opening."

"He has NEVER said that to me," Sydney mind-linked sadly to Marc, who was nervously waiting his turn to say goodbye to Akiiki.

"He just has a crush, it makes people do crazy things - as you might remember," Marc mind-linked back, trying to reassure her. "He definitely loves you but he just doesn't say it," he added.

"Well you don't say it very much either, you know?" she scolded in return.

"Well I do love you, sis. I'm sorry I don't say it as often as I should but I promise I will try to improve," he mind-chuckled back to her.

"I love you too, brother," Sydney replied. "We should all say it to each other more often, and you should DEFINITELY say it to Akiiki right now!"

"What's the use? In a few hours she will be on the other side of the world," Marc responded sadly. "We would both just be miserable. Just think how YOU would feel being that far away from Tyler all the time."

"I know it would be hard but I still think you guys can make it work. You both love each other and are being totally stupid about this," she replied angrily.

As Lucas retreated, Sydney moved in to give Akiiki a huge hug. "TELL HIM," she whispered urgently in Akiiki's ear.

"I can't, and what's the use?" Akiiki whispered back sadly. "We live a world apart."

"You're both being so stupid about this," Sydney whispered back fiercely, releasing Akiiki with a deep frown of frustration.

Akiiki slowly moved away from Sydney and stood in front of Marc, holding both his hands and staring at him intently with bright tears starting to slide down her cheeks.

"I will miss you so much, Akiiki," Marc told her sadly, as Mom watched their exchange intently. "I wish you could stay here forever."

"I will miss you too," Akiiki replied sadly. "I too desire many things for us that I dearly wish could come true," she added, giving Marc a huge hug which he returned gratefully.

"TELL HER!" Sydney mind-screamed at him.

"I'm sorry, I just can't. I know you don't understand," Marc replied quietly over their mind-link.

Marc and Akiiki separated slowly and said their final awkward goodbyes, with Mom and Sydney now both crying profusely as well. As they left with Dad, Marc went up to his room sadly and shut his door. Sydney and Lucas could both hear him sobbing softly but gave him space to work through his feelings.

Chapter 16.   Spies

It had been over a week since Akiiki left and most things were soon quickly back to their normal boring state for Marc and Sydney. Marc was missing Akiiki quite terribly today so Sydney had suggested another training session with their powers in an attempt to cheer him up. They had just been flying Yoda and Elle around Sydney's room with all their cat toys for a long time so now both cats were exhausted from all the excitement and had stretched out lazily on Sydney's bed. Every now and then one of them would meow sleepily and roll to a more comfortable position. However, they were also both keeping a watchful eye on another green scarab beetle which at the moment was crawling along the top of Sydney's mirror. Marc had spotted it earlier and flown it among the cat toys, but the beetle obviously did not appreciate the experience in the least and had quickly escaped.

Marc and Sydney were taking a break to recover from another one of their power experiments. After levitating the cats, they had experimented with levitating themselves and then each other. They quickly discovered that self-levitation required a lot of concentration to perform and Sydney's room was way too small for levitating each other very far without banging into something painfully. Both tricks were also extremely nerve racking and stressful so they gave up fairly quickly and decided to try it later somewhere bigger with a bit more room for error. Yoda and Elle had been watching them with great interest but now that the experiment was over the cats grew bored and sleepy again, occasionally meowing softly to each other but still watching the scarab beetle ever so closely.

Sydney was now experimenting with her cartouche in an attempt to trigger a new power. Marc was watching her distractedly as his feelings of loneliness and missing Akiiki had quickly started to return. Sydney made her cartouche appear by swiping over her right forearm and was now touching the individual hieroglyphics in different combinations and random orders. Sometimes the cartouche or the hieroglyphics themselves would change colors, but just as in all previous attempts, nothing felt any different in her mind or body and she was just not able to make anything interesting happen. She tried concentrating very hard after each combination was activated but she really just had no clue of what to do next. She also tried dragging the hieroglyphic symbols to rearrange them but they remained firmly in the same location but every now and then would blink or change colors.

After one of her random character combination attempts, a tiny spinning spiral galaxy full of bright stars and whorls of colorful space dust appeared inside the cartouche frame which was strangely mesmerizing and captivating. They both felt irresistibly drawn to touch the vibrantly moving surface of the cartouche. After shaking themselves out of the strange trance, they were both completely terrified so Marc made her swipe it off immediately before something crazy happened.

Trying to figure out their cartouche powers was extremely frustrating to say the least, but Sydney stuck with it after the galaxy vision for nearly an hour. Marc and the cats had lost interest long ago but Sydney still pressed on with her experiments. Finally, in an effort to try something different, Sydney touched both the falcon and the owl at the same time which made them both turn yellow but seemed to have no other effect. "Arrgghh, this is so annoying!" she complained loudly, startling Marc and both the cats.

"I'm hungry."

"Well then go make yourself a snack," she replied angrily. "Then hurry back and help me figure out these stupid combinations."

"What?" asked Marc in total confusion as he looked around at her. "I don't want a snack right now, did you want me to get something for you?"

"You just said you were hungry," she snapped back.

"No I didn't, I was just quietly sitting here thinking about Akiiki," he replied grumpily as the cats meowed to each other again.

"Hey my human is growling at yours again, this might get interesting."

"Probably not. These litter-mates are always hissing at each other but their claws never come out. Pretty boring to watch, if you ask me. I'm just happy the loud one is not here so we can nap."

Sydney whipped around and stared at both cats with her eyes wide open. "Holy crap, I can hear what the cats are saying!" she yelled. "Swipe your cartouche and hit the falcon and the owl at the same time," she instructed Marc. He excitedly followed her directions and his cartouche symbols turned the same yellow color as hers. They both stared at the cats intently, eagerly waiting for something to happen. Both cats stared back at the silly humans in obvious amusement.

"Uuummmm, why are the litter-mates staring at us like that?" meowed Yoda, looking over at Elle as his tail started twitching nervously.

"Beats me, maybe they are going to make us fly again – that is always fun," Elle meowed sleepily.

"Marc, did you hear that?" asked Sydney in amazement.

"Holy crap, yes. Let's try a mind-link on them to see if they can hear US," Marc replied excitedly as both cats were now staring at them with growing interest. "You try Yoda and I'll try Elle."

"Can you hear me?" they mind-linked to the cats, who both immediately jumped.

"Well I'll be a sewer rat, my human just meowed at me," meowed Yoda.

"Yes, mine too. Creepy. What do you think the litter-mates want from us?" meowed Elle, now staring at Marc with keen interest. "I just hope that stupid stinky dog is not coming back, the loud one is enough trouble for us."

"Ha, ha, no dog. Maisy is back home with Hailey and Jared. We just accidently learned a new power so now we can, ummm, talk to you," Sydney mind-linked to both cats. "We love you guys, you know that, right?" she added awkwardly. This felt more than a little weird. She and Marc had of course had hundreds of long conversations with both cats before, but this was now completely different since they could all actually understand one another for the first time.

Both cats jumped into their laps excitedly. "We love you too. You are our favorite humans," they both meowed.

"This power is almost as good as flying," meowed Elle.

"Are there any questions you always wanted to ask us?" asked Marc.

"Hmmm, where do you go almost every day for so long?" asked Yoda. "It gets lonely here."

"Oh, we have to ride that big yellow bus to school every day," explained Sydney. "School is mostly boring but sometimes we learn interesting things, and at least we get to see all of our friends there."

"Do you play with toys there?" asked Elle.

"No not usually, but sometimes in gym class," laughed Sydney.

"Do they have yummy treats there at skull?" asked Yoda.

"It's 'school,' not 'skull,' and no definitely not," Marc replied with a giggle. "Not unless you get some treats out of the vending machines," he added.

"Hey, I've always wondered," Marc began thoughtfully, "do you guys like your cat food? You always seem to go crazy when we give you treats like you are starving to death."

Both the cats looked at each other and meow-laughed. "Well, it's OK, but it gets pretty boring eating the same thing all the time," replied Yoda.

"Yeah, you guys seem to always eat something different every meal and it always smells very interesting," added Elle, who Mom often had to chase off the kitchen counters for "helping" too much as Mom was cooking.

"So think about how it is for us always eating the same thing – some more variety would definitely be purr-fect," Yoda said wistfully. "It doesn't seem fair compared to your meals."

"OK, we'll see what we can do," replied Sydney. "Sorry about that – we didn't know."

"Oh hey Elle, we have all been wondering something for a long time," Marc began, as Elle looked at him expectantly. "Why do you always carry around and hide your princess pony and the brontosaurus in closets and laundry bins all over the house?"

"Ha ha, that's her mothering instinct, she gets confused and carries them around and hides them like naughty little kittens," Yoda meow-snickered before Elle could respond.

Elle hissed at Yoda angrily. "Shut up, old grandfather!"

"So is that the reason - since you can't have real kittens of your own?" asked Sydney compassionately.

Elle turned away from them in embarrassment. "Yes, maybe I guess. I don't really know, sometimes it just feels like what I should do with them. It is hard to explain," she meow-whispered in reply.

"Oh, I'm sorry Elle!" replied Sydney. "Should we find some real kittens for you to adopt?" she asked.

"No, definitely not!" meow-laughed Elle and Yoda at the same time. "Kittens are too much energy and chaos for us," Elle added. "It's pretty nice with just the two of us, although old grandfather here does not like to play with me very often."

Yoda stuck out his tongue at her. "Your timing is always off – you always pester me to play when I am trying to nap or working on important business," Yoda snapped back.

"Yeah, as if – you are just old and grumpy!" Elle meow-laughed in response.

"Hummph," Yoda replied grumpily, making the twins chuckle.

"So are you guys happy and do you need anything?" asked Marc quite seriously.

"Yes we are happy most of the time, especially when you fly us – that is my favorite," said Elle. "But I need some more furry mice – the stupid stinky dog ate all mine this summer."

"I want more of the smelly dried grass – it makes me feel like a young kitty again," said Yoda, purring.

"Oh, catnip?" Sydney asked, giggling. "Sure, we'll ask Mom to take us to the pet store so we can get more stuff for you guys."

"And I need something with feathers to chase," Elle said wistfully.

"Well, Mom stopped buying anything with feathers because you always eat them off right away," Sydney laughed as Yoda meow-chuckled. Elle rolled her eyes in annoyance, reminding Marc of something he had always wondered about.

Marc stared at Elle and hesitated with his question. "So I know this is rude, Elle, but can you see out of your right eye at all?" Marc asked Elle curiously.

"No, not really. I can see some colors and tell day from night, but that is it," she replied. "It's always been that way so I am used to it. I can still catch mice and birds ten times better than old grandfather Yoda here," Elle explained proudly.

"AS IF, young kitty," growled Yoda angrily. "You just have your kitty energy but no skill yet to match me," he meowed as Marc and Sydney laughed at their posturing. "You are even louder than the loud one when you are stalking prey – it's no wonder you can never catch anything. You actually sound like a horse galloping you are so loud and unskilled. On the other paw, as a master of hunting, I stalk quietly and quickly and ALWAYS catch my prey."

"Oh yeah, well which one of us caught the last bird, hmmmm?" meow-countered Elle.

"That doesn't count!" meowed Yoda angrily. "I was chasing it and the stupid thing flew right into your mouth when you were yawning. You didn't even see it until it got stuck down your throat!" Elle simply stuck out her tongue at Yoda in response.

"Still counts, old grandfather," meowed Elle sarcastically, as the twins howled in laughter.

As if right on cue, the green scarab beetle dive-bombed Elle, flying right over her blind side as she swatted at it furiously but a little too late. "Where are all these nasty beetles coming from?" she asked angrily. "Today we have counted one for every claw. We chase them out of the house but more always come back. These are worse than the terrible stink bugs."

"I don't really know," replied Marc thoughtfully. "Dad thinks there may be some sort of nest nearby our house. But none of our other friends have seen them at their houses so I'm not sure where they are coming from."

Both cats suddenly froze. "Shhh, the loud one is coming," meow-whispered Yoda. A few seconds later Marc and Sydney heard thundering footsteps coming down the hall. They both reluctantly swiped off their cartouches just as Lucas burst through the door.

"Hey what are you two doing now? Is Marc planning a big hot date with booger big broken nose Becky?" Lucas teased. "Woooo hooo, he must be in luuuv. It's time for some big booger muuuchhaaass smmooocchhaass."

Now it was Marc's turn to resist using his powers on Lucas, as Sydney snickered in extreme amusement. "Yeah, very funny little brother, that's it. You found out our big secret. You are totally amazing," he declared, rolling his eyes.

"Ooooohhh, I knew it. Guess what? I'm gonna tell MOM aawwwlllll about it so she can plan your big first date," he taunted. "Then it will be you K-I-S-S-I-N-G booger big broken nose Becky all the time – just like Syd and Tyler!" Marc leapt up furiously to chase him down the hall as Sydney laughed hysterically at the chaos.

"KIDS, CALM IT DOWN UP THERE," yelled Dad from the downstairs couch as he and Mom were trying to watch TV. "You guys are supposed to be in bed – SETTLE DOWN!" Dad looked at the paused TV and then over at Mom. "Look dear – a new record," Dad said sarcastically. "We made it almost a whole two minutes into our show before we got interrupted - incredible," Dad added as they both started laughing at their own frustration.

The next morning, the entire house was awakened by squeals of joy from Lucas. The family quickly congregated on his room where they found him holding a beautiful orange and white cat on his lap. To everyone's great surprise, Elle and Yoda were also there actually napping at the bottom of his bed. Marc could not remember the last time he ever saw the cats willingly be this close to Lucas, much less be relaxed enough to take a nap. The new cat looked curiously at everyone standing in Lucas' doorway and meowed inquisitively.

"Oh Lucas, he is beautiful – where did he come from?" asked Mom as she dashed forward to pet the new cat, who immediately started purring loudly. He was very similar in size and shape to Yoda and must surely also be a Ragdoll or maybe a Himalayan, thought Sydney. He was all white with flame orange ears and tail, with a beautiful perfectly symmetrical orange face and gorgeous blue eyes. Everyone crowded around Lucas to admire him as Elle and Yoda both awoke to observe the action, although content to remain napping lazily at Lucas' feet.

"I have no idea, I woke up this morning and he was asleep on my chest. I thought it was Maisy for a second until I opened my eyes," Lucas replied. "Can we keep him, oh please, oh please?"

"He looks too gorgeous to be a stray, honey. Does he have a collar?" Mom asked nervously.

"No, no collar. He wants to be my kitty friend, can I keep him?" Lucas asked excitedly.

"Well, I suppose we can put up some 'found kitty' posters around the neighborhood to make sure he doesn't belong to anyone, then we can see," said Dad reluctantly. "And we'll have to take him to the vet to get checked out to make sure he is healthy." At the mention of the vet, Elle and Yoda both hissed loudly as the new cat meowed at them curiously.

"OK, it's a deal," said Lucas. "And I already named him – 'Mr. P' after your crazy King Tut sarcophagus."

"Well, now that's a great name – I love it," replied Dad enthusiastically as everyone laughed.

"Let's go find him some food and water," Mom said, admiring the gorgeous Mr. P as Lucas gently picked him up and went downstairs with Mom and Dad.

Marc and Sydney looked at Yoda and Elle nervously, extremely curious as to why they did not seem to care about a new cat suddenly appearing in the house. Sydney looked at Marc and they both swiped their cartouches, touching the falcon and owl at the same time to turn the hieroglyphic symbols yellow.

"Where did Mr. P come from and why are you guys both so chill?" Marc asked the cats.

Elle looked up at them sleepily. "Oh, we let him in the cat door last night. It's OK, he is a friend," she meowed, closing her eyes again.

"And he told us his human is far away, so nobody will come looking for him," Yoda meowed. "He's cool. Plus I think he likes the loud one so maybe he won't bother us so much anymore." Yoda rolled over lazily and promptly started snoring.

Sydney and Marc looked at each other nervously, swiped their cartouches off, and let the cats return to their nap as they walked downstairs. The whole situation seemed a little fishy but they were reassured by the fact that both Elle and Yoda did not seem to worry about the new cat in the least. And it definitely WOULD be nice for Lucas to have a new friend – he sure was always much less annoying to them when Maisy was around. Yes, maybe this would work out very nicely indeed.

Mom asked the twins to make some posters about the cat, so Sydney took a picture of Mr. P with her phone as he was sitting contentedly on Lucas's lap. She emailed the picture to Marc who quickly whipped out a nice "found kitty" poster from the home computer. "How many copies should I print, Mom?" he asked.

"Oh I don't know, maybe 25?" Mom replied. "You guys can go hang them up on the street signs and the neighborhood bulletin board today. I'll post it on the neighborhood Facebook page. We'll see what happens. He sure is a beautiful cat," she said wistfully, admiring Mr. P as he now stretched out lazily on Lucas' lap.

A few days later, they had received lots of compliments in response to the posters but so far nobody had claimed Mr. P. Mom and Lucas took Mr. P to the vet for a thorough check-up and to make sure he did not have an embedded microchip ID. Mr. P checked out perfectly with a clean bill of health and no detected chip so Mom was quite happy. But Mr. P definitely did not appreciate having his temperature taken and was quick to let the veterinary technician know exactly how he felt about her rudeness.

Lucas was absolutely ecstatic as he was so happy to have a new friend of his very own who was as cuddly and nice as his old buddy Maisy. To the utter amazement of Marc and Sydney, Mr. P genuinely seemed to thoroughly enjoy Lucas in return and the two were totally inseparable. Elle and Yoda also started hanging out more with Lucas and Mr. P since Lucas was much nicer to them when Mr. P was around. All in all, it was a definite win-win situation for everyone. Marc and Sydney did not get to see quite as much of Elle and Yoda as they would have liked, but overall it was a definite improvement over the usual constant Lucas chaos.

Mom and Lucas were running errands and Dad was giving a special public lecture on Tutankhamun at UVA today, so the twins and all three cats were spending the morning trying to rid the house of all the ever increasing and extremely annoying green scarab beetles. It was actually quite fun for all of them and they had an excellent battle plan in place. Marc and Sydney would levitate the beetles into their kitty carrier while the cats shut the carrier door and hunted down any stragglers or escapees who came within their range. So far they had collected three full carrier loads and then let them all go unharmed outside. After working diligently for most of the morning, it was thankfully becoming more and more challenging to find any beetles remaining in the house. When Elle finally gave the house the all-clear, they all went up to Sydney's room to relax and practice their powers.

"That was actually pretty fun," said Marc as he sat down in Sydney's chair, feeling fairly exhausted.

"Yeah, I'm just glad they don't stink like that awful stink beetle infestation we had a few years back," Sydney replied. "We pissed off a lot of green scarab beetles today, so that would have been nasty if they raised a stink. Plus luckily they don't seem to bite and their shells are so hard that the cats didn't hurt them. Good work all around, guys" she said as she sat on her bed surrounded by the three exhausted cats. They all meowed softly in response.

"So what do you want to work on, maybe shields?" asked Sydney. "I think I almost have your honeycomb shimmer shield figured out."

"Sure, we can try that," Marc replied. "Just don't levitate me, my head still hurts from last time you banged me into something. We need to find a bigger training area. I want to try your fireball again and Mom probably wouldn't want me to burn the house down today," he chuckled.

"Yeah, me too. I've also been working on a bow like Tutankhamun's but I've been scared to fire it in the house," she replied.

"Ohhh that would be really cool. I've also been working on explosive ninja throwing stars and want to try those too," said Marc. "Hey but first I want to show you something cool I figured out today - watch this," added Marc. He walked over to Sydney's wall, swiped his cartouche, and placed his hands on her wall. "Are you ready?" he asked.

"Sure, what in the world are you doing?" asked Sydney.

Marc placed his hands and feet higher and immediately began to climb straight up the wall and then hung upside down from the ceiling as Sydney gasped. "I call it the spider climb after my favorite superhero!" Marc exclaimed proudly. "I think it makes you lighter as well because I'm not straining to hold myself up, but it definitely tickles my fingers and toes – they are so sticky."

"Wow, that is amazing – how do you do that?" Sydney asked in awe, bending her neck strangely to look up at Marc.

"Just swipe your cartouche and think 'spider climb'," replied Marc. "At first I tried it as a 'gecko climb' but my fingers were too sticky to move easily – but I think gecko grab might come in handy for catching things or maybe gecko climb for walking up super smooth surfaces," Marc explained.

"OK, I definitely want to try that," Sydney said excitedly. "It really looks like fun!"

"Yes, definitely. So show me your fancy shield, little miss hot shot," Marc challenged, as he dropped gracefully back to the floor.

Sydney swiped her cartouche and concentrated on forming the shield. To Marc's surprise, a shimmering blue honeycomb bubble instantly formed around Sydney as she looked up proudly. "Yes, I did it!" she exclaimed as the bubble started to blink in and out. "Whoops," she said and returned to concentrating on the shield. It quickly reformed to its original shape.

"Let me try something," said Marc mischievously as he looked around the room. He located all the cat toys he could find and launched them at Sydney simultaneously from all directions.

"Hey!" she complained, but they were both amazed when every toy bounced off her shield with a small blue electric flash. "Awesome, it really works!"

"See if you can walk around now, that's where I have trouble keeping the shield in place," instructed Marc as he gathered the cat toys back up for another assault. Sydney's shield flickered as she stood up but then solidified as she began walking slowly around the room. Marc launched all the cat toys at her again and the shield held up perfectly up until the last few toys when her concentration was finally broken. A furry mouse covered with Elle's cat slobber smacked her right in the nose, startling her as she frowned in disgust.

"Nice, that was gross," she said, wiping her nose off as the cats all meowed hysterically.

"OK, my turn. Let's switch," said Marc eagerly. Sydney dropped the last remnants of her shield and used her powers to gather up the cat toys which were now scattered all over the room and were a little bit singed from the shield. Marc sat down and formed the shimmering blue honeycomb bubble around himself. "OK, ready!" he yelled as his bubble flickered momentarily and then snapped back into place.

Sydney snickered evilly and launched all the toys at him at once. His shield held only for the first few toys and the rest smacked into him from all directions, covering him in catnip dust, feathers, fake fur, and dripping slobber from multiple cats. Elle, Yoda, and Mr. P were all rolling over and meowing even more hysterically.

"Yeah, yeah, give me a break. LAUGH IT UP, FUZZBALLS! Obviously I need more practice," Marc said in annoyance. "Give me a chance to concentrate again."

Sydney tested Marc's shield several more times and he was able to eventually block most of the toy assaults but was just not able to hold it consistently at all whenever he had to move. They decided to try again later to give him a chance to recover. The cats had lost interest and were now hunting another green scarab beetle that had flown into the room a few minutes earlier.

"Crap, I thought we got them all," complained Sydney as she noticed the beetle. At that moment they heard the garage door open and soon Lucas was yelling for Mr. P. He quickly jumped off Sydney's bed and scampered downstairs to greet his best buddy.

"Marc, it's almost time for your soccer game!" yelled Mom from the bottom of the steps. "Come find your uniform and gear, and get a snack before we have to go. Sydney – you too! Tyler's mom is almost here."

"OK Mom, we're coming!" replied Marc as he raced out of the room leaving Sydney alone with the two cats. "See you later, Syd! Have fun with Tyler!"

"Yep, good luck at your game. We can practice some more tonight!" she yelled back as she walked to the mirror to make sure she looked presentable for Tyler. They were going to hang out with his mom at his house along with Nick and Kelly who were supposed to come over to watch a couple of movies. Nick was still nursing a sore knee from the last soccer game against Knuckles so Coach Carlos had ordered him to sit this one out.

Marc's team easily won their soccer game, but Marc had a super embarrassing moment after the game. Becky was there watching her little brother Robby's game on another field and had approached Marc nervously after the game.

"Hey Marc, great game," she said. "Can I talk to you about something?" she asked timidly.

"Sure, anything," Marc replied confusedly. He and Becky had not really spoken very much together one-on-one in the past so he wondered what was on her mind.

"So this is really awkward, but after Sydney's slumber party, Lucas told me that you have a giant crush on me," she said nervously.

"Oh crap, I'm going to totally pulverize him," said Marc furiously, smacking his fist into his other hand.

"So is it true then?" she asked quietly, staring at the ground.

"No, I like you a lot and everything Becky, but I always thought we were just good friends," Marc said awkwardly. "Plus, I have a crazy crush on Akiiki even though she lives on the other side of the world, so my romantic life is pretty messed up right now," he added sadly.

"Oh, thank goodness," Becky said with relief. "I saw how you and Akiiki were looking at each other, so I was pretty sure Lucas was pulling my leg. I didn't want to hurt your feelings but I have a boyfriend now. Sydney hooked me up with Wes and it's going great so far," she added excitedly.

"Cool, congratulations!" Marc said sincerely. "My crazy sister the match-maker! Wes is an awesome guy, and you guys make a great couple."

"Thanks," she replied. "Well, OK, I'll see you later. Looks like Robby's game is done, so we have to hit the road."

Marc watched her walk away as he thought longingly of Akiiki and tried to come up with a suitably nasty punishment for Lucas. He was completely stunned that his twerpy little brother would do something so purely evil and thoughtless. This was definitely a new low for Lucas.

"Are you OK, honey?" Mom asked as she walked over to him after the game. "It's pretty cool that Becky was here to see your game – you guys were amazing!"

"Oh, thanks Mom," Marc replied. "Yeah, I'm fine. Becky just came over to congratulate me too. Her little brother Robby is playing over on the other field."

"She is a very sweet girl, don't you think?" Mom asked casually.

"Sure Mom, Becky's cool but we're just friends," Marc replied sourly. "So don't go getting any romantic ideas, please."

"Hmmm, ok then, if you say so," Mom replied with a smile. "Are you ready to go?" she asked as Marc stopped to pick up one of the after-game snacks and drinks, waving goodbye to his teammates who had already started to scatter.

"Yep, whenever you are ready," Marc replied, still fuming about Lucas.

"Maybe a little fireball around the edges would do Lucas some good," he thought to himself excitedly.

"So how was the game?" Sydney asked later that evening when she got home from Tyler's.

"Oh the game was great, but you won't believe what Lucas did to me," Marc said with obvious annoyance. "Just check out this lovely conversation I had after the game with Becky," he said as he mind-linked the replay to Sydney.

"Oh, he did not!" said Sydney afterwards, completely shocked. "That could have really broken Becky's heart if she didn't have Wes already."

"Well, yeah, and HELLO - not to mention that it was supremely embarrassing for me!" Marc replied angrily. "You have to help me think of a good payback for the little twerp."

"Yeah, and I definitely still owe him for all the Tyler teasing," Sydney agreed. "At least he's gotten used to Tyler now and isn't quite as horrible to us as he was at the beginning. But I'm sure we can come up with something very interesting," she added with an evil chuckle.

"So how was Tyler's?" Marc asked. "Hopefully there was no kissing involved, and if there was – please don't replay that in your mind for me," he laughed.

"Ha ha, you sound like Lucas. I think I see where he gets it from," Sydney replied acidly. "It was just a really cool day - Nick and Kelly were there and we all just hung out and watched a couple of movies together and then got caught up with everyone's latest news. Nick's knee is actually almost back to normal since Kelly has been harassing him constantly and making him sit still and take it easy. Plus I haven't gotten to just TALK like that with Kelly for a long while, so it was nice," she added.

"OK, cool – that sounds pretty low-key," Marc replied.

"Tyler's mom was a little weird though – I think she may be worse than our mom with the romance stuff," Sydney added thoughtfully. "Every time she saw anybody holding hands she started giggling. I'm sure she must have been texting Mom a detailed report every five minutes," she said with a frown. "Grown-ups are so bizarre sometimes..."

"Tell me about it," laughed Marc.

"But I still wish you could have come with us, Mr. Soccer Star," Sydney added.

"Well, I always just feel like a fifth wheel, so it's OK. Maybe next time," Marc replied untruthfully. "Hey it's pretty late already and I'm beat from soccer – what do you say we skip powers practice tonight to just relax and try to think up a good payback for Lucas instead?" he asked.

"That sounds like a perfect plan – I'm beat too," Sydney replied.

That evening the twins had a long mind-link conversation and eventually devised a suitably mean trick to play on Lucas. The next morning they set their plan into motion as Lucas was downstairs watching morning cartoons.

"I'm really not sure why he's so terrified of this stupid thing," said Marc as he was holding a large clown doll from Sydney's collection. "I guess it is kinda creepy looking," he added, examining it thoughtfully. Suddenly the doll's head turned around to look at Marc as it raised its arms toward him, and he dropped it instantly with a shrill scream. "Ha ha, very funny!" he said to Sydney angrily, who was now laughing.

"Sorry – just practicing for later with Lucas," she replied.

"OK, well it definitely is MUCH creepier when it does that, so this should work," Marc said, picking the doll back up off her bedroom floor. He hid it behind his back as the two walked downstairs to the living room. Lucas was sitting on the couch with Mr. P curled up on one side of him and two of his teddy bears on the other side. Marc dropped the clown doll quietly behind the couch.

"What'cha watching, Lucas?" asked Sydney curiously as Marc stood beside her.

"Well, a stupid commercial right now, but 'Teen Titans' should be back on in a minute," he replied, looking over at her a little suspiciously. Marc quickly levitated the clown doll into place beside Lucas' teddy bears when he was not looking.

"OK, tell us if anything cool happens – we're going to the kitchen to find something to eat," Sydney replied cheerfully. They each grabbed a bowl of cereal and sat down at the kitchen table in clear sight of Lucas. Using his powers, Marc slowly turned the clown's head to stare at Lucas. Mr. P saw the motion and started growling deeply, which caught Lucas' attention.

"What's the matter, Mr. P?" Lucas asked the cat. He then looked toward his teddy bears and noticed the clown doll sitting beside them. "Very funny Syd!" he yelled, grabbing the doll and tossing it back behind the couch. "You know I hate that stupid clown doll!" he added.

"What are you talking about, dude?" Sydney asked. "I didn't do anything – what doll?" she added, yelling from the kitchen table and raising her hands in innocence. She and Marc carefully stifled their laughter so as not to give themselves away.

"Yeah, whatever – jerk-face!" mumbled Lucas in return, turning back to watch the TV. Marc levitated the clown doll back beside the teddy bears, this time moving the clown's arm to encircle one of the bear's necks. Mr. P growled again, annoyed that his nap was interrupted once more by the creepy clown.

Lucas looked over, saw the clown and immediately jumped off the couch to see if someone was hiding behind it to move the clown. He then looked into the kitchen where the twins were still sitting. "How did you guys do that?" he asked suspiciously.

"Do what?" Sydney asked innocently, smiling back at him. "We're just in here eating breakfast, dude."

Lucas was obviously quite bewildered. He then looked back over at the clown, which suddenly turned its head to stare at him and raised its arm menacingly to point at him. He immediately screamed and ran out of the room yelling for Mom. Marc and Sydney both started laughing hysterically. Mr. P ran over to Marc and sat down by his leg, meowing up at Marc accusingly and then scratching him on the leg before running after Lucas.

"Well, we don't need a cartouche translator for that," Sydney chuckled. "I'm pretty sure he told you to knock it off and leave Lucas alone!" she added, as Marc rubbed his scratched leg gingerly but still kept laughing.

"Oh, one more thing before Mom comes," Marc said, as he used his powers to stick both of the teddy bear heads down into the crack between the cushion and the back of couch, with their legs sticking up in the air. He and Sydney were just finishing up their cereal when Lucas dragged Mom into the living room, with Mr. P right behind them.

"There Mom – see? There he is – I swear he moved his head and pointed at me!" Lucas declared, now sobbing in terror and hiding behind Mom. "And look what he did to my bears!" he wailed.

"Marc and Sydney, will you guys stop teasing Lucas?" Mom scolded angrily. "This is ridiculous – you know he hates that creepy doll. And Lucas, it is just a doll and I'm sure it can't move like that."

"We didn't do anything – we've been in the kitchen the whole time, Mom - honest," declared Sydney innocently. "I haven't seen that doll in months – maybe Mr. P dragged it down here from my room," she suggested, as Mr. P meowed angrily at her in response.

"Maybe the doll is possessed by an evil ghost that's out to get you, Lucas," Marc suggested quietly. Lucas' eyes grew wide with fear and he hid further behind Mom.

"Marc! Really? Don't try to scare your brother like that," Mom responded angrily. "Don't listen to him, Lucas. Here, I'll put the doll in the closet so it won't bother you," she said, picking up the doll and putting it on the top shelf of the closet and then closing the door. She then turned back to Marc and Sydney. "I'm watching you two, so cut it out. Can't we just have a peaceful day for once?" she asked in exasperation.

Lucas rescued his teddy bears from the couch and then settled down nervously to watch his TV show again, turning around frequently to stare at the closet door.

"Alright dude – see you later then," said Sydney. "We're heading back upstairs."

"Maybe you should call the Ghostbusters," whispered Marc evilly toward Lucas. "That doll might get you if you don't."

"Very funny, jerk-face," responded Lucas nervously, still sniffling. "I know you did it somehow!"

When Lucas' attention turned back to the TV, Marc carefully opened the closet door with his powers and floated out the clown and made it sit beside the door. "That should freak him out," he mind-linked to Sydney as they walked back upstairs. Sure enough, a few minutes later they heard Lucas scream for Mom again. They kept up the trick for the rest of the day, moving the clown around occasionally to follow Lucas whenever he wasn't looking. Soon Lucas was a nervous wreck, looking back over his shoulder everywhere he went – until Mom finally blew her top and threw the clown in the trash can outside after ferociously scolding the twins again. When Mom wasn't looking, the twins gave each other an excited fist-bump – their prank on annoying Lucas was TOTALLY worth getting in a little trouble for.

That evening Sydney rescued the now-stinky doll from the trash and Marc put it in Lucas' bed, with the doll's head on his pillow. When Lucas went up to bed, they heard him yell and Mr. P meow loudly, and then heard his window quickly open and close. Sydney hurriedly looked out her bedroom window and saw that Lucas had thrown the doll out into the yard. She made sure no one was looking and then floated it up to her window and then put him back in her closet. She and Marc spent the rest of the evening laughing to each other about their trick, and replaying the various scared expressions on Lucas' face to each other. They were completely oblivious to the sounds of quiet sobbing coming from Lucas' bedroom.

They were both awakened the next morning by Mom yelling at them from the hallway outside their rooms. "Marc and Sydney, you two come out here now!" she demanded. The twins slowly and sleepily made their way out to the hallway and stood in their doorways. Mom and Dad were both standing there looking quite upset about something.

"What is it, Mom?" Sydney asked nervously.

"We were wondering which of you guys tracked in all the dust and mud?" asked Mom. "There's a muddy trail down the front walk, through the front door, up the stairs, and right to both of your rooms. Would one of you care to explain?" Marc and Sydney looked down at their feet and saw a clear trail of mud and dust just as Mom described, and looked at each other to see if either of them had any idea where it had come from. They both shrugged their shoulders.

"Wasn't us, Mom," said Marc confidently, as Sydney nodded her head in agreement.

"Really, well I find that hard to believe. Both of you guys get dressed and clean this mess up," Dad said angrily. "There's a bucket, cleaner, and brush in the closet to clean up the mud first and then the vacuum is downstairs after it dries."

"Oh, Dad. That is so unfair. How do you know Lucas didn't do it just to get us in trouble?" Sydney complained, as Lucas emerged sleepily from his bedroom to see what all the noise was about. He was a bit miffed that someone was making more noise than he was for once.

"Whatever it was, I didn't do it," declared Lucas. "I've been asleep all night long," he added, yawning widely.

"Well, there you go, and Dad and I certainly didn't do it either," said Mom. "You two get to work," she ordered as she and Dad headed back downstairs, being careful to avoid the muddy trail.

"Hmmmm, maybe that stupid clown doll of yours did it, Syd!" Lucas laughed. "What's that smell? Oh, I think I smell a little K-A-R-M-A!" he added, sniffing the air. Lucas snickered and stuck his tongue out at both of them as Mr. P meowed loudly and then scampered into Lucas' room as he shut his door.

Cleaning up the mud was very hard work and soon both of the twins were filthy, overheated, and grumpy from the effort. The mud was particularly gooey and simply did not want to release its Kung-Fu grip on the carpeted hallway and stairs, even with using their levitation powers to "lift off" the mud. So they poured on several bottles of carpet cleaner and took turns working it in with the brush and then dabbing up the wet sticky nasty mess. Elle and Yoda both sat nearby and watched them working with mild interest, since they had never seen them cleaning anything for this long before.

Marc had a sudden inspiration and asked the cats if they knew anything about the mess. Elle came over and tapped him on his cartouche arm with her paw. He and Sydney both activated their cartouches so they could communicate with her. "Well, do you know where this came from?" mind-linked Marc.

"Yeah, Mr. P tracked it in. We told him your mom was going to get mad," meowed Elle.

"No way. How can a cat track in this much mud and dust?" responded Sydney incredulously.

"Oh, not the cat Mr. P, the human Mr. P with the weird fur and funny walk," meowed Yoda. "He's Mr. P's human. We all let him in last night – he said he came to see Mr. P and to check on you two," he meowed proudly. "Do we get a treat?" he added hopefully.

Marc and Sydney stared at each other in complete terror. "Well, I guess we finally found the mummy – or rather he found us, I should say," said Marc.

Chapter 17.   Training

Marc and Sydney were both completely freaked out that the mummy was in their house and not ten feet away from them through their bedroom doors. They felt very lucky that the mummy had not attacked anyone or made an even bigger mess in the house than just the trail of mud. They gave strict instructions to Elle and Yoda to never let the mummy back into the house if it returned, but to come get them right away so they could figure out what to do. Over the next few days, the cat Mr. P refused to talk about the mummy or his relationship with it, so the twins were now very worried about him hanging out all the time with their little brother Lucas. However, they could not figure out a way to approach Mom and Dad with their concerns without sounding like they had both completely lost their minds. Their only reassurance was that both Elle and Yoda were not worried about either Mr. P in the least, and insisted that Mr. P was a very good cat friend and that they were both just being silly humans. In response, the twins were quite frustrated that the cats did not realize the danger that the mummy presented to the entire family, since they had never met an evil or dangerous human before in their very sheltered and pampered cat lives in their comfy house.

The whole situation was extremely worrisome and put a tremendous strain on the twins. Therefore, ever since the mummy's visit, they had been practicing their powers during every spare moment to prepare themselves for his return. After trying to find a bigger yet secluded place to practice, Marc had remembered a local hiking trail called Ragged Mountain which he and Sydney had hiked with their Scout Troop a couple of years ago before it had temporarily closed. It was within easy biking distance of their house and had only recently been reopened, so it was usually pretty much deserted. Also, one of the main water reservoirs for Charlottesville was within the park so there was a large handy source of water available to levitate just in case they caught anything on fire accidently during practice, which actually tended to happen quite frequently. It turned out to be a perfect practice area, and they went there almost every day for the next couple of weeks to hone their skills in seclusion.

Sydney had perfected her Tutankhamun bow, which was glowing a bright blue as she held it at the ready, with a shimmering quiver of blue arrows hanging from her back. She absolutely loved her new weapon and no matter how many arrows she fired the infinity quiver always remained full. The bow felt like a natural extension of her body and they worked together seamlessly, in absolutely perfect tune with one another. Sydney had even developed a wide assortment of different arrows, including freeze, fire, stun, grappling hook, and her favorite - explosive arrows.

Marc had nicknamed her Legolas after the amazing Elf archer in "The Lord of the Rings" trilogy. They had always laughed hysterically at the scenes in the movies when Legolas would rapid-fire arrows and never ever miss any of his targets, but now that was almost the case for Sydney. Today, as usual, she was practicing with pinecones that Marc would throw high into the air.

"OK, ready?" he asked.

"Yep, let them rip," replied Sydney as she watched the sky intently, hoping to break her record from yesterday. Marc immediately launched ten pinecones high into the air, purposely sending each rocketing in a different direction in an attempt to defeat her unerring Legolas aim. Sydney's arm moved in a blur from quiver to bowstring and shot ten arrows before any of the pinecones could reach the ground.

Nine of the pinecones exploded in a blue flash in mid-air but her last arrow just barely missed its target as the pinecone hit the ground and bounced away. "Yes! Nine, a new record!" she yelled triumphantly. "Tomorrow I'm switching to acorns!"

"Nice work, mighty she-elf," laughed Marc. "I have to admit I'm quite jealous. I just can't seem to get the hang of it like you can and I almost always miss by a few feet. I'm much better with my ninja throwing stars," he added, launching two at the closest pine-cones which exploded in a bright blue flash.

"Those throwing stars are really cool. You just need to keep practicing with your bow," Sydney reassured him. "Your fireball is much better than mine, so maybe the cartouche weapons just tune themselves to the natural skills of the warrior. You know I was always pretty good at archery in summer camp with the Scout Troop. You're good with soccer balls, so maybe that's why fireballs come more naturally for you," she laughed.

"Well, maybe," he replied, far from convinced. "Hey, hang on, I think I see something coming," he whispered urgently. They both stared intently back towards the hiking trail which they were practicing well away from as a precaution. Sydney was the first to spot the intruder.

"Oh, it's just that stupid nebby dog again. Looks like a Doberman from here," said Sydney as it walked off into the distance. The dog had first appeared several practices ago and now they seemed to see it almost every time. It would always keep its distance and never seemed to stay for long, so they just ignored it. "It must just be a stray or maybe it lives nearby."

"Yeah, I guess so. I just wish it would stay away," replied Marc angrily. "Every time I see it out of the corner of my eye, I think a person is there watching us, and it ruins my concentration. Oh hey, that reminds me – I found another cool new power yesterday, tap the falcon twice and think 'falcon sight' while you are looking at the dog."

"Well OK, that sounds pretty neat," Sydney replied with interest. She followed Marc's instructions and suddenly the dog seemed to be standing right in front of her, making her scream.

"See – instant binocular vision – pretty awesome, huh?" Marc declared excitedly.

"You should have warned me a little better," Sydney laughed in reply. "Definitely VERY cool, let me have a little look around. Yeah, the dog definitely does not have a collar. And I don't see or hear anything else, so let's keep going," Sydney suggested after scanning all around them and then swiping off her falcon sight. "Do you want to practice your fireball again?"

"Sure, you have fire extinguisher duty then," Marc replied. He focused on a lone dead tree in a wide clearing by the edge of the reservoir which was his usual target. "Ready?" Marc asked, carefully surveying the area to make sure the coast was still clear.

"Yeah, go for it," replied Sydney, lifting a huge scoop of water from the reservoir and dumping out a few fish and a badly startled frog.

Marc concentrated his power and made an open hand with his cartouche arm, aiming for the tree. A huge green fireball erupted from his fingertips with a deafening whoosh and blasted the entire tree backwards as it instantly burst into flames, and his arm cartouche glowed a brilliant green color.

"Nice!" yelled Sydney as she dumped the water onto the tree. "You almost knocked it out by the roots that time," she added admiringly.

"Yeah, that was really fun. I feel like a wizard from Dungeons and Dragons!" he said proudly. "Even the mighty Gandalf the Grey can't do massive fireballs like that!"

"Oh yeah, your balls are MUCH bigger than his," giggled Sydney, rolling her eyes. They both started laughing hysterically.

Sydney walked over to inspect the now-charred tree and stared at it thoughtfully. "You know, this tree was dead anyway and you've pretty much burnt it to a crisp over the last couple of weeks," she said to Marc. "I think we should maybe chop it into firewood, if you know what I mean," she added with a sly chuckle.

"Oh yeah, we keep forgetting to try throwing our swords!" Marc replied excitedly. "Stand back here near me and we'll give it a shot." They both swiped their cartouches and their glowing blue translucent swords materialized in their hands. Marc stared at Sydney's beautiful Samurai sword enviously, since he had not yet been able to craft anything other than the "standard" Egyptian hooked sword. "Oh well, mine is still super cool," he thought to himself happily.

"OK, we should start from the top and work our way down," Sydney said, confidently taking aim with her sword arm. "I'll take the very top and you hit beneath me. Are you ready?" she asked without taking her eyes off their charred target, which seemed to be shaking in fear due to the light breeze now blowing in the air.

"Yep, I'll count down from three," Marc responded as he started a countdown. When he hit "one" they both launched their swords simultaneously which flew spinning in a graceful arc and easily sliced twice through the top few inches of the tree, and then flew back towards them. The two chopped tips of the trunk arced slightly upwards and then fell straight down to the earth, as if the swords had sliced through with absolutely no resistance. Strangely enough, neither of them felt any fear as the deadly spinning swords returned and they both caught them effortlessly by the handle, without taking their eyes off the now quivering tree.

"Freaking ... awesome," they both said in amazement, admiring the wonderful swords glowing in their hands and their arm cartouches which were blazing a warm, bright orange.

"I think we need more practice," said Sydney gleefully. "Let's see how small we can make the pieces." They both launched their swords again and again, each time chopping off the topmost inch or two of the black tree trunk, until nothing was left but a pile of perfect little choppings piled closely around the stump of the tree.

"Wow, that was so much fun," Marc declared as they held their swords to inspect their handiwork. "We need to find some more dead trees around here," he added, scanning the nearby forest for another potential target. Sydney nodded in agreement excitedly.

Suddenly, Sydney's phone beeped, and she took it out of her pocket to see who it was. "Oh, it's a text from Dad - he says supper is almost ready and we need to come home," she said with disappointment. "Crap," she complained. They both swiped off their swords and gathered up their backpacks, surveying carefully to make sure any practice fires were out and they had left no trace of their practice session, except for the tiny firewood which they had stacked into a pyramid around the tree stump just for fun.

"Hey, we have another intruder," said Marc a few seconds later as he pointed at a green scarab beetle on a nearby tree. "So I guess they DO live in other places besides just our house," he chuckled.

"I hate those beetles, they are so annoying. Well, it's starting to get dark, are you ready to ride back home?" she asked.

"OK, sounds good," Marc replied as they walked back to the trail's edge to pick up their bikes to start the short journey home. As they walked past the tree with the beetle, they failed to notice that the entire back of the tree was covered with thousands of his beetle buddies, swarming in a giant green mass of riotous movement.

The next day the twins returned to Ragged Mountain for more training. They decided to practice levitation, since they had not attempted it since the last time in Sydney's room where they both had gotten banged around badly in the small space. They were warming up by practicing on some large boulders far off the main trail. Sydney was floating a particularly large one a few feet off the ground, checking carefully to make sure that there were no critters living underneath it.

"Done well you have, young one," said Marc in his best Jedi Master Yoda impression. "Remember, size matters not!" The both immediately started laughing and the boulder crashed loudly back to the ground.

"No fair! You messed me up!" she giggled. "Well, at least I didn't crush anybody," she added with relief. "Now stop teasing so we can concentrate." She shook her fist at Marc jokingly and then re-levitated the boulder.

Marc chuckled and levitated another nearby boulder which was even larger than hers. "This is too easy, how about a levitation battle instead?" he asked challengingly.

They both lowered their boulders. "What exactly do you have in mind?" Sydney asked suspiciously.

"Easy, we try to levitate each other while trying to stop ourselves from being levitated," he explained. "Like this," he added evilly, as suddenly Sydney felt herself flying up through the air.

"Hey, no fair! I wasn't ready!" she yelled angrily as she sped out past the bank and over the reservoir water. "Don't you dare!" she screamed at Marc as she was now dangling precariously upside down, staring at the dark, cold water far below.

"Oh, OK, I'll stop," said Marc mischievously, releasing her from his levitation and sending her plummeting toward the surface of the lake. Sydney caught herself just before she hit the water and levitated back to the shore with a wild look of utter fury on her face. Marc took several steps backwards as she approached, his eyes wide and wary.

"Let's see how YOU like that," she said angrily, holding out her arm toward Marc and sending him flying toward the lake, his arms flailing wildly. She flew him up about twenty feet over the water and then dropped him like a rock. Just before he hit, he raised his shimmer shield and bounced off the top of the water in a dry, shimmering bubble. He levitated himself back to shore warily, keeping his eyes on Sydney. He then dropped his shimmer bubble and gracefully jumped high into the air in a long arc, landing gently behind Sydney as she whipped around to follow his movement.

"What was that?" she asked warily.

"I call it a Jedi jump – just a little variation on levitation," he replied. "So OK, truce?" he asked, extending his hand for a peacemaking handshake.

"Oh no, I LIKE this game," Sydney replied with an evil twisted grin. They both suddenly jolted up into the air several feet and floated there unsteadily, as they tried to send each other off flying while struggling to maintain their own position. It was a perfect standoff of equal forces and they both started to sweat from the exertion, but refused to back down to each other in the slightest.

After a few minutes, they both heard a loud buzzing but maintained their complete focus on each other in their ongoing battle of wills, neither willing to concede. Suddenly Marc noticed a green scarab beetle land lightly on Sydney's shoulder.

"Hey Sydney, look out – there's a big green scarab beetle on your shoulder," Marc said breathlessly, straining from his effort.

"Oh, yeah – I'm so sure, Marc. You're just trying to distract – OUCH," screamed Sydney in pain. She instantly force-smashed the beetle with her fist and fell toward the ground awkwardly. Marc caught her with his powers just before she hit and lowered her gently to the ground.

"Crap - that really hurts!" Sydney complained, wiping at the green beetle goo which was all over her shoulder and running down her shirt. "I thought these stupid beetles did not bite," she added. Marc came over and helped her stand up gingerly, and then pulled the neck of her shirt aside to look at the bite as she looked away painfully. "This hurts worse than those nasty hornets who got me last summer," she said painfully.

"Oh Syd, it's already red and swollen," he said worriedly. "We should get you home for Dad to check on this."

"Um, never mind that - I think we have a bigger problem," she whispered. "Mr. Beetle Goo brought some friends, look!" They both turned to look at the forest around them. On every tree they could see, thousands of green scarab beetles were moving from the backs to the fronts of every tree trunk and their buzzing was getting deafeningly loud. Suddenly as one, the beetles all launched themselves at the twins.

"Oh crap – look out - shields up!" Marc yelled. They both raised their blue shimmer shields just in time and the beetles bounced off but immediately returned. Soon both shimmer shields were covered in beetles and all they could see was a mass of swarming green legs. "Are you OK, Syd?" Marc mind-linked since he could no longer see his sister who was encased in her own shield.

"Marc, I don't feel so well," Sydney said in a strange mind voice, as if she were struggling to stay awake. "I don't think ... I can ... hold my shield ... much longer," she added, her mind voice dropping to a barely audible whisper.

"Hang in there, Syd! I'm going to try a fireball to get us out of here," Marc mind-yelled back. "Try to hold your shield just a little longer so I don't get you too," he instructed. Marc concentrated carefully and soon had a blazing green fireball hovering over his right hand. "I need something a little different this time, and don't burn Syd or myself," he said to the fireball. The fireball shimmered back at him, almost as if it were winking. He laid it carefully on the ground at his feet and said "OK, on three." He counted to three in his mind and dropped his shimmer shield. At the same time, the fireball blossomed into a giant blazing ball, instantly incinerating all the beetles in range of the twins and then blowing out.

Immediately after the explosion, Sydney's shimmer shield blinked out and then disappeared completely as she fell towards the ground awkwardly with a moan of pain.

"Crap, crap, crap – stay with me Syd!" Marc yelled as he rushed over to catch her just before she hit the stony earth. "Syd!" he screamed.

"It's OK," she mumbled quietly. "I'm ... just so ... sleepy, I need ... to take a little ... nap," Sydney whispered, barely coherent and fading fast.

At that moment Marc heard more beetles buzzing nearby and quickly looked around, surveying the area carefully. Most of the beetles had been destroyed but more and more were arriving with every passing second, landing on the nearby trees and watching him carefully. He knew he had to move – and quickly.

Sydney was now completely out but still breathing deeply. He checked her pulse and it was slow but steady, and her temperature felt normal. He carefully levitated her in front of himself and started the hike back toward the bikes. Unfortunately they had moved further off the trail than usual today to reach the large boulders, so he knew it was at least a five minute walk back to their bikes. Several times a few beetles swarmed to attack them, but Marc was able to raise his shimmer shield to drive them off. Most of the beetles simply flew from tree to tree, following the twins closely. Marc got the eerie feeling that they were contentedly leading him somewhere.

As he slowly approached their bikes, he realized the beetle's deadly plan in utter terror. The tiny clearing where they had concealed the bikes was surrounded by trees full of swarming beetles, easily ten times the number they had just faced in the forest. And worse yet, several Doberman dogs were chewing on their bike tires which he could see from this distance had all been hopelessly shredded. Sydney was still completely out and he knew he was on his own to protect both of them.

He touched his cartouche and concentrated with all his might, closing his eyes. "I need some beetle bombs, like the Holy Hand Grenade from Worms, but they have to spread like a furious fireball when they explode," he thought carefully. "But not harm people, trees or bikes," he added quickly in his mind. He carefully visualized the effect he wanted as the buzzing of the beetles grew ever louder. He opened his eyes and was extremely pleased to see about twenty shimmering silver balls materialize around his feet. He picked one of them up carefully and gave it a close inspection. It was about the size of a golf ball and had a glowing red cross design which he knew instantly was Templar. "Cool, I see these have been used before," he thought to himself in awe, fondly remembering all the stories he had heard of the brave and valiant Knights Templar which gave him a mighty dose of courage.

He levitated the beetle bombs around himself and Sydney in a tight spinning circle and approached their bikes. The dogs backed away but then formed themselves into a growling ring to surround the twins, gnashing their teeth viciously at Marc. Marc glanced down quickly at the bikes – yep, all four tires had been shredded. "Dad is going to be pissed, he hates changing bike tires," Marc thought to himself bitterly. "Hmm, that gives me an idea – if we get out of this we will need a quick rescue." He turned to keep an eye on the dogs and beetles and mind-commanded his phone in his pocket to send Dad a text message:

Dad, this is an emergency. Sydney got a bad bug bite and is really hurt. She has passed out cold. Our bike tires were chewed up by dogs, can you come rescue us? Meet us in the Ragged Mountain parking lot – ASAP!

Dad was usually good about responding to texts, and Marc was immensely relieved when he heard his phone beep a few seconds later. He read the reply text with his mind:

No problem, on my way. Be there in five minutes, keep an eye on Syd and treat her for shock. We can take her straight to the UVA hospital.

Marc breathed a deep sigh of relief. At that moment everything went crazy. All the beetles simultaneously launched themselves at the twins as the dogs charged them at the same time. Marc instantly triggered all the beetle bombs and there was a blinding flash of light and a deafening explosion as all the bombs went off at once. The dogs were instantly incinerated and the bomb blast rocketed through the air to obliterate all the beetles in an ever-expanding bubble of death and destruction which extended as far as Marc could see and then blinked out.

As his eyes recovered from the brightness, Marc looked around carefully and yelled "YES!" triumphantly. Sydney stirred in the air, still being levitated in front of him. "Syd, are you OK?" Marc mind-linked to her.

"Just so tired, turn off … those lights and stop … being so … loud, please. You're worse … than Lucas," she replied groggily as she quickly fell back asleep. Marc chuckled to himself and levitated her and the bikes down the path to the parking lot, moving as rapidly as he could. He was overjoyed to see Dad's truck lights turning the corner into the empty parking lot as he arrived. He dropped the bikes and held Sydney gently in his arms.

Dad quickly arrived and checked Sydney over. Marc showed her the bite area which was still very red and swollen significantly more than it was the last time he had checked. She stirred a little and Dad helped Marc get her into the truck carefully and buckled her in. He and Marc started loading in the bikes when suddenly one of the Doberman dogs appeared on the path. It was limping and badly burnt but growled at them both fiercely. Dad jumped in front of Marc reactively and Marc quickly conjured a beetle bomb and help it up for the dog to see. The dog instantly turned tail and ran back up the path.

"Is that what chewed up your bike tires like this?" Dad asked, still keeping an eye on the path. Marc dissolved the beetle bomb and quickly levitated the two bikes in the truck.

"Yes, come ON let's GO, Dad. Syd says they are Dobermans that must live around here," Marc replied in frustration, as Dad still watched the path.

"That's not a Doberman, Marc – that's an Egyptian jackal, and a very big one at that," Dad declared in confusion. "But how in the world did it get here?" he asked as he jumped in the truck and sped out of the parking lot.

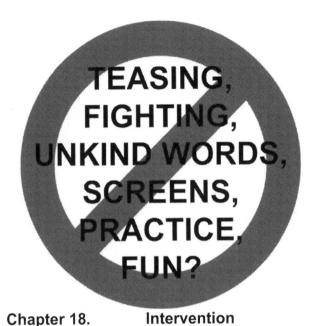

Chapter 18.   Intervention

The twins finally arrived back home after a long stay in the UVA Hospital Emergency Room. The doctors had treated Sydney's bite wound and put her on strong anti-biotics, but had been unable to detect any sign of venom in her system. Marc had described the green scarab beetle in extensive detail and even drew a very meticulously accurate picture, but the doctors had not been able to find anything like it in their on-line venomous creature database. Sydney had slowed recovered and was still groggy but had started to feel much better, so they had released her from the hospital with a long set of directions for Dad.

Mom was waiting for them on the porch as they arrived, and helped Sydney into the house with great concern as Lucas watched curiously from around the corner. She settled Sydney onto the couch and made her a cozy nest of blankets. Marc and Dad returned from the garage where they had stowed the wrecked bikes.

"Can I get you anything, honey?" Mom asked worriedly as she carefully looked Sydney over and checked her wound bandage.

"Maybe just a water, I'm so thirsty," she replied. "Thanks, Mom," she added gratefully. Mom and Dad both headed off to the kitchen together, deep in conversation.

"OK, I don't remember anything after the beetles swarming our shields," Sydney mind-linked to Marc, staring at him intensely. "What the heck happened?"

Marc filled her in on the details via mind-link along with some replays of the craziest parts, as Mom soon returned with a large glass of ice water. Sydney had a look of complete terror on her face and had to hide it quickly from Mom. "Thanks, Mom," she said looking away, as Mom placed the glass on the table beside her.

"Marc, keep an eye on her, please," instructed Mom. "I want to go over the doctor's directions with Dad."

"Sure Mom, no problem," Marc replied. "I'll be her protector, guardian and defender forever," he chuckled as Sydney stared at him and instantly started tearing up. Luckily, Mom hurried off quickly to meet Dad in the kitchen.

"Thanks – you saved us tonight, brother," Sydney said tearfully. "We are SO lucky to have gotten out of that."

"Nah, it wasn't luck – it was SKILL," Marc laughed in reply. "For once, all my powers worked exactly like I wanted them to," he added via mind-link.

"Yeah, I loved those beetle bombs – that was really quick thinking," Sydney replied. "Now I want to play Worms again – I freaking love that game, even more so now!"

At that moment, Lucas appeared mischievously around the corner and walked over to stand staring mockingly at Sydney. "What's the matter with you, dork? You got bit by a little bug and crashed your bike?" he taunted, acting out a crazy scene of her dancing around and tripping over herself clumsily. "Another visit to the Emergency Room – you are such a stupid klutz. The UVA doctors must be SOOOO sick of seeing you in there all the time – ha ha!"

Marc completely snapped. Sydney mind-linked "NO" but it was too late. From several feet away, Marc force-punched Lucas without thinking and sent him flying over the coffee table into the other couch, screaming in shock and fury and landing hard. Marc immediately reached painfully for his cartouche, which was flashing red and burning his arm like never before.

"Whoops, you OK Lucas?" Marc asked sheepishly. "That was totally automatic, Syd – I couldn't stop it," he mind-linked apologetically to Sydney.

Lucas quickly scrambled to his feet and charged Marc with his fists flying in fury in full berserker mode, yelling at the top of his lungs. They met with a furious smack and were knocked backwards into the couch, screaming and pummeling each other as they twisted in a riotous whirlwind of uncontrolled fury. Sydney jumped to her feet to pull them apart but immediately found herself too dizzy to stand and stumbled into the coffee table, scraping her leg badly and landing hard on the floor in pain.

"KIDS, KNOCK IT OFF," yelled Dad, as he and Mom ran instantly back into the room. Everyone froze and Marc pushed Lucas off himself angrily. "We leave you for two seconds and you're already trying to kill each other?" Dad yelled. Lucas' nose and Sydney's leg were both bleeding profusely, as was Marc's top lip which was stuck in his braces painfully.

After an instant of assessment, Dad ran to Sydney to help her first and whipped out a tissue to hold on her bleeding leg. At the same time, Mom ran to Lucas and tilted his head back, pinching his nose, leaving Marc standing alone, seething and furious. Marc attempted to pull his lip out of his braces but it wouldn't budge so he just stood there trying to catch the dripping blood as best he could and ignoring the pain, his lip stuck upwards in a comical sneer. At least his cartouche had stopped burning and now quickly faded away.

"I've got this, Dad," said Sydney weakly, sitting up and reaching for her leg to apply pressure. "Go help Marc," she added, pushing Dad towards Marc with a worried look.

Marc held up his chin so Dad could survey the damage. "Oh great job on this Lucas - you guys have no idea how much money we spent on your teeth," Dad said angrily. "Marc, this is going to hurt," he warned as Marc stiffened. Dad gingerly grabbed Marc's lip and yanked upwards, freeing it from the braces but starting a fresh stream of blood. Marc did not make a sound but simply endured the pain silently. "Hold your head back, we need some towels," said Dad as he ran off to the kitchen. He quickly returned with clean dish towels for all of three of them, which they took sheepishly and applied to their various wounds.

"OK, EVERYBODY SIT! FAMILY MEETING!" Dad yelled after their immediate medical crises were resolved. The kids all sat down quickly. Marc kept as far away from Lucas as he possibly could, as they shot each other looks of pure hatred and fury.

"AND NONE OF THAT!" Mom yelled, as she snapped her fingers to interrupt their stares. The boys slowly turned to instead look at her angrily. The kids quickly realized that they had NEVER seen Mom and Dad this furious so the boys both immediately dropped their belligerent attitudes. Mom and Dad were both shaking angrily with their eyes closed, obviously counting to ten (or maybe a hundred, or possibly a thousand) to calm themselves.

"Oh crap, this is going to be bad," Sydney mind-linked to Marc worriedly.

"No doubt. Stupid little twerp Lucas – it's all his fault," Marc mind-linked back to her.

"Well, you shouldn't have lost your temper like that, you could have really hurt him," Sydney replied, looking over at Lucas who was defiantly holding back tears and still pinching his bloody nose.

"Yeah, I know. I'm glad the cartouche stopped me," Marc replied guiltily. "I was so angry and stressed out from the battle and the hospital and I just totally lost it. So stupid."

Mom and Dad both opened their eyes and looked at each other, steeling themselves with a quick nod. The kids all waited on pins and needles for the explosion. "OK, this is the last straw. We don't know what is wrong with you guys but you are all siblings and are supposed to treat each other with kindness, respect, and even a little love," Dad explained in a calm voice. "Your mom and I have brothers and sisters and we NEVER fought constantly like you guys do. You guys are always trolling and roasting each other, arguing, teasing, and now fighting and all bloody. Actually, we rarely ever hear any of you saying anything nice to each other. You guys are siblings and you are the main family you each will have one day after Mom and I are gone, and you need to learn how to get along and support each other through good times and bad. Like it or not, you are stuck with each other for life!"

"Syd and I get along just fine," complained Marc stubbornly. "It's him that's the problem – he doesn't get along with anybody."

"Is not!" Lucas retaliated immediately. "And I get along just fine with Hobie and ALL the cats and Maisy! The stupid twinnies here are the problem," he added as he pointed at Marc and Sydney. Sydney HAD been feeling a little sympathetic toward him but now stuck out her tongue at Lucas. Mom coughed ominously and they all shut up, refusing to look at each other.

"Well, I agree, Marc - you and Syd HAVE been getting along remarkably well lately," Mom said carefully. "But there are THREE of you and you ALL need to learn to get along. And everybody hiding out in their own rooms on screens does NOT count." All three of the kids snorted.

"So starting tomorrow we are going to have some new rules around here. You can call it an intervention," said Dad as they all groaned loudly. "Number one – you are all grounded for two weeks, and no screens starting now. Marc and Syd, hand over your phones." The twins immediately started a strong concerted protest.

"Mom - I use my phone for homework," Marc declared loudly, beating Sydney to the punch.

"Mom, you guys can't do this to me – I text and talk to Tyler all the time!" Sydney complained. "He is going to dump me!"

"Marc – nice try. All I ever see you doing on your phone is watching stupid meme videos and playing games. And Sydney dear, Tyler can come over anytime he likes; you two will figure it out," replied Mom as she took their phones. "Which brings us to rule number two. Starting tomorrow, the three of you are going to spend ALL your free time in this room TOGETHER learning to get along." This instantly brought loud complaints from everyone.

"How am I supposed to visit with Tyler if these two are in the same room with us?" Sydney yelled hysterically.

"You will learn to cope, Sydney," replied Dad. "Just include Marc and Lucas in whatever you and Tyler are doing."

Lucas made a disgusted face and pretended to barf. "What do you mean exactly? There's no way I'm kissing Tyler – that's all he and Syd ever do!" Marc and Mom immediately started laughing uproariously.

"IT ... IS ... NOT!" yelled Sydney loudly, lunging over Marc in an attempt to viciously punch Lucas before Dad intercepted her.

"Well, you gotta admit - it kinda is sometimes," mind-linked Marc, still chuckling.

"Oh shut up, you're not helping matters!" Sydney mind-linked back to him with a nasty glare.

"And Marc, we don't want you to feel lonely either, so your dear Becky can come over anytime she wants," said Mom in a soft, understanding tone. Now it was Lucas and Sydney who started laughing hysterically, as Marc's face turned a brilliant red and he gave them both the evilest of evil eyes.

"Mom, it's not like that at all. I told you weeks ago - Becky and I are just friends," Marc explained. "We always have been. And plus she already has a boyfriend – Wes," he added awkwardly. "Lucas just started that rumor to embarrass me." Lucas was now making covert kissy-faces at him, and Marc was strongly tempted to force punch him again - no matter what the cost.

"Well, I guess I need to have a little talk with Wes' mother about him stealing girlfriends," Mom mumbled angrily to herself in a barely audible whisper, before putting on her happy face.

"Oh honey, I'm sorry she was not the ONE," replied uber-romantic Mom, obviously in complete denial of his explanation. "But don't worry, you will find your soul-mate one day – you just have to keep looking."

Marc rolled his eyes at Mom as Sydney snorted. "Well I already did - but she's now halfway around the world from me," he thought to himself depressingly. He quickly found his thoughts drifting to his beloved Akiiki. "It just isn't fair to find someone who is absolutely perfect for you and then immediately lose them like that," he thought to himself bitterly.

"So what exactly are we supposed to do all locked up together in here for two whole weeks?" asked Sydney skeptically.

"Well, you can play board games, go outside together, watch TV, or hey – even read some books," Dad responded. "I never see you guys reading anything that isn't homework. Doesn't anyone read books anymore? You guys are always stuck on your stupid screens."

"Hey, we could play Mario Kart on my Switch!" said Lucas happily.

"No fair – you would always win!" complained Sydney. "And Dad - we read books for fun on our phones now all the time," Sydney added. "You and Mom need to get with the times."

"No sorry, I said no screens, so that includes the Switch and no books on your phones," replied Mom. "And board games, NOT video games. Watching TV is the only 'no screens' exception, but you have to ALL agree on what to watch and your time is limited," she added. Lucas was mortified that his hopes for a loophole had been so quickly squashed.

"OK, now rule number three. Starting now, there shall be no unkind words to one another, no teasing, no fighting, no taunting, no looking at each other funny or anything like that," Dad declared. "Any violations whatsoever mean another day of being grounded for EVERYONE." They all groaned and rolled their eyes.

"So in summary - learn to cooperate and get along or you will ALL be grounded forever," Mom added. "Now everybody off to bed!" They all put on their best fake smiles and headed upstairs to bed, carefully keeping their distance from each other to avoid any temptations toward violence.

Marc and Sydney spent the next few hours in mind conversation from their rooms complaining to each other bitterly, but not coming up with any good ways to avoid their upcoming grounding. The next morning they all managed to be civil towards each other and were able to make it to school without any further incidents. Sydney broke the bad news to Tyler who thankfully took it in stride and reassured Sydney that it would all be OK and they could get through the next couple of weeks. Then of course they kissed and Marc had to look away in exasperation. "Arrggghh, this is going to be rough trapped in the same room with them for two weeks," he thought to himself bitterly.

When they returned home after school that evening, they found that Mom and Dad had apparently been quite busy in the new family "intervention room." One of the couches had been moved out and the other was pushed against the wall, and there were now three small desks and a chair for each, labeled with their names. There was also a new bookcase stocked full of all the family board games, several bins of Legos, and a large collections of books from throughout the house.

"Oh man, this is depressing," said Marc, as the three of them stood surveying the new room in disbelief.

"Hey, Mom even moved my teddy bears in here - that was really nice of her," said Lucas as he ran over to inspect his desk area excitedly. "And she brought down all my Pokémon cards and my Star Wars and Indiana Jones Legos – excellent!" he exclaimed.

"Oh yeah, real nice," Sydney snickered. The twins rolled their eyes at each other, still struggling to cope with the thought of spending most of the next two weeks trapped in this room with each other.

"Oh no, it gets even worse," Marc declared, just noticing the schedule Mom had posted in the hallway. "She has got to be kidding – this is awful," he moaned. Sydney joined him to check it out, and they read it together.

School Day Schedule

7:00am – 7:30am – Wake up, get ready for school

7:30am – 8:00am – Breakfast (dining room)

8:00am – 4:30pm – School

4:30pm SHARP – Report to intervention room

4:30pm – 6:00pm – Homework time (intervention room)

6:00pm – 6:30pm – Dinner (dining room)

6:30pm – 7:30pm – TV time (intervention room)

7:30pm – 10:00pm – Games and sibling bonding (intervention room)

10:00pm – Report to bedrooms for night

"Games and sibling bonding?" snickered Sydney. "Oh this is going to be horrible – look at the weekend schedule! She even has homework time built in there too – this has to be a terrible joke!" The weekend schedule looked particularly dreadful to them both:

Weekend Schedule

9:00am – 9:30am – Wake up, clean up your rooms

9:30am – 10:00am – Breakfast (dining room)

10:00am SHARP – Report to intervention room (or church on Sundays)

10:00am – 12:00pm – Games and sibling bonding (intervention room)

12:00pm – 12:30pm – Lunch (dining room)

12:30pm – 4:30pm – Games and sibling bonding (intervention room)

4:30pm – 6:00pm – Homework time (intervention room)

6:00pm – 6:30pm – Dinner (dining room)

6:30pm – 7:30pm – TV time (intervention room)

7:30pm – 10:00pm – Games and sibling bonding (intervention room)

10:00pm – Report to bedrooms for night

"I haven't gotten up at 9:00 on a Saturday morning for years!" Marc complained. "No fair – that's my only real sleep-in day!" They both groaned loudly as Lucas came over to investigate the schedule.

"Let's see, it's 4:30 now on a school day, so we're supposed to start homework now, cool!" Lucas said excitedly, carrying his school backpack over to his desk and getting out his books and homework.

"How is this at all cool?" Sydney asked him in disbelief. "Do you actually like this schedule?" she asked incredulously.

"Oh yeah, it looks pretty good," replied Lucas. "We're all stuck in here together, so we should just try to make the best of it. AND we could all use some help with our time management skills. Especially you two – Mom says you are both horrible procrastinators," he snickered.

"Oh can I PLEASE force punch him again?" Marc mind-linked to Sydney. "Just a real quick one – maybe Mom wouldn't notice."

"No, you had better not – he would tell on us and we would all get another day of jail time," she mind-linked back, laughing. "But it was definitely a good thought, I can't believe he is not complaining about this."

"Hey Syd, can you help me for a minute with my math homework?" Lucas asked pleasantly. "Mrs. Smith didn't explain this very well and I don't think I understand it."

Sydney looked at Marc in total shock. "He has never asked me for help with ANYTHING before, holy crap!" she mind-linked to Marc. "Ummm sure, Lucas, just show me what you are working on," she replied, pulling up her chair beside his as Marc looked on in complete bewilderment.

"OK, where did Mom hide the real Lucas? This is obviously a cyborg replacement on the 'goody two shoes' setting," Marc mind-linked to Sydney, as he walked over to his desk to start on his homework. "See if you can find the OFF switch or at least a volume control." She mind-laughed back at him.

"See? I have to do all these," Lucas said sadly, showing Sydney a sheet of about 25 problems. "But there are numbers and letters, and she said something about getting all the letters together but I don't know if I'm supposed to spell something or what," Lucas complained.

"Oh, cool – you guys are starting some basic algebra," Sydney said, looking over the problems. "These are not that bad at all. The letters are called 'variables' and basically they represent a number you are trying to solve for. So all of these just have one variable so you just move all the variables to one side of the equation and put all the numbers on the other side."

"But they all have at least two letters in the equation – look," complained Lucas, pointing to the first problem. "See, this one is $2x = x + 4$, I don't get it."

"Since the x letters are the same, they are both the same variable so you just have to get them to move where you want them," Sydney explained.

"Well how do I do that?" asked Lucas. "Do I just ask them to move politely, or what?"

"The biggest rule in algebra is that whatever you do to one side of the equation, you have to do the same thing to the other side, or else they won't be equal anymore," Sydney explained.

"OK, I suppose," replied Lucas tentatively.

"So let's try to get all the x letters on the left hand side of the equation, and all the numbers on the right hand side, OK?" Sydney instructed. "We'll write it down step by step, and then you will get it. So what happens if we subtract x from both sides of the equation?" she asked.

"Um, two x minus one x leaves one x, I guess," Lucas replied. 'And one x plus four minus one x leaves just four I suppose," he continued.

"Right, so what are you left with then?" Sydney asked.

"Ummm, x equals four?" he replied tentatively.

"Exactly, that's the right answer, so you are done with that one," Sydney praised.

"Oh, OK – that wasn't too bad I guess," Lucas admitted.

"And if you ever want to check your answer, you can just plug it back into the original equation," explained Sydney. "So two times four equals eight on the left, and four plus four equals eight on the right, so you know the answer is correct since they are equal."

"Oh, that's pretty cool," replied Lucas excitedly. "Watch me do the next one on my own then," he continued.

At that moment, Mom and Dad walked into the room and did a double-take. "It was so quiet in here I didn't think you guys were home yet," Dad exclaimed. "So what do you think of the layout and schedule – any questions for us?"

"No, we get it Dad," Lucas said. "Hey, Syd is helping me with homework so you and Mom need to keep it quiet," he added as they both laughed.

"OK, fine then," Mom replied as they walked out of the room smiling. "See – I told you it would work," Mom whispered a little too loudly to Dad, making Marc scowl.

"Well, it's only been like ten minutes, so we'll see if they actually survive the evening together," Dad whispered back. "I won't be holding my breath. Help me see what we can scrounge up for dinner tonight – I SO miss Marion's cooking," he lamented.

"Oh shut up," Mom laughed, punching him in the shoulder as they entered the kitchen.

"OK, this one is x equals seven, right?" Lucas asked Sydney much more confidently.

"Yes, great job, see I told you they were not that bad," Sydney replied.

"OK, I SO got this. You can work on your homework and I'll just call you if I need you," said Lucas, concentrating on his next problem. "Thanks for helping, sis!"

"No problem, dude! Anytime!" Sydney replied happily, smiling over at Marc.

"Wait until you see how much Spanish homework Senor Poolay gave us," Marc complained, quickly turning Sydney's smile into a frown.

"Just lovely!" Sydney replied sarcastically. "Let's just work on it together and we can hopefully knock it out quickly." The homework was not that difficult, but the sheer volume of work made it quite tedious and they had just barely finished when Mom called everyone for dinner.

"Wow, this looks great, Mom!" Sydney said as they all sat around the loaded dining room table.

"Thanks – Akiiki sent me the recipe since Marion said this was one of your Egyptian favorites," Mom replied, which brought a nice smile to Marc's face. "You guys did great helping each other this afternoon, so Dad and I actually had time to cook something nice tonight for a change," she added, smiling at Dad. Everyone quickly dug in for dinner, and they all had a nice conversation about how everyone's day had been and were able to catch up on each other's latest news. After dinner, the kids helped clean up the table and then returned to the intervention room for the rest of the evening.

"That was the nicest family dinner we have had together in months, thanks dear," said Dad, giving Mom a kiss on the cheek. "I think this crazy plan of ours might actually be working," he added excitedly.

"Fingers crossed," Mom replied happily. "So far so good!"

"OK, the schedule says we have an hour of TV time, what do you guys want to watch?" Lucas asked the twins back in the intervention room.

"I don't care," said Marc. "Why don't you check to see what is on tonight? I guess we could always watch Netflix if there is nothing good on regular TV."

"Or we could just skip TV and move straight to 'sibling bonding' which is next on Mom's schedule," snickered Sydney. "Maybe she means with superglue to bond his lips together," she added via mind-link to Marc, making him start laughing. "That might be pretty fun."

"OK, I'll keep that in mind," replied Lucas seriously as he started flipping through the TV channels to find a program they could all agree on. "All these hundreds of TV channels and nothing good is ever on," Lucas mumbled to himself. After several frustrating minutes of searching, he finally found a nice documentary on Bengal Tigers which the twins agreed to watch, mainly because Lucas was so obviously excited about the show that they at least knew it would keep him quiet for an hour.

"Wow, that was a really cool show," declared Lucas after it was over. "It makes me want to visit my tiger friends at the DC zoo again," he added wistfully. At that moment Dad came in the room carrying a huge box.

"OK guys, 7:30pm – time for sibling bonding and games," Dad declared excitedly as the twins both groaned. "I found this box of old artifacts you guys can help me sort through for some good, quality family bonding time." Both the twins instantly perked up and grew excited.

"Cool, what have you got in there, Dad?" Marc asked curiously.

"Ah yes, ladies and gentlemen, please prepare yourselves to be completely astounded and amazed," Dad cackled in his showman voice as he opened the top of the box. "For I bring to you, my beloved children, many amazing tomes of untold entertainment and infinite wisdom inside this box, all with no batteries, cords, or Wi-Fi required," he added as he reached slowly inside the box, enjoying the moment of anticipation. Lucas was totally captivated and started clapping loudly but both twins' excitement had quickly turned to skepticism.

"Behold! An ancient artifact I believe was once called a BUUK," Dad declared, holding up a thick hardcover book. Lucas instantly frowned, now suddenly realizing where this bad dad joke was really heading.

"Yeah, big deal, Dad – it's the second 'Harry Potter' book," said Sydney sarcastically. "I told you we still know what books are and we read them on our smart phones now," she added with a deep frown. "Plus it saves trees!"

"Oh, but this is not just ANY second 'Harry Potter' book," Dad replied excitedly, ignoring Sydney. "Your mom and I waited outside a bookstore here in town for HOURS to be among the first to buy this very book on its US release day. We then flipped a coin every morning for over a week to see who was going to get to read it each day. I have NEVER seen any of you guys that excited about reading a book – you are too occupied with your silly screens to really enjoy the wonder of reading a good book for the first time."

Mom laughed from the doorway of the intervention room. "So did you tell them the part where you cheated and tricked me with a two-headed coin for the first few days?" Mom asked with a giggle. "I didn't think I was EVER going to get to read it."

"Well, perhaps I may have just possibly failed to mention that little part," Dad added sheepishly as the kids all laughed uproariously.

"Well, don't let me interrupt," Mom snickered. "By all means, please continue your astounding excavation!"

"So as I was saying before being so rudely heckled by the surprisingly lovely lady over there," Dad continued as he rolled his eyes at Mom, "there are some really great books in here that I think you all may thoroughly enjoy during your glorious time together in the intervention room. There are not just the newer 'Harry Potter' books in here, but also all my very favorite books I loved when I was your age."

"Ha ha, Dad – that's impossible - they would have disintegrated by now since you are so ancient," Lucas replied, feeling badly cheated by Dad's little trick. Dad stuck his tongue out at him and started stacking up the books into different piles on the table for them.

Sydney moved to stand beside Dad and peered curiously into the box, starting to gain interest. "What is that tattered little paperback there?" she asked, pointing to an ancient and battered little book near the bottom of the box.

"Ah, yes – this is the book that started it all for me," Dad said lovingly as he picked it up gently and showed her the cover. "'The Hobbit' by J.R.R. Tolkien," he announced proudly. "This was the first really long book that my big brother Ed forced me to read in the fourth grade."

"Forced you to read?" Marc asked curiously, picturing his Uncle Ed strapping a young Dad to a chair with his eyes clamped open like in the opening of Robot Chicken.

"Well yes, I suppose I was a bit like you guys seem to be and wasn't that interested in spending time reading big long books," Dad explained. "I told him it looked stupid and I didn't want to read it, but he kept pestering me for weeks so I finally caved in. And of course I loved it and then immediately read all of the 'Lord of the Rings' trilogy and after that all kinds of science fiction and fantasy books. See, here they are," Dad added, reaching in for three more extremely tattered and yellowing paperbacks.

"Geez, Dad – what did you do to them?" Sydney asked disgustedly. "Our school librarian would faint if she saw the pitiful shape these books are in."

"Well I read them all about a hundred times, so I guess that takes a toll after a while," Dad laughed. "And they're getting old and a bit fragile like me I guess. Oh, here's another of my favorites – this is a cool illustrated version of 'The Hobbit' based on the cartoon movie," Dad said excitedly. He turned to a marked page and opened it up to show the scene of Bilbo finding the One Ring. "See, I even had grandma embroider this scene onto the back of a shirt for me – that was so cool!" Dad remembered fondly.

"Cartoon movie?" Marc mind-linked to Sydney as she shrugged in confusion.

"I think he's finally gone off the deep end," Sydney mind-linked back, making a crazy sign with her finger beside her head. Mom saw her crazy motion and started giggling, giving her a big thumbs up in response.

"Oh here Lucas, you will love these," Dad said, making a stack of large colorful books. "This is my all-time favorite comic strip – 'Calvin and Hobbes'. It's about a young boy around your age whose best friend is a TIGER!"

"A tiger? Really Dad?" Lucas asked skeptically as he moved in for a closer look. "You're just trolling me, right?"

"No, see – here's a cover picture – the boy is Calvin and the tiger is Hobbes," Dad replied, holding up one of the books. "I actually was campaigning hard to name you Calvin when you were born, but Mom vetoed me," he added as Mom smiled at him.

"Excellent!" said Lucas, grabbing the whole stack and heading over to the couch to start reading them feverishly.

"Ohhh, look what I found in here!" Sydney exclaimed excitedly. "You've got first edition hardcovers of all the 'Twilight' series, too," she teased.

"Oh, those are Mom's - definitely Mom's, yep," Dad replied a little too quickly. "I don't know how they got in there," he whispered.

"Nice try. Actually, those are both of ours," Mom laughed. "We had to flip a coin to take turns reading those too."

"Oh, the truth comes out Dad!" Sydney giggled. "Apparently you are also a hopeless romantic just like Mom!"

Dad shrugged nonchalantly, admitting defeat. "OK maybe, but at least I was Team Edward while crazy Mom was Team Jacob." Mom rolled her eyes at him.

"Well, I was Team Bella all the way," Sydney snickered. "Both of those guys were just way too high-maintenance and high-drama for her, and she was just lucky it turned out so well in the end!"

"Well that is quite true - I never thought of it that way," Mom chuckled.

"Oh, you'll like these Marc," Sydney said, pulling more books out of the box. "Dad has a few old Star Wars books in here. Gee, I've never even heard of any of these, Dad."

"Oh, yeah those were some of my favorites – 'Splinter of the Mind's Eye', 'The Courtship of Princess Leia', and 'The Han Solo Adventures'," Dad replied excitedly.

"Ewww, 'The Courtship of Princess Leia' – who would want to read a book with a bunch of goopy romance, hand-holding, and kissing?" Marc asked disgustedly.

"Oh, I don't know," Sydney replied thoughtfully. "I think it would be interesting to see exactly how Han and Leia fell in love," she added, looking intently at the front and back cover.

"No thanks – yuck!" Marc replied, now examining the other two Star Wars books closely.

"OK, come on dear, let's leave the kids alone," Mom said quietly to Dad, grabbing his hand.

"Alright, so you guys have fun checking these out – I've got a bunch of other great books in there like the 'Xanth' series, the 'Chronicles of Narnia', the 'Chronicles of Pyrdain', and 'The Elves and the Otterskin' series," Dad said excitedly as he and Mom started to walk out of the intervention room while Elle and Yoda came in to investigate. "They are all really good reads and will open up your imaginations much better than all those silly screens."

"Yeah, yeah, whatever - thanks Dad!" Sydney scowled, as Marc kept digging deeper into the bottom of the box. Elle and Yoda were now both desperately trying to jump inside the box to see what all the excitement was about, so Marc had to fend them off while he was exploring.

"Syd, I don't believe it!" Marc exclaimed suddenly, lifting something out of the box carefully. "I just found indisputable evidence that Dad may actually once have been cool," he added in an awed voice. "Look – he made his own Mines of Moria campaign for Dungeons and Dragons when he was our age!" Marc held up the obviously hand crafted notebook which had a color pencil drawing of Gandalf and the Fellowship of the Ring facing the Balrog on the Bridge of Khazad-dum with Dad's name on top of the cover under the title. They quickly carried it over to the table and opened it up to investigate.

"Oh man, this is so detailed and awesome," Sydney exclaimed. "This must have taken him a long time to make," she added, spreading out and admiring all the dozens of hand-drawn maps and Dad's typed instructions for the Dungeon Master.

"Yeah, and hey look - it says '1982 to 1983 (age 14)' on the cover. Holy crap - Dad is freaking ANCIENT!" Marc snickered.

"This is hilarious – look he has a special character sheet for Gimli the dwarf," Sydney chuckled, pointing to his "special attack" description. "It says if you roll a natural 20 he chops his opponent's head off - but only if they are 8 feet tall or under. That's quite a reach for a Dwarf!" They both started laughing uproariously, attracting Lucas' attention.

"What did you guys find?" Lucas asked curiously.

"Dad made a cool Mines of Moria Dungeons and Dragons campaign when he was my age," answered Marc, showing Lucas all the drawings.

"OUR dad made this? Lucas asked incredulously. "This is way too cool for him, you're kidding me, right?"

"Nope, it's legit," Sydney laughed.

"Hey I have a crazy idea – what if we invite our friends over tomorrow to play it?" Marc asked. "I've never played a home-made campaign before – it might be fun."

"Yeah, that would be cool," Lucas replied. "My buddy Hobie plays all the time, he would love it."

"And we can invite the whole D&D club from school," Sydney added. "Tyler and the gang will get a kick out of this," she chuckled.

For the rest of the evening, Marc and Sydney looked over Dad's old D&D creation while Lucas was happily reading through the stack of Dad's Calvin and Hobbes books, giggling uproariously every few pages. Before they knew it, Mom and Dad came in to remind them it was time for bed.

"Good night, guys!" Lucas yelled happily as he ran upstairs to his room, precariously juggling the entire stack of books he was reading.

"Good night, dude!" replied Sydney, with a big smile at Marc.

"I guess that wasn't so bad," Marc said thoughtfully.

For the next week and a half Tyler, Hobie, Nick, Kelly, Becky, Wes, Jorge and Lodi all come over to play D&D every evening after dinner, as well as weekend afternoons and whenever they could all get together. Lucas had insisted on playing Gandalf, and his buddy Hobie desperately pleaded to play Frodo since he was a big Lord of the Rings fanatic. Marc and Sydney both shared Dungeon Master duty so it worked out perfectly with nine players to play each of the nine members of the Fellowship of the Ring. Mom and Dad often came in to watch their crazy antics and Dad's "cool" factor suddenly went through the roof, much to Mom's amusement. Mr. Worzboi, their teacher from school who led their D&D club, even joined them a few evenings since he had heard all their excitement at school.

A couple of days later, the group had nearly finished the campaign and now faced the mighty Balrog on the Bridge of Khazad-dum. Lucas had gotten a little over-excited and jumped on the table and held out his hands dramatically. "You cannot pass!" he yelled at the top of his lungs, at which point everyone started laughing hysterically and gave him high-fives as he jumped back down. The battle with the Balrog was really tough and nearly everyone was down to just a few hit points left. Dad had cleverly/evilly given the Balrog "magic reflection" powers so

Lucas' first fireball had bounced back and nearly fried Tyler's poor Aragorn character. Eventually they defeated the Balrog by a narrow margin and limped their way out the Mines of Moria to end their campaign on the borders of Lothlorien.

"Wow, that was really cool, Dad," Marc praised as all the friends packed up their dice and books and chuckled about all their crazy adventures on the long campaign.

"Yeah, I really like how you mixed in the Tolkien story with all the crazy random monsters and creatures," Jorge said admiringly to Dad.

"Yeah, as I remember, I had just gotten the latest Monster Manual so I spent several days pulling out all my favorites to stick into the game," Dad laughed.

"I loved all your pictures and maps, too," added Becky, who was helping Wes pack up all their gear. "It must have taken forever for you to draw."

"Thanks, it was definitely a lot of fun to make," Dad replied as Mom rolled her eyes. "You guys did much better than my friends – none of them made it past the Balrog and they were mad at me for weeks," he snickered.

After they bid farewell to all their friends, the kids returned to the intervention room to finish cleaning up before they heading to bed. "Guys, Dad and I are really proud of your behavior and cooperation over the last two weeks," Mom said excitedly.

"Well, thanks Mom," replied Sydney. "Surprisingly, it was actually a lot of fun."

"Yeah, I didn't realize how much time I've been wasting on screens," added Lucas. "We should have a family game night in here at least once a week."

"That would definitely be fun," replied Marc enthusiastically. He thought about Lucas' screens observation and realized that he himself had been just fine over the last two weeks without watching all the silly internet memes and playing video games all the time, at least when he wasn't practicing with Sydney before their punishment. All in all, their forced "jail" time had been very interesting. And Yoda and Elle would definitely be happy that tomorrow they could resume their powers training.

Chapter 19.   Trap

Lucas' favorite night of the year was finally here – Halloween. He had decided about a month ago after long and careful deliberation that he was going to be Chunk from "The Goonies," so Mom had found him a great costume and also a "Team Chunk" trick-or-treat bag and he was TOTALLY thrilled. Lucas had been counting down the days until Halloween, and the last week or so had seemed to him to move at a standstill.

Sydney had been pushing her plan for going as Han and Leia from Star Wars, but Tyler had eventually convinced her that instead they should go as Mike and Eleven from Stranger Things, his favorite TV show of all time. They had gone shopping with Mom at the Halloween store and found a nice costume for Tyler with Mike's 80s-style green striped shirt, nerdy backpack, a black 80s haircut wig, and a big plastic walkie-talkie. Sydney's Eleven costume came with a pink dress, blue jacket, green/yellow striped white 80s tube socks, a long blonde wig, and a fake box of Eggos. Sydney really liked the costume except for the wig which made her head miserably itchy in a matter of minutes every time she wore it, so she was quite worried about wearing it for a couple of hours straight on Halloween night. But Tyler loved her costume, so she swore to herself to suffer through in silence for his sake.

Marc was still feeling quite lonely and was missing Akiiki very badly, but Sydney was forcing him to go out trick-or-treating with them whether he liked it or not. Marc had reluctantly agreed, mainly because he knew Sydney would pester him relentlessly otherwise, so he had opted for an Indiana Jones costume complete with a whip, jacket, and cool authentic fedora hat. Dad of course was totally thrilled with his choice and told the twins he was going to join them for Halloween as Indy's father, but luckily Mom had intervened to talk him out of it.

Sydney was still laughing about the conversation between Tyler and Lucas at the costume store a couple of weeks ago as they were shopping around for their costumes. For several days before, Tyler had been trying to convince Lucas to dress up as the demo-gorgon from "Stranger Things" to coordinate with their Mike and Eleven costumes, and he was pushing hard again at the store.

"Dude, come on – it will be great," Tyler had argued. "You're already a little monster most of the time and the mask would look so cool on you. And look, the face/mouth flaps even open and close just like on the show and you can still see out the eye holes," he added, excitedly holding up the mask to show Lucas.

"Hmmm, no thanks, Tyler," Lucas had replied, hugging the Chunk costume bag he had found immediately upon arrival at the store, since he had already scoped it out a few days before. "I already told you - I'm going as Chunk – he's my favorite character from The Goonies. Check it out – my costume looks just like him – brown checkered pants, a loud black Hawaiian flower shirt, and his red slick jacket from the movie."

"Why would you want to dress up as Chunk?" Tyler had argued. "You don't even have any truffle to shuffle – you're too skinny," he had teased. "A demo-gorgon would be much more exciting."

"Hmmm, actually I have an even better idea for you, Mr. Smarty Pants," Lucas replied seriously. "How about YOU dress up as Sloth and be my 'Goonies' partner? You are already so ugly you won't even need a mask," he added as everyone laughed hysterically. "Just wear a Superman shirt and some suspenders and you'll look just like him!"

"Hey, no way dude! I don't look like Sloth at all, right Syd?" asked Tyler angrily, remembering how hideously ugly and deformed Sloth was in the movie. "I mean, look at my fantastic hair – Sloth barely has any – just a little wisp on top!"

Sydney carefully surveyed him up and down for several moments before responding, as Tyler flashed his most dazzling smile and struck his best model pose. "Well, I don't know – I think Lucas is totally right. You DO look just like Sloth!" as everyone howled in laughter and even Tyler started giggling.

Tonight Lucas had been fully dressed in his costume and pestering Mom to let them start since around 4:00pm, but somehow Mom had miraculously held him back until the "normal" trick-or-treating start time of 6:00pm. Mom had given Tyler and the twins strict orders to stay with Lucas constantly as they went trick-or-treating around the surrounding neighborhoods, and to watch out for cars – especially since lots of trick-or-treaters from distant places were always dumped off every year.

"Why do I have to stay with these losers?" Lucas complained. "I'm a big boy – I could just go by myself."

"Well Chunk, they are going to keep an eye on you to keep you safe," Mom replied patiently. "We wouldn't want One-Eyed Willy to get you now, would we?" she asked.

Lucas rolled his eyes dramatically. "Mom, One-Eyed Willy is the Goonies' friend – not the bad guy!" he said in exasperation at Mom's total movie ignorance. "Honestly Mom, you are hopeless – one of these days I am going to disown you," he complained. He grabbed his trick-or-treat bag and ran out the front door. "Come on, twerky teenagers – we need to hurry up before all the good candy is gone!" he yelled.

Tyler and the twins quickly grabbed their bags and costume accessories and headed out after Lucas. Everyone's costumes had turned out great but Sydney's head was already starting to itch from her Eleven wig, but she did not complain since she didn't want to make Tyler feel guilty. By the time they had hit all the houses on their street, the neighborhood was getting quite crowded. There were lots of amazing costumes, and checking them out was one of the twin's favorite things about Halloween. Marc pointed out a boy in a cool homemade Rubik's Cube costume, and Tyler saw several characters from the action movie he and Sydney had seen for their first date. To Marc and Lucas' tremendous disgust, the couple had started a game of kissing whenever anyone saw one of those costumes.

There also seemed to be an extraordinary number of Egyptian pharaoh, queen, and mummy costumes this year – probably due to their parents' discoveries this summer which had been all over the news for months. However, their favorite group was four friends in awesome homemade Ghostbusters costumes, plus a crazy-acting girl in a slasher costume who didn't seem to really match them. It seemed to Marc that it would have made much more sense for her to have dressed like Janine, their cool Ghostbusters secretary. The party of five friends returned their stares curiously, particularly focused on Tyler and Sydney which creeped them both out a little.

When they reached the last street of their neighborhood, Lucas stopped suddenly and doubled over by the edge of the road, swaying awkwardly. Sydney and Tyler rushed over to him to see what was going on. "Syd, I think … I ate … too much … candy – I don't feel … so good," he wheezed, ending with some dramatic barfing noises and then dropping a giant pile of fake barf between Tyler's feet. Tyler jumped back quickly and started to turn a little green until he realized Lucas was totally pranking him.

"Nice one, little bro!" yelled Sydney, giving Lucas a double high-five. "Just like we planned," she added as they all laughed at Tyler's reaction. Sydney smiled at him slyly and then gave him a kiss of apology which he reluctantly accepted.

"OK, fine – you two got me. But I think someone should be worried about payback a little later," he whispered in Sydney's ear.

Sydney stared into his eyes fiercely. "Bring it Mike, I'm sure Eleven can handle it!" she whispered back with a mischievous smile.

Over the next couple of hours, they hit two more nearby neighborhoods and then decided to head back for home as everyone's bags were literally overflowing with candy and they were all getting a little tired. As they reached the entrance to their neighborhood, Lucas looked back excitedly at someone who was following them. "Hey check it out, guys! Somebody's dad dressed up as a mummy – that's the coolest mummy costume I've ever seen. He's even got the walk down perfectly."

They all turned quickly to check out their lurching pursuer, and Marc and Sydney knew instantly that it was no costume but that Mr. P had finally tracked them down. "That's Mr. P, we need to get home quickly," Sydney mind-linked in a panic.

"I know! Crap crap crap!" replied Marc over the mind-link as they both stood frozen in fear.

"Come on, Tyler – let's go say hi and get a better look," said Lucas, grabbing Tyler's hand and dragging him forward toward the mummy.

"NO!" Marc and Sydney both screamed simultaneously. "Uhh, I just got a text from Mom and she said we need to hurry home for … um … ice cream!" added Marc, thinking fast about what would get Lucas to cooperate.

"Ahhh, OK then. Candy AND ice cream – excellent!" Lucas said, turning around and walking back towards the twins with Tyler following reluctantly. "You're not trolling me, right?" he asked Marc a bit suspiciously as Marc shook his head.

"That really is a cool costume, come on Syd – can't we check it out?" Tyler said, turning back. "It would only take a minute."

Sydney stared back at him nervously, as the mummy was continuing its slow staggering advance and getting ever closer to them. "Actually, I have a … romantic um, surprise for you back home, so we should get going Ty," Sydney said awkwardly, reaching for his hand.

"Ohhhh, I DO like surprises," Tyler replied, happily taking her hand as they all now hurried back toward home.

When they got back to the house a few minutes later, Tyler's mom was already there waiting for him. "Shoot! Why is she here so early?" he lamented.

"No worries, I can give you your surprise later, my love," replied Sydney, giving him a quick goodbye kiss on the cheek. "I'll see you tomorrow, Mike," she added.

"OK, good night, and you make an awesome Eleven!" he replied, heading over to his mom's car and hopping in. She stared after him worriedly as their car pulled out of their driveway and turned down the street. Sydney quickly ran back to the road and looked back the way they had come. To her great dismay, she could see the mummy still lumbering after them in the distance.

"Marc, get Lucas inside, the mummy is still coming behind us," she mind-linked to Marc who quickly ushered Lucas through the front door. Sydney gave one last scan of their perimeter using her falcon vision and then followed them into the house, locking the front door behind her and then running through the house to lock all the other doors. When she returned to the kitchen, Lucas was arguing with Marc and Mom.

"Marc said there would be ice cream!" Lucas was wailing at Mom, who looked very confused.

"Why do you need ice cream when you have about twenty pounds of candy in your bag?" Mom asked curiously.

"Well, he was REALLY good tonight so I told him he could have some," Marc added to support Lucas' pleas.

Mom looked at them both thoughtfully for a moment. "Well OK, I guess it wouldn't hurt," Mom said with a smile. "Just don't eat too much and get sick," she warned. Lucas then started laughing happily and excitedly started into a long play-by-play run-down to Mom about his little prank on Tyler.

While Lucas and Mom were occupied, Marc and Sydney hurried back to the front door and saw the mummy now standing across the road from their house just staring at them. "Crap, what does he want, do you think?" Marc whispered worriedly.

"Well, us - I guess," Sydney whispered back. "Keep an eye on him for a minute, will you? I've got to get this stupid wig off – it's driving me nuts. I just wore it to make Tyler happy but I can't concentrate with it on."

"Sure no problem, just hurry up. I'll keep an eye on Mr. P," Marc replied, not taking his eyes off the mummy with his falcon vision. "Dang he is UGLY, it looks like he is all dried up and almost falling apart," he added.

Sydney was back in just a few minutes, and had changed out of her costume into shorts and a T-shirt but was scratching her head in annoyance. "Much better," she whispered as she rejoined Marc and watched the mummy carefully. Lucas' cat had followed her back down the stairs and was now staring out the front window curiously beside them.

Lucas suddenly came crashing towards them. "Hang on Mom, I'll show you - I left the bucket of fake barf on the porch," he yelled as he pushed the twins out of the way and jerked the front door open wide. During the chaos, the cat bolted through the open doorway before anyone could stop him. "Mr. P, come back!" yelled Lucas in dismay as the cat ran straight across their yard and then across the road towards the mummy. Lucas started to run after him but Sydney grabbed his jacket and held him back.

The mummy smiled at them grotesquely and then slowly reached down to pick up the cat. With a last evil look at the twins, he then turned and disappeared through the neighbor's bushes. "Hey, ugly mummy - come back here – that's my cat!" yelled Lucas, struggling ferociously against Sydney's restraint. The twins glanced at each other and then nodded desperately.

"Lucas, you stay here with Mom, Syd and I will get Mr. P back for you," Marc said as convincingly as he could. "Don't worry, he will be fine," he added, as Lucas had started crying dramatically.

"What's wrong with Lucas?" Mom asked worriedly, joining them by the door.

"Oh, Mr. P ran out the front door and across the road – Marc and I are going to go find him," Sydney explained. "It's OK, we'll be back soon," she added as the twins headed out the door to follow the mummy.

"OK, well, be careful," Mom yelled after them, holding Lucas' hand and heading back into the house.

"Hurry up, he can't have gone far," whispered Marc as they reached the other side of the road. "Be ready with your shimmer shield and bow just in case," he warned.

"Yep, I'm on it," Sydney replied, now searching the bushes there they had last seen the mummy. "Um, do you remember this trail?" Sydney asked curiously, pointing down a narrow creepy looking path she had uncovered behind the bushes. "I don't think I've ever been this way before, but this must be the way he went," she added worriedly.

"I have a bad feeling about this," replied Marc as he joined Sydney and they started walking cautiously down the trail. They followed it across the block and then stopped at the next road, looking around carefully before moving into the open. They could see the strange trail continuing across the road from them. They both suddenly jumped as they heard a loud evil voice beside them.

"Oooohhh, look guys, it's the special twinnies," said Knuckles as he and his gang of cronies approached the twins from down the street, carrying several big boxes of eggs and toilet paper. "What are you two creeps supposed to be dressed as? Big losers maybe?" he added as all the cronies started chuckling appreciatively.

"Now is NOT a good time, Alec," replied Sydney angrily. "Why don't you and your little gang of misfits just keep moving out of our way, and go pull your silly egg and TP pranks somewhere else?"

"Oooohhh, big talk from a useless slimy girl," Knuckles replied. "In case you haven't noticed, we have you two losers outnumbered," he added, waving his arm at his cronies Kyle, Will, Matt, Drew, and Harlow. They all flexed their muscles, cracked their knuckles, and tried to look tough and scary.

Marc and Sydney both started laughing hysterically. "Oh, that is a good one, Alec," Marc snickered. "You guys are just pitiful – you couldn't intimidate a flea!" All the cronies now shuffled around and stared at each other uncertainly, their massive bully egos suddenly shattered by the twin's rude response.

"Will you idiots just keep moving and get out of our way before this gets ugly?" Sydney added. "We're on an important mission here and have to get back to it."

Knuckles was not pleased and all of his now-confused cronies stared at him awkwardly, waiting for instructions from their leader. He motioned them to move around the twins, enclosing them in a circle. "Not just yet, girl - I've been waiting for this for a long time. It's time for little payback for all your nasty tricks on us," Knuckles said menacingly. "We'll try to leave a few of your bones unbroken so you can crawl back to your momma – eventually," he snickered evilly.

"Syd, look out!" Marc yelled as he force-smashed a green scarab beetle that had been flying towards the back of her neck. They both instantly raised their shimmer shields as a huge swarm of green scarab beetles had suddenly appeared, attacking everyone indiscriminately.

"What's this? More nasty tricks!" Alec screamed as he and his cronies started to scatter in terror. They all yelled in pain as one by one they were bitten and quickly dropped to the road.

"Marc – beetle bombs! Hurry!" yelled Sydney. "The beetles are going to kill them all!"

Marc conjured a large pile of beetle bombs and the twins dropped their shields, simultaneously scattering the silver bombs in all directions and setting them off instantly with a blinding flash. When he and Sydney opened their eyes, they surveyed their surroundings carefully and were pleased to see that all the beetles were gone. "Come on, we have to get these idiots out of the road to safety!" yelled Sydney, as she levitated half of Knuckles gang toward the bushes. Marc quickly levitated the other half and then checked the vital signs on each boy carefully before hiding them all in the bushes, while Sydney acted as lookout.

"OK, everybody is stable but they are all asleep," Marc declared. "It looks like they all got at least three bites, so will probably be out cold for a while. Come on, we need to keep moving," he urged. They hurried back across the road to where the trail they had been following continued.

"Trust me, they are all going to have a very nasty headache when they wake up," Sydney snickered. "I sure never thought we'd be rescuing cronies today – what a weird and bizarre day!" she added.

"Tell me about it," replied Marc. "And I have a bad feeling it is about to get a whole lot weirder!"

They moved cautiously but quickly down the trail which was now entering a wooded area behind their neighborhood. Suddenly Sydney bent down and picked something up from the trail. "Hey Marc – I found Mr. P's collar – we are definitely on the right track," she said excitedly as she shoved the collar into her pocket.

"I have a bad feeling the two Mr. P's are leading us right into a trap – I've never trusted that stupid cat after the mud incident," Marc replied angrily. "Why don't we just leave them both and tell Lucas we couldn't find him?"

"No, he would be devastated and you know it," replied Sydney. "We have to see this through," she added nervously. "Plus we don't know for sure – the cat may really be in trouble." As soon as the words left her lips, they heard a loud growling and a blood-curdling cat scream not far ahead on the trail. "Crap, hurry up!" yelled Sydney, forging ahead quickly.

Suddenly they reached the end of the woods and the trail opened to a large cemetery. "Oh crap, you have got to be kidding me," yelled Marc. "Of course we end up in a cemetery on the spookiest night of the year!" he complained.

"Look – there he is!" yelled Sydney. Among the tombstones ahead, the twins could see the cat Mr. P surrounded by six Egyptian jackals who were launching themselves to attack the poor cat. Sydney instantly conjured her bow and before Marc could blink, the six jackals were hit by exploding arrows and disintegrated into a large cloud of jackal goo.

Marc ran forward to check on the cat, who was obviously badly injured. There was no sign of the mummy, but Marc noticed several green scarab beetles on the nearby tombstones who were watching him warily. "Are you OK, Mr. P?" he asked, picking up the cat gingerly and touching the falcon and owl on his cartouche so they could communicate.

"It's not too horrible – but they got my back leg pretty badly," Mr. P mind-meowed weakly to the twins. "I don't think I can walk, but never mind me. You are both in terrible danger – this is a trap!" he warned ominously. "You need to run NOW! Make sure Lucas is safe..." He then gasped in pain and passed out.

"Crap!" yelled Sydney. "Now what?" she added, looking around carefully. There was no sign of the mummy but more beetles were quickly assembling and she could see more jackals running toward them in the distance. "Marc – we need to get out of here – FAST!" she yelled and then screamed in terror. A blackened hand had a firm grip on her ankle, and the attached arm was quickly rising from the mound of dirt at her feet. She reactively shot an exploding arrow through the arm, blowing it to smithereens but the blackened hand was still attached to her ankle, as she stumbled backwards in a panic.

Marc moved to stand back-to-back with Sydney, kicking the zombie hand off her leg and carefully cradling the unconscious cat under his arm. All around them from beneath every tombstone, zombies were slowing rising up from their graves, now free from their long slumber and eager to feast upon the twin's living flesh. At that moment, the first wave of scarab beetles launched themselves at the twins, with several large jackals now also nearly upon them. "Shields up!" yelled Marc as they were overwhelmed by the swarming beetles. "You know, I'm getting really tired of these stupid bugs!" Marc yelled angrily. "Sydney, on three," he mind-linked to his sister who was out of sight behind the mass of swarming beetles. "One ... two ... three," he mind-linked and then dropped his shield, setting off the pile of beetle bombs he had conjured. All the beetles and all the nearby jackals were incinerated, but the zombies all continued to move toward the twins unfazed. Marc carefully laid the unconscious cat on the ground nearby and conjured a small shimmer shield dome over him to protect him from further harm.

"Marc, it's the human clause you added to the beetle bombs, the zombies still register as humans so the bombs don't affect them!" Sydney yelled. "Try your sword attack!" she mind-linked as she notched the first arrow to her magical bow. Two zombie heads exploded grotesquely as her first two arrows unerringly hit their mark, but the now detached zombie bodies still kept staggering blindly forward towards her.

Marc was having slightly better luck. He launched his boomerang sword and chopped four zombies cleanly in half with his first attack. Unfortunately the eight separated zombie parts kept flopping and dragging themselves forward, undeterred in their hungry pursuit of the twins. "Syd – this isn't working, they just keep coming. Let's try fireballs," Marc mind-linked nervously. "On three again," he added. As he finished his countdown, they both launched their best fireballs into the crowd of zombies, with a far better effect. The zombies disintegrated instantly, but as the fireballs faded, more zombies were quickly advancing behind their fallen comrades, joined by numerous jackals and another swarm of green scarab beetles not far behind.

Then both their phones beeped. "Oh PERFECT timing," Sydney yelled as she blasted several nearby zombies. "Can you check – I haven't figured out the phone link yet, and it's probably Mom."

Marc checked his phone with his mind-link while crafting more beetle bombs. "Yep, it's Mom – she wants to know if we found Mr. P and if we are OK. That would clearly be a YES and a giant NO, but what should I really tell her?" he asked sarcastically.

"Just tell her we ran into some very old friends and we might be a while but the cat is fine," Sydney replied, thinking fast. "We definitely don't want her driving around the neighborhood looking for us." Marc sent Mom the text and launched a new round of beetle bombs with another giant flash.

"Man, I'm going to have to start wearing sunglasses when I use these things, I'm getting a migraine from all the flashes," Marc complained. "What exactly are we going to do?" he whispered to Sydney. "The zombies just keep coming so we should probably get out of this graveyard, but the beetles are more dangerous in the trees and we're too far from the road. And obviously we can't go home or everything would just follow us – I'm sure the jackals could track us anywhere we went."

"Just keep blasting, we'll figure it out," Sydney whispered back, instinctively shooting two jackals who had just leaped over a tombstone to attack them. "Help me make a fence around us with our shimmer shields - that should help to hold them back far enough so they can't overwhelm us with numbers."

"Good idea, sis," Marc replied, working with her to create a five foot tall shimmer shield fence in a wide circle around them. He then fireballed the inside of their new enclosure to clear out any stragglers. This tactic seemed to work well –

Marc kept lofting a steady stream of beetle bombs and fireballs over the fence while Sydney took care of anything that foolishly jumped the fence.

Marc and Sydney continued to fight a long and valiant battle but the forces of darkness were slowly closing in upon them as they struggled to maintain their shimmer shields and keep up their offensive attacks. Then suddenly the army of the living and undead paused ominously and made way for their leader, the mummy Paatenemheb, who parted them like Moses parting the Red Sea. Slowly he staggered toward the twins as all his mighty warrior creatures moved out of his path in fear and respect of his horrible powers. One of the zombies who Marc had earlier slashed in half was too slow to crawl away and the mummy kicked him violently, scattering what was left of the zombie's rotten corpse across the ground.

"Well, this is it, Syd. He's finally found us. Let's light this nasty old snot rag up – on three," said Marc. "One ... two ... three!" The mummy waved one hand and both their best attacks fizzled out uselessly as he drew closer and closer. "Again!" yelled Marc but nothing happened.

"He's blocking our powers, I can't shimmer shield either," yelled Sydney in a panic, as their shimmer fence flickered out completely. The mummy was now close enough that they could see him smiling grotesquely. "I guess we'll just have to do this the old-fashioned way," she screamed defiantly, raising both her fists as the mummy slowly lurched forward.

"OK, you take left and I'll take right," advised Marc who stood at the ready. The mummy waved his other hand and suddenly neither of them could move a muscle but stood completely frozen in place. This time they heard a dry chuckle from the mummy and were soon overwhelmed by the strong smell of natron, oils, and long-rotten flesh as he slowly reached for them.

"Well, it's been an honor fighting beside you. I love you and I couldn't ask for a better sister," lamented Marc. "But crap, I wish I could see Akiiki again."

"Goonies never say die," said Sydney fiercely. "We are not giving up – as soon as he releases us - we smash him, so be ready. And I love you too, brother."

The mummy grasped their right arms firmly with his bony, rotten hands and they both blacked out instantly.

Chapter 20.   Tutankhamun

Marc and Sydney awoke to find Asim and Akiiki looking over them worriedly, with a blazing sun shining behind them.

"Oh crap, are you guys dead too?" Marc asked groggily.

"We're not dead, we're just on Tutankhamun's afterlife plane," replied Akiiki. Oh thank goodness you are ok – we were so worried," she added. "Are you hurt at all?"

"No, we're fine," replied both Marc and Sydney as they slowly sat up.

"Where did you say we are?" asked Sydney as she looked around in disbelief. Marc and Sydney saw the beautifully encased Great Pyramid in the distance, and realized they must be in ancient Egypt, just like their dream so many months ago. They then noticed the three Egyptians and a familiar cat standing behind Asim and realized they were not alone.

"This is Tutankhamun's afterlife plane," replied Asim as the twins stood up carefully. "Let me introduce you – this is Tutankhamun, his wife Ankhesenamun, and of course this is Mr. P, sorry - I mean Paatenemheb." Tutankhamun tried to stifle a snort as Mr. P scowled at him.

"I am sorry, my friend," said Tutankhamun, turning to Mr. P. "That crazy Howard Carter shortened my name too, which was quite annoying at first, but your nickname is just a single letter which is really quite sad." Mr. P shrugged and laughed softly.

The twins had both instantly recognized Tutankhamun from their vivid dreams, and now remembered Mr. P as one of the burly generals from the dream. But they had never seen Ankhesenamun before, except from the paintings and afterlife bling from Tutankhamun's tomb. She was absolutely gorgeous with long, dark black hair and strikingly blue eyes. However, she was dressed like a modern rock star in a skirt, high leather boots, and a wild blouse, with a beautiful intricate jeweled Horus necklace as the only object on her that would identify her as an ancient Egyptian.

"It is our pleasure to finally meet you," said Tutankhamun formally, as all three of them bowed to the twins. "We have been watching you for a very long time, along with your friends Akiiki and Asim here. As Asim said, this is my wife Ankhesenamun and you already know my good friend Mr. P," he added with a chuckle.

At that moment Akiiki rushed forward to give Mr. P a giant hug as he scowled in bewilderment. "Thank you for saving them, I am forever in your debt," she said, tears now streaming freely down her face.

"Saving us?" asked Marc and Sydney confusedly.

"Yes, but it would have been much easier to rescue you if you were not always trying to destroy me," Mr. P said with a laugh, as Akiiki released him from her hug. "I know my mummy form was not very pleasant but that was the easiest way to stay for so long in your plane to keep an eye on you," as the cat Mr. P purred fondly, rubbing around his ankles.

"Yes, well, sorry about that but we thought you were the bad guy all this time," said Marc apologetically as Sydney shrugged.

"I must say - you two are quite dangerous," Mr. P chuckled. "I thank Isis for building in a cartouche override among friends!"

"So where is your mummy now that you are here?" asked Sydney curiously.

"Oh, I brought it here with me but I am hopefully through with it now, so I will ask Osiris to find a nice spot for it in that cemetery near your house - just in case," Mr. P replied. "It's definitely a little weird having two bodies for my soul to choose from at the moment," he laughed. "By the way, thank you for bringing my mummy home with you – it will be much more peaceful there in Charlottesville than being on display in some museum with millions of visitors," he added with a wink toward Tutankhamun with a sly smile. Tutankhamun frowned back at him in annoyance and stuck out his tongue at Mr. P.

"Tutankhamun, this is your afterlife plane?" Sydney asked as she looked around in wonder. "This is just like the dream where we first saw you months ago. The Great Pyramid looks absolutely perfect, not at all like it looks today."

"Yes, this is how the Great Pyramid looked in my lifetime," Tutankhamun replied. "Egypt shall always be my home, so I crafted this plane as I like to remember her. And of course all the objects from my tomb came with me in the afterlife," he added, pointing to the meteorite dagger at his waist. "This dagger was one of my most prized possessions on the material plane, so I am happy that it now joins me here as well."

"Is there only one afterlife plane?" Marc asked curiously. "Where is everybody else?" he added as he looked all around them.

"Oh no, there are infinite afterlife planes for mortals, and infinite planes for all the Gods – including your one God - as well," Tutankhamun explained. "When you pass from one of the material planes, you may craft your own afterlife plane or live with loved ones or even live among the Gods, and visit other afterlife planes as you like. It is really quite wonderful. Ankhesenamun and I are content to stay here most of the time, but we often visit allies in other planes and also welcome many visitors here. My father Akhenaten now spends most of his time in the afterlife plane of Aten, Egyptian God of the Sun-Disk, but he still visits us here from time to time. Also, Howard Carter and his Egyptologist friends visit us often to learn the ways of ancient Egypt - and to correct their own old research theories," he added with a chuckle. "Like me being a cripple, walking with a cane and having a club foot – what idiotic notions," he snickered in total amusement.

"Allies? So who are you at war with?" asked Sydney. "I'm afraid we thought Mr. P was leading all the scarab beetles, jackals and zombies who have been after us," she added sheepishly, with a big grin toward Mr. P, who smiled back in return.

"No, they are all drawn to your cartouche power. The main war is between the evil Set and Horus, the Falcon God of the Pharaohs," Tutankhamun explained. "Osiris is the brother of Set and husband to Isis. Set was insanely jealous of Osiris' power and murdered his brother, scattering the parts of his body all across Egypt so he would be denied an afterlife. But Isis gathered up the pieces to resurrect her husband and together they had their son Horus. But again Set murdered Osiris and banished him to the underworld where Set's son Anubis was the ruling God and could bend Osiris to his will. But Set's plan backfired as Osiris then wrestled dominion of the underworld from Anubis. Now Horus forever seeks his revenge and constantly battles Set for control of all of Egypt, and also to keep Set away from Horus' beautiful wife Hathor, the Goddess of love."

"Hey, that is just like our last camel ride in Cairo!" exclaimed Akiiki.

"Yes, exactly. I gave my friend Tarek the camel master a little extra inspiration that day," said Tutankhamun with a smile. "The war has been raging for many thousands of years," said Tutankhamun bitterly. "Originally Horus and Set fought for domination of Egypt, but now the war has spread to all of the material planes and also for control over the afterlife planes. We, of course, fight on the side of Horus," he added, waving his arm to indicate Ankhesenamun and Paatenemheb. "We fight to maintain Maat – the balance of light and dark power in the universe."

"Are you all Asim warriors?" asked Marc curiously, eyeing Akiiki and Asim with keen interest as well. Everyone nodded.

"Yes, we were all Asim cartouche warriors in the material plane and now continue in the afterlife," Tutankhamun replied, activating his arm cartouche. "Our cartouche bracelets replicated when we crossed to the afterlife, but you and Sydney have our originals now. And Akiiki and Asim have Paatenemheb's original plus a spare he was guarding."

"So when did you find yours?" Sydney asked, turning excitedly to Asim and Akiiki.

"We found them a couple of days after I got back to Egypt from visiting you. They were in Tutankhamun's two life-sized tomb guardian statues that Dad was restoring," replied Akiiki. "We were alone in the GEM conservation center one night while Dad was working late to install a display in the Tutankhamun hall, and we saw a glowing blue cartouche on both of them. Marc, I remembered your story from the butterfly room at the museum, and I knew immediately what they were," she added with a dazzling smile at Marc. Akiiki and Asim both swiped and then held out their right arms which had a very familiar blazing blue Asim cartouche.

"Marc and Sydney, I have already explained this to Asim and Akiiki, but you must clearly understand the responsibility and the danger before you continue on the path of the Asim warrior," said Tutankhamun in a serious voice. "It is a heavy burden to bear and full of risk not only to yourselves but also to your families and loved ones. Ankhesenamun, Paatenemheb, and I were all betrayed and murdered in our mortal lifetimes over the power of these cartouches."

"Betrayed?" asked Sydney warily.

"Yes, Paatenemheb and I were murdered in a chariot ambush led by my supposedly trusted advisors Ay and Horemheb during a battle in Lower Egypt," explained Tutankhamun. "But their betrayal of Ankhesenamun was far greater. They did not want her to become a powerful Pharaoh like Nefertiti, so they thwarted all her plans to claim what was rightfully hers and forced her to marry Ay who then became Pharaoh. Only a few weeks later he had her killed and her body was fed to the jackals so she would be denied an afterlife," said Tutankhamun, now overcome with rage.

"Tutankhamun journeyed through the Duat once again to battle Anubis in order to rescue me," Ankhesenamun explained. "Otherwise I would have been trapped there in agony for all eternity," she added as she grasped Tutankhamun's hand with a smile.

"Yes, Anubis still holds a terrible grudge against me for rescuing you. And I will never forgive Ay and Horemheb for their treachery," continued Tutankhamun. "Now they both serve as generals for Set, so I will never stop fighting them. After their terrible betrayal they erased my cartouche from the kings list and from all my mighty temples including Karnak and Luxor, botched my mummification, stole my Grand Tomb which would become Ay's, and stuffed me instead in a tiny nobleman's tomb, not even fit for the least of the Pharaohs. But their plan backfired as now I am the most famous Pharaoh of all time," he added with a wry smile.

"What a horrible betrayal for you all - I am so sorry," replied Marc sadly. "What did you two decide?" asked Marc, now staring intensely at Akiiki and Asim.

"Well, we've already been here for a couple of hours and saw your whole graveyard battle," replied Akiiki. "So we already accepted instantly, obviously," she added a bit sheepishly.

"Yes, they both begged me to teleport them down to help you, but I told them Mr. P had it under control," Tutankhamun laughed. "But please do not take this decision lightly, we lost three recruits in battles with Anubis and Set only last week. It is a dangerous life you would lead – not only for yourselves but also for all your family and friends. You will soon discover that the cartouche powers are definitely more of a curse and a terrible obligation instead of a gift as they may at first seem."

"I ACCEPT," said Marc and Sydney simultaneously, then looked at each other and giggled. Marc walked over to Akiiki and held her hand with a giant smile.

"So you can teleport between planes?" Sydney asked. "Is that how we got here?"

"Yes, I teleported you here along with my cat friend," Mr. P explained as the other Mr. P meowed gratefully. "Asim warriors can pass between any of the material and afterlife planes, but it is very dangerous and advanced magic. For now we will handle the teleportation for you, so you must promise not to attempt it on your own until you have completely mastered your cartouches," he added seriously.

"Yes definitely, if performed incorrectly, you can be forever lost in the Duat," added Tutankhamun. "You must also remember that your body is always healthiest in its natural plane, so it is not wise for you to stay a long time in any of the afterlife planes or you may begin to fade out of existence." The four twins looked at each other warily.

"How is Mr. P?" Marc asked. "He was hurt pretty badly by the jackals," he said, now looking carefully at the cat, who seemed to be fully recovered.

"Ankhesenamun healed him when you arrived," Tutankhamun explained. "Her cartouche gift is healing." Ankhesenamun smiled at them all modestly.

"Cartouche gift?" asked Akiiki. "What is that?"

"The cartouche bracelets were created by the Goddess Isis, the weaver of fates, and Thoth, the Egyptian God of magic and writing," explained Ankhesenamun. "Since Thoth was master of both magic and writing, he thought it clever to mark each warrior with the Asim cartouche to activate and control their powers. But along with the mark and powers, Isis gives each warrior a special talent or gift, which is usually based on a skill they already possess. I was a healer in my childhood, so my cartouche gift is magical healing. I was able to easily heal our little friend Mr. P here," she added, stroking the cat's head fondly, as he began to purr loudly.

"What are OUR cartouche gifts?" asked Sydney excitedly, looking at the others to see if they already knew theirs.

"They have yet to be revealed," replied Tutankhamun. "Although I have a feeling yours may be archery which is also my gift. Mr. P's cartouche gift is battle strategy, which was of course magically augmented from his role in my army as my wisest general." Mr. P chuckled appreciatively.

"So how were we doing strategy-wise before you rescued us?" Marc asked Mr. P curiously. "We used a shimmer shield fence to hold them back, but the zombies were starting to overwhelm us."

"I think it was a very effective strategy, two Asim warriors have actually never faced that many enemies before without reinforcements," Mr. P replied proudly. "And Marc, I really like those beetle bombs of yours - you'll have to teach me that power. I hate those scarab beetles – I've been bitten hundreds of times," he added as the cat Mr. P meowed in agreement. "Actually, between Anubis' jackals, beetles, and snakes it seems like something is always trying to bite me," he chuckled.

"I would be honored to teach you," replied Marc with a broad smile. "I conjured them from one of our favorite video games, but I'm not sure where the Templar cross on them came from. I assumed the Knights Templar must have imagined them before I did. Anyway, I should probably modify them to work on zombies – I designed a 'no harm to humans' feature which seemed like a good idea at the time but backfired on us badly in the cemetery."

"Speaking of zombies, what will happen to the zombie bodies we battled?" Sydney asked Tutankhamun. "They used to be loved people with families who miss them, and now their graves and remains are destroyed. We didn't have a choice," she added sadly.

"Osiris is the protector of graves and cemeteries and now rules as the God of the Underworld, so he will restore the zombies to their resting places, and they will again be at peace," Tutankhamun replied solemnly. "I'm sure Osiris will be quite angry with Anubis for disturbing them – this is a horrible new tactic Anubis has not dared to use in many centuries."

Tutankhamun turned to face Marc and Sydney. "Before the cemetery battle, we were answering questions from Akiiki and Asim about their cartouche powers," Tut began. "Do you have any questions so far or were your instruction manuals clear enough?"

"Instruction manuals?" Sydney and Marc both asked simultaneously, confused.

"Yes, your instruction manuals are written directions cross-referenced by both the name of the power and the cartouche color, and show the hieroglyphic character activation sequence, warnings, and any special usage instructions," Tutankhamun explained. "We spent many centuries creating them and perfecting them, so most cartouche warriors learn very easily and quickly with practice."

"Ummm, ours did not come with any instruction manuals," Sydney replied. "We've just been winging it." Mr. P slapped his forehead in disbelief.

"Syd, your manual was written all over the outside and inside of Mr. P's sarcophagus," Akiiki replied. "We could read it in the GEM Conservation Center after we received our bracelets. Our manuals were written on a huge stack of papyrus scrolls in Tutankhamun's guardian statues – that's why their 'skirts' were so large. The bracelets and the scrolls in the statues were all shimmer cloaked which is why they were never discovered."

"Rut row, we never went back to see the sarcophagus after we got our cartouches," Marc replied, looking over at Sydney. "But Dad did a full 3D scan inside and out so we can ask him for all his pictures when we get home," he added sheepishly. Mr. P started chuckling at their dilemma.

"Interesting. Well, you've been doing remarkably well with your powers - quite miraculously in fact - with having no instructions or proper training," Tutankhamun said appraisingly. "Hmmm, we have an urgent mission for you all, so perhaps a little basic training is in order - Asim and Akiiki, can you please show them some of the basic powers?" he asked.

"Sure, so what do you guys already know?" Asim asked the twins.

"Let's see - shimmer shield, arm shield, archery, levitation, translation, force punch, beetle bombs – obviously, mind-link, ninja throwing stars, Jedi jump, spider climb, gecko grip, sports finesse, falcon sight, and fireballs," replied Marc, counting off on his fingers. "I think that's it so far, right Syd?"

"Also shimmer swords," Sydney replied. "Those are awesome. Plus the galaxy cartouche that I was never able to figure out."

"Galaxy cartouche?" asked Tutankhamun curiously. "I have never heard of this - can you please show us?"

"Yes of course, I memorized the combination – it was very complex," replied Sydney, tapping her cartouche hieroglyphic characters in a blur of speed. Immediately, a tiny spinning spiral galaxy full of bright stars and whorls of colorful space dust appeared inside the cartouche frame. Everyone leaned over her arm curiously for a closer look at the vibrantly moving surface of the cartouche. They all felt themselves falling into a strange trance, until Sydney quickly swiped it away.

"Amazing - I have never seen that power before," said Ankhesenamun excitedly. "I felt strangely and inexplicably drawn to touch the galaxy cartouche though - it was so beautiful and irresistible. I will ask Isis and Thoth what that power does, but for now I would not repeat that again – it felt very powerful and dangerous," she added, looking at Tutankhamun and Paatenemheb worriedly.

"Yes, I thought so too, so this is only the second time I have tried it," replied Sydney. "I will definitely heed your warning - thanks. OK Asim, how about those powers – do you and Akiiki know all those as well?"

"Hmmm, actually I don't know most of those powers and I've read the whole manual from front to back many times," Asim responded confusedly. "Let's just start from the beginning. Here's a super important one – first one in the manual," Asim explained, demonstrating slowly on his arm cartouche. "Swipe from top, then falcon, reeds, cloth, then owl," he said, touching each of the cartouche characters as he said their name. The cartouche flashed a bright blue and then returned to normal. "So that sets up a powers cloak around you, so that the forces of Set and Anubis will not be drawn to your powers when you use them."

"Oh, is that why all the nasty green scarab beetles and jackals followed us everywhere?" Sydney asked in amazement.

"Yes, the scarab beetles, scorpions, jackals, baboons, and other servants of Anubis are all drawn to the power of the cartouche," replied Tutankhamun. "It is one of the primary ways they track down cartouche warriors, and then call reinforcements for battle. This is a very important magic and you should use it before beginning any serious cartouche spells. But low-power spells like mind-link and translation do not generate a large enough powers signature for them to detect, so you do not need to cloak for those."

"The cloaking worked really well for us," Akiiki added. "We were able to practice for the last few weeks completely undetected."

Marc and Sydney both followed Asim's instructions, and both cartouches flashed. "OK, got it," they both exclaimed proudly. "What's next?"

"Well, this one is just a variant on the mind-link, but we have found it useful," Akiiki explained. "So it's just a downward swipe and then you think 'holo mind-link'," as she stared at Asim. A small holographic image of Asim's head and shoulders then appeared floating above her now yellow cartouche, and she appeared in the same form above Asim's yellow cartouche and waved to everyone. "So it's almost the same as mind-link except that you can also see the person you are talking to, which is nice sometimes."

"Oh, that's really cool," Sydney exclaimed. She and Marc got it to work on the first try and made funny holo-faces at each other, as everyone laughed.

"This will be another really good power, but I'm not very good at it yet," said Asim. "It's a full body cloak to make yourself invisible. Swipe from top, then falcon, owl, falcon, then owl," he said, again touching each of the cartouche characters as he said their name. He instantly disappeared, but there was still a barely perceptible shimmer where he had been standing. "The problem I have is when I move, watch this," he explained. Suddenly they saw a more noticeable contorted image of his body as he moved slightly, like looking through a pebbled glass shower door. "I can't hold it very well when I move - oh and remember there is no shield with it – only invisibility."

"I used this shimmer cloaking power most of the time when I was guarding you guys - I was always nearby," Mr. P chuckled to Marc and Sydney. "Let's just say my mummy form would have been a little too conspicuous otherwise, except of course on Halloween night," he laughed.

To Asim's great surprise, Marc and Sydney both got it to work perfectly on their first try and could even maintain the cloak as they walked around. "Sorry, we've been practicing with holding shimmer shields while moving, so this feels very similar," Sydney said apologetically when she saw his expression.

"Most excellent," exclaimed Tutankhamun, as Mr. P looked very pleased as well.

"Oh, this one is one of my favorites so far," said Akiiki. "I'm not sure if this is what you guys meant by your 'falcon sight' power, but this one is a bit like a video reconnaissance drone that you can control and monitor. So it's a swipe from the top, four falcons, and then think 'falcon'." Her cartouche changed to a warm golden brown color, and instantly a beautiful brown Egyptian falcon appeared, gripping her cartouche arm gently with its talons. She then stared at it and nodded, and then the falcon took flight and headed over to circle the top of the Great Pyramid. "So you access the falcon-sight just like using a mind-link," she explained, closing her eyes and moving her arms reflexively as the falcon banked and turned back toward them. "Then mind-link 'return' when you want him to come back," she added as the falcon landed gently on her cartouche arm again a few moments later.

"Ohhh, he's gorgeous!" Sydney squealed in delight as she moved closer to admire the exquisite bird, who gazed back at her inquisitively and gave a piercing falcon shriek. "What do you guys like to talk about?" Sydney asked. "He must have some amazing stories to tell."

"Very funny, animals don't talk Syd," Akiiki chuckled, rolling her eyes.

"Sure they do, we talk to our cats all the time," Sydney replied. "Here – everybody do this – swipe down, then falcon and owl at the same time," she instructed as the hieroglyphic symbols turned yellow. Everyone else followed her instructions and gazed interestedly at the falcon, who was now staring curiously at Akiiki. "Go on, it's OK," mind-linked Sydney.

"I am pleased to serve you Mistress Akiiki, my name is Third Eye of Horus," said the falcon in their minds, with a formal bow toward Akiiki, who almost dropped him in delight.

"Oh, the pleasure is mine," Akiiki responded. "I'm so sorry – I did not know we could talk to each other, my beautiful dear friend Third Eye of Horus," she added, stroking the falcon's head affectionately.

"That power is not in the instruction manual," said Asim. "I'm sure I would have remembered that one."

"You are correct, it is not in the manual," Tutankhamun replied, as Ankhesenamun stared at him worriedly.

"Why – is it banned?" asked Marc, noticing their reaction.

"No, animal speak is not banned or forbidden by the Gods, but Osiris feared that it would tempt cartouche warriors to enslave animals as Anubis has done to build his army," Tutankhamun explained.

"Oh, I would never do that," Akiiki said, staring at the falcon fondly.

"Can you summon other creatures?" Sydney asked as she and Akiiki continued to stroke the falcon who was obviously enjoying their attention immensely.

"Any creature that was properly mummified can be summoned from the afterlife – falcon, ibis, monkey, cat, snake, tiger, crocodile, bull, and hippopotamus," answered Mr. P. "If they agree, they will answer your summons and perform your bidding. But some animals are not plentiful or can be uncooperative, so they may choose not to respond."

"Also some are very dangerous and unpredictable – hippopotami, crocodiles, and bulls in particular have a very short fuse and often turn on the summoner," added Ankhesenamun.

"And do not summon the beetle, baboon, jackal, scorpion, or dog – they are now all servants of Anubis," warned Tutankhamun. "Your mind will be open to Anubis in their presence if you summon them."

"On man, creature summoning is so cool - I can't wait to try it!" exclaimed Marc.

Well, just be careful when you do," laughed Sydney as she gave the falcon a final petting on his head. "And be sure to warn me first if you conjure anything dangerous."

"Well, goodbye for now, my friend," Akiiki said to Third Eye of Horus who then bowed once more and gave another piercing falcon shriek in farewell. She swiped her cartouche again and the falcon disappeared with a small blue flash.

"So once we summon a creature, animal speak must be OK since we didn't get a red cartouche, right?" Marc asked timidly.

"What's a red cartouche?" asked Akiiki curiously. "Asim and I have never seen one of those."

Tutankhamun and Mr. P started laughing. "Your cartouches have a built in morality override, so if you try something against the rules, your attempt is blocked and you get a burning red cartouche on your arm as a reminder," Ankhesenamun replied, as everyone snickered. "I guess Marc and Sydney must have broken many more rules than you two."

"Hmmm, I suppose we DO both have a bit of a troublemaker streak in us," Marc giggled. "And missing the instruction manual did not help our case either, so it's not TOTALLY our fault since we were learning as best we could."

"Perhaps you are right," Ankhesenamun chuckled.

"OK, what else should we show you?" Asim asked. "Oh, here's one that might be helpful with the flying scarab beetles. So it's a swipe from the top, tap twice on the reeds, and then think 'sandstorm'." His cartouche changed to the color of sand, and a small swirling sandstorm appeared beside him, which immediately created a strong wind all around them. "After you conjure it, you can steer it with your mind and then also adjust the intensity. I've never tried a big one, but it should knock any flying beetles way off their course." He swiped his cartouche again and the storm immediately dissipated.

"That might be interesting to mix with my fireball," said Marc, who had been watching with keen interest. "I can teach you that one, but it takes a little practice."

"NO!" exclaimed Tutankhamun immediately. "That one is also not in the instruction manual because it is so dangerous. A cartouche warrior caused the Great Fire of Rome and did not survive the fury of his own unleashed power. Marc - you have extraordinary fire control, but Asim and Akiiki are not ready."

"Well, OK, but it's one of my favorites," Marc replied, sorely disappointed. "Maybe after you guys have more training," he said to Asim and Akiiki sadly.

"Can you help me with levitation?" Akiiki asked to cheer him up. "I'm not very good at it," she admitted with a dazzling smile. Marc felt better instantly.

"Sure, I would love to," he replied excitedly. "What do you want to start with?" he asked, looking around for small objects to levitate. "Here, how about this small rock?"

"OK, I can probably handle that," she replied confidently. She concentrated intensely, staring at the rock, and gradually it started to wobble upwards for a few inches until it dropped back to earth. Akiiki gave an exhausted sigh. "See, not very good," she lamented.

"Hmmm, you're just overthinking it," Marc replied encouragingly. "Just concentrate on the rock - and only the rock – block everything else from your mind. Then just visualize where you want it to go. Give it another try."

Her second attempt was much better but the rock only levitated a few seconds before falling again. "You're making me nervous," she whispered to Marc in embarrassment.

"Well, you need to block me out of your mind then," Marc chuckled back.

"Easier said than done," Akiiki thought to herself bitterly. "Come on, I can DO this," she thought, breathing deeply to calm herself as she closed her eyes.

"Try it again," Marc said enthusiastically. This time the rock rose quickly and started a tight orbit around Akiiki's head. She opened her eyes with a wide grin, watching the rock still spinning around her head. "There, nicely done!" Marc said, returning her smile and reaching over to hold her hand. The rock instantly wobbled out of orbit and smacked into Sydney's nose.

"Whoops, sorry Syd!" Akiiki said. "Marc distracted me – luckily it was a small rock."

"Yeah, no problem, it happens to me with Tyler all the time," she laughed, rubbing her nose.

"See, that was great," Marc said. "Let's find something a little bigger to practice on," he added, looking around again before locating a suitable object. "Hmm, why not?"

"Tutankhamun, do you mind if we lift that?" Marc asked, pointing towards the Great Pyramid of Khufu. All three of the ancient Egyptians started laughing.

"Sure, by all means, please be my guest," Tutankhamun replied with a broad smile.

"Like THAT is going to happen," chuckled Mr. P as Ankhesenamun snickered.

"Marc, are you crazy?" exclaimed Akiiki, her eyes wide with disbelief. "I could barely lift a little pebble and you think I can lift a giant pyramid?"

"Sure, it is mind over matter," Marc said. "As the great Jedi Master Yoda says, size matters not!" he added in his best Yoda voice. "The process is the same, just concentrate on the pyramid and block everything else from your mind. If we mind-link we can combine powers and work together so I can help you. We will just lift it straight up, hold it there for a few seconds, and then set it back down again very gently. Are you ready?" he asked.

"Sure, I guess," she said unconvincingly. Mr. P snickered loudly. Ankhesenamun punched him in the arm with a frown, and motioned for him to be quiet.

"Who is this Master Yoda?" Tutankhamun mind-linked to Ankhesenamun and Paatenemheb.

"He is their elderly cat," replied Paatenemheb in confusion.

"Strange. If this actually works, perhaps you should bring him here for a little field trip to teach us his wisdom," Tutankhamun replied over the mind-link. "I have not used the animal speech in centuries, perhaps there is something important we are missing."

"Yes, perhaps," replied Ankhesenamun, watching Marc and Akiiki intently.

"Remember – mind over matter," Marc replied, holding her hand and linking to her mind. "Oh, your mind is so beautiful, very different than Syd's," he said, looking at her in wonder.

"Hey! What's that supposed to mean?" interrupted Sydney angrily.

"Whoops, sorry, I got distracted," Marc replied.

"As have I," Akiiki said as they both felt their minds spinning and intertwining together into a strange and marvelous web, their eyes mesmerizingly locked together.

Marc blinked quickly to break the tantalizing trance they were both falling under. "OK, sorry – let's concentrate. Visualize the pyramid and block everything else out," Marc mind-linked to Akiiki as they held both hands and regained their focus. "OK, ready, on three," he said over their mind-link. "One, two, three..."

To everyone's complete amazement, the Great Pyramid of Khufu slowly rose out of the desert sands and floated in place perhaps fifty feet into the sky.

"By Isis, I don't believe it!" exclaimed Mr. P.

"Have you ever seen raw power like this?" Ankhesenamun mind-linked to Tutankhamun and Mr. P worriedly.

"No never, I can barely levitate a few single stones of the Great Pyramid, and yet they have easily lifted the entire pyramid," Tutankhamun replied in awe over their mind-link. "The total weight is over six million tons!"

"We should consult Thoth - perhaps Marc has tapped some unknown power by following his own path through the cartouche," Mr. P mind-linked nervously in reply. "Or perhaps Master Yoda has led him to a more powerful route."

"Yes, I think perhaps you are correct, you definitely need to bring me that cat," Tutankhamun replied. "Thoth and Isis are confident in the Prophecy of Four but the twins' immense power will be challenging for them to control. There is much that can go wrong very quickly, I fear. I am also worried about Sydney's galaxy cartouche – that is powerful and dangerous magic I have simply never seen before. Paatenemheb my friend, you must help Ankhesenamun and I keep a close watch on them at all times."

"Perfect, Akiiki," said Marc. "OK, now let's set it gently back down." Slowly the Great Pyramid returned to its original position.

"Wow, that was amazing, thanks!" Akiiki said, awkwardly giving Marc a giant hug. "And we definitely need to try that mind-link again soon," she whispered gently in his ear. "It was getting VERY interesting," she added mischievously, as he felt himself getting dizzy from her sweet warm breath in his ear.

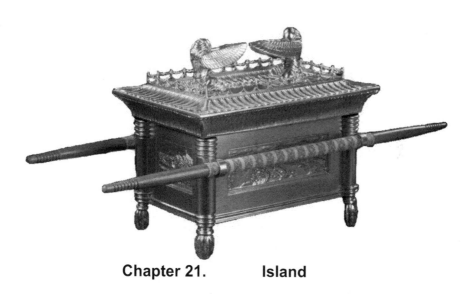

Chapter 21.   Island

"Our time is running short, are you ready for the mission?" Tutankhamun asked the twins urgently. They all nodded nervously and waited for his instructions. "We need you to retrieve three cartouche bracelets from one of our high security vaults on your plane. They have been safe there for many long centuries but the vault will soon be compromised so we need to remove them before that happens. If we can remain undetected by Set and Anubis, it will hopefully be a quick in-and-out mission, and Mr. P will teleport there and back again with you and will also stand guard while you access the vault. Ankhesenamun and I will also monitor the operation closely from here and bring reinforcements or a rescue if needed."

"OK, sounds pretty straightforward – where is the vault?" Sydney asked.

"It was built by Horus many centuries ago for cartouche bracelet storage, but was then also later used by the Knights Templar and others as a secure vault for their religious and cultural artifacts," Tutankhamun explained. "It is on a small island called Oak Island, just off the southern shore of the land you call Nova Scotia, Canada."

"Do you mean THE Oak Island from Dad's favorite TV show?" Marc asked excitedly.

"Yes, the very same," replied Tutankhamun. "The show and their excavations are the main problem, actually. Their persistent drilling has finally reached the top of the vault and they have unknowingly predicted the contents and also the connection to the Knights Templar, so we fear Anubis and Set may soon realize the true treasure being held there – the cartouche bracelets."

"So there really is a vault full of treasure in the Money Pit?" asked Akiiki.

"Well yes, of course," replied Tutankhamun. "It was a perfectly secure location for Horus until about 300 years ago when treasure seekers started digging all around the island, primarily searching for pirate gold. The upkeep since then has been quite annoying – misdirecting their efforts, planting false leads, causing equipment breakdowns, triggering tunnel collapses, redirecting exploratory boreholes, and re-filling the pit with seawater whenever they got too close. Honestly, it's been a bit exhausting," he explained.

"So how do we get inside the vault, do we just teleport in?" Asim asked.

"No, the vault and the flooded entrance tunnel are both shimmer-shielded, and require four cartouches to enter and exit," explained Mr. P. "I will take you to the entrance and wait for you there. You will need to swim through the pitch dark entrance tunnel. Akiiki and Asim – do you know the aqualung and torchlight spells?" They both nodded yes. "Excellent."

"Your cartouche magic is limited once you are inside, so you will have to exit the same way," added Tutankhamun.

"So where are the cartouche bracelets inside the vault?" Marc asked. "Do we have to search around for them or will it be obvious?"

"They are on top of the three primary religious artifacts in the vault, you should be able to find them easily with torchlight," Mr. P explained. "Akiiki – yours is on top of the Ark of the Covenant, Sydney – yours is in the Holy Grail, and Asim – yours is hanging from the Jerusalem Temple Menorah."

"You're kidding, right?" asked Marc incredulously.

"No, the vault is the final resting place for most of the treasures collected by the Knights Templar and others," Tutankhamun replied. "But take only the bracelets, and leave the rest for the Lagina brothers and their team – they have been admirably persistent and the artifacts belong in museums for all to admire. They hit the top of the vault a few months ago but of course the shimmer shield knocked all the teeth off their drilling caisson, blocking their progress. Once Horus removes the shimmer shield, they will finally enter the vault this digging season. The bracelets are the REAL treasure in the vault, obviously, so we need to remove them before that happens."

"Oh, that reminds me," added Ankhesenamun. "Please move the Temple Menorah to the east by five feet, otherwise one of the treasure seekers' boreholes this season will damage it badly." Marc stared at her curiously, wondering how she could know that with such certainty.

"What should we do with the bracelets?" Sydney asked curiously. "Will we get knocked out when we touch them?"

"Just place them on your right wrist and your cartouches will cloak and protect them," Mr. P replied. "Only your first bracelet causes blackouts – the cartouche assimilation process simply overloads your mortal systems."

"This all sounds very complicated, you sure we are the right ones for this mission?" asked Akiiki skeptically.

"Of yes, the Prophecy of the Four says you are the ones who will finally return the bracelets to action in our war," replied Ankhesenamun confidently.

"So I take it we are the Four?" Sydney asked curiously.

"Yes, Isis has foretold your arrival," Ankhesenamun replied mysteriously, as Tutankhamun frowned at her.

"If you are ready, please hold on to one of my arms tightly," instructed Mr. P.

"Good luck to you all," said Tutankhamun. "Have no fear – we will be watching your progress closely." With that, the twins held on to Mr. P and they instantly blinked out of existence and re-materialized on Oak Island.

Marc immediately recognized their new surroundings. "We're on the east side of the triangular shipwreck swamp!" he exclaimed excitedly. "Dad would flip out if he knew we were here – 'The Curse of Oak Island' is one of his favorite shows!"

Sydney laughed, looking around carefully for any enemies. "Yeah, well I think Mom is getting pretty frustrated with it – every week they find some tantalizing new clues but never any of the massive treasure hoard they say is there. At this point she just watches it to humor Dad."

Akiiki giggled. "Well, you heard Ankhesenamun - make sure your mom watches next season because they will find the vault and all its treasures. Your dad's obsession will be totally vindicated."

"I just hope those treasure hunters are not working late tonight to see us," Asim said nervously.

"No, all mortals except for you four are off the island at the moment," replied Mr. P, with a chuckle. "Horus arranged a little research field trip to get them out of our hair for the night, in case anything goes badly."

"Excellent, I don't want any innocent bystanders getting hurt," Sydney said with relief. "Our luck with avoiding trouble has not been going so well lately."

"True that!" agreed Marc ruefully as the others laughed.

"So far so good," Mr. P whispered, as he activated the power concealing sequence on his cartouche. "OK, that should conceal any powers we may need tonight. Follow me – the cloaked entrance is over here," he added as he led them down a narrow path beside the swamp, which ended in a small, nondescript puddle of water. "Here we are, everybody in," he instructed gruffly, surveying their surroundings carefully. They all shrugged and moved to stand in the middle of the puddle, forming a tight circle and facing each other.

"Now what?" Asim whispered.

"Stack your cartouche hands on top of one another, and the gate will open," Mr. P instructed, still scanning around for enemies. "Be ready with your aqualung spells, the first step is a doozy," he chuckled. "I'm going to cloak as soon as you are in. Keep an open mind-link between the five of us so I can keep in touch with you. We may not have much time, so don't dilly-dally in there – the vault can be quite overwhelming."

"Marc and Syd, you must hold on to our hand at all times for the aqualung spell to work," Akiiki said as she and Asim punched a complex sequence into their cartouches. Marc grabbed Akiiki's left hand with his eagerly, but Sydney felt very strange reaching for Asim's hand.

"Don't worry, I'll protect you Syd," Asim said, not understanding the real reason for her reluctance, but smiling at her reassuringly.

"Ha. More likely, I'll be protecting YOU," she replied with a laugh.

"Well, you are certainly an incredible warrior, so you're probably right," he whispered back with another wide smile. "How about you have my back, I'll have yours, then. Deal?"

"Deal," she replied, grabbing his hand in a fierce handshake and then not letting go.

"This feels a little stupid," Marc said doubtfully as he held out his cartouche hand over the puddle, and the others stacked their hands on top.

Asim was the last to place his hand and he hesitated momentarily. "Everyone ready?" he asked, as they all nodded. As soon as he touched Sydney's hand, the puddle dropped out from under them and they fell into a deep water-filled room. It was a miracle that none of them screamed in shock from the abrupt drop. Akiiki and Marc kept their hands locked together, as did Sydney and Asim, and the Egyptians awkwardly swiped their cartouches to activate their lights. As they looked around the room and slowly calmed down to breathe normally with the strange aqualung spell, they saw a long, completely water-filled narrow corridor descending into darkness ahead.

"OK, everybody stay together and swim carefully," Akiiki instructed over their mind-link. Swimming along the downhill slope while still holding hands proved to be very difficult, and soon everyone was quite tired and they made little progress.

"Hey Syd, I have an idea," Marc said over mind-link. "Use gecko-hands to pull ourselves down the wall – that will be easier than swimming at this weird angle."

"Great idea, replied Sydney, activating her cartouche. Her hands did not look any different but as she touched the wall, her hand stuck like glue and she was easily able to pull herself and Asim down along the wall, releasing and repositioning her hand. She looked back over her shoulder and saw Marc and Akiiki also making excellent progress behind her in the same way.

"Thanks, this is much better," Asim mind-linked to Sydney, as she returned a smile in the dimly lit corridor.

Even with the magical assistance, it took them several minutes to reach the bottom of the long corridor. When they finally reached the end, they could see a chamber above them through a glowing shimmer shield hatch in the ceiling. Akiiki tried to push through the shield with her cartouche hand but it held firmly in place. "How do we get up there?" she mind-linked.

"Stack hands again," instructed Asim. It was a little more difficult to do underwater since they could not let go of their breathing partner, so they stacked hands in pairs. They were instantly ejected upwards into the chamber above, everyone landing on their feet and somehow totally dry. The shimmer shield was now on the floor beside them. Akiiki let go of Marc's hand and stepped on it experimentally, but it was solid once again. They all took deep breaths of the stagnant air, which was still preferable to the strange aqualung spell.

"Wow, that was amazing, but it feels great to breathe normally again," Marc said.

"Not as amazing as where we are," replied Asim, brightening his cartouche light to give a better view of their surroundings. "This place is incredible!" They all looked around completely awestruck. As their eyes grew accustomed to the bright light, they saw that they were in a fairly small chamber which was stacked high with treasures of every imaginable variety, size, shape, and color.

"WOW. I wonder how the Knights Templar managed to collect all this stuff, since they suffered so many crushing defeats in their misguided Crusades?" Marc asked, as everyone looked around in amazement. "Hey, how do you activate the cartouche light?" Marc asked Akiiki excitedly. "I want to take a closer look around."

"Oh yeah – sorry," replied Akiiki. "You swipe down and then think 'torch', and then think what brightness setting you want. Just don't think 'full blast' or 'brightest' because it will be absolutely blinding." Marc and Sydney both activated their lights on low and then they spread out to start exploring the small chamber.

"Wow, after a lifetime of searching I have finally found it!" declared Marc almost immediately.

"Found what?" Sydney asked excitedly.

"I finally found a place that is messier than your room!" Marc declared, laughing hysterically.

"Ha ha, very funny!" replied Sydney irritably, sticking her tongue out at him. "But I think you may be right, this looks like a treasure garbage dump." They were immediately able to locate the "big three" treasures they were searching for which were isolated in the center of the room on an ancient wooden table. But all around the walls, other treasures were just stacked in precarious piles on shelves or more tables, with not even a square inch of the actual walls visible, and barely any space for them to squeeze into to explore. It totally reminded Sydney of their kitchen pantry, which had once had a sense of organization but had since been defeated by years of the family just hurriedly shoving items in wherever they would fit. Every now and then Mom and Dad would do a "pantry purge" to throw out expired or undesirable items, but that obviously had never been done in this chamber.

"Wow, this totally reminds me of the Room of Requirement or the Gringott's Lestrange vault from Harry Potter," Akiiki declared in awe. "It looks like the Knights Templar spent many years just stockpiling all their greatest treasures in here haphazardly. I'm glad they left our three treasures in the center, otherwise it would take us forever to dig through all this treasure."

"Yeah, you guys grab your cartouche bracelets while I have a quick look around," Marc instructed. The others gathered around the central table to start the search, but just as Mr. P had said, the bracelets were right on top of the big three treasures. They each spread out to inspect their assigned treasure.

Akiiki's artifact, the Ark of the Covenant, was the largest of the three and was placed in the exact center of the vault. It was absolutely breathtaking to behold, a solid gold chest with four short legs, intricately beautiful panel decorations, two long wooden carrying poles, and an exquisite ornate golden top with two angels facing each other with outstretched wings. Her cartouche bracelet was hanging on the angel's wings so she very gently lifted it off and placed it on her wrist, as Asim and Sydney watched nervously. Instantly it shimmered and then cloaked into disappearance. "Weird, I can't see it, but I can still feel it on my wrist," she whispered, feeling around the edges of the bracelet.

"Hmm, papyrus scrolls, Inca gold, a kingly sword with a broken blade, Shakespeare manuscripts bound in leather..." Marc whispered to himself behind them as he explored the treasure-filled walls.

"OK my turn," said Sydney, reaching for the rough, non-descript goblet which had a shiny golden interior cup surface. "A humble cup for a humble carpenter," she whispered as she found her cartouche bracelet inside and placed it on her right wrist. It immediately cloaked itself just as Akiiki's had done seconds ago. "Um, is it just my imagination, or do the Ark and Grail look EXACTLY like the ones from the Indiana Jones movies?"

"Yeah, the props master was probably a Templar Knight," laughed Asim.

"Or maybe he borrowed the originals out of here to shoot the movies," Akiiki giggled.

Marc was continuing his inspection behind them, excitedly talking to himself. "Old books – I can't read the titles but man - they look ancient, I swear those look like Marie Antoinette's lost jewels, Spanish pieces of eight, Greek and Roman scrolls, a gold and silver mechanical owl, a pirate compass, does that book say King Solomon?, a bust of Alexander the Great…"

Asim stood beside the large Menorah from the Jerusalem Temple, which was solid gold and stood over five feet high. The Menorah had six delicate rounded branches curving out from the central post with a total of seven lamps at the top, each shaped like an almond flower with ornate buds and blossoms. The two-layer stepped base was hexagonal and also made from solid gold, with lovely almond-themed carvings to match the lamps. Asim carefully retrieved his assigned cartouche bracelet which was hanging from the central lamp, placed it on his wrist and watched it shimmer-cloak into nothingness. "Cool," he exclaimed as he felt the invisible outline of the bracelet on his wrist.

"A bunch of silver Athenian Owl tetradrachms, Ming Dynasty vases, Samurai armor, a Viking sword, a bust of Nefertiti, small Egyptian obelisks, a smooth golden ring – hmm that one looks familiar, a Pegasus helm…" Marc continued his narrative as he explored. "Guys, you retrieved your new bling, now come on - check this stuff out with me!"

Suddenly they all heard Mr. P's voice in their minds. "Hurry up in there, we've got lots of company arriving! Fantastic - plus the big guy is here now, oh this is just great."

"Asim – move the Temple Menorah to the east by five feet, as Ankhesenamun instructed," yelled Akiiki. "We can't leave until it is moved, otherwise it will be destroyed." Asim struggled to move the heavy Menorah per her directions, but it took precious seconds since his attempt at levitation was blocked in the vault.

"Hurry up, come on!" Marc exclaimed when it was safely moved. "Everybody stand on the hatch and stack hands!" They all moved quickly to get back to the hatch and stand in a tight circle.

"Who's the 'big guy' I wonder?" asked Asim as he put his hand on top of the stack, dropping everyone through the shimmer shield and back into the water. The retraced their awkward swim which was far easier moving up the passageway as quickly as they could using the aqualung spells and then assembled hurriedly under the exit hatch.

"OK, everybody be ready with shields and weapons, we don't know what's up there," instructed Marc. "And be careful. Stack hands on three..."

They were expelled through the hatch back to the surface in a smooth arc, each landing gracefully on their feet with shimmer shields up, facing one of the four compass directions. They were completely unprepared for what they saw. A huge shimmer shield bubble as big as a house was overhead, easily containing all of them and the hatch under its protection. The entire top surface of the bubble was crawling with green scarab beetles, and they could see packs of jackals wandering around the edges searching for openings, along with several pirate zombies who had risen up out of the shipwreck swamp.

"Oh man, Mr. P makes it looks so easy," Sydney exclaimed, admiring the giant shimmer shield.

"Well, he's been practicing for what? 3,400 years?" Marc replied.

"Hey, a little help here?" Mr. P called breathlessly. They all turned to see Mr. P in the center of the shimmer dome, whacking at three Egyptian Cobras with his sword while obviously struggling to keep the dome in place. Marc incinerated the snakes with a massive green fireball, which parted gracefully to pass around Mr. P.

"Thanks, Marc," said Mr. P, moaning painfully. "They burrowed under my shield and one of them got me before I saw them. I can't hold this shimmer dome much longer, you guys need to get ready. Prepare ... your ... attacks. Reinforcements are coming, you just have to ... hold them off." Mr. P was obviously fading fast from the Cobra venom.

"Crap, I hate snakes! Why did it have to be snakes!" screamed Sydney, looking around for more nervously and conjuring her bow. "Oh, and don't let those beetles bite you – they will knock you out cold, believe me, I remember," she said, rubbing her old neck bite in painful recollection.

"Um, friends, I think I found the big guy," Akiiki said fearfully. "Look!" she screamed, pointing off to their south. They could see a giant twenty foot tall humanoid shape with a head of a black Jackal, walking around the base of the shimmer dome and attacking it with lightning strikes from his black, fiercely clawed hands.

"Oh great, it's Anubis!" yelled Asim. "He's a little hard to miss!"

"The bigger they are, the harder they fall," yelled Sydney fearlessly. "I've got my bow, you guys ready your weapons, the shimmer dome is starting to fade." Marc quickly crafted several hundred beetle bombs and stacked them into a large pyramid with his powers.

"What are those?" Akiiki asked curiously.

"These are beetle bombs, when the shield drops, you can levitate them out in all directions and then trigger them to explode at the same time," Marc quickly instructed. "I didn't have time to take off the human protection clause, so they won't hurt us but they also won't work on those pirate zombies."

"OK, got it!" Akiiki replied.

"Asim, I want to try a combo attack by combining our powers," Marc said, turning to Asim. "Make a bunch of those whirlwind sandstorms circle the dome base and I'll fill them with fireballs to wipe out everything else."

"Yep, I'm on it," Asim replied, swiping his cartouche and concentrating his powers.

"I can't ... hold it ... any longer, guys. Sorry..." moaned Mr. P as the shimmer dome blinked out. Immediately all the beetles and jackals came swarming in toward them.

"NOW!" yelled Marc. Sydney let loose with her bow taking out the closest pack of approaching jackals and pirate zombies, while Akiiki instantly spread the beetle bombs which burst into a massive, deafening explosion. While that faded, Asim and Marc sent several giant fire/sand whirlwinds spinning around the outside perimeter of the old dome base, throwing out globs of molten glass and incinerating everything in their path.

At that moment, four cartouche warriors teleported in, one blinking into existence protectively beside each of the twins. Tutankhamun and Ankhesenamun appeared next to Marc and Sydney, while a handsome man in revolutionary garb with a ponytail blinked into place beside Akiiki. Another young man with black hair and a mustache dressed a bit like Indiana Jones appeared beside Asim.

As soon as he caught sight of them, the giant Anubis charged at the group angrily. "Ankhesenamun, get Paatenemheb out of here before he dies in this plane!" Tutankhamun yelled urgently. She ran to Mr. P and they both instantly blinked out of existence. "Shields up!" yelled Tutankhamun to the other two warriors, who restored the shimmer dome just as Anubis hit the boundary. He tried to force his clawed hands through the shield, which bent inwards but held firm. He roared in frustration and started slowly pacing the perimeter, staring at them all fiercely while nonchalantly patting out a molten glass fire burning on his arm.

"Hello again, Anubis my friend," said the pony-tailed warrior. "You picked a glorious day for a battle."

"Hello Thomas, my presidential friend," replied Anubis sarcastically. "I just couldn't resist capturing so many cartouche bracelets in a single easy stroke," he chuckled evilly.

"Hmm, you and what army? It appears that all of yours has been reduced to ashes," taunted the other cartouche warrior with the mustache.

"It is no matter, Howard my friend, I can always summon more if I need them," Anubis replied. "But a mighty God of Egypt against seven mere mortals – four of them babies – you don't stand a chance against my wrath. Hand over the Asim bracelets, all of them, and I may spare you. Otherwise I will just remove the bracelets from your dead arms – I care not. Your fight is useless. Resistance is futile." The four twins looked at each other cautiously – none of them had ever been trolled by a God before and they did not quite know how to respond.

"We politely decline," Tutankhamun replied fiercely. "The Four have been assembled and now fight with us. Your days are now numbered."

"Oh yes, the mighty Four that Isis is always babbling on about. Sydney, Marc, Akiiki and of course the namesake Asim." Anubis stared at each of them creepily as he said their names, as if he were carefully memorizing their faces. "Excuse me if I'm not impressed, what a waste of bracelets," he laughed.

Sydney's hands moved in a flash and before they knew it, three arrows were sticking out of Anubis' nose and he roared in pain and anger.

"Whoops, sorry about that Anubis - just a reflex reaction," yelled Sydney fiercely. "I don't like dogs, especially big ugly ones who talk too much. Hmmm, I guess I'm just more of a cat person. Say hello to my home-girl Bastet for me." Anubis pulled the arrows out of his nose gingerly and stared at Sydney in absolute unbridled fury.

"Be careful, Syd," Akiiki group mind-linked to her.

"Nice shot," mind-linked Tutankhamun.

"How did you get them through the shimmer shield?" asked Marc curiously.

"Well, I made micro-holes in the shield ahead of them, obviously," she replied over the mind-link.

"Brilliant," Asim replied admiringly.

Anubis quickly regained his composure. "You will regret that young Sydney, be sure to say hello to Tyler and little Lucas for me – I'm sure I'll be seeing them both VERY soon," he snickered evilly. Sydney scowled back at him fiercely.

"OK guys, we need to teleport out of here quickly before any of his buddies show up," Tutankhamun instructed over the group mind-link. "We can't teleport through the shimmer shield, so we'll have to drop it first and then instantly teleport out together before Anubis can reach us. Just for extra cover as a precaution, the Four should conjure a nice parting gift for our dear big friend – I thoroughly enjoyed the fiery sandstorms – that should work nicely."

"OK, got it," everyone responded.

"Thomas, please teleport the girls; Howard, please teleport the boys. The twins all slowly and nonchalantly grabbed the arm of their assigned ride so as not to raise suspicion from Anubis. All at the same time, on my count. Three, two, one... NOW!"

Asim and Marc instantly launched a massive firestorm which enveloped the entire group as they felt themselves blinking away. But suddenly, Anubis' head rose through the flames with his clawed hand reaching for Sydney's cartouche arm. She twisted her body wildly, somehow maintaining contact with Thomas while shooting an explosive arrow directly into Anubis' right eye. He roared in pain and fury as the arrow exploded, spattering her side with Anubis goo as he struck out blindly with his talons, ripping deeply into the right side of her ribcage before she blinked out completely.

Chapter 22.   Promises

"Ankhesenamun, Sydney is hurt!" yelled Thomas, carefully supporting her with one arm as they blinked into Tutankhamun's afterlife plane. Ankhesenamun was just finishing her work on Mr. P and came running over quickly as the others arrived nearby. She hurriedly conjured a low couch and Akiiki helped Thomas lay Sydney carefully upon it. Sydney's shirt was shredded on her right side, with four wide gashes on her ribs oozing blood, and her entire right side covered with black bloody specks of Anubis goo.

"Hang in there, Syd," Marc said worriedly as he held her left hand tightly.

"Oh, I'm OK – it just stings a little," she replied bravely. "So can you heal me or are Anubis' claws poisonous?" she asked Ankhesenamun, who was busily cleaning her wounds.

"Well, to be honest we don't know," Ankhesenamun replied cautiously. "Nobody has ever survived one of his attacks, except for Tutankhamun when they fought for me in the Duat."

"Oh, great. Well, that's VERY reassuring," Sydney replied painfully.

"You'll be fine, Syd – it doesn't look that bad," Akiiki said as she was assisting Ankhesenamun. "Asim had a nasty bike crash once and it was much worse than this looks," glancing up worriedly at her brother.

"OK, now please remain as still as possible," Ankhesenamun said as she held her hands over Sydney's wounds. She began chanting quietly in a language they did not recognize, and her cartouche began to glow brightly, bathing Sydney's side with a blazing purple light.

"Oh, that tickles," said Sydney, immediately feeling the pain diminish to be slowly replaced with a warm glowing tingle.

"Shut up and hold still," Marc whispered. Sydney stuck out her tongue at him, as Ankhesenamun continued her work for several minutes.

"There, how does that feel?" Ankhesenamun asked.

"Much better, thanks," Sydney replied, stretching her arm upwards to test her side.

"I'm afraid you will have some faint scars from this," Ankhesenamun said as she gave Sydney's side a close inspection.

"That's OK – it was totally worth it!" Sydney replied fiercely.

"Oh crap - what is THAT?" Akiiki said worriedly, pointing at Sydney's shirt and startling everyone.

"Tutankhamun, we have a little complication," Ankhesenamun replied, the fear palpable in her quivering voice. All over Sydney's side, the black Anubis goo specks were slowly congregating together and taking shape before their eyes.

"Oh, that is TOTALLY disgusting," said Marc as Sydney began to panic.

"Holy crap – just tell me what is happening to me, you big doofus!" Sydney yelled at him.

"It appears that Ankhesenamun's healing has also reformed all the Anubis splatter that was all over your shirt," replied Tutankhamun. "Do you remember where you hit him with that explosive arrow?" he asked.

"Yeah, right in his eye exactly where I aimed, of course," Sydney replied confidently.

"I thought so," Tutankhamun replied, as everyone watched the grotesque spectacle before their eyes. Slowly the mass of oozing flesh began to take shape and formed itself into a large eye, surrounded by a black hairy eyebrow and parts of Anubis' cheekbone. "Mr. P, please fetch me a box quickly," he instructed as the healing process completed and the eye blinked at them angrily. "Are you well healed, my friend?" he asked Mr. P as he handed over a small wooden box with a hinged lid.

"Yes, of course I am fine, thanks to your beloved," Mr. P replied with a smile at Ankhesenamun. "But you must lock away the eye – it is probably still linked to the mind of Anubis who is surely quite angry right now."

Tutankhamun reached down carefully and pulled the eye up from Sydney's shirt, holding it aloft for all to see. "Wait, hang on a minute before you put it away. May I?" Sydney asked, gingerly grabbing the grotesque eye and turning it towards her face. She waved at it and blew it a big kiss, as everyone laughed in surprise. The pupil of the eye narrowed to a fierce vertical slit and the surrounding flesh seemed to scowl at her angrily.

"Too bad I didn't blast off his ear as well – I could have given him a nice verbal message too," Sydney said as she roughly dropped the gruesome eye into the box and Mr. P closed the lid.

"Mistress Sydney, you are either very brave or very foolish for taunting Anubis," Tutankhamun chuckled in surprise.

"Well, a little of both, obviously," she replied with a nervous laugh.

Asim looked at her sternly. "You need to be careful – it is not wise to mess with the Gods - they are quick to anger and have no patience with mortals." Sydney stared back at him curiously, missing the silent exchange between the ancient Egyptians.

"Did any of Anubis' flesh or blood get into Sydney's wound?" Tutankhamun asked Ankhesenamun worriedly over mind-link.

"No, I cleaned her wound thoroughly, but I fear some of her blood may have mixed into Anubis' reformed eye," she replied worriedly over mind-link. "I was certainly not expecting that and have never seen anything like it before."

"We shall need to watch her carefully to be sure there is no contamination," Mr. P added via mind-link, as the three nodded. "And we must also consult Thoth to see what we should do with Anubis' captured eye in case it has now assimilated her blood. Right now we need to keep everyone calm."

"Well, Horus will LOVE this story!" exclaimed Tutankhamun loudly, capturing everyone's attention. "Set stole both of Horus' eyes many centuries ago and there was an epic battle between them before Horus was able to win them back."

Tutankhamun turned to Thomas and Howard. "Mr. Jefferson and Mr. Carter, thank you for answering my call and coming to our aid," he said, as they both bowed in return.

"It was our pleasure, no thanks are needed," replied Thomas.

"And it has been a great honor to fight with the Four," added Howard with a bow toward the twins.

"I am afraid I must ask you both for another favor," replied Tutankhamun guiltily.

"You have but to name it, old friend," replied Howard with a smile, as Thomas nodded in agreement.

"Can you return the twins to their homes safely for me, and keep a close watch on them along with your mortal and afterlife cartouche allies?" Tutankhamun asked seriously. "I fear that Anubis will be seeking a swift and brutal revenge, and I will need you to cloak the twins and their families and friends from his spies."

"Of course, it would be a great honor," replied Thomas with a smile. "My old revolutionary friends have been looking forward to another glorious mission. And I will warn the mortal warrior musician friends of Charlottesville on the material plane."

"The Egyptologists will protect Cairo and her twins, as always, my friend," replied Howard warmly. "And I will warn Zahi, Tarek, Evelyn and the other mortal Egyptian warriors."

"You both have my eternal thanks," replied Tutankhamun, bowing low.

Tutankhamun now turned to the twins. "Sydney, Akiiki, and Asim – your cartouches will cloak and protect the extra bracelets you are guarding. They cannot be harmed by anything on your earth. You must now seek out the chosen warriors for your foster bracelets – when you find them, they will be revealed by a blue Asim cartouche floating above their heads. When you see this sign, your bracelets can be released and you can deliver them to their new warriors and share your instruction manuals. Do you understand?"

"Yes," they all replied simultaneously.

"However, we cannot foresee how long it may take you to find their matches, so be patient," Ankhesenamun added. "Sometimes the search may take many years but you must be ever vigilant."

"Marc, I have another mission for you, Thomas, and Sydney after your return home," Tutankhamun continued. "Your presence has now been revealed in Charlottesville and I fear Thomas' cartouche bracelet in his Monticello home will now be in danger. Several artifacts have already been stolen from there over the years by servants of Anubis, but I fear their search may now be redoubled after our victory today."

"So that's what happened to your first Great Pyramid of Cheops!" Akiiki exclaimed, looking over at Thomas.

"Yes, it was the most obvious sign of my connection with Egypt, but as you know, luckily I selected a more subtle artifact to serve as the guardian of my bracelet," Thomas replied.

"Yes, your rotating book stand," Sydney exclaimed. "Marc and I saw it when we visited with Akiiki!"

"Exactly," Thomas replied. "One of my favorite inventions, I must say. I still use it every day in my afterlife Monticello," he added with a wide grin. "Now the original is slightly repurposed for an even greater mission," he chuckled.

"Marc, Thomas' bracelet shall be your responsibility," Tutankhamun instructed. "Mr. P and Thomas will contact you in a few weeks when the plans have been set, so be ready."

"What about the cartouche bracelet in the cat mummy at the Smithsonian?" Marc asked, as Akiiki listened with keen interest, now piecing together some of her strange experiences during her recent visit with the twins.

"Oh, that one is WELL guarded," laughed Howard. "The other mummies on display there are all guardians of the cartouche and will spring to life to protect it if threatened. The crocodile and bull are particularly grumpy and vicious when awakened, so I pity the fools that choose to face their wrath. Plus I'm sure you noticed Rick, the burly museum guard?" he asked.

"Oh yeah, I remember – he gave us the evil eye when we lingered too long near the mummy," Sydney replied. "I suppose he is a cartouche warrior as well?" she asked excitedly.

"Yes, one of our finest," Mr. P replied. "Special Forces, you might call him. And there are many others nearby in Washington DC who can instantly provide backup if needed."

"Mr. P, Howard, or Thomas will be bringing you all back here for training every few weeks, so that the Four can hone your skills together and work cohesively as a team," Tutankhamun explained. "And I am making arrangements for your families this summer so that you can all be together on an exciting new mission," he added, smiling at Marc and Akiiki who were nearly jumping for joy as they listened intently and stared excitedly at one another. "I'm sure you will all enjoy Italy very much."

The cat Mr. P ran over to Sydney's leg and stared up at her intently. She touched the falcon and owl on her cartouche so they could communicate. "Please, can you take me back to live with Lucas? I have grown quite fond of him and can help to keep him safe," Mr. P mind-meowed as Sydney mind-forwarded his question to the others.

"That would be fantastic," she replied. "We would love to have you live with us for as long as you like. We would all be honored to have you join us." Mr. P meowed appreciatively.

"And you two need to read your instruction manuals," Paatenemheb scolded both Marc and Sydney with a fierce scowl.

'Yes sir," they both laughed. "We'll get those scans from Dad and start studying right away!" Marc added.

"It has been a long day and a glorious battle. Are you ready to return home now?" Tutankhamun asked them all kindly, as the twins stared at each other with wide smiles of joy.

"Oh no, please wait," Akiiki exclaimed. "I nearly forgot in all the excitement! In his letter, Lucas said I was supposed to do something first!" She immediately ran to Marc and kissed him fiercely, knocking them both stumbling backwards but with their lips never parting. As everyone woo-hooed, a few seconds later they released each other and stood holding hands, both visibly wobbly on their feet but supporting each other happily.

"OH MY. I take back everything bad I ever said about Lucas," Marc said breathlessly. "Akiiki, I love you and I should have told you long ago," he added, staring deep into her gorgeous green eyes.

"I know," Akiiki replied, pausing dramatically. "I love you too," she added with a dazzling smile, as Sydney began crying tears of joy.

"FINALLY!" yelled Ankhesenamun, startling everyone. "Oh thank Hathor and Isis! You two were taking FOREVER to fulfill your romantic destiny." She ran over and hugged Akiiki and Marc tightly, totally catching them by surprise as they awkwardly returned her hug, both still stunned and reeling from their first kiss.

"Oh Akiiki, thank you for inviting me to your wedding – you were so stunningly beautiful and your dress was simply breathtakingly exquisite, if I do say so myself," Ankhesenamun said proudly. "One of my best creations, I must say. And Marc, you were so handsome in your tuxedo and it was just such a glorious and splendid day for both happy families. Oh, and your children are so darling, and they will become the mightiest…"

"AHEM," Tutankhamun interrupted as Marc and Sydney stared at Ankhesenamun and each other in shock and joy. "Ankhesenamun my love, they are still mortals, do not spoil their adventure," he scolded with a smile.

"But Tutankhamun my love, Isis has already woven their fates and I have seen," she replied, bubbling with excitement. She now turned to Sydney and Asim whose eyes grew wide in fear. "And YOUR children! They too shall be the mightiest of the mighty and shall rule…"

"AHEM," Tutankhamun interrupted again, now laughing. "You are doing it again, my love."

"Whoops, sorry," she replied, still overjoyed and obviously flustered. "I'm just so excited. The Prophecy of the Four says the sons and daughters of the four Asim twins shall have special power above all others," she said with a smile at the shocked twins. "You ALL have a wonderful adventure ahead," she concluded with a low bow.

Marc and Akiiki were now staring at each other intensely, overcome with joy that they would now be together and reeling in happiness from their revealed destinies. Suddenly Marc gave her a mischievous grin, which she returned suspiciously. "Well, since it has already been foretold and we have already wasted enough precious time," he said, releasing one of Akiiki's hands and dropping to one knee. He stared at his free hand in deep concentration and quickly closed it tightly when a bright flash appeared.

"Marc, what are you doing?" yelled both Sydney and Asim, his crazy plan suddenly dawning on both of them as they slowly recovered their senses.

The eyes of both Akiiki and Marc were now locked together as she waited intently, tears of joy now forming in her eyes. "I know we are young, but I love you with all my heart forever and want to spend the rest of my life with you - will you marry me?" he asked, placing a shining golden ring on her right ring finger.

"Yes," she replied happily, staring at the beautiful ring, which had a large center diamond with their names written in intricate golden cartouches on either side. It was absolutely breathtaking. Sydney and Ankhesenamun had now started crying in earnest, while Asim and the other males were still completely lost in shock.

As Marc released her right hand and stood up, she closed her free hand tightly and concentrated for a long moment. Akiiki then dropped gracefully to one knee. "It is our tradition that my beloved also receives an engagement ring," she said sweetly as she slid a matching silver ring onto his trembling right ring finger. "This ring symbolizes an eternal unbroken love that has no beginning and no end, as is my love for you. Will you marry ME?" she asked with a dazzling smile and flash of her gorgeous green eyes.

"Yes," Marc declared immediately, pulling her up into his arms for another long kiss as everyone now cheered happily.

"I am so happy for you two, I have been trying to get you together for ages," Sydney wailed loudly in joy. Akiiki and Marc now stared at Sydney and Asim happily.

"Tutankhamun, can you marry us?" Marc asked excitedly.

Tutankhamun started laughing. "No, I do not have that power, but I suppose I could summon a priest," he added thoughtfully, smiling at Ankhesenamun.

Akiiki quickly grabbed Marc's hand. "HELLO – beautiful wedding dress - remember?" she asked him intently, pointing to her now tattered, bloody, and dingy clothes.

"Oh yeah, I guess we should wait, huh?" he asked her sheepishly as she grinned back widely.

"I think that would be wise, your families would be sorely disappointed if you did not," Ankhesenamun answered, now laughing uproariously. "Wedding ceremonies are an important spectacle and a glorious celebration of your everlasting love."

"Mortals – always in a hurry!" chuckled Mr. P.

"I truly hate to disrupt this glorious moment, but the twins must return to your homes," Tutankhamun said sadly. "You have been gone for a long while and your families will be worried. Thomas and Howard, can you take them home please? Mr. P will be your backup."

"It will be our great pleasure," Howard replied.

"We are all so happy for you – true love is such a beautiful thing," Thomas added blissfully. "Personally, my luck in love was quite poor, as I lost several loved ones far too early during my lifetime. But my afterlife reunited with my wife Martha and all our children and grandchildren has been amazing. I wish you both the best."

Marc and Akiiki enjoyed another long kiss of farewell, and promised to mind-link each other as soon as they returned home. A few short moments later, everyone teleported away, leaving Tutankhamun and Ankhesenamun alone holding hands.

"You know, you really should stop your meddling," Tutankhamun said. "Hathor and Isis will be upset that you are doing all their work," he chuckled.

"I just can't help it - you know I'm a hopeless romantic," Ankhesenamun replied. "Besides, today was the first engagement day that was foretold in the Prophecy of the Four - I only gave them a little nudge."

"Hmm, yes I remember when you nudged me – I think I still have the scars somewhere," he replied, looking himself over playfully.

Ankhesenamun stuck out her tongue at him. "Be nice or I will nudge you again," she threatened with a smile.

"I did like the rings – did you meddle there as well?" he asked.

"Oh no - both rings were conjured from their love - I had nothing to do with it," she replied. "But they were absolutely perfect. I am glad to see the tradition we started in ancient Egypt still lives on – the giving of rings is our most beautiful and lasting legacy," she added wistfully.

"Yes, they are a wonderful symbolism of everlasting love like ours," Tutankhamun replied. "So when is their blessed wedding day, my lovely apprentice of Isis and Hathor?" he laughed.

"Hey, sometimes a girl needs a little hobby!" Ankhesenamun giggled back at him. "Their wedding is not for another four years, on a gorgeous sunny day in early June," she answered wistfully. "So they have plenty of time, but the next few weeks are going to very interesting when their families discover the rings," she laughed. "But their love and devotion is strong and forever unwavering, so they will be just fine soon enough."

"Yes, it will be very interesting to watch, indeed," laughed Tutankhamun. "I'm sure their parents will be quite shocked about making such a serious commitment at their young age; I certainly can't imagine how that would feel with our daughters," he added thoughtfully.

"Hmmm, yes I agree completely. Where are they, anyway?" Ankhesenamun asked, looking around. "I haven't seen them since this morning when Mom stopped by."

"They are both down by the Nile playing with Nefertiti, I can hear them laughing from here," Tutankhamun replied. "We should definitely introduce them to the twins next time."

"Yes, that would be very nice," she replied.

"You know - I think you scared Sydney very badly today with your Isis vision," Tutankhamun said, placing his arm around her waist.

"Yes, I think both she and Asim were a bit shocked, I got carried away in all the excitement and probably should not have said anything," Ankhesenamun reflected guiltily. "Sydney's future is not as clear as that of Marc and Akiiki; she has some difficult choices to make very soon and she must let her heart be her guide. The faces of her children will keep changing in my visions until she finally decides," she added worriedly.

They both stared after the twins, lost in thought as they stood together in silence for several long moments. "Well, the end has now begun, my love," Ankhesenamun said wistfully.

"Yes, the tides are finally turning in our favor after all these many centuries," Tutankhamun replied. "Shall we deliver Sydney's present to Horus? I think he will be very interested to see it, and it to see him as well, perhaps."

Mr. P had already said farewell once the coast was clear, and then had teleported to Egypt to guard Howard and the twins. Thomas was now walking Sydney and Marc down the road to their house. "Be cautious, but have no fear – my old friends and I will be keeping an eye on you," Thomas said kindly. "I will always be nearby if you need me – just call me over mind-link. Farewell for now, my friends." He gave each of them a long hug and then a salute before he teleported away.

"Hold still!" Sydney laughed, trying to put Mr. P's collar back on as he struggled to jump out of Marc's arms as they reached the end of their driveway. "You know Marc - you amaze me, a few weeks ago you couldn't even tell Akiiki you love her and now you two are engaged?"

"Isis has already woven our fates together, so who am I do deny our glorious destiny of love?" Marc replied, still giddy with happiness and staring fondly at his silver engagement ring.

"Very funny," Sydney replied sarcastically. "Mom is going to FLIP."

"Which is exactly why we're not gonna tell her, duh!" Marc replied.

"Well I hate to burst your bubble but I think Mom and Marion are going to notice your fancy new rings fairly quickly," she laughed.

"No worries, we can just take them off until we're ready to break the news," Marc replied as he reached to remove the ring from his finger. He instantly yelped in pain and saw that his arm cartouche was glowing red. "Uh oh, maybe we can at least cloak them, then," he said, concentrating on the ring. He yelped again and received another red cartouche for his effort, the ring remaining firmly in place on his finger and completely visible. "OK, OK – I get it!" he said angrily to the cartouche, rubbing his throbbing arm gently. "I suppose I could just do a full body cloak around Mom and Dad, but they would probably quickly get suspicious of having an invisible son."

"Hmmm, maybe SOME promises are not meant to be hidden," laughed Sydney.

"Oh crap - you're right, this will be tricky," Marc replied, his confidence now suddenly shaken. "Maybe we'll call them friendship rings?"

"Well, most friendship rings don't have a giant diamond like Akiiki's and yours – I see you two didn't think this through very far, huh?" she asked.

"Maybe not, but Isis and Hathor will guide our way," he replied with a chuckle.

"I think traditionally you are supposed to ask her father for permission first, too, before you ask her," Sydney laughed. "She'll probably get into a lot of trouble for this crazy little plan of yours!"

"Whoops, I totally forgot about that part," Marc replied. "Sallah is cool though, so I think he and Marion will be OK with it after the initial shock - as long as we take our time. And you have to cut me some slack – this is my first marriage proposal, you know! You're the one who is always telling me to be spontaneous in love, anyway! So this is all partly your fault!"

"OK fine - I can accept that," Sydney laughed. "Well, no matter what, I'm truly happy for you both, brother," she said joyfully. "Mom told me once that she instantly knew she and Dad were meant to be together, just like magic. It must be the same for you two."

"Yes, I have never felt more strongly about anything in my life," Marc replied.

"And I know she has been in love with you from the first time you met - I could see it so obviously in Egypt but you didn't have a clue until the slumber party, you big doofus," scolded Sydney.

"Well, I'm not very good at all of this romance stuff," Marc replied, chuckling. "You may need to help me for a while, oh mighty matchmaker."

"No problem – I still owe you for helping me with Tyler. I never would have made it through without you," Sydney replied seriously. "And overall you did just fine with Akiiki after you finally clued in, brother. But now I'm really worried - what do you think Ankhesenamun meant about Asim and I?" Sydney asked fearfully. "I don't know what that means for Tyler. Asim is like a brother to me - that is all. And we're apparently having kids together?"

"Well, just ask her about it next time we see her," Marc replied. "There is no sense in worrying about it. Honestly, I really like her but she TOTALLY creeps me out with her future visions from Isis, but we both owe Ankhesenamun our eternal thanks for saving your life. She and Akiiki both lied to you Syd – your wounds from Anubis were REALLY bad. I'm pretty sure you would have died if it had not been for her healing gift," he added as he looked at Sydney fearfully.

"Yeah, I know," replied Sydney. "I could totally see the fear in Akiiki's eyes when they were both working on me. I just hope it finishes healing OK on its own, something feels a little off inside," she added worriedly as they entered their front door. "We've definitely gotten ourselves into some serious danger with these cartouches, but I still think it is totally worth it."

Marc nodded in agreement. "Yep, I'm ALL in too. I totally owe Anubis a big payback for attacking you, and I can't WAIT to give it to him," he added, smacking his fist into the palm of his other hand. Sydney chuckled and gave Marc an enthusiastic fist-bump.

They found Lucas on the front couch, anxiously awaiting their return. Mr. P immediately squirmed wildly and meowed loudly so Marc released him to scamper happily into Lucas' lap. "Oh guys, thank you so much – I can never repay you," Lucas said tearfully. "I know I'm mean sometimes but I'm really sorry and I love you guys – you know that, right?"

"Yeah dude, no problem," Marc replied. "We've both been pretty awful to you too and we're so sorry as well. Let's call an official truce, ok? We love you too, and I owe you BIG TIME for that letter you wrote to Akiiki," he added.

"Yeah, deal - I'm totally down with a truce. And I know you and Akiiki are in love, and maybe someday she will be my sister – that would be really cool with me," Lucas replied excitedly as Marc gave him a big hug.

"Thanks, that means a lot to me, little brother," Marc replied.

"Oh, wait a minute - nice engagement ring!" Lucas said mischievously as he spied the shiny silver ring on Marc's finger. "Looks like my plan worked even better than I thought it would. How did you two manage that? You haven't seen each other in weeks."

"Um, we exchanged them by mail, but PLEASE let me handle it with Mom," Marc said nervously.

"No worries, I can keep a secret for you and your muuuchhaaass smmooocchhaass BELOVED," he snickered. "What's up with Syd?" Lucas asked, looking at her curiously as she stared back at him robotically. Marc shrugged his shoulders.

"Syd, what's wrong with you?" Marc said over mind-link, now getting very worried. "You haven't said a word since we got home. Are you OK?"

"It's Lucas – we have a problem," Sydney replied mechanically over their mind-link, pointing at Lucas.

"Well, snap out of it and show me," Marc replied. "I don't see anything."

"Here, look through my eyes," she replied weakly, sending him the image that now haunted her vision and had paralyzed her mind. A large glowing blue Asim cartouche was floating over Lucas' head. Sydney's Oak Island cartouche bracelet was destined for him.

"Oh, holy crap, you have GOT to be kidding me," was all that Marc could say in response.

Join the Four on their next adventure:

CARTOUCHE CHRONICLES 2: PURSUIT IN POMPEII

Live out your own Cartouche Chronicles adventures!

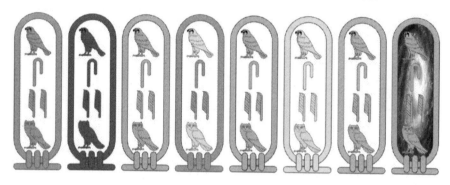

Awesome cartouche stickers and temporary tattoos in assorted colors (for different powers) available ONLY on my official website at:

www.cartouchechronicles.com

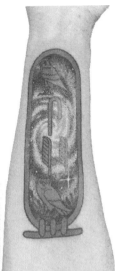

About the Author

Eric Cutright's "real job" is being a safety consultant and safety assessor for the rail and mass transit industry, both designing systems and performing detailed hardware and software safety analyses on advanced computer-based train control systems such as Communications Based Train Control (CBTC) for the NYCT Metro in New York City and various Positive Train Control (PTC) systems for the US rail industry. He was a co-founder of Rail Safety Consulting (now part of TUV Rheinland) and holds a BS, MS, and PhD in Electrical Engineering (EE) from the University of Virginia. Eric was also just one pesky class away from an undergraduate minor in Archaeology at the University of Virginia (summer fieldwork that would have been AMAZING but would simply not fit into his EE summer research schedule). He is also now proudly serving as the Scoutmaster for Scouts BSA Troop 1028 in Charlottesville, Virginia – a truly remarkable group of young men, young women, siblings, and parents.

Eric's fondest career wish is to have writing more Cartouche Chronicles become his "real job," and to inspire young readers to ditch their device screens every now and then to experience the joy of reading books just for fun. There is also still so much we can learn from our fascinating past, so he hopes to foster more interest in the amazing world of archaeology all around us. He dreams someday of having a heroic action figure made of him (with some cool accessories) for his inspiring and often challenging and underappreciated role as "bad joke Dad" in the Cartouche Chronicles.

Eric lives in Charlottesville, Virginia, with his lovely wife Marsha, four amazing and ever-entertaining teenage boys Kyle, Marc, Luke, and Eagle Scout Alec, two cats Yoda and Elle (just like in the books), crazy little demo-dog Luna, and an ever-changing variety of other critters (e.g. snakes, turtles, newts, dragons, and frogs) at any given time.

Check out his official Cartouche Chronicles series website and contact page at:

www.cartouchechronicles.com

References and Credits

Illustration Credits

Front Cover:

> Cartouche title and author artwork copyright Eric Cutright
>
> Original ASIM cartouche artwork copyright Eric Cutright
>
> All character photographs by Eric Cutright
>
> Author's cat Yoda
>
> Sydney's bow: Saluki Bow Company - Scythian Horn Bow
>
> Jewel beetle, family Buprestidae. Getty Images/Corbis
>> Documentary/Darrell Gulin
>
> Green fireball effect, www.youtube.com
>
> The Goonies Chunk costume by FUN costumes
>
> Goonies Team Chunk Tote Bag by CafePress
>
> Baby Ruth, Nerd, Laffy Taffy and Chunky candy by Nestle, 3 Musketeers
>> candy bar by Mars Chocolate
>
> Indiana Jones hat by Disney
>
> Stranger Things Eleven tube socks by Spirit Halloween, Netflix official
>> merchandise
>
> Egyptian papyrus crafted and pressed by Boy Scout Troop 1028 in
>> Charlottesville, VA during Eric's Archaeology Merit Badge class
>
> Mummy hand ground breaker (heavily customized) by Bristol Novelty
>
> Background: University of Virginia Cemetery, photograph by Eric Cutright

Inside Cover:

> Cartouche title and author artwork copyright Eric Cutright
>
> Tutankhamun Funerary Mask, Photoshop sample, Sandro Vannini
>
> 1 Discoveries – Tutankhamun Funerary Mask, Photoshop sample, Sandro
>> Vannini
>
> 2 GEM – Grand Egyptian Museum design artwork, Heng Pehang Architects
>
> 3 Humps – USA Today, Medioimages/Photodisc
>
> 4 Homecoming – Author's cats Yoda and Elle, photograph by Eric Cutright,
>> original Yoda and Elle cartouche artwork copyright Eric Cutright

5 Trouble – Original blue ASIM cartouche artwork copyright Eric Cutright

6 Champion – JUJU Athletics Elemental Red Fire Dodgeball, buy it on
www.amazon.com

7 Dreams – Tutankhamun's "Anubis the Dog" statue, original sculpture by The
Revival Art Company, UK, photograph by Eric Cutright

8 Crush - Original red ASIM cartouche artwork copyright Eric Cutright

9 Powers – Chewbacca bracelet: a ThinkGeek exclusive, original blue and
green ASIM cartouche artwork copyright Eric Cutright, photograph by
Eric Cutright

10 Visitors – Akiiki photograph by Robert Radifera Photography
(www.radifera.com), Charlottesville Airport (CHO) photograph by Eric
Cutright

11 Rematch – BoBin 3D Soccer and Fire PVC Wall Stickers Break through the
Wall Waterproof Removable Room Decals Murals Wall Poster, buy it on
www.amazon.com

12 Butterflies – Blue Seahorse, Carousel on the National Mall, Washington,
DC, picture from http://www.nationalcarousel.com/Album.htm

13 Tigers – Sumatran Tiger Damai, Smithsonian National Zoological Park, by
Mehgan Murphy, copyright Smithsonian Institution, 2011

14 Godzilla – Wilderness Systems Pamlico 145 Tandem Kayak (buy it on
www.austinkayak.com), Bending Branches paddle, Shark Teeth Mouth
Decal Stickers Kayak by weldecals (buy it on amazon.com),
Brontosaurus by Douglas, My Little Pony by Aurora World, author's cat
Elle, photograph by Eric Cutright

15 Monticello - Thomas Jefferson replica bookstand, made by Eric Cutright,
photograph by Eric Cutright, Original ASIM cartouche artwork copyright
Eric Cutright, learn more about Monticello at www.monticello.org

16 Spies –Jewel beetle, family Buprestidae. Getty Images/Corbis
Documentary/Darrell Gulin

17 Training – Marc and Sydney at Trout Pond, WV – Eric's favorite camping
area, photograph by Eric Cutright

18 Intervention - Original intervention artwork copyright Eric Cutright

19 Trap – Goonies Team Chunk Tote Bag by CafePress, Baby Ruth, Nerd, Laffy Taffy and Chunky candy by Nestle, 3 Musketeers candy bar by Mars Chocolate, photograph by Eric Cutright

20 Tutankhamun – Sun God Re', original sculpture by Veldon Simpson, Innerspace Luxor Las Vegas, 70/777, photograph by Eric Cutright

21 Island – Scale Indiana Jones Ark of the Covenant, Sideshow Collectibles, from https://www.sideshowtoy.com/collectibles/product-archive/?sku=400037&archive=y

22 Promises – Ramose and Wife, original sculpture by Veldon Simpson, Innerspace Luxor Las Vegas, 311/777, photograph by Eric Cutright

Author Picture:

Eric's ASM Galaxy Cartouche Tattoo by Ben Miller, Ben Around Tattoos, Charlottesville, VA, www.benaroundtattoos.com

Indiana Jones hat by Disney

Fake "for Dummies" book series artwork by Wiley

Stranger Things Action Figures by Funko

Jor El figure by LEGO

NYCT Subway Train model, NYCT Museum gift shop

Snowy Owl figurine by Pot Belly's

Egyptian Cubit measuring rule from British Museum

BB-8 lamps by ThinkGeek, Intertech

BB-8 robot by Sphero

Photograph by Marc Cutright

Thanks from Charlottesville – "Charlottesville VA We Are One" logo, original artwork copyright Eric Cutright

Back Cover:

Cartouche title artwork copyright Eric Cutright

Original ASIM and other cartouche artwork copyright Eric Cutright

All character photographs (except Akiiki) by Eric Cutright

Akiiki character photograph by Robert Radifera Photography (www.radifera.com)

Author's cats Elle and Yoda

Friend's dog Mia

Indiana Jones hat by Disney

Jewel beetle, family Buprestidae. Getty Images/Corbis
  Documentary/Darrell Gulin

Egyptian papyrus crafted and pressed by Boy Scout Troop 1028 in
  Charlottesville, VA during Eric's Archaeology Merit Badge class

Tutankhamun Funerary Mask, Photoshop sample, Sandro Vannini

Charlottesville VA We Are One logo, original artwork copyright Eric Cutright

Background: University of Virginia Cemetery, photograph by Eric Cutright

Pop Culture References

All pop culture references are copyright of their respective owners and are intended as a homage to my favorite influences. There are numerous "Easter eggs" buried for fun in this book just waiting for discovery by an attentive reader. Please refer to disclaimer at front of book for copyright usage under fair use act. Precise usages/themes are provided in parentheses:

Calvin and Hobbes (Moooochas Smooochas, dinosaur museum, tigers at zoo) – Copyright Bill Waterson (my all-time favorite comic strip)

Curse of Oak Island (Curse of Oak Island, Laginas) – Copyright History Channel

Dungeons and Dragons (Dungeons and Dragons) – Copyright Wizards of the Coast

Ghostbusters (Ghostbuster, Janine) – Copyright Columbia Pictures

Godzilla (Godzilla, Mothra, Rodan) – Copyright Toho Company

Harry Potter (Harry Potter, Harry Potter and the Order of the Phoenix, Luna Lovegood, Room of Requirement, Gringott's Lestrange vault) – Copyright J.K Rowling and Warner Brothers Entertainment

Indiana Jones and the Raiders of the Lost Ark (Sallah Mohammed Faisel el-Kahir, Marion, Indiana Jones, Ark of the Covenant, Holy Grail) – Copyright Walt Disney Company, Paramount Pictures

Legos (Lego), Copyright The Lego Group

Liverpool FC (Liverpool, Mohamed Salah, Premier League) – Copyright Liverpool FC and Premier League

National Geographic (National Geographic Magazine) – Copyright National Geographic

Netflix (Netflix) – Copyright Netflix

Nerf (Nerf gun, Nerf darts) – Copyright Hasbro

New England Patriots (Patriots, Tom Brady, Gronk) – Copyright National Football League, New England Patriots

Nintendo Switch (Switch, MarioKart) – Copyright Nintendo

Party of Five (party of five hidden Easter egg) – Copyright Columbia Pictures Television.

Pokémon (Pokémon cards) – Copyright Pokémon and Nintendo

Robot Chicken (Robot Chicken) – Copyright Nickelodeon Adult Swim

Rubik's Cube, Copyright Erno Rubik

Spiderman (Spidey sense) – Copyright Sony Pictures, Marvel Studios, and Disney

Star Trek (Star Trek, USS Enterprise, Captain Kirk, Spock, Resistance is futile) – Copyright CBS Studios, Paramount Pictures

Star Wars (Star Wars, Jedi Master Obi-wan, Rey, Padme, lightsabers, Yoda, Jedi Master Yoda, R2-D2, size matters not, laugh it up fuzzball, Han, Leia) – Copyright Walt Disney Company

Stranger Things (Stranger Things, Elle, Eleven, 011, Mike, Demo-gorgon, Demo-dog) – Copyright Netflix

Superman (Superman) – Copyright DC Comics

Teen Titans (Teen Titans) – Copyright Cartoon Network, Warner Brothers Entertainment, and DC Comics

The A-Team (I pity the fools) – Copyright NBC

The Fifth Element (The Fifth Element, Leeloo, variation on "me protect you") – Copyright Sony Pictures

The Goonies (The Goonies, Goonies Never Say Die, Chunk, Sloth, One-Eyed Willy, Truffle Shuffle) – Copyright Warner Brothers

The Greatest American Hero, TV show 1981-1983 (variation on powers without an instruction manual) – Copyright ABC

The Hobbit and The Lord of the Rings (Hobbit, Lord of the Rings, Bilbo, One Ring, Legolas, Gandalf, Balrog, Frodo, The Fellowship of the Ring, You cannot pass, Bridge of Khazad-dum, Lothlorien) – Copyright JRR Tolkien

The Mummy – 1999 Version (Evelyn, Rick) – Copyright Universal Pictures

Twilight series (Twilight, Bella, Edward, Jacob) – Copyright Stephenie Meyer

University of Virginia (University of Virginia, UVA) – Copyright Rector and Visitors of the University of Virginia

We Bought a Zoo (a few seconds of terror leading to true love) – Copyright Twentieth Century Fox.

Worms (Worms, Holy Hand Grenade) – Copyright Team17 Software Ltd

and of course my favorite Pittsburgh word – "nebby" (translation: nosy, prying, meddlesome)

Recommended Reading

Books on King Tutankhamun and Ancient Egypt

If you would like to learn more about King Tutankhamun or Ancient Egypt, here are some of my very favorite books on these topics:

Biesty, Stephen. (2005). *Egypt in Spectacular Cross-Section*. Italy: Scholastic.

Faulkner, Raymond. (1994). *The Egyptian Book of the Dead: The Book of Going Forth by Day*. San Francisco: Chronicle Books.

Freed, Rita. (1988). *Ramesses the Great*. Memphis: Boston Museum of Science.

Garolla, Federico. (1988). *The Egyptian Museum Turin*. Italy: Grafica – Gorgonzola.

Hawass, Zahi. (2000). *The Mysteries of Abu Simbel: Ramesses II and the Temples of the Rising Sun.* Egypt: The American University in Cairo Press.

Hawass, Zahi. (2003). *Secrets from the Sand: My Search for Egypt's Past*. New York: Harry N. Abrams Inc. Publishers.

Hawass, Zahi. (2004). *The Curse of the Pharaohs: My Adventures with Mummies*. Belgium: National Geographic Society.

Hawass, Zahi. (2004). *The Golden King: The World of Tutankhamun*. Washington DC: National Geographic Society.

Hawass, Zahi. (2005). *Tutankhamun and the Golden Age of the Pharaohs*. Washington DC: National Geographic Society.

Hawass, Zahi. (2005). *Tutankhamun – The Mystery of the Boy King*. Washington DC: National Geographic Society.

Hawass, Zahi and Lehner, Mark. (2017). *Giza and the Pyramids.* New York: Thames and Hudson.

Hobson, Christine. (1987). *The World of the Pharaohs: A Complete Guide to Ancient Egypt*. New York: Thames and Hudson.

Mascort, Maite. (March/April 2018). The Search for Tutankhamun. *National Geographic History, Volume 4, Number 1,* pp. 28-39.

Mayes, Stanley. (2003). *The Great Belzoni: The Circus Strongman who Discovered Egypt's Ancient Treasures*. New York: Tauris Parke Paperbacks.

Phillips, Graham. (2003). *Atlantis and the Ten Plagues of Egypt: The Secret History Hidden in the Valley of the Kings*. US: Bear and Company.

Reeves, Nicholas. (1990). *The Complete Tutankhamun: The King, The Tomb, The Royal Treasure*. New York: Thames and Hudson.

Siliotti, Alberto. (1997). *Guide to the Valley of the Kings*. Italy: Barnes and Noble Books.

Symonds, Matthew (December 2017/January 2018). How the Pyramids Built Egypt. *Current World Archaeology, Volume 8, Number 2*, pp. 24-29.

Tiradritti, Francesco. (2000). *Egyptian Treasures from the Egyptian Museum in Cairo*. Italy: White Star Publishers.

Ziegler, Christiane. (2002). *The Louvre Egyptian Antiquities*. Paris: Editions Scala.

Books on Archaeology

If you would like to learn more about archaeology in general, here are some of my very favorite books on archaeology (and potential clues to future *Cartouche Chronicle* settings). Note that many of these are older versions from my younger days, UVA archaeology classes, and museum tours so may be out of print, but there are many OTHER great books on archaeology for all levels of interest on www.amazon.com .

Anderson, R.G.W. (1998). *The British Museum*. London: British Museum Press.

Ashe, Geoffrey. (1987). *The Quest for Arthur's Britain*. US: Academy Chicago Publishers.

Biers, William. (1988). *The Archaeology of Greece: An Introduction*. US: Cornell Paperbacks.

Cassini, Silvia. (1998). *Pompeii*. Italy: Electa Napoli.

Clayton, Peter and Price, Martin. (1988). *The Seven Wonders of the Ancient World*. US: Dorset Press.

Coles, Byrony and John. (1989). *People of the Wetlands: Bogs, Bpdies, and Lake-Dwellers*. New York: Thames and Hudson.

Crump, Donald. (1986). *Splendors of the Past: Lost Cities of the Ancient World*. Washington DC: National Geographic Society.

De Franciscis, A. (1995). *Pompeii: Monuments Past and Present*, Italy: Vision Roma.

Deiss, Joseph Jay. (1985). *Herculaneum: Italy's Buried Treasure*. New York: Harper and Row.

Dickinson, Mary. (1994). *Wonders of the Ancient World: National Geographic Atlas of Archaeology*. Washington DC: National Geographic Society.

Fagan, Brian. (1985). *The Adventures of Archaeology*. Washington DC: National Geographic Society.

Gallenkamp, Charles. (1985). *Maya: The Riddle and Rediscovery of a Lost Civilization*. US: Viking Penguin Inc.

Grant, Michael. (1986). *Greece and Rome: The Birthplaces of Western Civilization*. New York: Bonanza Books.

Higgins, Reynold. (1997). *Minoan and Mycenaean Art*. London: Thames & Hudson.

Hobson, Christine. (1987). *The World of the Pharaohs: A Complete Guide to Ancient Egypt*. New York: Thames and Hudson.

Irlando, Antonio. (1997). *Pompeii: Everyday Life in the Town Buried by Mount Vesuvius 2000 Years Ago*. Italy: Casa Editrice Fortuna Augusta.

Kenyon, Kathleen. (1979). *Archaeology in the Holy Land*. New York: W.W. Norton and Company Inc.

Landels, J.G. (1978). *Engineering in the Ancient World*. US: University of California Press.

Lessing, Erich and Varone, Antonio. (1996). *Pompeii*. Italy: Terrail.

Macauley, David. (1979). *Motel of the Mysteries*. Boston: Houghton Mifflin Company.

MacDonald, David. (January 1965). Oak Island's Mysterious "Money Pit." *Reader's Digest*, pp. 136-140.

Marx, Robert and Jenifer. (2009). *The World's Richest Shipwrecks: A Wreck Diver's Guide to Gold and Silver Treasures of the Seas*. US: RAM Books.

Matz, Erling. *Vasa: 1628*. Stockholm: The Vasa Museum.

McIntosh, Jane. (1988). *The Practical Archaeologist: How we know what we know about the past*. New York: Facts on File Publications.

Metraux, Alfred. (1970). *The History of the Incas*. US: Random House.

Panetta, Marisa. (2004). *Pompeii: The History, Life, and Art of the Buried City*. Italy: White Star Publishers.

Sullivan, Robert. (2015). *Secrets of the Ancient World: Antiquity's Most Intriguing and Enduring Mysteries*. New York: Time/Life Books.

Thomas, David. (1979). *Archaeology*. New York: Holt, Rinehart and Winston.

Throckmorton, Peter. (1987). *The Sea Remembers: Shipwrecks and Archaeology*. New York: Weidenfeld & Nicolson.

Various Editors. (1981). *The World's Last Mysteries*. US. Reader's Digest.

Wells, Susan. (1997). *Titanic: Legacy of the World's Greatest Ocean Liner.*
New York: Time/Life Books.

Westwood, Jennifer. (1987). *The Atlas of Mysterious Places.* New York:
Weidenfeld & Nicolson.

Magazines on Archaeology

If you would like to learn more about archaeology in general, here are some of
my favorite magazines on archaeology:

Archaeology, www.archaeology.org, Archaeological Institute of America, US.

Biblical Archaeology Review, www.biblicalarchaeology.org, Biblical
Archaeology Society, US.

Current World Archaeology, www.world-archaeology.com, UK.

National Geographic History, www.nationalgeographic.com, US.

My Favorite Just-For-Fun Books

I love reading science fiction and fantasy books just for fun, here are some of my absolute favorites of all time, plus some young reader books I enjoyed in my early years:

Anything Star Wars (three of my favorites are the lesser-known *The Courtship of Princess Leia* by Dave Wolverton (1995), *The Han Solo Adventures* by Brian Daley (1992), and *Splinter of the Mind's Eye* by Alan Dean Foster (1978)).

Alexander, Lloyd. *The Chronicles of Pyrdain* series.

Anthony, Piers. *Xanth* series.

Boyer, Elizabeth. *Elves and the Otterskin* series.

DiTerlizzi, Tony and Black, Holly. *The Spiderwick Chronicles*.

Grahame, Kenneth. *The Wind in the Willows* (a gift from my beloved Aunt Ava)

Lewis, C.S. *Chronicles of Narnia* series.

Meyer, Stephenie. *Twilight* series.

Potter, Beatrix. *The Tales of Beatrix Potter* series (Peter Rabbit and Mrs. Tiggy-Winkle were my favorites).

Rowling, J.K. *Harry Potter* series.

Tolkien, J.R.R. *The Lord of the Rings* trilogy and *The Hobbit*.

Finally, here's a cool young adult fantasy series from some friends of mine in Charlottesville, VA:

Klintworth, Nathan and Buck. *Henry Hawthorne* series.

Thanks from Charlottesville

    May the hideous terrorist acts of August 2017 in Charlottesville, Virginia never be repeated anywhere in the world. _We are one_ city forever united against the insanity of those terrible days. Moreover, across the world _we are one_ people – every one of us created by God in His image and each of us equal in His eyes regardless of race, color, gender, religion, status, or any other artificial category of human differentiation. The madness needs to stop. God surely desires that no group should foster hatred or seek domination over any other, and it is my greatest hope for humanity that we can ALL someday follow His exalted will, and live together and love one another as one people.

    Thanks for the thoughts, prayers, and emotional support to Charlottesville (particularly from the US entertainment industry) as we struggled to recover from the aftermath of those horrible events in our beloved city – it was truly appreciated. My family and I are proud to call Charlottesville our forever home.

25934870R00157

Made in the USA
Columbia, SC
04 September 2018